Union Clues

FELICITY RADCLIFFE

DEDICATION

To the one and only Chef, with love.

CONTENTS

DAWN

TWO YEARS LATER

ACKNOWLEDGMENTS

So many people helped me write this book. I am grateful and hugely indebted to you all.

The amazingly talented Val Littlewood designed the cover. Thank you so much, Val.

A few brave friends volunteered to make cameo appearances in the story. Thank you, Dorothy and Bob Bennett, Hannah and Chris Marsh, Chris and Ian Harriman, Patrick Shears, Jim Packer and Mike Hall.

I am lucky enough to have a wonderful, creative and eagle-eyed group of readers who worked hard to help me refine the original manuscript. Thank you, Chris and Ian Harriman, Kay Beal, Sally Runham, Mike Hall, Julia Pearson, Helen Findley, Joanne Lewis and Kate. I take full responsibility for any errors that might have slipped through.

My fellow writers in Huntingdon Writers' Group are a constant source of inspiration. Thanks, in particular, to my role model Georgia Rose and the incredibly meticulous Sally Runham.

My friends in the book club provide encouragement, laughter and Prosecco – not necessarily in that order. Maggie Tebbit, Jackie Digby, Ellie McKenzie, Rosalind Southgate, Julia Pearson, Sue Tebbit, Eileen Swanson, Janice Harding, Katy Smith, Emma Penniall and Sarah Fussell – I couldn't have written this without you.

My colleagues and fellow scriptwriters at HCR104fm are another source of inspiration. Thanks, in particular, to Jean Fairbairn, poetess extraordinaire, Helen Kewley and Sue Rodwell-Smith.

Finally, a huge thank you to everyone who follows me on social media, reads my short stories and poems – and to those who bought my first novel, 'The Dark Side of the Book Club', helping to raise money for Cancer Research. This book is different from 'Dark Side', but I hope you enjoy it anyway.

STELLA

1 SLUMMY MUMMY

'Question?'

That's the title of the email to my husband. As I scan the brief contents I tell myself there's nothing to worry about, but I'm not convinced.

Alex, my husband, is a fairly clever man. You don't become as powerful as him without being reasonably bright. I assume that Jennifer, his communications manager and the sender of the email, is smart too. As her job title suggests, she clearly understands the power of words and uses them with subtle economy, unlike me. The email exchange reads as follows:

Jennifer: *'What shall we do when Leviathan ends?'*
Alex: *'Don't you worry – I'll work something out.'*

That's it. You probably think I'm making too much of this; that I'm just a paranoid wife. Indeed, both Alex and Jennifer would instantly come up with plausible explanations if challenged, effortlessly demeaning me as a deluded woman who has got nothing better to think about and who has lost touch with professional life.

Jennifer might claim she was merely concerned about how the team will secure its next assignment once the Leviathan programme finishes in a month's time. Alex might say they were referring to the wrap-up party they intend to organise for the hundreds of consultants and clients who have worked on the programme over the last five years. In either case, the email exchange would be proven innocent. Even I might have thought it innocuous – apart from one word. *You.*

That single word makes me doubt my husband, despite his brusque response. He could have written 'don't worry', but he didn't – he wrote 'don't you worry'. That slight glimmer, that bat squeak of affection, is easily discernible to me. After all, I have over twenty years of training in decoding Alex's oddly impersonal messages and greedily hoarding every possible scrap of emotion, no matter how subtly expressed. That one was never going to get past me.

I wonder if Jennifer noticed it too and basked in the glow of Alex's imperfectly concealed warmth. Probably. The woman is a communications specialist, after all. On the other hand, her professional skills make it likely she would also have picked up on the rather patronising tone of 'don't you worry' and, even more concerning for her, his use of 'I' rather than 'we'.

Neither comes as a surprise to me. These days, Alex is used to being in charge and making things happen, but is less accustomed to making decisions together, as part of a special team of two. It wasn't always this way but gradually, over the years, things have changed. It used to be the two of us against the world but lately, more often, it's the two of us against each other. Now, quite possibly, there is a third person in this relationship, as another doomed wife once said.

I should log off at this point, but you know how it is. Having loosened the scab, I can't stop picking. First, I check the time of Jennifer's message and find it was sent at 6.36pm the previous Friday. The programme team finishes early on a Friday night, so Jennifer would have been on her way home. I picture her on the train, travelling west across the Pennines to her home in Manchester from the Leviathan headquarters in Leeds. Probably on her second can of gin and tonic, with her guard down, she couldn't resist pushing for some expression of commitment from my husband.

Alex, on the other hand, would have been heading in another direction, south to King's Cross. Diligently fielding work emails and bracing himself for the stressful rush-hour journey across London to our home in Surrey, he quickly fobbed her off with a carelessly worded one-liner. An email whose tone, on both sides, implies to me a well-established affair, rather than the first flush of passion. The realisation causes a sudden stab of pain in my stomach.

I cast my mind back to the time when Jennifer first joined Leviathan - just over a year ago, I think. The previous communications manager had lost the confidence of the client, an occupational hazard on a programme as big, complex and politically sensitive as Leviathan. Right from the start, Alex was full of praise for Jennifer, calling her a 'breath of fresh air'. At some point shortly afterwards, I now recall, he stopped talking to me about her – a sure sign, I figure, that their relationship had moved beyond the purely professional. The question is – will the affair end next month, along with the Leviathan programme? Or will Alex 'work something out', as he promised her?

Abruptly I slam my laptop shut, suddenly desperate to silence my obsessive train of thought. I tell myself I have no proof. It could be nothing. Not for the first time, I chastise myself for hacking into my husband's email account. 'You only got what you deserve!' screams my inner voice – always my worst critic. But do I deserve this? And is there anything to deserve, anyway?

One thing's for sure; it's time for wine. In the corner of our kitchen is a large, stainless steel, glass-fronted wine fridge, where Alex keeps his vintage wines which, according to him, require precise temperature control. So-called 'weekday wine', the type normally guzzled by me, and sometimes by the children, when Alex is away, is kept in the garage in litre bottles and transferred to the food fridge as and when required, which is pretty often these days.

I pull open the door of the wine fridge and survey the rows of treasured bottles. Quickly I make an informed choice, aided by long years of listening to boring conversations about wine between Alex and his friends. A Puligny Montrachet Premier Cru 2011, perfectly chilled and with dew clinging invitingly to the bottle's sloping shoulders. To complement this superb vintage, I pull from the kitchen cupboard a battered tumbler, rendered practically opaque by thousands of dishwasher cycles. I slosh the exquisite white Burgundy into this unworthy vessel until it is almost full, then take a hefty swig.

As I wander back to my seat at the island in the middle of the kitchen, my eye is drawn towards our noticeboard. Not for us the kind of noticeboard I see in my friends' houses – covered with Post-it stickers bearing hastily scribbled reminders, dog-eared takeaway menus, children's drawings and tickets to events attended decades previously. No; our noticeboard displays a tasteful collection of family photos, carefully curated and arranged by Alex and designed to show visitors what a happy, successful family unit we are.

In the middle of the board, taking pride of place, is a photo of the paterfamilias himself, dressed in his off-duty uniform of pristine chinos and polo shirt. His honey blonde hair is artfully ruffled, to conceal his incipient bald patch, and his body looks pretty good, I have to admit, thanks to his personal trainers in London and Leeds. Unusually, he is alone; in most of the other photos, our son Hugo is right next to him. In the older shots, Hugo is a miniature version of his father, apart from his hair colour, but in the more recent photos he is taller and slimmer than Alex, much to the latter's annoyance. As I work my way through my first tumbler of wine, I examine my son's face in each of the photos, looking at the cute, lopsided smile which, sadly, so often fails to reach his eyes.

Hugo went away to university last October and I still miss his calm, oddly polite presence every day. I miss having someone to watch Strictly Come Dancing with and I especially miss our little private jokes. We text every day and FaceTime at least once a week, though, and he always seems happy enough. He's studying business management at the University of St. Andrews, which Alex is fond of calling 'the Oxbridge of Scotland', to mask his disappointment that Hugo has not gone to Oxford or Cambridge, like most of his expensively educated classmates at Dulwich College. Alex has no room to talk, though – his alma mater is decidedly red brick. There's only one Oxbridge graduate in the family, and that's me. Are you surprised?

Secretly, I'm glad Hugo chose St. Andrews. Scotland is far enough away, I figure, to allow him to escape his father's influence and work out what he wants to do with his life. I suspect business management is not his true calling and hope he'll eventually switch to a subject about which he is truly passionate. Talking of passion, I also hope he has more luck with his love life now he's at university. His few attempts at relationships with girls have not worked out well so far. My son is a good-looking young man, with my dark hair and unusual, pale blue eyes, inherited from his father. He has never been short of admirers, all of them attractive, confident young women, but invariably he has ended each relationship after just a few weeks. According to him, none of these girls was 'quite right'. I really hope that now, having left his all boys' school behind and living and studying alongside a variety of young women, he'll come to understand them better, have more realistic expectations and find friends and lovers who put a genuine smile on his face – one which always reaches his eyes.

While I refill my tumbler, I scan the noticeboard for our daughter, who makes fewer appearances on the board than her older brother. As I look at a photo taken in Cornwall last summer, my heart lifts. Imogen, her long blonde hair braided in cornrows and with henna tattoos on her tanned arms, gazes openly back at me, as though daring me to tell her to wash them off. Although she's more rebellious than her brother, which admittedly is not difficult, Immo causes me fewer worries. A talented artist with a burning ambition to be a textile designer, she has been allowed far more academic freedom than her brother, precisely because she's a girl and so doesn't bear the burden of fulfilling Alex's expectations by following in his footsteps. It can still be a sexist world in our household, but in this respect it has benefited my daughter. We constantly row about all the usual things – clothes, make-up, choice of boyfriends, alcohol consumption, smoking and whether she can leave Alleyn's School and go to the local comprehensive. Nevertheless, we're both confident in the strength of the love that exists between us, no matter how noisy our rows, which generally occur during the week, when her father is away. In fact, when it comes to Alex, we both maintain a conspiracy of silence. On more than one occasion I have gently held back Immo's hair while she has vomited into the toilet after one too many Woo-Woos, promising 'not to tell Daddy' - and I have always kept my promise. Alex made a fuss about the henna tattoos and would be horrified if he knew about the real one on his daughter's right shoulder. To him, his 'Minnie' is the beautiful, artistic and charmingly quirky daughter whom he confidently expects to marry someone rich and have children of her own, just like her mother. As I refill my tumbler and notice I will soon need a second bottle, I know just what you're thinking, and you're dead right. Look how that has worked out for me.

As I finish the bottle, I take a reluctant look at the photos in which I make an appearance. Invariably, my smile is just a shade too bright and my body is partially hidden – either concealed behind my husband or children or swathed in baggy clothes. It's not that I'm fat – I can be objective about myself, even after a bottle of Burgundy's finest. On a good day I can wear a size twelve, although I do opt for a fourteen when I want to feel more comfortable. Still, I reason, I'm a perfectly respectable size for a forty-seven-year-old mother of two, so why do I try to airbrush myself out of every family photo, these days? I used to be so vibrant and self-assured. When did my confidence ebb away? How did it happen? A fat tear trickles down my face and plops into my empty tumbler, reminding me to get some more wine. This time, though, I stick to the 'weekday wine' in the food fridge. I figure that's all I deserve.

Making a start on my second bottle, I try to recall happier times and pinpoint the time when things started to change for me. Looking back to when I first met Alex, I remember how different everything was in those days and how I was the one in control. I take a gulp of wine and wince at the taste, which seems so bitter compared with its vintage predecessor. Then I cast my mind back to the first time I saw Alex, at my firm's welcome party for our new graduate trainees. Dressed in his brand new, slightly shiny M&S suit with the too-long sleeves, earnestly shaking hands with the partners, nodding vigorously in response to everything they said and trying so hard to impress. I recognised him immediately from the photo in his profile given to me by HR and strode over to introduce myself.

'Hi David.' I smiled at the partner with whom Alex was attempting to ingratiate himself and held out my hand to the new joiner. 'You must be Alex. I'm Stella. I've been assigned to you as your buddy – to help you settle in at the firm.'

'Well aren't you the lucky one, Alex?' remarked David. 'Stella is one of our rising stars. Like you, she joined as a graduate trainee and, only a few years on, she's successfully managing a workstream on one of our most important IT projects. You'll gain a lot from buddying up with her, Alex. Watch and learn!' With that, David moved away to join another group, leaving Alex and me to get acquainted.

It wasn't love at first sight; at least, not for me. I admit, Alex was extremely good-looking, and I was the envy of many of my female colleagues for having lucked out with such a cute buddy. However, whilst I appreciated his looks and physique, he seemed way too straight for me and, in any case, I preferred to keep work and play separate in those days. At the time I was dating a much older man called Sean, a director of one of the big multi-national record companies. He wasn't as aesthetically pleasing as Alex, but he was a lot of fun. He took me to some amazing gigs, where we got to go backstage and meet countless celebrities. At twenty-four, I fancied myself as a sophisticated woman of the world: successful IT consultant during the week and rock chick at weekends. A twenty-one-year-old graduate trainee was not my style at all.

Meanwhile, Alex was playing the long game. After the end of our three-month official buddying period, he made sure he had a legitimate reason to keep in touch by asking me to be his mentor. He was dispatched on assignment to Reading whilst I remained in London, but he ensured we met regularly for drinks after work on the pretext of him asking my advice about his role on the project. When he could afford it, he took me out to dinner and always insisted on paying, even though I was earning more than him. Every day he sent me charming, funny texts and I gradually came to appreciate the dry wit behind the serious façade. Before I knew it, he was part of the fabric of my life; a good friend who always made me smile.

Gradually we started to share details of our personal lives. As the only child of a single mother, I have always been fascinated by large families, so I inevitably found Alex's family stories irresistible. The sprawling Pitulski clan, with its Polish heritage, colourful history and even more exotic characters, sounded so beguiling to me when described by Alex, one of the family's success stories, who was adored by his parents and sister. He also introduced me to Polish cuisine, including the cheese and jam sandwich much beloved by the Pitulski children and which is still my favourite snack. Not long afterwards, when Sean abruptly ditched me for a gorgeous backing singer, Alex consoled me on numerous occasions with industrial quantities of Polish vodka. He was happy to let me cry on his shoulder and to listen patiently whilst I repeatedly, and I'm sure tediously, dissected my broken relationship, trying to work out what I had done wrong.

Being dumped hurt me far more than it should have done. A more resilient woman would have blamed Sean, a notorious commitment-phobe who, despite his age, had never had a long-term relationship in his life and had a history of jumping ship as soon as a potential new conquest presented itself. A strong person would have chalked it up to experience and moved on. However, as far as I was concerned, the break-up was all my fault; proof that I was still, deep down, the unattractive outcast I had been at school. For some reason, I thought, Sean had found me intriguing when he met me at my friend Helen's party, but it was clearly only a matter of time before I was found out and he saw me for what I really was. I figured I had got above myself by imagining, quite wrongly, that I was worthy of dating someone so sophisticated. The confidence which had led me to dismiss a graduate trainee as potential boyfriend material disappeared in an instant when Sean left me, and I was transported right back to my gawky teenage self.

When I was a teenager at school, complete with puppy fat, braces and dodgy dress sense, boys only dated me for a joke, or as a dare. I eventually found this out when the popular girls who put them up to it thought it would be amusing to enlighten me. Later, when I went up to Cambridge, I lost the braces and reinvented myself by slimming down and adopting a veneer of nonchalance when confronted with the opposite sex. I had a few relationships during my university years, but the men I really liked were not keen on me and those who were interested didn't hold my attention for very long. In truth, looking back, I was far more interested in my studies, developing a fascination with maths and technology which I still have to this day.

Sean was the first man in my life who had really got under my skin. During our eight-month relationship I fell for all his lines and allowed myself to believe I was different from his previous girlfriends. I really thought I would be the one to change him and cure him of his aversion to long-term relationships. With hindsight, I know I was doomed to fail, but I'm sure you've made a similar mistake at least once, by thinking you could convert someone who was fundamentally unsuited to monogamy. It's a story as old as time; the irresistible lure of the bad boy, made even more potent when the girl in question still thinks of herself, deep down, as the ugly nerd whom the boys only dated as a dare, to amuse the cool girls they really fancied.

During the months following my split from Sean, Alex worked hard to rebuild my confidence. He constantly told me I was beautiful. At weekends he took me shopping, helped me choose countless new outfits and boosted my self-esteem by telling me how great they looked on me. With his encouragement, I had a makeover – I got a different haircut and started booking myself in for regular manicures and facials. I also joined the same gym as Alex and embarked on a regular exercise programme. The two of us would compare notes after our sessions and I felt a glow of satisfaction at reaching each new milestone. Colleagues and friends all told me how great I looked. Gradually, without consciously realising it, I put Sean behind me and moved on.

Now I no longer spent all my weekends at gigs with Sean, my social life was improving too. I received a lot more invitations to parties and dinners, often taking Alex with me as a convenient 'plus one'. He was always delighted to accept and having a companion did make it easier to socialise with my friends, most of whom were in relationships. People started to assume that Alex and I were dating and neither of us did anything much to put them right. One Saturday night, after a dinner party, Alex and I shared a taxi home. We had both drunk a lot of wine over dinner, especially me, and of course the inevitable happened. The taxi dropped us both off at my flat and that was it until Sunday evening, when Alex briefly went home to pick up his work clothes for Monday, plus his laptop, and bring them back to mine.

From the start, I appreciated the fact that Alex didn't play games and was open about his devotion to me. After my opposite experience with Sean, this was both a comfort and a relief. Everything about my relationship with Alex felt easy and natural compared with his predecessor. My friends all liked Alex, whereas most of them had mistrusted Sean and a few had actively loathed him. There was no negative impact on our careers; on the contrary, our colleagues were pleased to see us both so happy. We liked a lot of the same things – books, films, restaurants, plays – even music. Alex finally convinced me I didn't need someone like Sean beside me to be deemed interesting. We had similar professional ambitions, too. Everything just seemed to fit, as though it was meant to be. I began to see that being with someone like Alex, who fitted so easily into my world, made far more sense than to be with Sean, who inhabited an alien universe and had a completely different set of values.

Gradually, my feelings for Alex grew. We had great sex, got on extremely well and hardly ever argued. I was the envy of all my friends for having such a good-looking partner and people were constantly telling me I looked better than I ever had. The word 'glowing' was often used. Really, what was not to like?

Fast forward a year. Like me when I joined the firm, Alex rose rapidly through the ranks and we were soon generally regarded as peers, although our performance could not be compared directly, as we never worked on the same project. However, despite this supposed parity, Alex still frequently sought my advice and claimed to be in awe of my intellect, honed at Girton College, where I had studied maths and physics. Alex, on the other hand, saw himself as less academic than me, having graduated in business studies. Gradually, though, his confidence in his ability increased, bolstered by the unofficial old boy network in our firm.

As Alex and I both grew more successful and student poverty became a distant memory, we began to travel, taking increasingly extravagant trips. Mini breaks in Europe were followed by a touring holiday in California, a safari in Tanzania and then two weeks in a luxury all-inclusive resort in Mexico. It was there, on a picture-perfect evening, as the peach coloured sun dipped below the turquoise waves crashing onto the white sand at Tulum, that Alex proposed. In the shadow of the imposing Mayan ruins on the cliff top, he went down on one knee and produced a showy diamond engagement ring. At the time it felt incredibly romantic and, overwhelmed with surprise and joy, I had no hesitation in accepting. Looking back, though, I can see that the rock chick was already long gone. Hindsight's a wonderful thing, isn't it?

Our friends and colleagues were pleased for us and the Pitulski tribe, predictably, was noisily delighted. Only my mother sounded a gentle note of caution, 'are you sure you're not just drifting into it, darling? Is it what *you* actually want?' but she was nearly two hundred miles away in Macclesfield and her warnings were drowned out by those around us. Wedding preparations proceeded apace, with Alex's London-based relatives providing most of the practical assistance. Wanda, his mum, helped me choose my dress and his sister Eva, who was between jobs at the time, helped organise my hen do, make-up and flowers. We even had a Catholic ceremony to please his family; not being particularly religious, I raised no objection. Even when required to attend a pre-marriage course, I dutifully went through the motions without dwelling much on the content. Before I knew it, we were married – less than three years after that earnest graduate trainee first shook my hand at our firm's welcome party.

From the start, marriage suited Alex. He seemed to grow in stature and become more self-assured the minute we returned from our honeymoon. Colleagues hinted to me that his management style had changed, becoming more directive and less collegiate, but I had no first-hand evidence of this, as we continued to work on different projects. His teams did not always welcome the new approach by Alex, but the firm's partners did – and so did the client sponsors. He got things done, after all, and ultimately that was what mattered.

As Alex became increasingly autocratic, he did not make many new friends at work, but he did deliver significant cost savings and productivity improvements. The projects he directed made his client organisations leaner and fitter, with more profits to reinvest in the business and reward the board of directors. In turn, as his clients became richer, they re-hired Alex and recommended him to others. Each referral enabled Alex to sell yet more work to new and existing clients and his success acquired its own momentum. He was on a roll.

While all this was happening, I was still doing well. I was highly regarded by my clients and seen as a 'safe pair of hands' by the partners in our firm. However, when those same partners were looking to admit newcomers to their closely guarded ranks, it was Alex who was invited to submit his partner case, not me.

By this time, my husband was regularly raising the subject of starting a family. I wasn't very keen as I felt I was at a pivotal point in my career and couldn't afford to take time out. Nevertheless, as was increasingly the case, Alex got his way in the end. A few romantic nights in with a lovely meal, excellent wine and a few shots of that Polish vodka, culminating in supposedly spontaneous lovemaking sessions initiated by Alex, with my cap forgotten in the heat of the moment, and Hugo was on his way.

After that, the speed of my transformation into an under-confident wife increased dramatically. Hugo was a sickly, sensitive baby, so I only went back to work part-time after my maternity leave, as he hated to be separated from his mummy. I have to admit, the feeling was mutual, and Alex's family were experts in fanning the flames of my guilt, having had a lifetime's worth of training from the Catholic priests and nuns. So I put my career on the back burner, whilst Alex forged ahead with his, eventually making partner on his second attempt at the tender age of twenty-eight – one of the youngest partners ever in our firm. To celebrate, we bought a large house in Surrey which needed a lot of work and, less than two years later, I was pregnant again. Imogen was a strident and demanding baby and I had a clingy toddler to contend with too, along with a full-scale house renovation project to manage. Quitting work seemed like the only option and by now, Alex easily earned enough to finance our lifestyle.

After I stopped working, the years flew by in a whirlwind of play dates, SATs, report cards, after school clubs, interior design and all the other elements which fill the life of a well-to-do wife and mother in the stockbroker belt. During this time, I watched a lot of my friends, who were in a similar position, lose sight of their marriages and let their children devour their every waking moment, but I was determined not to fall into that trap. It was difficult, though, as by now Alex was directing huge programmes which were usually based in other parts of the country, so he was mostly away during the week. At weekends, I tried to make up for his absence by cooking his favourite meals, arranging 'date nights' and organising social events with friends. Every Friday evening I waited for him, all fragrant and gussied up like an archetypal 1950s housewife on the cover of a knitting pattern. My hair, nails and make-up were always freshly done and the well-worn, mismatched underwear I usually flung on during the week was replaced by something lacy, slinky and silky from Agent Provocateur or La Perla. As my husband walked in the door I invariably greeted him with a kiss and a gin and tonic, clinking with ice cubes, but as the years went by his kisses became as cold as the drinks I poured him and it seemed like nothing I did was good enough. Alex criticised everything – the way I looked, the dinners I prepared with such care and the nights out I arranged so thoughtfully. My confidence, already at a low ebb, sank still further, until eventually I came to dread the weekends and look forward to Monday morning, when it was just me and the children once again.

So weekdays became my favourite time, but however much I loved my children and enjoyed their company, I couldn't escape the nagging thought that this was not the life I had wanted for myself. I mourned the loss of my career and wondered how, without consciously signing up to it, I had effectively become a single mother – albeit a wealthy one. I attempted to silence the intrusive voices in my head with copious quantities of alcohol; a solution which never works, as I'm sure you know, although that didn't stop me from trying repeatedly. As the years passed and my children grew less dependent on me, wine o'clock gradually started earlier, but I didn't really notice – or I pretended not to.

Fast forward again to the present day and Alex is preparing for the successful rollout of the final phase of the Leviathan programme, which he has directed for its entire five-year lifespan. As its name suggests, Leviathan is massive – the biggest and most successful IT implementation in the history of the UK public sector. Barring a major disaster in the final few weeks, it will be seen as a resounding success – unlike the myriad failed IT programmes which have embarrassed the UK government in the past. Every phase of Leviathan has been implemented, on time and within budget, at each location across the country. Sure, there have been a few technical glitches along the way, but Alex's teams resolved them promptly under his leadership. Suffice to say that, when Leviathan wraps up, it will cement my husband's reputation as one of the most formidable programme directors of his generation and that senior partner promotion will be a slam dunk.

So there we have it. The earnest graduate trainee in his shiny M&S suit has been replaced by a 'heavy hitter' with a wardrobe full of Gieves & Hawkes, a legendary career and probably a gorgeous mistress as well. Meanwhile, the Cambridge graduate with the promising career and sparkling social life has turned into a slummy mummy, slumped in her beautifully appointed kitchen at one o'clock in the morning, working her way through her second bottle of wine. Funny how things turn out.

As I clumsily refill my tumbler with 'weekday wine', the kitchen door suddenly crashes open behind me and I jump in alarm, spilling wine onto the polished silestone work surface of the island, from where it drips lazily off the edge onto the slate tiles below. Imogen stares with disdain at the growing puddle of wine at my feet, then at me and my tumbler.

'What are you doing, Mummy? Why are you down here so late, getting lashed on a school night? And what's with the panda eyes – have you been crying? What's the matter – is it Hugo? Oh. My. God. Has something happened to him…?'

Quickly I hold up my hand to quell Immo's mounting panic. As I'm sure you know from experience, teenage girls are great at spinning a drama out of nothing, and my daughter is a drama queen par excellence. 'No, darling – it's nothing. Hugo's fine. I'm just feeling a bit down – that's all. Sorry I woke you. Go back to bed, otherwise you'll be tired in the morning.'

Imogen is not so easily fobbed off. 'OK then – if it's not Hugo, then it must be Daddy. He's the only other reason you'd be getting wrecked in the middle of the night.' As I open my mouth in an attempt to prove my relative sobriety, my daughter puts up her hand to silence me, pulls up a stool and sits down facing me, putting on her best 'concerned and mature' face. 'It can't be easy for either of you, what with him being away all week. You must miss each other so much.'

I find it touching, her unshakeable faith in the strength of my relationship with Alex. I struggle to find a reply which will sound sober and will not give away the true reason for my tears. 'You're right – it's not easy' is the best I can do.

'Well, booze is hardly going to help, as you've told me on more than one occasion when my head has been down the loo. Right – here's what you need to do. Step One – Holiday and Makeover. When Daddy comes home at the weekend, sit down with him and book that three-week holiday you keep threatening to have once his project is over. You don't need to worry about me – Sam's mother has already said I can stay with them. Then, once it's booked, you'll have a month to turn things around. Go back to Fat Club and lose those ten pounds you say you've put on – although I can't see them, I have to say. Whatever - if it will make you feel better, then it's worth it. Get your hair and nails done while you're at it, have a spray tan and buy a whole new holiday wardrobe. Then you'll look sick, you'll have a great holiday, and you and Daddy will reconnect. Step Two – Career. When you get back from holiday, start that new business you keep talking about – Digital Whatever. No more putting it off. Hugo has gone and I don't need much of your time any more. Now's your chance, so take it! There you go – sorted. Don't thank me – you can pay my consultancy fee in Asos vouchers.'

I have to smile at my daughter's optimism – her youthful conviction that a person's problems can easily be tackled and overcome by taking a few practical steps. Experience has shown me things are rarely that simple. I have to admit, though, she does have a point when it comes to the holiday. Maybe a decent break, just the two of us, will give Alex and me a chance to reboot our relationship and make a fresh start. Perhaps a luxury 'fly and flop' holiday, with lots of restorative sunshine, plenty of good wine and the chance to have some real, honest conversations, might convince Alex to call time on his affair, if he is having one, and help me remember all the reasons why I married him.

I reach over to my daughter and ruffle her already dishevelled hair. 'OK, Dr. Immo. I'll follow Step One of your plan. When Daddy comes home at the weekend we'll book that holiday – I promise. Meanwhile, I'll start over at Fat Club. They meet on Wednesday nights, which is handy. I'll pop along tomorrow evening and re-join, then I'll book in for hair, nails – the full works. I'll have a total overhaul of the bodywork. Prepare to see a radical transformation in my appearance over the next few weeks!'

In some ways, but not all, Immo is as serious as her father. 'Don't get ahead of yourself, Mummy,' she cautions me gravely. 'First step – cutting back on the weekday wine. Do you know how many calories are in that stuff?' She screws the top back on the bottle and puts it in the fridge. Then, grabbing a glass from the nearest kitchen cupboard, she returns to her stool and pours half the contents of my tumbler into it. 'There you go – already a fifty percent calorie saving. Cheers!'

'Now you are taking advantage,' I remonstrate, 'but cheers, anyway.' I smile at my daughter and we clink our glasses together. 'Here's to luxury holidays!' I proclaim, feeling marginally better.

'To luxury holidays,' echoes Imogen, 'and new beginnings.'

'Here's hoping,' I tell myself as I swallow the last of my wine. 'Right, Immo – finish up your wine and go back to bed. It is a school night, after all.'

2 LOCKED AND LOADED

By Friday night I'm feeling much more positive. Sheryl, the group leader at Fat Club, was delighted to welcome back a prodigal daughter at Wednesday's meeting. By the way, Fat Club is not its real name, obviously. A few of its more sporadic attendees, myself included, call it Fat Club, mainly so we can all say, 'First rule of Fat Club? Nobody talks about...' You get the picture. Anyway, after two days back on the diet, I am already feeling lighter and slimmer, although experience tells me this is probably all in my head and will not necessarily translate into a lower number on the scales at next week's weigh-in. Whatever, as Imogen would say. I'll take any good feelings I can get. Also, by some minor miracle, I managed to secure a hair appointment at my busy local salon. Honestly, it's often easier to get an audience with the Dalai Lama than to book a cut and colour with Jeanette, my stylist, so I really lucked out and am now sporting a tasteful, yet slightly edgy bob, my dark hair subtly highlighted with rich auburn. I have also had my nails done, so I'm looking rather more polished than before. I have decided to leave the spray tan until nearer the holiday. These things only last a couple of days on me at best, so I'll retain my customary pallor for a few more weeks before temporarily getting transformed into an Oompa Loompa in preparation for the beach.

Talking of beaches, I have spent the time I would normally waste hacking into Alex's email account more profitably over the last few days, on an exhaustive search of luxury holiday websites. After checking out every exotic location, from Puerto Rico to Penang, I have finally found my idyll of choice – a tiny, remote island in The Maldives, accessible only via seaplane. A small cluster of exquisitely appointed huts, constructed in polished teak in a supposedly traditional design, perch on stilts over an azure sea that is so clear, you can see the outlines of manta rays gliding lazily through the water. From the balcony of each hut, with its sun deck and foaming jacuzzi, the lucky occupants can easily descend their own private staircase and lower themselves straight into the warm water. I can so easily imagine myself snorkelling in leisurely fashion away from the steps, with the ocean as my own private aquarium. I actually feel the sun's heat on my face and stomach as I doze on an imaginary sun-lounger, interrupted only by the welcome shock of a cold glass on my belly. It's an early evening cocktail, mixed from our private bar by a tanned, relaxed and smiling Alex. I can almost taste the luscious cuisine in the fine dining restaurants and feel the cool, crisp cotton sheets of our king-size four-poster on my bronzed body, scented with fragrant oils from a couples' massage earlier in the day. Bliss. A holiday like this is just what we both need…

My dreams are interrupted by the sound of Alex's key in the lock and my mind immediately snaps back to the game plan I drew up earlier. Clearly, I figured, it would be counter-productive to try and discuss holidays the moment Alex walks in the door, stressed out after a busy week and with his mind still focused on work. Instead I offer my husband a friendly greeting, trying not to feel disheartened by his cursory peck on the cheek when he sees me for the first time after a week away. I press a large gin and tonic into his hand and position myself directly underneath the downlights in the kitchen, all the better to show off my restyled, newly highlighted hair, just to see if he will notice. Yes – I know what you're thinking. 'Who is she trying to kid?' Again, you're dead right. Of course he doesn't notice a thing. But then again – does your other half notice when you have your hair done? Just saying…

'What's for dinner?' Alex enquires.

'I made Nasi Goreng. I thought we hadn't had it for a while, and I fancied something a little exotic.' I know, I know. Pathetic attempt to use food to conjure up a holiday mood.

'OK – I'll choose a wine to go with it. I'm thinking perhaps a Sauvignon Blanc – or maybe I'll push the boat out and open that bottle of Puligny Montrachet I've been saving. I've had a successful week up in Leeds, so I think I deserve it.'

'I think the Sauvignon Blanc will go better with the Nasi Goreng than the Puligny Montrachet,' I counter hastily. 'Also, I'm planning on getting sea bass next weekend for our lunch party, so perhaps we should save the Puligny Montrachet for our guests; it would really complement the fish.'

'Alright, if you say so,' Alex replies grudgingly. 'Open the Sauvignon Blanc while I go and get changed.'

Phew, that was close. I now have a week to replace the exquisite vintage I necked so casually on Tuesday night. As I open the wine and finish cooking the food, I try not to think about Alex's failure to say 'please' or 'thank you' and just hope he will not notice I've used a Fat Club recipe.

Dinner passes off uneventfully. I ask Alex how Leviathan is progressing through its final stages and make a few suggestions which, to my ears, sound pretty apposite and insightful. I have always tried to stay up to date with the world of business and still consider myself well-informed, despite my many years away from the workplace. These days, though, I note sadly, it's always me who offers Alex my opinion. He doesn't ask my advice any more.

After dinner I pour us two large Armagnacs. Sheryl would not approve, but it's all part of my plan. I'll do extra exercise tomorrow, I promise myself. Then, before Alex has a chance to retreat to the living room to watch TV, I tentatively broach the subject of the holiday. Taking his silence as evidence of at least some interest, I quickly grab my laptop and click through my carefully curated sequence of photographs depicting one tropical paradise after another and culminating in my preferred option of The Maldives. I hope Alex will agree with my top choice but in reality I would be delighted if he went for any of the resorts I have selected.

As I reach the end of my presentation I glance at Alex, trying to gauge his reaction, but his face is oddly expressionless, and he remains silent. 'So – what do you think?' I ask eventually, when he does not volunteer an opinion. 'Which option do you like best?'

Alex turns and looks me directly in the face for the first time since he returned home. 'None of them,' he answers flatly.

'I don't understand.' As I reply, I hear a note of desperation in my voice and I don't like it, but I press on anyway. 'I've picked a varied selection of the best luxury holidays in the world. I think they're all great and would be happy with any of them. Surely there must be one you like?'

'That's just it – I don't want a luxury holiday,' Alex states firmly. 'I do want a three-week break when Leviathan wraps up. God knows I deserve one. But I don't want to spend it lying on a sun-lounger worrying about what's happening back at the office. I want to do something really relaxing, but active, which takes my mind off work entirely.'

'You don't have to lie on a sun-lounger' I reply, sounding a little frantic now, I have to admit. 'There are loads of activities on offer at all the resorts – diving, tennis, water-skiing, golf…'

Alex puts up a hand to silence me. 'It's no use. I've been thinking about this quite a bit recently and I've decided what I want to do. I want to hire a narrowboat.'

'A…what?' I stare at my husband in amazement.

'The clue's in the name,' he replies drily. 'It's a boat and it's narrow. You use it to explore the canal network. It's the most relaxing thing ever.'

'How do you know?'

'Do you recall me talking about Dosia – my girlfriend whom I met at Polish Club, when I was at school?'

How could I forget? Dosia was Alex's first love. A beautiful girl and a talented musician, she broke the heart of eighteen-year-old Alex when she called time on their two-year relationship, leaving him for a trombone player in her youth orchestra. However happy Alex's family members were when we got engaged, I secretly think they would have been even happier if he had married Dosia, an eminently suitable girl who shares his Polish heritage. Dosia's memory is wheeled out occasionally by Alex; usually as a metaphorical stick to beat me with if I do something which doesn't match up to my husband's exacting standards. I suspect he has never really got over her. 'Yes, of course,' I eventually reply.

'Her family used to own a narrowboat and I went on it with them quite a few times, on various holidays. I really enjoyed it and I'm sure I can still remember how to steer and moor the boat, so there's no problem there.'

'But what about me?' I wail. By now I really hate my tone of voice but I'm powerless to change it.

'You work the locks, of course. That's how it's done – the man steers the boat and the woman works the locks. I know all about locks, though. I'll teach you.'

'That's not what I mean,' I counter, amazed he is being so obtuse, not to mention sexist. 'What I mean is – don't I get to express a view about what sort of holiday we have?'

Alex glares at me. 'Stella,' he begins in the terse, clipped tone he always uses when he is getting angry. 'Answer me this. Which of us has just spent five years directing the largest, most high-profile IT transformation programme in the UK? Can you imagine how stressful that has been and how much has been at stake – including my entire career? Don't you think I deserve to have the holiday of my choice?'

For a moment I fall silent, tempted to back down – but only for a moment. I'm not a complete doormat; not yet. 'I haven't exactly been idle for the last five years, Alex. I've supported our children through GCSEs, A levels and going to university. I've kept the whole domestic side of things running smoothly, while you have effectively been an absentee husband and father. It hasn't been easy for me, either.'

Alex dismisses my argument with a wave of his hand. 'No comparison,' he says glibly. 'Anyway, it's my salary that pays for – what did you call it – the domestic side of things, so I'm calling the shots. I'm sorry if that sounds harsh, but there it is. You can go on a girls' trip with your friends later in the year,' he adds, adopting a tone which is clearly meant to be conciliatory, but just sounds patronising to me.

This supposed concession makes the red mist descend; a rare occurrence for me, as I'm normally pretty even-tempered. 'Well that's big of you!' I screech. A small voice in my head tells me I sound hysterical and out of control, but I can't stop now. 'That would be really convenient for you, wouldn't it? To get me out of the way for a while, so you can…' I break off suddenly, as I realise I have no proof, and trading wild accusations won't help my cause.

My husband's face has turned red and his lips are compressed into a thin, hard line. 'So I can … what?' he challenges, his tone quietly menacing. 'Do explain precisely what you mean.'

The two of us stare wordlessly at each other. The telepathy which still exists between us, despite the precarious health of our long marriage, tells us a line is going to be crossed if we choose to carry on and we both know if we cross that line, there will be no going back. By silent, mutual consent, we both step back from the brink.

'I'm going to bed,' I mutter angrily. 'You go ahead and book the bloody holiday on the barge, or whatever it's called.'

'It's called a narrowboat,' Alex reminds me as I walk away from him. 'You'll enjoy it, I'm sure,' he adds, suddenly magnanimous in victory, but my back is turned as I leave the room and I don't bother to reply.

Early on Monday morning, Alex returns to Leeds after a tense weekend. Luckily Imogen was mostly out with friends and was plugged into her headphones while she was at home, so she was oblivious to the frosty atmosphere in the house.

To avoid further conflict, Alex communicates solely via our family WhatsApp group until Tuesday evening, when an email arrives in my inbox containing the fait accompli - a booking confirmation for our forthcoming holiday. Apparently, we are to pick up our narrowboat from a place called Allenby Marina, located near the village of Allenby St. Giles, somewhere in Leicestershire. Not quite The Maldives, then. Still, at least I'll save money on that spray tan, I reason grimly, as I contemplate the prospect of three rainy weeks clad in tracksuit bottoms, a parka and a pair of wellies. Très glam.

I admit I do perk up slightly when I see a picture of the boat itself. Painted in suitably aquatic shades of blue and green, it has a cosy looking double bedroom, a reasonably well appointed kitchen and a decent shower room, plus gas central heating and a solid fuel stove, so I apparently won't be roughing it as much as I feared. In an attempt to make the best of things, I try to overlook the mention of a pump-out toilet, which sounds horrific. I resolve that, whatever has to be pumped out to wherever, I'm not bloody doing it, whatever Alex might say. I figure I generally live in the shit, so I'll be damned if I'm going to pump it around the place as well.

As I pour myself a reasonably diet-friendly gin and slimline tonic, I grudgingly acknowledge that overall, the narrowboat doesn't sound as bad as I feared. I imagine there will be plenty of canal-side pubs, so at least I'll be able to cheer myself up, even if the boating is boring. I also try to ignore the name of our allotted vessel. 'Two's Company' hardly seems appropriate for Alex and me right now, but who knows? Maybe we can work things out on this holiday. After all, we have been together a long time, and something tells me we still have the remnants of a relationship worth salvaging. At the very least, we owe it to ourselves to give it a go.

The next evening, I head back to Fat Club and am cheered to discover I have lost three pounds, so I decide to stay for the group pep talk rather than scuttling away immediately after being weighed, as I tend to do if I have failed to lose weight or, worse still, have gained further poundage. As we share stories about our dieting ups and downs over the last week, I find myself telling the group about our forthcoming holiday and am astonished at the enthusiastic response I receive from my fellow dieters, several of whom have taken a break on the canal network. Sandy recounts a magical night moored in Stratford upon Avon, where she and her husband enjoyed an evening aperitif on deck, followed by an excellent performance of 'A Midsummer Night's Dream'. Helen and Paul enthuse about the wildlife they spotted on the Oxford Canal - herons, a kingfisher and even an otter. All of them recall cosy canal-side pubs and blissful evenings spent moored in the middle of nowhere, enjoying genuine off-grid time with a barbecue and a glass of wine. Buoyed by my slimming success and their upbeat stories, I almost begin to look forward to this holiday. Almost.

The rest of the week passes off uneventfully. When Alex comes home on Friday, we head straight out for dinner with friends at our local Italian restaurant. A convivial evening with good food, lots of wine and constant laughter helps to ease the remaining tension between us but still, when Alex disappears into his study after breakfast the following morning, I feel relieved he is out of my way and I can relax. Does that sound dreadful to you? Anyway, even if it does, the peace does not last long. An hour or so later, I get the call.

'Stella? Can you come in here? I've got something to show you.'

As I walk into the office, I see Alex has hooked his laptop up to our large monitor and I stare, puzzled, at the diagram on display. 'What's that?'

'That, Stella, is possibly the first ever animated model demonstrating how to operate a lock on the canals. I got one of our interns, Jamie, to produce it. His work on Leviathan had come to an end but there was no point in sending him back to London when we are this close to the final rollout and we might need extra skin in the game, so I thought I'd test his programming and user experience skills instead. He's done a superb job I have to admit. Prepare to be impressed! Right, let's start from the beginning, as they say.'

Oblivious to my open-mouthed stare, Alex clicks away on his laptop and an introductory image appears. 'Essentially,' he continues, 'the model comprises four scenarios. Number one – travelling uphill when the lock is in your favour. Scenario two – again travelling uphill, but this time the lock is against you. Three – travelling downhill, with the lock in your favour. Can you see where we're going with this?'

Wordlessly I nod, not trusting myself to speak.

'Last of all, scenario four – downhill with the lock against us. Easy. Right, let's look first at scenario one.' With a decisive click and a proud flourish, Alex displays the first view of his beloved model. 'As you can see, the boat is approaching the lock, which will enable it to travel uphill. As the diagram shows, the lock is empty of water, which means our boat can pass straight into it without you having to empty it first. The lock is therefore deemed to be in our favour, which means we have priority. When we're going downhill, the opposite is true, that is, if the lock's full, we have priority – but I'm getting ahead of myself. Back to scenario one. The person working the locks – i.e., you – gets off the boat at the lock moorings. Meanwhile the person steering the boat – i.e., me – waits on the back counter with a nice cold glass of white wine, or a gin and tonic.'

Alex laughs cheerily at what is clearly his idea of a joke. I remain stony-faced, but he fails to notice, so wrapped up is he in his precious model.

'Right, so you approach the lock and open the gates,' he continues. Another click and the gates on the model lock swing open. 'I steer the boat in and you shut them behind me. Then you run to the other end of the lock…'

'Run?' I interrupt.

'Well – trot, maybe. Anyway, you hurry. Then you open the paddles on the lock – ground paddles first, obviously, then gate paddles.'

'Obviously.'

Oblivious to my sarcasm, Alex presses on. 'As you can see from the model,' he proudly proclaims, 'the lock fills with water when the paddles open and the boat is lifted up.'

The model boat bobs jauntily on a rising tide of water and I feel a grudging admiration for Jamie's programming skills.

'Once the lock is full and the water level inside the lock is exactly the same as it is on the canal outside, you can swing the gates open and allow the boat to exit the lock.'

'And then I can get back on the boat?' I enquire hopefully. This all sounds far too much like hard work to me.

'No - not yet. First you have to close all the paddles and shut the lock gates behind the boat as it departs. That's an important rule to remember – always leave every lock with the gates and the paddles closed, so no water can escape.'

Alex pauses, takes a drink from his coffee mug and gives me a self-satisfied smile.

'So there you have it – the basic principles of how to work a lock. A fine example of beautiful, simple engineering, making full use of the weight and power of water. Despite all today's sophisticated technology, no one has ever found a better way than this to move boats up and downhill. Sometimes the original designs are still the best. It's perfectly easy to understand, don't you think?'

'Well,' I respond carefully, 'I'm sure it will make sense when I do it for real.'

'Don't worry if you haven't quite got it yet,' Alex reassures me, with genuinely no idea of how condescending he sounds. 'Let's carry on and run through scenarios two to four. I'm sure that will help reinforce the learning.'

I can almost feel you raising an eyebrow in disbelief, but it's true, I swear. My husband really does use phrases like 'reinforce the learning' when talking to his own wife. Long years spent working as a consultant can do that to people, especially if you embrace the jargon as enthusiastically as Alex has done. While he drones his way through the remaining scenarios, the water drains in and out of the model lock, the gates and paddles open and close, the boat goes up and down and I zone out completely. In truth, the principle seems simple enough, especially to someone who once graduated with a 2:1 in Maths & Physics, so I figure it's bound to be even easier in practice. As Alex keeps talking, I run through the to-do list for tomorrow's lunch party in my head. Being a successful hostess is my most immediate concern; the locks can wait. Looking back, I now realise if I had paid more attention on that Saturday morning, things might well have turned out differently. It's like I said earlier – hindsight's a wonderful thing.

3 PRAISE THE LEVIATHAN

The next day the weather is warm and sunny, with just a gentle breeze. Perfect, benign conditions – just right for a Sunday lunch party under the big tree in the garden, with a bunch of affluent couples not unlike ourselves. Despite my recent weight loss, I don't feel quite confident enough for my white skinny jeans; although I can wriggle into them, my reflection in the mirror is still far too reminiscent of a pygmy hippo for my liking. However, my navy polka dot palazzo pants look better than they have in ages, so I combine them with a plain white T-shirt, classic white sneakers and some red lipstick and I'm good to go.

As our guests arrive, air kissing me with apparent delight and pressing chilled champagne bottles and fragrant flower bouquets into my hands, I think fleetingly of how long I have known them all. Although we have all been on the same party circuit for over a decade, I'm not sure I could call any of them a true friend. Sure, we often shared babysitters when our children were younger and one or two of them have pulled a few professional strings for Alex, but I think of what my Mum might have said, were she still alive. If the doctors told me I had cancer, would I call any of them for support? Probably not. Still, they are good fun and sometimes, on a sunny Sunday, that's enough.

The sea bass goes down a treat and allows Alex to show off his griddling skills to our appreciative guests. I try not to think of the 'prick with fork' joke as I serve my homemade salads and breads which require far more effort and skill. I fill glasses with the sneakily replaced Puligny Montrachet, followed by numerous other vintage bottles from the wine fridge. Later, as our guests are demolishing my Tropical Pavlova and I am picking out bits of mango, trying hard to be 'good', the talk turns to our forthcoming holiday. Just like at Fat Club, everyone seems to think three weeks on a narrowboat is a terrific idea although, unlike my fellow dieters, none of this lot has ever actually ventured onto the canals.

'Club Med Exclusive's more my style, to be honest,' admits Roger, Alex's favourite golfing partner, 'but it sounds like an ideal way for you to recuperate, old boy. This bloody programme has taken it out of you – I think some downtime is long overdue.' Raising his glass to his friend, he proposes a toast, 'To a speedy recovery for our poor overworked friend here!'

The others raise their glasses and chorus, 'To Alex!' while I do my best to join in enthusiastically.

Later, as I wobble into the kitchen with a precarious trayful of plates and glasses, Roger's wife Madeleine collars me on her way back from the downstairs loo.

'Stella – I'm glad I've caught you on your own. Are you OK?' she asks me, taking the tray from my hands and looking furtively around her to make sure no one else is within earshot. 'I don't mean to pry, but you don't seem your usual bubbly self and you're looking a bit pale and drawn. Have you lost weight?' Without waiting for an answer, she places her hand on my arm and whispers, 'I know everyone's concerned about Alex, but you need to look after yourself as well. Also, this boating holiday – are you sure you're OK with it? I wouldn't have thought it was your thing.'

'It's not, to be honest,' I admit to her, 'but I think I owe it to Alex to do what he wants, after his five years of hard labour on Leviathan.'

'Oh, you are an angel, Stella.' Madeleine pulls me in for a hug. 'You're a much better wife than me.'

'I'm really not, Mads, but thanks anyway,' I mumble into her carefully tousled mane of hair.

'No problem,' she replies, stepping back and giving me a solicitous look, her head tilted to one side. 'Call me if you need anything – or even if you don't. I'm always around.'

'Will do.' As she walks away from me, back towards the garden, I call after her, 'Thanks again, Mads,' and, without turning around, she raises a casual arm in silent acknowledgement. Well, what do you know? Sometimes people just up and surprise you. I automatically dismiss her comments about looking pale and drawn, along with the ridiculous suggestion that I am a good wife. Instead I focus on what, for me, is the highlight of our conversation - Madeleine noticed I have lost weight! The thought keeps a smile on my face for most of the day.

The few weeks which separate the lunch party from the start of our narrowboat holiday just seem to fly by. Along with Leviathan, the academic year is drawing to a close, so all three members of my family need my support and I have little time left to focus on my own troubles. It's probably just as well.

Imogen's end of year school report makes very good reading, which I would not have predicted a year ago. I had been concerned she would coast through the first year of sixth form, much like her mother did. However, without wanting to sound boastful, I've always been very good at cramming for exams, so I had no difficulty in turning things around during my A level year, whereas Immo's GCSE results were distinctly average, so I concluded she would probably struggle with the same approach. I've therefore been nagging her for most of the year about the importance of keeping up with her schoolwork, but it appears I need not have bothered. Despite her apparently casual attitude, it seems Imogen has been working harder as the year has progressed, now she has given up the subjects she hates and can focus on what really inspires her. Her teachers are all hugely impressed with her progress.

To celebrate her success, I buy my daughter some of her beloved Asos vouchers and treat her to afternoon tea with a glass of Prosecco, followed by a spot of pampering at our local spa. I also email her school report to Alex, copying in Immo.

His response is predictably effusive, 'Well done Minnie. Keep up the good work, Daddy.'

Meanwhile Hugo has passed his first-year exams with no problem, although I get the impression university life has not absorbed him as thoroughly as I would have liked. The best piece of news I receive from Scotland is that my son has got a vacation job as a camp counsellor at a children's summer camp in the US. Apparently, an American student called Rob, who lives in his hall of residence, recommended him to some people he knows back home. Although I'm disappointed I won't see much of him over the summer, I'm even happier that he has a challenging and hopefully fun opportunity lined up.

As predicted, the Leviathan programme is coming to a triumphant close. The final rollout went smoothly, and Alex is now busy directing the wrap-up activities, among them the party to which he and Jennifer might or might not have been alluding in their ambiguous email. The event has been scheduled for the Friday before we are due to leave on holiday and the big surprise for me is that I have been invited. Plus-ones are not generally issued for work events at the firm and the forthcoming party is no exception. However, Alex has decreed that I and the wife of the client sponsor should be there to help present the prizes and, I quote, 'present a human face'. Cue a couple of hastily scheduled appointments at the nail bar and the beauty salon, to get my human face un-creased. I also indulge in a flurry of online shopping; I figure I deserve a new outfit as a reward for winning my half stone award at Fat Club. I order a size twelve cocktail dress which fits perfectly when it arrives, so I feel pretty good about myself when I sit down at my laptop on the day before the party to trawl through Jennifer's social media accounts.

I have checked her out before, of course. You wouldn't believe me if I denied it, would you, so what's the point? In her online photos she looks lovely, with her long red hair, blue eyes and slender figure. Strangely enough, this does not bother me; I am more disturbed by the unremitting dullness of her posts. Her life outside work seems to consist of a monotonous succession of Saturday morning Park Runs and cinema trips with her young nephews, with just the occasional girls' night out thrown in for good measure. No young woman's life could be this boring, I figure – particularly when she lives in a vibrant city like Manchester. Jennifer has got to be hiding something. In line with company policy, there is of course no mention of Leviathan, nor are there any references to a partner.

Up until now I have only read Jennifer's recent posts, searching for any hint of her possible involvement with Alex. This time, though, I decide to go back in time and look at her earlier posts. It has never seemed relevant before, but now I might actually be going to meet her, I feel the need to know more about her history. So back I go, through month after month of tedium, until an Instagram post abruptly brings my weary scrolling to a halt.

In the photo, our Jen poses for a selfie with a cute guy. They both adopt the time-honoured selfie posture – heads pressed together, necks craning upwards to avoid jowls, lips pouting. The caption reads, 'Just chillin' at home with my BFF'. Yeuch! I continue to scroll back in time and estimate that the same man features in around one third of her posts over a period of three to four years. His name is Stefan. It's clear to me he is more than just a friend, although nothing explicit is said. Eventually, when no new information reveals itself, I give up and start rewinding towards the present day, just in case I've missed anything. That's when I realise all mentions of Stefan, across every social media platform, simultaneously cease ten months ago, not long after Jennifer became part of the Leviathan team. Is it just a coincidence? I've no idea – but I promise myself I will find out. As a first step, I resolve to make sure Jennifer and I meet at the party on Friday.

Easier said than done, as it turns out. The huge, glittering ballroom of the hotel in Leeds is packed with hundreds of people; it seems like every person with any connection to Leviathan is there. Finding one individual in this throng, without making it look too obvious, is definitely a challenge. I make a conscious effort to relax, figuring it's going to be a long night and I have plenty of time to track her down.

In preparation for the prizegiving Alex quickly introduces me to Lois, the wife of his client sponsor, before dashing away to speak to someone more important. A gym-honed blonde in her late fifties, Lois is sporting an on-trend jumpsuit, making me feel rather dated in my sequinned cocktail dress. She exudes genuine warmth, though, which I rarely encounter in Surrey when meeting someone for the first time.

'Your hair looks fantastic!' she exclaims. 'Did you have it done here in

Leeds? If so, you've got to tell me the name of the salon!'

When I oblige her with the name, she smiles knowingly. 'Good choice – I hear they've got a lovely team of stylists in there.'

'Yes, it does seem so,' I agree, 'they're certainly very friendly. The stylist who did my blow dry found out more about me in half an hour than my regular stylist has in ten years – and she told me all about her life, too. I received chapter and verse on her ex-husband, her new boyfriend, her mother's hip replacement – the lot.'

'That's how we roll, here in Leeds!' Lois laughed, the phrase sounding slightly odd to me when spoken in her Yorkshire accent. 'Friendly, curious and not afraid to speak our minds!'

'Well, I like it.' I clink glasses with Lois and we both accept refills from a passing waiter. 'It makes a refreshing change,' I add, silently making an exception for Madeleine, whose genuine concern at our lunch party came as such a surprise. Just then my reflections are interrupted by my husband's voice booming through the PA system, announcing the prizegiving is going to take place in a few minutes. Lois and I dutifully make our way to the stage, where we are miked up and given our instructions.

The prizegiving is an informal affair, designed to raise a few laughs and remind people of the lighter moments which punctuated the five-year relentless slog. There's a prize for the best practical joke, the funniest karaoke performance, the most inventive excuse for being late – you get the idea. None of the prizes is directly related to work. I recognise the hand of Alex behind all this; I'm familiar with his tactics, after all these years. When people talk about Leviathan in the months and years to come, this is what he wants them to recount – the team spirit and the fun, not the hard graft and the sacrifices. This is the folklore he wants to attach to his programme. No doubt Jennifer, as part of her communications role, will be helping him with this.

After the prizegiving, I am of course clearly identifiable as Alex's wife, so I get ambushed by one Leviathan team member after another, eager to tell me how brilliant they think Alex is, and how much they have enjoyed working for him. They all seem genuine enough and, as I watch my husband working the room, taking time to greet each of the consultants and clients, I can't help but feel impressed. Whatever difficulties Alex and I have experienced recently, I have to acknowledge his incredible achievement in making a success of the Leviathan programme. Few other people could have managed it – including myself, I reluctantly admit. I accept a fresh glass of champagne from a waiter and turn to greet the next person, who has tapped me on the arm, doubtless wanting to sing Alex's praises.

Of course, I'd have recognised her anywhere. Long red hair and blue eyes – tick. Willowy figure – another tick. As she holds out her hand, I remember to pretend not to know who she is and wait for her to introduce herself.

'Hi, I'm Jennifer – comms manager on Leviathan. I'm glad you were presenting the prizes – it made it so much easier for me to stalk you afterwards!'

I must look alarmed, or guilty, or probably both, at her use of the word 'stalk', because she puts her hand on my arm and leans in, treating me to a whiff of Chanel No. 5. It's one of my favourite perfumes too, funnily enough.

'Don't look so worried. I just thought I'd save you for a minute – from all the other members of Alex's team coming up and telling you how fabulous they think he is. Don't get me wrong; he's done a great job, just like we all have, but I'm willing to bet no one has told you he couldn't have done it without you.'

'You're right,' I mutter, completely wrongfooted, 'no one has mentioned that.'

'I thought as much. Well anyway, it's true – he could *not* have managed without you. Fact. It's time someone said it, in my opinion. I also wanted to say how much I admire you. I know how much you've given up for him.' Smiling at me, Jennifer raises her glass and clinks it heavily against mine. 'Congratulations, Stella. It's all over now, and you can have your husband back at last.'

I raise an eyebrow. 'Only until the next programme starts, of course.'

Jennifer dismisses my comment with an airy wave of her hand and I fleetingly wonder how much she has had to drink. 'Don't think about that tonight – just enjoy! Anyway, I must let you circulate. You look amazing, by the way. It has been lovely to meet you. I do hope we meet again.'

With that she is off, air kissing and hugging her way through the crowds. As I watch her go, I wonder if I have been wrong about her, and about Alex, all along. Only her casual comment about me getting my husband back leaves a slight trace of doubt in my mind, but I immediately chastise myself for being so suspicious. I resolve to go on holiday with an open mind and a positive attitude towards my apparently brilliant husband who, as people have continually been telling me, desperately needs a break.

4 WELCOME TO ALLENBY

On the following Friday, the day before we are due to begin our odyssey on Two's Company, I pack up the car, diligently following the detailed list emailed to me by Alex. I then add what is, for me, a remarkably restrained amount of practical clothing, plus a basic selection of skincare and cosmetics, reasoning that luxury items will not be required on a trip like this. As I look around my walk-in wardrobe, barely altered by the removal of my holiday garments, I sadly contemplate the items for which I will have no use this year. No sundresses, swimsuits, sarongs or sandals for me, unless you count my well-worn Fit Flops. Too bad, but I must not 'dwell', as Alex calls it. I tell myself briskly that self-pity is a most unattractive quality and I won't gain anything by being miserable. Luckily, this last thought reminds me not to forget my pills.

Without really noticing it happen, I have become the type of woman who carries a special bag for her pills; all the little helpers which enable a perimenopausal insomniac with a tendency towards melancholy – I won't dignify it with the term depression – get through her days and nights. When it comes to my medicine bag, I have no intention of packing light for this holiday. I figure I will need all the chemical assistance I can get. In they all go – the packets of anti-depressants, sleeping pills and strong painkillers blagged from my GP, along with an array of herbal remedies and mood boosters purchased from health food shops in a perpetual triumph of hope over experience. Best to be prepared.

Finally, I'm ready to depart, as is Immo, who has been packed for hours and is eagerly looking forward to three weeks with her best friend Sam and her family. At precisely the agreed time, a gargantuan SUV rumbles up the drive and Harriet, Sam's mum, strides purposefully towards our front door. Close behind her is Sam herself who, with her long blonde hair and carefully cultivated, beetle-black eyebrows, is a carbon copy of Immo.

Whilst our daughters might be clones, their mothers have very little in common. Harriet, who originally trained as a Norland nanny, is a hyper-organised supermum to her brood of four, of which Sam is the eldest. I'm sure that, back in the day, she was a force to be reckoned with on the school hockey team and was undoubtedly a prefect, possibly even head girl. Her bombastic self-assurance brings back unpleasant memories of being bullied relentlessly at my comprehensive for being a nerd and, even more unforgivably, a female nerd. I'm polite to her but keep contact to a minimum. Imogen, of course, thinks she's wonderful, but then again, I remember idolising my best, or rather my only, friend's mum when I was at school, wishing my mum was more like her. As I wave them off, lock the house and prepare to depart for Leicestershire, I say a silent 'sorry' to my mum's memory and wonder what she would say if she could see me now. Nothing I would enjoy hearing, I suspect.

As I get into my car, I quickly cheer up at the prospect of a rare treat – a long car journey on my own. I have always enjoyed driving, which is a bonus when you're a consultant who has to go wherever the client wants. I'm picking Alex up at Leicester station later on, as he is working at the firm's London headquarters today and pointed out, quite reasonably in my view, that it was a waste of his time to travel back to Surrey, only to head north again straight afterwards. Although this plan allowed him neatly to sidestep the packing, I was happy to comply, as it means a few precious hours with just me and my playlists for company.

As I drive away, I begin playing my latest compilation, prepared especially for the journey. 'Girls on Tour', it's called, because it features all my favourite female artists, especially the ones whom Alex hates. As our house disappears in the rear-view mirror, Chrissie Hynde begins to serenade me with 'I'll Stand by You'. I hurriedly shuffle the tracks and wonder how that particular song made it onto the playlist.

Alex has booked our accommodation for tonight. By now, my expectations of our holiday have been well and truly managed, so I haven't even bothered to Google the hotel. I'm therefore astonished when, after a half hour drive from Leicester station, we arrive at a gorgeous country house hotel, surrounded by rolling parkland. Immaculate lawns sweep down to a tranquil lake, iridescent in the light of the warm evening, and a herd of deer grazes peacefully under the trees. As we step out of our car, a valet swoops down the stone steps to take care of our bags. Then, as we enter the imposing reception, all polished wood panelling and glittering chandeliers, we are each offered a glass of champagne. Apparently, the purpose of this is to assist us through the check-in process, which is hardly onerous, as the reception staff are a model of quiet efficiency.

Shortly afterwards, Alex joins me as I stand on the balcony of our cavernous bedroom, gazing out over the parkland. 'Good choice of hotel,'

I offer.

'Well, you deserve it.' He looks over at me and smiles. 'I know you're not exactly looking forward to boating, so I thought you could do with a little luxury, before we set off. Look, I have a few work emails to take care of – then I'll put my out of office message on and that will be it. Why don't you go and have a nice relaxing soak in the jacuzzi, before we go down to dinner?'

The jacuzzi in our bathroom is easily big enough for two and, as I step into the fragrant, frothing water, I recall a time when Alex would have been eager to join me. I push the thought firmly from my mind and luxuriate in the bubbles, then dress for dinner in a tunic and leggings – the most appropriate outfit I can muster from my pared-down holiday wardrobe.

As I reappear, Alex quickly and decisively flips his laptop shut. 'Perfect timing – I'm all done,' he announces proudly. 'You will not see this laptop again for the rest of the holiday, I promise. Come on – let's go to dinner.'

Over aperitifs, followed by a sumptuous tasting menu with wine pairings, we discuss Immo's surprisingly good school report, Hugo's forthcoming trip to the US and the various proposals for the future IT change programmes that Alex will undoubtedly direct, if and when they sell. We also talk about our friends and Alex's family; we even touch upon current affairs. The elephant in the room, tomorrow's departure on the narrowboat, is studiously avoided by both of us.

Later, in bed, my husband initiates sex. This a rare occasion for us, these days. Usually it's me who makes the first move and I have become used to being rebuffed quite frequently amid protestations from Alex that he is too tired. Recently, I admit, I haven't often bothered to try. Tonight, therefore, is a very welcome change. It really is. I hate that term 'making love' – don't you? As though love is something which can easily be manufactured with the help of a few drinks and some racy underwear. I don't know quite what Alex and I are making tonight. Amends, perhaps? Whatever it is; while it doesn't match up to the passion of our early days, it is a good start to our holiday, I think. An auspicious beginning. I sleep better than I have in ages.

Next morning, I feel quite cheery as I put on my first boating outfit, comprising my oldest Breton top, as battered and well-loved as a childhood teddy bear, plus a pair of baggy cargo pants. At breakfast I chomp my way through the lavish buffet, as Alex reassures me I will burn loads of calories when working the locks. I don't entirely buy his theory – I'm not going to be running a marathon, after all – but the pancakes and full English win out in the end. No surprise there.

Happily, the sun is shining as we depart for Allenby Marina, which makes it slightly easier to leave the haven of the luxury hotel. On the way, we pass through the pleasant village of Allenby St. Giles, basically a cluster of houses and a church, pub and shop, all perched on a modest hill overlooking a lush valley. It's vaguely reminiscent of the Cotswolds, minus the tourists, celebrities and politicians. As we head down the hill, Alex points out the shining ribbon of canal which snakes across the valley floor. From this distance it is indistinguishable from a river and I revise my expectations of something much more industrial. There's nothing dark or satanic about this place, that's for sure.

Soon we turn a corner and I'm treated to my first sight of the marina itself, directly below us. My first impression is that it's so much bigger than I expected. There must be at least two hundred narrowboats down there, moored in orderly rows alongside wooden jetties. The site is surrounded by well-tended lawns dotted with picnic tables, where groups of boaters appear to be enjoying an al fresco breakfast. It all looks very agreeable I have to admit. A few minutes later, as Alex pulls into the car park and stops next to what is clearly the marina office, I find myself hopping eagerly out of the car, keen for a closer look at the cornucopia of vessels before me.

There are boats of every style and colour, from the clearly traditional red and green variety, festooned with colourful accessories and overflowing plant pots, to the grey, riveted type that even I recognise as faux-industrial. They look impressive, but I'm positive no one has ever transported coal in those things. There are a few boats which appear to be stuck in a 1970s style time-warp – I'm vaguely reminded of the Mystery Machine from Scooby Doo – whilst several others have clearly not seen a lick of paint since The Everly Brothers were in the Top Ten. Then there's the names. I suddenly feel grateful for the rather twee name given to our boat; clearly it could have been much worse than Two's Company. True, I do spot some rather clever Latin names like Festina Lente, but they are far outnumbered by some truly terrible homegrown efforts, created by mangling our wonderful language. I know, I'm an annoying pedant, but do indulge me for a moment and you'll see what I mean. For instance, Meander is plastered over the side of one boat. 'Me and 'er'. Give me strength. I puzzle for a second over Thistledome until I realise it translates as 'This'll do me'. Christ. Boozer's Glory cheers me up, though, and I search around for other fun names until the strident voice of my husband interrupts my idle musing.

'Stella! Come on; stop daydreaming!'

I follow him dutifully into the marina office, where we are greeted warmly by a barrel chested, liberally bearded man clad almost entirely in Allenby Marina branded merchandise. I'm sure that, if he were to roll up his sleeves, I'd find the marina logo tattooed on one leathery bicep, possibly two.

'Morning, folks – welcome to Allenby Marina! I'm Ron. Are you lovely people here to pick up a hire boat?'

'Yes, we are,' Alex replies. 'The name's Pitulski.'

'Ah – so now we know! When your booking came over the Internet, we were wondering how to pronounce that one – weren't we, Joyce?' Ron looks over at a tiny woman with a halo of curly grey hair who is sitting at a desk in the corner, half hidden behind a huge computer screen.

'Yes, we were,' agrees Joyce 'and now we know it's dead easy – you just say it how you spell it! Where does it come from, me duck – the name?'

'It's a Polish name,' says Alex tersely. 'My parents are from Poland, but I was born and brought up in London.'

'We have some lovely Polish people around here, don't we, Ronnie? Very hard workers. I won't hear a word against them. There's even a Polish section in our local Tesco. I got you some really tasty sausages from there, Ronnie, do you remember?'

'I'm sure Mr. Pitoolski doesn't want to talk about sausages and would just like to see his boat' Ron answers firmly. 'This way, Mr. P. She's moored right outside, on the wharf.'

'I'm Alex, and this is my wife Stella.' Clearly Alex wants to prevent any further mention of our supposedly troublesome surname.

'OK, Alex and Stella. Let me show you around your boat, then I'll take you out for your free lesson. It'll last around an hour. We'll cruise down the cut for about half a mile, then we'll go through the first lock, turn her around in the winding hole and bring her right back to base. After that, you should be all ready to start your adventure!' Ron beams at us, his kindly face lighting up at the thought of the fun he is convinced we are going to have.

'No, you don't understand. We don't need any instruction. I'm a very experienced boater and I have already given my wife some in-depth training on how to work the locks. If you could just take me through the controls, in case they are different from the other boats I have steered, that will be quite sufficient. Oh – and please show my wife where all the cupboards are, how the cooker works – those kind of things.'

'Are you sure?' Ron looks deeply concerned. 'I'm a bit worried about just letting you go off on your own. Most people say they find my lessons very helpful. A few have even confessed they would have ended up in a right pickle, if it wasn't for me.'

'We'll be fine.'

'Alright then – if you're sure. In that case, let's start with the engine and the controls.'

'Stella, can you bring the bags on board, while Ron and I are in the engine room? It will save time – then he can show you around the boat.'

I can't believe Alex has asked me to lug the bags in by myself. Well actually I can – and I bet you can, too. So much for last night's romantic interlude. I find it even easier to understand why he was so rude to this kind man and why he has rejected his offer of a lesson which would have been so helpful to me. Nowadays, my husband hates being told what to do at the best of times and will be particularly reluctant to take instruction from Ron following the casual display of benign racism in the marina office. As ever, my needs come a poor second to his feelings.

As I struggle in with the last of the bags, Ron is just concluding his explanation of the engine and controls. Clearly relieved to be talking to me rather than my husband, he then guides me around the boat, which is remarkably well equipped. The kitchen even boasts a pestle and mortar, plus one of those handy devices for removing the skin from garlic cloves. I couldn't be more surprised. Encouraged by my positive reaction, Ron proudly demonstrates the ingenious, space-saving cupboards and shows me in detail how to work the cooker, shower and toilet. Meanwhile Alex lurks impatiently behind us, obviously eager to be off. When Ron starts explaining to me how to work the gas central heating, he can bear it no longer.

'Look, Ron, I don't mean to be rude – but it's July. We really are not going to need the gas central heating. If you don't mind, we'd just like to be on our way.'

Looking hurt, Ron drops the boat keys into Alex's outstretched hand. 'Right you are. I'll see you in three weeks.' Smiling at me, he proffers a business card. 'Here's the phone number for the marina, my lovely, just in case you need us. It'll be either me, Joyce whom you've met, or my business partner Eddie who answers the phone. We're always here to help. I'll be off, then. Bye now – have a nice holiday.'

Once he has gone, Alex sighs with relief. 'Christ, I thought we were never going to get rid of him. Right – let's get going. Just stick the food in the fridge – we can unpack the rest of the stuff later on.'

'OK - me duck.' I'm hoping a little humour will help Alex recapture last night's good mood, rather than making him even more tetchy. It could go either way, I think. As it turns out, I'm rewarded with a thin smile. Clearly, we're not out of the woods just yet.

As I shove the last of the food into the fridge, which of course seems tiny compared with our American-style behemoth back home, Alex fires up the engine. Unexpectedly, I'm suddenly filled with a sense of anticipation. Whilst this is far from being my ideal holiday, it's exciting to be doing something new. I trot through to the rear of the boat and join Alex as we set off.

The exit from the marina looks unfeasibly small to me. To make things even more difficult, it is spanned by a footbridge overhead, making it impossible to see if any boats are travelling past on the canal outside.

'Stella – go back through the boat and stand on the prow. If you see any boats coming, yell "stop". If I don't hear from you, I'll assume I'm clear to pull out. Off you go – quick!'

I scuttle obediently through the boat to the area at the front which, according to Ron, is rather unpleasantly named 'the cratch'. From there, I manage to scramble clumsily onto the prow of the boat. As I attempt to stand upright, I narrowly avoid hitting my head on the footbridge as the boat starts to pass underneath it. I hear Alex yell something, but I can't make out what he is shouting. It's probably just as well. I hastily duck down and look left and right for boats, but thankfully the canal is deserted, so I cling to the roof of the boat with one hand and give Alex a cautious thumbs-up with the other.

Alex wasn't lying when he said he knew how to manoeuvre a narrowboat. As I watch, he guides Two's Company smoothly through the narrow gap under the footbridge, then pushes the tiller decisively to the right. The boat swoops across the canal in a graceful arc, making a perfect left turn. I feel quite proud of him, until I realise with a start that we never actually discussed whether to turn left or right. It appears I have just embarked upon a three-week holiday with absolutely no idea of where we're going.

I retrace my steps to the back of the boat and resume my place alongside Alex. 'Nicely done, Cap'n!' I begin breezily, using my best Captain Pugwash accent. Although I'm annoyed at not being consulted, I decide it's not worth starting a fight just after we have set off on our holiday. My husband, however, has no such qualms.

'I wish I could say the same for you,' he growls in response. 'You nearly took your head off on that footbridge. I must say, for an intelligent woman, you can be a real klutz sometimes.'

'I suppose that's why you didn't see fit to consult me on the route,' I fire back, all thoughts of peace-making instantly forgotten. Of course, there is always the possibility Alex doesn't actually have a plan and just turned left on impulse, but I dismiss this thought immediately. My husband always has a plan and he doesn't do impulsive.

'I didn't see much point, to be honest,' Alex replies. 'You don't know the area, nor do you know how to interpret a waterways guidebook. Also, I wasn't sure you'd want to be consulted. After all, you haven't actually shown much interest in this holiday, now have you?'

I have two options here. Option One – lose my temper and yell that my lack of interest is hardly surprising, given his autocratic approach to planning this holiday. Option Two – bite my tongue, pour us both a glass of wine and ask him to show me the guidebook and the route. Swallowing my pride, I choose the latter. I just don't feel up for a tempestuous start to our holiday, which could herald three weeks' worth of rows or, even worse, stony silences and protracted sulks – Alex's speciality. I count to ten as I watch the pleasant Leicestershire countryside drift past, then suggest a glass of Sauvignon Blanc and a run-through the itinerary.

'OK, but just a small one for you,' warns Alex. 'You need to stay focused, ready for the locks.'

Without bothering to reply, I head down to the kitchen, or rather the galley, as I'm apparently supposed to call it. I quickly down a large, surreptitious glass of Sauvignon Blanc, then pour two more and take them up to the back counter for Alex and me.

'Right, so here's the immediate plan,' he begins, pointing to a page in the guidebook. 'We're currently heading south east on the Leicester Arm of the Grand Union Canal. There's Allenby Marina, where we started – can you see it?' He points to a capital M, surrounded by a square, and I nod. 'Obviously we've only got half a day left today, so we'll moor around here, near this aqueduct. It looks like a nice rural place to stop for the night – lots of peace and quiet. Then, tomorrow, we'll head through Foxton. It's a famous canal centre with a really picturesque staircase. There are great views from the top and the pubs aren't too shabby, as I recall. We'll call in to one of them for a drink if we have time, then head on down the Grand Union.'

Alex pauses to sip some of his wine and flip to a different page in the guidebook. I consider asking him what on earth a staircase has got to do with boating but decide to keep quiet for the moment.

'OK, so this is the overall plan for the whole three weeks.' Alex points to a map of England, where waterways twist their way across most of the country. 'We continue down the Grand Union, all the way to Norton Junction, just here, which marks the end of the Leicester Arm. After that we turn right and travel through the lovely village of Braunston, where we turn left onto the Oxford Canal and proceed as far as we can until the halfway point in our holiday, when we turn the boat around in a winding hole and cruise back to Allenby. Who knows, we might make it to Oxford and, even if we don't, there are loads of beautiful places to see along the way.'

Oxford is very nice, don't get me wrong – but I could drive there from my house in under three hours, M25 and M40 permitting. Still, I guess that's hardly the point. It's all about the journey, not the destination, I tell myself firmly. In an attempt to show interest, I ask Alex to flip back to the original page in the guidebook showing today's portion of the journey and peer closely at the map, trying to understand the notation.

'So why is the canal shown as a red stripe and a blue stripe?'

'The red line alongside the blue line of the canal denotes the towpath. You'll see it sometimes switches sides, so the red line tells you which side of the canal the towpath is on.'

'OK. So, what are those little black arrows, here and there on the canal?'

'Those, Stella, are the locks. The U-shaped arrows mark the winding holes, where the canal has been widened out so you can turn a narrowboat around. Note as well that all the bridges are numbered, so we can use them as way markers, to show us exactly where we are at any one time. Clever, isn't it?'

I look up from the guidebook and scan the canal ahead. Right on cue, a small brick-built bridge appears in the distance. From here, it looks far too narrow for our boat to go through, but as we get closer, I see it will be wide enough, although with little room for error. I'm sure that won't bother Alex, though. On the apex of the bridge I spot a plaque with a number on it and strain my eyes to read it as the boat glides closer.

'That looks like – Bridge 84.'

'Correct.'

I look down at the guidebook. 'Then, right after Bridge 84, there's one of those arrows.'

'That's right, Stella – your first lock.'

'And we're mooring – down here.'

'Right again.'

I count the arrows on the map and attempt to quell my rising panic. 'Alex – there are seven arrows between here and the place where we are mooring tonight. That means I have got to do seven locks!'

'Well done, Sherlock. I thought it would be best to break you in straight away, so you can put into practice what you have learned from my presentation and from Jamie's model.'

The bridge is now upon us and is just wide enough for our boat to pass. As Alex confidently steers us through the narrow gap and we emerge on the other side, I see a row of bollards on the towpath to the right. Just beyond them, in the middle of the canal, our way forward is barred by an imposing set of lock gates, topped with two very heavy looking black wooden beams, tipped with white. I stare at them and my stomach does back flips, but not in a good way, like it does when you meet someone you really fancy. No – this is bad. Very bad indeed. I realise with a sinking feeling that I can remember precisely nothing about Alex's presentation or Jamie's model. If Alex wants to 'break me in', he's about to do a fabulous job.

5 BAPTISM OF FIRE

My husband slows the boat right down and pulls in towards the canal bank, alongside the bollards. 'Right, Stella – off you get,' he commands.

Imagine a chubby penguin wearing a Breton top. That's what I undoubtedly look like as I launch myself across the small gap which separates the back of the boat from the towpath. I land heavily, jolting an ankle, but it could have been worse. I congratulate myself for not falling in the water and start hobbling off towards the lock, until Alex calls me back.

'Stella! Haven't you forgotten something?'

'What's that?'

'Your windlass, Stella – to open and close the paddles? You won't get very far without it.' Alex holds up a heavy-looking metal object, a scornful look on his face. As I walk shamefacedly back to the boat and take the windlass from him, he scathingly says, 'Focus, Stella. I knew I shouldn't have let you have that glass of wine.'

Without bothering to reply, I grab the windlass from his hand and stomp off towards the lock. On the way, I give myself a stern talking-to. 'Really, how hard can this be? You're a Physics BSc after all, Stella – you can work it out. Go on – make Alex wind his neck in by actually doing this thing properly.'

As I reach the lock, I see it's full of water and, mercifully, some of my supposedly in-depth training comes back. I remember I need to empty the lock, let the boat in, close the gates and then re-fill it, thereby lifting up said boat. Easy-peasy. I locate the ground paddles on either side of the gates and recall that I need to open them first although, for the life of me, I can't remember why. 'Who cares,' I say to myself, 'just get the bloody things open.'

I push the windlass onto the spindle of the nearest paddle and try to turn it. Nothing – it won't budge an inch. Christ alive, these things are stiff.

37

I push harder, until I hear a shout from Alex. I look round at him, cup one hand behind my ear and he obligingly yells more loudly.

'Other way!'

Oh – right. I switch the windlass around and push in the other direction. This time, the windlass begins to turn and, as if by magic, the lock begins to empty. Good-oh. I'm getting the hang of this. I rotate the windlass happily and look ahead of me down the canal, where a beautifully decorated boat has just pulled up alongside the bollards on the other side of the lock. I'm delighted to see that the two occupants of the boat are waving at me. How friendly everyone is, on the canals. It's going to be just like they said at Fat Club – relaxing and oh, so friendly. I feel even cheerier when I see one of the occupants, a woman, jumping off the boat and running towards me, windlass in hand. I call out to her:

'No need to rush! I've got this – although some help would be nice.'

As she gets closer, I see that, contrary to my expectations, the woman does not look friendly. Not friendly at all.

'What the hell are you doing?' she yells at me by way of a greeting.

'I'm – I'm just emptying the lock, so our boat can go through.'

'Didn't you see us coming? We have got right of way – the lock is in our favour.' As she speaks, the woman glances briefly at our boat below, then back at me. 'Hire boaters. I might have known. You lot don't care which boat has the right of way, nor how much water you waste…'

I hurriedly cut her lecture short. 'Look, I'm sorry. I didn't mean to be inconsiderate; it's just that this is my first ever lock and I forgot about rights of way. I was just concentrating on working the lock properly. I do apologise.'

The woman appears unmoved by my grovelling apology. 'If it's your first ever lock, then you must have departed from Allenby Marina,' replies the super-sleuth of the canal network.

'Yes, that's right. My husband and I have just started our holiday.'

'Well, we're going there now to buy diesel. While we're filling up, I'll call in at the marina office and give Ron and Joyce a piece of my mind. They have no business letting beginners like you take a boat out without proper instruction. Now you help me refill this lock and get our boat through. While we're doing it, I'll provide you with the guidance which Ron should have given you, but obviously didn't!'

With that she marches off to the far side of the lock, before I have a chance to defend poor Ron. With brusque hand signals she shows me how to close my paddle then open the one at the other end to re-fill the lock. After that, once the water is level, we shift the heavy wooden gates to let her boat in, by pushing our backsides against them. I find I can do that bit quite well; having a sizeable posterior is sometimes useful, I reflect ruefully. However, I do find the whole business surprisingly strenuous, but I console myself with the thought that, with six more locks to go after this one, I'm likely to burn off all the pancake and sausage calories from breakfast.

After what seems like ages, the lock has been re-filled and then emptied, with Miss Marple's boat in it, so it's time for her to head north towards Allenby. Without a word of goodbye, she runs off to join her husband on the boat. 'So much for friendliness,' I reflect, thinking sadly of poor, kindly Ron whom I have unwittingly dropped right in it.

I wait for Alex to steer our boat into the lock, uncomfortably aware that he's bound to have witnessed the whole pantomime. As he passes me, his face like thunder, he calls out, 'That went well, Stella! Clearly you've forgotten everything I taught you about rights of way.'

I'm not going to let him get away with that – not after my humiliation at the hands of Miss Marple. 'Well, if you had let me have the lesson with Ron, maybe I would have remembered!' I fire back.

'That's no excuse!' Alex retorts. 'My training was perfectly adequate – it's just that you still seem to be suffering from baby brain, even though our youngest will soon have left school! Go and shut the lock gates behind me – if you can manage to do that.'

Red-faced and furious, I storm off and close the gates. Next, I open the paddles and fill the lock, just like old grumpy knickers on the other boat showed me, staring fixedly at the rising water level and trying hard to calm down. Once the lock is full, I laboriously push the gates open, then shut them again behind the boat once it has exited the lock. With Miss Marple's harshly delivered advice still ringing in my ears, I remember to close all the paddles before leaving the lock, as she taught me, before running along the towpath to catch up with Alex on the boat. As I draw alongside, though, I discover he has no intention of stopping for me.

'There's no point in you getting back on!' he calls as I puff my way along the towpath. 'It's not far to the next lock – you might as well walk. Oh – and Stella?'

'What?' I glare at him, white-hot rage coursing through me.

'You forgot your windlass – again.'

Cue a frantic dash back to the first lock, followed by a ragged sprint to the next one, to prepare it for the boat's arrival. As I run, I wonder how on earth I am going to get through the next three weeks. Before I left home, I had imagined boredom was going to be my main problem. Right now, though, boredom seems like nirvana compared with the exhaustion and indignity I've suffered so far. Grimly I accept that, if I'm to survive this ordeal without drowning in self-pity, I need to make what Immo calls an 'attitude adjustment'.

A few minutes later I reach lock number two, repeatedly humming 'Anger is an Energy' under my breath. John Lydon is an unlikely mentor for me, I admit, but the song helps me channel my rage and lends a tense, febrile strength to my muscles. I blitz my way efficiently through the next lock, slam the final gate shut with a resounding 'thunk' and am jogging away, filled with a grim satisfaction, when I hear Alex's voice shouting:

'Stella – you've left the bloody paddles up! The gate has bounced open as well – you shouldn't have slammed it so hard.'

'I'll slam you against something hard, if you're not careful' I mutter angrily to myself as I stride back to the lock, close the paddles and shut the wretched gate.

As I march towards lock number three, I discover that, if you walk briskly, you actually catch up with a narrowboat on the move. As Ron told me earlier, narrowboats have a maximum speed of four miles per hour and etiquette decrees that they travel even more slowly when passing moored boats, to avoid disturbing the occupants. Although I feel like strangling Alex right now, I can't deny he is always courteous to strangers, if not to his wife. A few boats are tied up at the side of the canal, so he slows right down as he approaches them, and I quickly draw alongside Two's Company. This is unfortunate, as I would much rather avoid my husband right now. I stare fixedly ahead as I march along the towpath, determined not to make eye contact as I stew in my own righteous indignation. Alex, though, has other ideas. Although he never apologises to me for anything, I can tell he feels he has been too hard on me as he holds out his version of an olive branch.

'Stella – the next two locks are quite close, but after that there's a bigger gap. Why don't you get back on the boat then, so you don't have to walk too far?'

'No,' I respond flatly. 'I'm going to walk between all five remaining locks. After all, you're the one who is always saying I should take more exercise.'

'Suit yourself.'

Alex looks rather hurt at my rejection of his peace offering and I feel the urge to give in and smooth things over like I usually do, but I resist the temptation and am actually relieved when I turn a corner and see the gates of lock three ahead of me.

I concentrate hard and work the lock in silence, but my head is full of Miss Marple's stridently delivered advice. I've had more enjoyable earworms, I have to say. 'Always leave each lock with all gates and paddles closed!' is the mantra that repeats in my head, over and over again. I'm determined not to make a mistake this time. I will not give Alex the satisfaction of shouting at me again. As I open the gates and he steers the boat out of the lock, I keep my head down to avoid his gaze and beetle around, closing the paddles on both sides. I then shut the gate on the far side of the lock, deploying my backside to shift the heavy beam. 'Nearly there,' I think as I retrace my steps and start to close the final gate on the towpath side. 'Paddles down – check. Gates almost done…'

It's then I hear my husband shouting at me yet again and I look up, puzzled. What the bloody hell have I done wrong now?

'Stella! Leave that gate open! Look – there's another boat coming! Open your eyes!'

I look ahead of me down the canal, see another boat cruising towards us and quickly revise Miss Marple's mantra. Clearly 'always close all the gates' really means 'always close all the gates, unless another boat is coming'. Makes sense, I suppose. I see Alex greeting the occupant of the boat as they pass each other, and I hurry back to the far side of the lock to open the other gate. Unfortunately, this earns me another tongue-lashing.

'Leave that one shut, Stella! She can go through on one gate!'

It seems as though I can't do anything right. I look on in mute anger as the pretty blonde woman at the tiller steers her boat expertly into the lock through the narrow gap left by the one open gate. She gives me a friendly smile, which takes me by surprise and prompts me to call out to her.

'I'm sorry I started closing the gates! I didn't see you coming.'

'That's no problem,' she replies with another smile. 'Your husband explained you're just learning the ropes. You're doing great! Would you mind closing the gate behind me? I'm a solo boater, so it would be a big help.'

I'm aware that my mouth has dropped open in surprise. 'You mean – you do all this by yourself? Working the locks, steering the boat – the lot?'

'Yes – it's fine.' Expertly she flicks a rope over a bollard to steady her boat as I run to close the gate. 'I get plenty of nice people offering to help – and there's no one else on the boat to shout at me!' She gives me a cheeky wink as she jumps onto the towpath to open the paddles.

As I contemplate her long, tanned legs in their denim shorts, I imagine she does indeed get many offers of assistance. I can't feel jealous, though, either of her competence or her lovely legs, as I'm so grateful for her kindness. Her warmth stays with me, cheering me as I make my way to lock number four, which is clearly visible just ahead.

On my approach to the lock I pass some more moored boats and marvel at how colourful they look in the afternoon sunlight. One is a veritable market garden, with tubs full of salad leaves and tomato plants crammed into every available space on the roof and deck. Another rather shabby craft has so many bicycles, logs and folding chairs on its roof that I'm surprised the owner can see over them to steer the boat. Mind you, the thing looks as though it hasn't moved in about twenty years, so maybe this isn't an issue.

Happily, the lock is in our favour, so I open the gates to allow Alex to drive through, then shut the first gate. As I go to shut the second, I'm treated to the sound of two voices shouting at me in unison. Here we go again. What have I done wrong this time? One of the voices belongs to Alex, naturally. The other person I have apparently riled is the man at the tiller of Market Garden, which has just pulled out into the canal from its mooring place.

'Wait!' yells Alex. 'That boat wants to join us!'

Obediently I keep the second gate open and wait for Market Garden to arrive. As he attempts to enter the lock, it's clear the old man at the tiller is not as skilled as the gorgeous blonde from lock three. His boat hits the narrow opening on both sides with a couple of resounding clunks and he glares at me as though this is somehow my fault.

'You didn't exactly make that easy for me, love,' he grumbles, and I realise he was expecting me to have reopened the first gate for him. Clearly you can't win at this boating lark. Before I have a chance to reply I'm joined on the towpath by a frail, elderly woman, presumably his long-suffering partner.

'Sorry about my husband,' she begins, 'he can get a bit tetchy at times.'

'I can relate, believe me,' I reply and smile gratefully at her. Maybe the canals are quite friendly after all. Together we close the gate, enclosing the two boats, then walk to the front of the lock to open the paddles and fill it. After I've opened my ground paddle, I glance across at my companion and see she has already finished opening hers and is sitting calmly on the balance beam. It's then that my competitive instincts kick in. I can't believe this fragile-looking woman, who must be at least twenty years my senior, can work the locks more quickly than me. I rush over to my gate paddle, hurriedly fit the windlass onto the spindle and push hard. Happily, it is a lot less stiff than the ground paddle and I attempt to demonstrate my relatively youthful vigour by rotating my windlass as rapidly as possible. Sadly, I fail to notice the sign on the lock warning boaters that gate paddles must not be opened until the lock is at least half full. So keen am I to prove myself that I also fail to see that my companion has not opened her own gate paddle yet. Talk about pride coming before a fall – or rather a waterfall, in this case.

Instantly a noisy torrent of water issues forth, gushing through my gate paddle and causing Market Garden to ricochet crazily between the walls of the lock and our boat. Water cascades across its prow and splashes liberally into the cratch. Several tomatoes are shaken from their stems and plop into the murky depths of the lock. Predictably, Alex yells at me, but thankfully I can't make out what he is shouting due to the noise of the water. Meanwhile my elderly companion climbs nimbly across the lock gates, showing remarkable agility for her age.

'Just close the paddle for a minute, dear,' she gently advises.

I do as she says, and the torrent subsides. By now, however, I am welling up and could easily produce my very own flood of tears, with minimal encouragement.

My companion must have noticed my distress as she puts her hand on my arm and says in a calm, soothing voice, 'The gate paddles on these locks can be quite fierce, dear, if you're not used to them. Don't worry, there's really no harm done, apart from a small amount of water in our cratch, which will dry out in no time in this sunny weather. I suggest you have a nice big gin once you moor up and forget all about it. Right – looks like it's time to open the gates and let our two grumpy old gits out. Or maybe we should just leave them there – and go down the pub?'

'Tempting,' I laugh, suddenly feeling much better. 'Unfortunately, we have three more locks left to do before we moor up, so I'd better crack on.'

'Lucky you. We're going to get as close as we can to Foxton tonight. My husband likes to have his tea early, which is why we were moored up back there, then he prefers to carry on boating until it's practically dark. Strictly speaking, you're not supposed to run your engine after eight o'clock at night, but he takes no notice. He doesn't care about disturbing other people. Personally, I'd like to sit on the towpath and enjoy the evening sun in weather like this, but I get no choice in the matter.'

For a moment I feel thankful for Alex and his love of an early evening drink whilst on holiday. I feel even more grateful that I will have the company of this feisty and efficient lady through my final three locks. I'm amazed that I could ever have thought her frail.

Even in the company of Maud, my new best friend, I still manage to get it wrong a few times. At lock number five I leave a windlass hanging from a gate spindle and Maud gently explains to me how said windlass could easily spin off and become a lethal metal projectile. Apparently, a friend of hers had his nose broken by a flying windlass and another bruised his hand very badly. Who knew boating was such a dangerous pursuit? If I had wanted to take up an extreme sport, I would have gone for something more glamorous, like volcano boarding. Then, at lock number six, I find myself on the wrong side of a balance beam as it unexpectedly springs back, and I narrowly miss being bounced right into the lock. This incident earns me another dire warning from Maud about the possibility of drowning through being sucked down into the depths of the lock by the current created from the flow of water through the open paddles. I begin to suspect that Maud has a love of all things macabre, but I'm still sorry to bid her goodbye when we finish the seventh and, for me, the final lock of the day.

'I wish you could join me for that large gin,' I say as I prepare to take my leave.

'So do I, but you never know – we might run into each other again. It's a small world, on the canals!' With that, Maud trots off to catch up with her boat and boards it with a sprightly leap.

I reflect that it is just as well she is so fit for her age, as her husband barely slows down to let her back on. By contrast, Alex has brought Two's

Company to a halt a little further down the canal and is waiting for me.

'Right, there's not much further to go, then we can moor up for the night. In the meantime, I thought you could use a glass of this.'

From behind his back, my husband produces a bottle of fizz and two glasses. I glance at the label and notice it's a decent brand of champagne, not Prosecco.

'I put it in the fridge while we were doing the first lock, so it should be nice and cold.' Expertly he pops the cork, pours two glasses and hands me one. Then he clinks his glass against mine. 'Here's to you. I know this afternoon hasn't been easy for you, but well done for surviving your first set of locks. Tomorrow should be easier.'

Alex is an expert at this – making me burn with hatred for him one minute, then wrong-footing me the next with his unexpected kindness. Often, I'm easily won over, but not this time.

'Alex. You have spent the entire afternoon yelling abuse at me. You can't expect me to forget all about it, just because you pour me a glass of champagne.'

'But Stella – I have to shout when I'm on the boat and you're on the towpath, or you'd never hear me. Also, when you make a mistake whilst working the locks, you have to put it right quickly. There's no time for niceties. Don't take it personally. You actually did pretty well out there. Now just relax and enjoy your champagne, while I find us a nice place to moor.'

Sensibly, Alex shuts up at this point, restarts the engine and the boat resumes its leisurely progress down the canal. The early evening sun bathes the surrounding countryside in a golden glow which is more flattering than any Instagram filter. Just ahead of us, a heron stands sentinel on the towpath, then flaps lazily away as we approach, circling behind the boat to resume its vigil on the opposite bank. A moorhen darts nervously in and out of the reeds then, just around the next bend in the canal, we pass a pair of swans gliding serenely along. Meanwhile I drain my first glass of champagne, accept a refill offered promptly by Alex and suddenly the world doesn't seem quite so bad.

'This looks like a good place – just after the aqueduct. Pop up to the front, Stella, then jump off the prow with the rope in your hand, as I pull alongside. That's all you need to do – just keep hold of the rope and I'll tie her up.'

This time I jolt my other ankle as I jump off, but the pain is muted by my champagne-induced glow and the relief of having survived my first day's boating. True to his word, Alex expertly ties the boat to the metal piling and sets up two folding chairs on the towpath.

'Let's finish off the champagne and relax for a bit, then I'll fire up the barbecue. You can go and have a shower if you like, while I cook. The water will be nice and hot as the engine has been running for a few hours. It's the engine that heats the water up.'

I can feel my anger dissipating under the combined offensive of several glasses of champagne, Alex's offer to cook dinner and the prospect of a nice hot shower. It's simply too exhausting to stay mad at him. I give in and decide to play nice, but without sounding too grateful. 'Sounds like a plan.'

We quickly empty the bottle of champagne and I float off soon afterwards to check out the shower room. I have been bracing myself to rough it during this holiday by washing in a miserable dribble of a shower, returning home less clean than Immo after her first trip to Reading Festival last summer, but I'm pleasantly surprised. As promised by Alex, the water is hot, and the pressure is pleasingly strong. I have a leisurely shower, then leave my hair to dry naturally as I unpack our clothes and put them away.

Fifteen minutes later I'm feeling nicely refreshed. I'm wearing a new set of clean, albeit scruffy clothes and I have even bothered to put on a touch of slap and a squirt of perfume. I fling open the bedroom curtains, confident I look presentable enough, should anyone be passing by on the towpath and happen to look in. That's when I see Alex, tapping away busily on his phone as dinner sizzles on the barbecue beside him. I plug my own phone into the charging point at the front of the boat, then stick my head out of the window.

'Can I bring you a glass of wine?'

My husband puts down his phone just a little too quickly. 'Thanks Stella – that would be good.'

I pour two large, chilled glasses of Picpoul and take them outside. Alex accepts his glass with a smile.

'Great, cheers. I'll take this with me while I have a shower – if there is any water left, that is.'

'I was wondering about the capacity of the tank while I was showering.'

'Not wondering hard enough to take a shorter shower, I notice. You were in there ages! We'll have to fill the tank tomorrow, due to your extravagance.'

I look over at my husband, expecting him to appear displeased, but instead he just has a cheeky smile on his face. Well what do you know – he just made a joke, of sorts. Clearly the champagne has had a mellowing effect on him as well.

'Right – I'm off.' He slips his phone into the back pocket of his jeans. 'Can you keep an eye on the ribs, please? I don't want them to burn.'

'Sure, but may I borrow your phone? I need to FaceTime Immo and mine is just charging up.'

Am I imagining things, or is there a slight hesitation before Alex agrees? Maybe, but he taps in the passcode anyway and hands the device over to me, looking happy enough. Bless him. Does he really imagine I don't know the code for his phone? As I take the phone from him, I reflect on the power which comes from being constantly underestimated.

As soon as Alex is out of sight, I check his texts and see he has neither received nor sent a text message since yesterday. Next, I go to WhatsApp and discover he has just had a conversation with someone called Jonathan, who is complaining he has not yet received an update on the project. What project could this be? As far as I know Alex has not yet secured a follow-up to Leviathan; programmes of that size take months, if not years, to sell. However, it's highly likely he has a smaller project running which he hasn't mentioned to me. Ever the professional, Alex replied promptly to Jonathan just a few minutes ago, telling him he's on holiday but will provide an update as soon as possible.

Satisfied I know the reason for the hurried tapping and not wanting to be caught snooping, I FaceTime Immo, who has spent a totally inactive day sunbathing in the garden with Sam and is about to go and hang out with her and a few other friends in the family's large 'den'. They are clearly having a wonderful time doing absolutely nothing. I envy them their teenage luxury of wasted time and the illusion of an endless supply of it stretching ahead of them.

Dutifully, Immo remembers to ask me how our holiday is going, and I recount all my embarrassing boating mishaps. My daughter laughs at my blunders, which helps me to process them and put them behind me. She knows from experience that our shared hilarity can help wipe the egg from my face and I love the way she wants to help me feel better.

While we are talking, Alex reappears, and I motion for him to come and join us. Immo instantly switches to the more grown-up, slightly formal persona she adopts with her father, asking him if he is managing to relax and if his work colleagues are leaving him alone.

'Yes, they are, Minnie – thanks for asking. There's one client called Jonathan who is hassling me a bit, but I should be able to keep him off my back with minimal effort.'

'That's good to know. Oh, and Daddy – no one says "hassle" any more, by the way.'

'Thanks for the heads up, Minnie. I'll just take my Zimmer frame and go check on the barbecue.'

'No worries – have a nice dinner. I've got to say goodbye anyway. Just remember - you tell Jonathan, or whatever his name is, that if he doesn't let you enjoy your holiday in peace, he'll have me to deal with!'

'I probably won't pass on that message as he's a fee-paying client, but I appreciate the sentiment. Right, I'm off – talk to you tomorrow.'

Alex disappears and Imogen and I sign off in a flurry of 'love yous' in the modern fashion. I recall that my Mum never said she loved me – at least, not until near the end – but I always knew she did, no matter how badly I behaved. I really did. As I click the red button and Immo's face disappears, I hope she does too.

As the sun sets on our first day of boating, Alex and I enjoy a peaceful barbecue. In the manner of so many long-married couples, we don't feel the need to talk much. We discuss Hugo's forthcoming trip to the US, but for the most part we keep silent. As I gaze up at the sky, which is streaked through with pink and gold, I feel grateful that my husband isn't treating me to a recap of the afternoon or trying to hand out boating tips. Long may it continue.

When it gets too chilly to remain outside, we check out the DVD collection on the boat, refill our glasses and decide on Notting Hill, which we both have seen about a million times before. The fact that we can watch films on the boat is a welcome revelation to me and the undemanding comfort of a good old Richard Curtis romantic comedy is a perfectly soothing way to end a day which has definitely had its moments.

Now I know you aren't supposed to take a sleeping pill if you've had a skinful of wine and champagne. After all, there is a warning on every pack. Tonight, though, not for the first time, I ignore the advice of the NHS. I'm not a great sleeper at the best of times, and tonight I need oblivion to help me face day two of boating. Also, despite the relative peace of our first evening together on the boat, I'm not in the mood for any more 'make amends' sex. As Alex opens out the large double bed which fills the entire width of the cabin, I hurriedly take off my make-up, clean my teeth and gulp down a couple of pills, then go and join him. After that, everything goes blank, which is just fine by me.

6 WELL MET

Next morning, I wake to the welcome smell of coffee and toast and the less agreeable sound of my husband's voice, urging me to get up.

'Come on, Stella, get going! We've got a long way to go today and lots of locks ahead of us!'

Deep joy. I struggle out of bed, groggily throw on the first T-shirt and pair of shorts I can find, bundle my bird's nest of hair into a scrunchie, then shuffle into the galley in search of that toast and coffee. As I gratefully inhale the steam from my first mug, Alex seats himself next to me and shoves the guidebook under my nose. Clearly there is going to be no chance for me to wake up gradually over a leisurely breakfast.

'Right, here's the plan for this morning. We have five locks in a kind of flight, although they're a bit spread out. Lock number one is not far off, then there's quite a big gap before lock number two, so you can get back on the boat then, if you like.'

How generous of him. I remain silent, defiantly cramming peanut butter toast into my mouth. Sod the calories; I'm bound to burn them off anyway, by running around getting everything wrong.

'Locks two, three and four are quite close together, then there's another gap, so you get a second chance for a rest. After that there's just one more lock, then you can relax properly all the way to Foxton. We won't worry about Foxton yet; we'll discuss it at lunchtime. Oh, I almost forgot! After the five locks we go through a tunnel. That'll be an interesting experience for you. Right – let's head off. I'll go up to the back counter and start untying.'

I can't imagine how the tunnel thing is going to work and I'm vaguely concerned about why we need to worry about Foxton, but I push these thoughts to the back of my mind and focus on my more immediate problem, namely the five locks which are coming right up. Five wonderful opportunities for me to make mistakes and be shouted at all over again. I can't wait. I refill my coffee mug, add a generous slug of whisky – don't judge me – and join Alex at the back of the boat.

As I emerge into the pale, hazy morning sunlight I see Alex has already untied and is pushing the boat away from the bank. As he jumps back on, he guns the engine and gasps breathlessly, 'Did you see that, Stella? A boat just came past us. If we hurry, we can catch them up and partner them through the locks. That means half the workload for you.'

I'm not sure this is entirely welcome news. I think I would rather do all the work myself than have another Miss Marple scrutinising my every move. Even a pleasant companion like Maud, with her overactive imagination, would get a bit wearing after five locks. I say a silent prayer for a lovely, understanding lock buddy and, for once, the man upstairs is listening.

As we approach lock number one, I see both gates are open, and the boat Alex was chasing is waiting patiently inside. I grab my windlass – I'm not about to forget it a third time – swig the last of my illicit, whisky-laced coffee and jump off the boat onto the towpath.

When I arrive at the lock, I see a genial-looking, bearded man about my age standing beside it. He tips his wide-brimmed boater's hat in a friendly greeting and calls out to me.

'Perfect timing! I thought I was going to be doing all these locks myself. How lucky to have someone to share the work; it looks as though it's going to be a hot day.'

'You might not think yourself quite so lucky, once we get going,' I reply. 'This is only my second day's boating and I think I made every possible mistake yesterday. I'll try not to repeat them today but, being realistic, I'm pretty likely to screw up again.'

'No worries!' my companion says cheerfully. 'You and your husband are just learning; that's absolutely fine. We all had to learn at some point. I'll talk you through everything and I'll help you out if you need it.'

'Thanks, but you don't quite understand. It's just me who's learning. My husband is already an experienced boater – he used to go boating as a teenager. That's what I'm finding so difficult.' Feeling only slightly disloyal, I confide, 'He's not the most patient of men and, because he knows what he's doing, he has forgotten what it's like to be a beginner. That's why I get such a hard time from him, whenever I mess up.'

At that moment, Two's Company glides past us into the lock, with Alex concentrating hard to ensure he does not lose face by hitting either the other boat or the side of the lock. In the boat goes, sweet as a nut. I see the look of satisfaction on my husband's face and glance at my new companion as if to say, 'See?'

'Right, let's close the gates behind them, then we'll go to the other end and fill the lock,' my companion explains. 'Afterwards, once we've finished this lock, I suggest we walk to the next one together. On the way, I'll explain to you how I know your husband is not half as good a boater as he thinks he is.'

Well, now I am intrigued. I copy my companion carefully and we complete the first lock without incident. As he sets off, Alex calls over to remind me I can come back on board, but I decline his offer and walk off with my new friend, who introduces himself as Chris.

'OK, let me tell you why your husband still has a lot to learn about boating,' Chris begins. 'Take a look at the tiller of your boat. Do you notice he has draped the mooring rope around the tiller pin, so it hangs down?'

'Yes – what's the problem with that?' I try not to appear too gleeful as I glance over at Two's Company and see that Alex looks pretty pissed off. Clearly my decision to walk away with Chris has not gone down very well.

'The problem is, if the rope comes free and falls into the water, it could easily get wrapped around the propeller, bringing your boat to a standstill and taking hours to disentangle. I once had to saw a guy's mooring rope off the prop with a breadknife. That's not the worst of it, though. Say, if the rope also gets hooked around the foot, or arm, of the person at the tiller, then slips into the water and wraps itself around the prop. In a situation like that, the person can get dragged into the water and mangled pretty comprehensively by the prop. Like they were in a Moulinex. Granted, it doesn't happen very often, but when it does, it's pretty gruesome. You might want to warn your husband.'

'Thanks, that's very – illuminating,' I reply, thinking that Chris's macabre imagination puts Maud's to shame, and resolving to choose my moment carefully before telling Alex he's doing something wrong. Thankfully, though, the conversation then takes a less alarming turn. We discuss our respective families and I learn that the man at the tiller of Chris's boat is his brother, who is going through an acrimonious divorce and needs a break. Chris is divorced himself, but apparently has an amicable relationship with his ex, with whom he shares custody of their two children.

While we complete the next three locks, Chris and I work well together, as he calmly explains how the locks operate and why each particular step is performed. I don't hear a word from Alex the whole time and my confidence in how to work the locks soars. In between, I chat away happily about Imogen and Hugo. As I proudly mention Hugo's job in the US, I suddenly realise I haven't heard from my son for the last couple of days, which is unusual. I figure, though, that he's busy preparing for his trip and I decide not to worry. Instead I just concentrate on the locks, working methodically through each step. I'm starting to see how people can find this relaxing.

As Chris and I begin the relatively long walk to lock five, my phone vibrates in the pocket of my shorts. I pull it out, take a look at the screen and, feeling slightly relieved, smile at Chris. 'Well, what do you know? His ears must have been burning. It's my son!' I put the phone to my ear and listen quietly to Hugo as he tells me his news.

Chris must find my long silence odd as he looks quizzically at me more than once. At one point, presumably noticing the expression on my face, he indicates that he will drop back to give me some privacy, but I shake my head. I don't want to be alone at this particular moment.

Eventually, I find a voice of sorts.

'No, honestly – I'm absolutely fine. All I want is for you to be really, genuinely happy in life and you can only find happiness if you're true to yourself,' I babble. 'I'm so glad for you – it's just that, being realistic, I worry your life will be a bit more challenging, given what you've just told me, than I would have liked. Having said that, things are changing fast, so that's getting less true every day. Silly me. Anyway, whatever happens, I'm here for you and I love you. Never forget that...OK of course, I'll tell him - when the time is right...No – I understand – no, I don't think you're wimping out. One step at a time...OK, that's fine – off you go. Keep in touch, darling. I love you...No, love you more! Bye.'

As I put my phone back in my pocket, Chris quietly says, 'I don't want to pry, but that didn't sound like a trivial phone call.'

At this precise moment, I feel profoundly grateful that this stranger is beside me, rather than my husband. 'My son just told me he's gay,' I manage. 'Now he has told me, I realise there is a part of me which has always known. I kidded myself he had just never dated a girl who was right for him, but deep down I knew. I'm honestly fine with it – I just don't know how I'm going to break it to Alex. He's rather traditional about these things – it's all to do with his family background.'

When I look at Chris, I see he's smiling broadly. 'Well, I think it's brilliant that he feels able to tell you, safe in the knowledge that he can rely on your love and support. After all, it wasn't long ago that men would deny their true selves, marry women and have children with them, only for it all to implode years later, with disastrous consequences. I should know – that's what my Dad did.'

I stare open-mouthed at him as we reach lock five.

'Look, if you ever need to talk, just Google the name of my boat – Baleine – plus the word "narrowboat", then follow the links to my website and blog. You can reach me that way.'

As we open our final set of paddles and the lock fills up, I call across to him,

'Baleine? Doesn't it mean whale, in French?'

'Sure does,' Chris laughs. 'I'll tell you the story behind the name, one of these days. In the meantime, enjoy the rest of your holiday!'

With that, we open the gates, close our paddles and jump aboard our respective boats. Conveniently, two other vessels are waiting to enter the lock, so we don't need to close the final set of gates. Baleine departs ahead of us and is clearly a bit faster than Two's Company, although that's not saying much where narrowboats are concerned. Nevertheless, Chris and his brother rapidly disappear into the distance and another fleeting canal friendship comes to an end.

'Well that all went quite smoothly,' Alex comments afterwards, as we drift peacefully along the canal.

Somehow, I manage to answer him, although my voice sounds strangely distant to me as I speak. 'Yes – it was much easier the second time around, and Chris was very helpful. He explained everything really well.'

'Glad to hear it,' replies Alex tersely. 'And did this Chris explain what you need to do in order to prepare the boat for a tunnel?'

I shake my head and see a look of grim satisfaction on Alex's face. Why must my husband always be so competitive, whether appropriate or not? I wonder how I'm ever going to find the right way, or the right moment, to tell him about Hugo.

'Right, so you need to walk through the boat and turn on all the lights, including the one in the cratch at the front,' orders Alex. 'Then, when we are in the tunnel, you must stay within the profile of the boat at all times, so you don't bang your head on the tunnel walls. I suggest you come and stand next to me – that's the safest place for you.'

Gratefully I escape downstairs to turn on the lights and pour myself a large glass of wine as I pass through the galley. I know, it's way too early, but I think you'll agree these are trying circumstances for me. As I gulp it down, I stare through the front window of the boat at the Stygian gloom of the tunnel mouth, which looms ever larger as our boat approaches it. Water vapour issues from its gaping maw and the noise of our engine echoes back towards us in an ominous roar. It feels as though we're about to be swallowed whole and, at this precise moment, that would suit me just fine.

In the end, twenty minutes in the dark gives me some much-needed respite. Alex is fully occupied, as we pass several boats going the other way, and I stand at his side in silence as he focuses on the task in hand. As I am fast discovering on the canals, the dimensions really shouldn't work, but somehow do. The tunnel looks far too narrow to allow two boats to pass, but each time they manage to edge past each other with literally inches to spare.

Finally, we emerge once again into the sunlight. All around, the landscape appears unnaturally vivid after the velvet darkness of the tunnel. The trees are a particularly luminous green, birdsong sounds louder than usual, and the sky is a fluorescent peacock blue. Faced with this onslaught of nature, I resolve to put things into perspective. After all, my son is healthy, with great prospects. People face infinitely greater challenges than me, every minute of the day. I know millions would swap their lives in an instant for mine, with its first world problems. I resolve to get over myself and tell Alex about Hugo later on today. After all, he is his father. He deserves to know. In the meantime, I crawl onto the roof of the boat and stretch out on its sun-warmed surface, flecked with droplets of water from the tunnel. I shut my eyes and try to think of nothing.

I must have dozed off, because all at once I find my dreams invaded by a cacophony of competing sounds. Dogs bark, children scream, people laugh and a voice coming over a tannoy announces the imminent departure of a boat trip. Startled, I abruptly sit up, wondering what has happened to my rural idyll, and find myself in a busy canal basin. All around me, boats jockey for position and a large pub, with a packed beer garden, lies immediately ahead. To our right is what looks like another watering hole, again with a busy garden, plus an ice cream shop next door. People are swarming everywhere. After the darkness of the tunnel and the calm of the canal, it's an unwelcome assault on the senses. Alex, however, appears unfazed.

'Welcome to Foxton!' he cries happily. 'It's just how I remember it. On hot days like this, half of Leicester decamps out here. Let's tie up over there on the left, beside the beer garden, then you can go off and find the lock-keeper.'

'Why do we need a lock-keeper? We haven't had one of those before.'

'True, but things are a bit different here. As I mentioned yesterday, Foxton Locks is a staircase, so you need to get permission from the lock-keeper to go up or down. See that lock over there, next to the pub?'

I nod, feeling confused.

'That's Foxton Bottom Lock – the start of the staircase. If you walk over there once we've tied up, then make your way uphill, along the path beside the locks, opposite the side ponds, you'll find the lock-keeper somewhere around. He'll be dressed in blue, with a red buoyancy aid. Just tell him you want to book our boat in. He'll explain what to do and tell you how long we have to wait before we can go up.'

I'm really none the wiser as I stumble off the boat and make my way across to the bottom lock via one of the many standard-issue brick bridges which span the canals around here. As I reach the lock, I note with alarm that it looks different from those I've done so far. It's half the width, for a start, which means only one boat can fit in at a time, so no partner for me. I reflect gloomily that I'll miss Chris and his wise counsel.

I follow Alex's instructions, locate the path to the right-hand side of the locks and trudge uphill. As I make my way past the locks, I note to my dismay that there are no gaps between them; they all seem to blend into each other, with the top gate of one lock forming the bottom gate of the one above it. Suddenly the penny drops and I finally realise what Alex meant when he referred to a staircase. 'Typical,' I think to myself. 'Just when I'm starting to get the hang of this lock business, they go and move the goalposts, big time.' My stomach lurches in anticipation of more lock trauma ahead, which is the last thing I need right now. I feel some relief, however, when I spot a man who is clearly the lock-keeper and who appears to be helping a boat through the locks. Maybe I'll get some assistance, after all.

'Good afternoon!' I call out as I approach, trying to sound as normal and cheerful as I can. 'I've been told I need to book our boat in.'

'You at the bottom, coming up?'

'Er – yes.'

'Name?'

'Stella Pitulska.'

'That's an unusual name for a boat, but then we do get all sorts of daft names.'

'Oh sorry, no – that's my name. You need the *boat* name – right. Two's Company – that's what the boat is called.'

'Glad we've sorted that one out. I take it you've never done these locks before?'

'No – this is my first boat trip.'

'OK, no problem. We'll help you out. The one thing you've got to remember is – red before white.'

I look blankly at the lock-keeper who consults his notebook then, ignoring my puzzled face, announces,

'You've got about a forty-five-minute wait, then you'll be following a boat called Freefalling – now that is a daft name. Just look out for them and when they enter the bottom lock, you get ready and go in next, alright? Either I'll be there to help you, or one of my colleagues will give you a hand.'

'Thanks. It's a song, by the way.'

'What is?'

'Freefalling – by Tom Petty. It's a great tune – you should check it out. Personally, I've seen much worse boat names, and this is only day two.'

The lock-keeper looks at me as if I have gone mad - and maybe I have. Without a word, he moves on to the next lock and I return to the boat.

'We have to wait forty-five minutes, then follow that boat, called Freefalling, over there,' I announce, trying to sound as though I know what I am talking about.

'OK, perfect,' Alex replies. 'Let's nip over to the pub and grab a drink and a sandwich while we wait.'

As I'm sure you have noticed by now, Alex is not someone who likes to be kept waiting, so I tell him I'm amazed at how calmly he's reacting to the news of the long delay.

'Oh, forty-five minutes counts as a short delay, around here,' he breezes. 'Boats often have to wait for two to three hours if the locks are busy, so we're in luck. Come on – let's go and eat lunch.'

I order a large glass of wine and a fish finger sandwich. Normally this would be a guilty treat for me, invoking happy memories of childhood Saturday mornings when Mum would fill barm cakes with fish fingers and brown sauce, as a weekend breakfast treat. Today, though, as I sit in the sunny beer garden surrounded by happy families, I can't stop thinking about Hugo and I can only pick at my food, although I empty my wine glass rather quickly. I know I should tell Alex our son's news but right now, I just can't find the words. To be perfectly honest, I'm afraid of what his reaction will be. I decide to wait until this evening, when we will have more time to discuss it, and focus for the moment on the immediate challenge presented by the so-called staircase.

'Alex – the lock-keeper mentioned something about red before white. Do you know what he was talking about?'

'Yes, I do. When you're doing a staircase like this, you always need to remember to open the red paddle before the white one. You'll see they're painted in the appropriate colours. If you get it wrong, you'll flood the side ponds, which is not good news, especially on a busy day like this when they are surrounded by tourists. There's even a rhyme about it: *"red before white and you'll be alright – white before red and you'll wish you were dead".'*

Great – more death and destruction on the supposedly peaceful and relaxing canals.

'Sounds wonderful,' I mutter through gritted teeth, glancing at my watch. 'Looks like we have time for one more drink before I face the staircase, or whatever it's called. I'll go and join the queue at the bar.'

We are just finishing our second drink when we see Freefalling heading towards the bottom lock.

'Time to go!' Alex immediately jumps up and sprints away towards our boat.

7 AMATEUR ALCHEMY

For once I've managed to think ahead and bring my windlass with me, so I only have a gentle, if not entirely sober walk to the bottom lock, which is on the other side of the pub. When I arrive, I see a different lock-keeper waiting for me.

'Hi, I'm Fred,' he calls. 'I hear from Gordon that you might be in need of some help – am I right?'

'You are indeed. I'm new to boating and these locks look so different from the ones I did yesterday.'

'A little different, but fundamentally the same,' Fred replies enigmatically. 'Don't worry – I'll help you out.'

And he does. We work our way methodically up the first few locks in the staircase, with Fred carefully demonstrating each time how to open the red paddle first, followed by the white. However, although we make no blunders, it's abundantly clear we're proceeding too slowly for the hire boat behind us. Its occupants are demonstrating their displeasure by standing around, hands on hips, staring up the hill towards us with faces like thunder.

'Don't mind them,' Fred reassures me. 'They weren't happy with having to wait for an hour at the bottom. If they wanted to get somewhere fast, they shouldn't have hired a narrowboat.'

You can say that again. I'm gradually getting used to the slower pace, though, so I'm pleasantly surprised when, through my slight wine fog, I notice we're about to start the second last lock. I'm right behind our boat, walking over the small bridge leading to the red and white paddles on the far side of the lock, when I hear the distinctive ringtone of Alex's mobile. He's the only person I know who uses Apex; I guess he just likes the name and thinks it's appropriate for him.

I see my husband pull his phone from his pocket, look briefly at the screen, glance quickly left and right, then answer the call. As I step off the bridge and walk over towards the paddles, I'm conscious I'm entering his line of sight. Instinctively, Alex looks up as I pass by and, just for a second, our eyes meet. In that instant I know. Whoever he's talking to, it's not a client. The guilt is written all over his face.

Suddenly it's all too much for me; first Hugo, and now this. Of course, I suspected both, but to have the two of them confirmed as reality on the same day is something else entirely. My eyes fill with tears and my body starts to bend in on itself, as if to shield me from the pain. Frantically I try to pull myself together. I can hear my mother's voice in my head, urging me to be brave and not to make a scene in public. Dashing the tears from my eyes with one grubby, oil-stained fist, I blindly fit the windlass onto the spindle and begin to turn the handle. Grimly I resolve to get through the remaining locks somehow and put my problems to one side, if only for a few minutes.

It's then I hear the urgent shouts from Fred, the friendly lock-keeper, and the impatient crew of the boat below. I can't work out what's happening, until I look down at my windlass and discover to my horror that, in my distressed state, I've walked right past the red paddle and opened the white one instead. I had just one rule to follow and I've broken it. I see water pouring over the rim of the side pond below, soaking the feet of the tourists on the adjacent path and causing them to scramble urgently up the slope, yelling in alarm and indignation. Fred rushes over to me, pushes me out of the way rather roughly and seizes my windlass. Quickly he closes the white paddle, opens the red one and calls out an apology to the spectators as the water level in the side pond begins to subside. Meanwhile I stand helplessly on the bank, sobbing. I can hear Alex yelling at me, but the sound barely registers.

After a few minutes, Fred returns. 'I'll see you through the last two locks, love,' he says calmly. 'Why don't you get back on your boat, make yourself a nice cup of tea and have a sit down. You'll feel better in no time. There's no permanent harm done – the punters down below got a bit of a soaking, but they'll dry out soon enough. It'll give them something to talk about in the pub. Anyway, one thing's for sure – you'll never make that mistake again. Just chalk it up to experience.'

I make my way shakily to the front of the boat. I can feel Alex's eyes on me as I walk, but I refuse to look at him and climb into the cratch, out of sight. Ignoring Fred's suggestion of a 'nice cup of tea', I go straight to my bag of pills and swallow two strong painkillers. They were prescribed for my dodgy ankles, so they're not designed to deal with the sort of pain I'm feeling right now, but I'm hoping they will at least take the edge off. As I wait for them to kick in, I'm vaguely aware of the boat rising up through the remaining locks, then cruising off down the canal. Not for long, though;

after a couple of minutes Alex kills the speed, pulls in to the bank and ties up. I hear him walking down the steps from the engine room and know he's about to confront me, so I brace myself.

'Stella! What in God's name was that all about? I have never been so embarrassed in my life! What the hell were you thinking?'

I stare at my husband, feeling oddly calm as I ignore his ranting.

'So, Alex. Exactly how long have you been having an affair?'

'I don't know what you're talking about – and don't try to change the subject.'

'I'm talking about that phone call back there. You weren't speaking to a client – I could see it in your face.'

'Don't be ridiculous. It was that client Jonathan I already told you about.'

'I don't believe you!'

'Well, that's your problem.'

'Alex. Swear to me you are not having an affair.'

'Stella, I'm not having an affair, I swear. I wouldn't do that to you, even if you were to flood all the side ponds in Leicestershire. So, dry your eyes, calm yourself down and we'll go and enjoy the twenty-one miles of lock-free cruising stretching ahead of us. You'll get another chance to tackle a staircase when we reach Watford, the next set of locks, but I'm imposing a drinking ban on you before you attempt that particular feat. In the meantime, let's put that last mistake down to the half-litre of Chardonnay you drank at lunchtime and forget it, OK?'

I feel confused. I know what I saw, or at least I think I do, but Alex has flatly denied it and has let me off my latest boating mistake a lot more lightly than I expected. He's being unusually forgiving, all things considered. I don't know what to think. The pills are really taking effect now and I'm starting to feel a bit weird. I need to clear my head.

'Look, Alex, I want to get some fresh air. I'm going to go for a little walk, to calm down, before we carry on. I'll be right back.'

'Good idea,' Alex smiles at me. 'Did you spot the café back there? They do wonderful ice creams, if I remember correctly. Go and get yourself one, to eat while you walk. I'll see you in a bit.'

Ice cream. What am I – six years old? Given the state I'm in right now, I fear I'm rather beyond salted caramel.

'See you later, Alex.'

I climb up the steps to the engine room and leave via the back of the boat. I walk a few yards along the towpath towards the café, then stop for a moment to look at a statue on the grass verge at the side. It's a life-size model of one of the horses which were used to pull the original working narrowboats, before the invention of the diesel engine. I rest my head against the horse's neck and feel an odd kinship with this beast of burden who, I imagine, was every bit as downtrodden as I currently feel.

I'm about to walk on, but then something stops me. Call it a sixth sense, call it whatever you like, but a voice in my head urges me to return to the boat. I nearly ignore it, but then decide not to. I quietly retrace my steps and, as I step onto the back counter, I hear my husband's voice coming from the bedroom below. Gingerly I move forward and sit down on the engine room steps so I can listen to what he is saying.

'Look, for the last time – I know it's difficult, but you mustn't call again. She's getting suspicious…No, not specifically of you. I don't think she suspects you; not after your Bafta-winning performance at the wrap-up party. But she suspects someone – and that's bad enough…I know, but it's only three weeks, then we'll see each other again…No, of course not – what are you saying? There's no chance of me patching things up with Stella. It's over…Look, we've been through this before. You have to be patient. Just wait until Imogen finishes her A levels next year – then things will be different. I can't afford to disrupt her education. If you had children you'd understand.'

How thoughtful of him.

'…Oh angel, I know it's hard for you. It's hard for me, too…What do you mean? I've done everything you asked. You stipulated no romantic holiday destinations, so, where am I? Leicestershire. That's got to mean something…Yes, well – when we're together properly, I'll take you somewhere really nice. In fact, I've already been looking at places for us to go. There's this amazing luxury resort in The Maldives. Very secluded. I think it will be perfect for the two of us. How does that sound?…Good. Glad to hear it. Look – I've got to go. She'll be back soon. I'll see you in less than three weeks. Stay strong – that's my girl…Love you too, Jen. Bye.'

My first reaction, on hearing this conversation, is relief. Now I finally know the truth and no longer have to question myself, I feel curiously light, as though my bones are made of aluminium. Then I feel hard, and immediately afterwards I feel vulnerable. I feel vengeful, frightened, alone, sick, scared, angry and desperately sad, all in quick succession, and I know I can't trust myself right now, so I force myself to keep sitting silently on the engine room steps as Alex wanders about below. I sit, I wait, I think – and I make plans. Then, finally, when I feel ready to act, I walk down the steps. Jen might be able to deliver a Bafta-winning performance, but I'm going to go one better, with a real Oscar winner. I bet Meryl Streep is shitting herself.

'Hi – you were ages!'

'Sorry, Alex. I just needed some time to myself.'

'Feeling better now?'

'Much better, thanks. Look, I'm sorry for what I said earlier – for accusing you like that. I was just stressed out over what happened, back there at the locks. I wasn't thinking rationally, but that's no excuse. It was wrong of me. Can we put it behind us?'

'I think that would be best. Let's forget it ever happened and enjoy a nice long stretch of lock-free cruising.'

'Yes, let's. Tell you what – I'll mix us a lovely Pimms to enjoy as we go along.'

'Sounds like a plan.'

A few minutes later we set off on the next leg of our journey, standing side by side on the back of the boat, glasses in hand. As we emerge from under our first bridge, I see a young man kneeling on the towpath, his camera fixed to a tripod positioned carefully on the uneven ground. He looks up from behind the camera as he spots us, his face lighting up at the prospect of a perfect 'golden hour' shot, illuminated by the glorious light of the early evening sun.

'May I?' he calls.

'Of course.' Alex nods graciously in the photographer's direction.

The young man fires off as many shots as he can in the few seconds available to him before we pass by. As he focuses on his task, I try to imagine the scene through his eyes. Two smiling people, enjoying an early evening drink on their narrowboat, framed by the attractive arch of the traditional brick-built bridge and with the boat name, Two's Company, underneath them, as if to highlight their apparent harmony. Maybe he is hoping to sell the image to the Canal and River Trust, for use in one of their ad campaigns. Who says the camera never lies?

Soon afterwards we leave Foxton behind and drift along through open countryside. After a while I glance over at my husband, perched on the skipper's seat to my right with his legs dangling nonchalantly, one hand on the tiller and the other clutching his almost empty tumbler of Pimms. I have always thought his face so handsome in profile, with his patrician Roman nose and his blonde hair brushed back from his face, showing off his chiselled high cheekbones. I look at my gorgeous husband and am suddenly overcome with such a rush of loathing that it takes a huge effort to remain silent. I feel shocked, but strangely energised, too. I didn't realise I was capable of feeling so strongly about anyone apart from my children, and I like the idea that I can still surprise myself. As Alex drains his glass, I can hardly trust myself to speak and only manage one word, 'Refill?' I receive a nod in response; clearly neither of us is feeling very talkative.

Glasses in hand, I head down to the galley. I pour a large measure of Pimms into both glasses, add a hefty slug of gin to my husband's drink, then get the pestle and mortar out of the kitchen cupboard. Next, I walk into the bedroom to find my bag of pills. Once back in the galley, I liberate some of the pills from their blister packs by breaking the seals with the sharp edge of my thumbnail and pushing each pill through its foil cover. I place the pills in the mortar and gently push down with the pestle, enjoying the satisfying crunch as the casing of each pill gives way under the pressure. I grind the pestle this way and that, crushing the pills finely and taking care to ensure not even a speck of the precious powder escapes. As I work, I explain to an imaginary Alex exactly what the pills are for. 'These, my darling, are for getting your girlfriend to give a supposedly Bafta-winning performance at the wrap-up party, so I wouldn't suspect her. So you could protect her. Is that the only reason you invited me – to throw me off the scent? Also, you lying, cheating bastard, they are for having sex with me when you had already decided our marriage was over. Oh yes – and for swearing to me you were not having an affair. I think that's enough to be going on with, for the moment.'

Once I'm satisfied the powder is fine enough, I carefully tip it into my husband's glass. For good measure I add some more neat Pimms, straight from the bottle, to make the liquid nice and dark. Finally, I give both glasses a good stir with their swizzle sticks, decorate them liberally with strawberries, cucumber slices and mint leaves, then take them up to the back counter. 'Cheers, darling,' I say warmly, smiling at my husband as I hand him his glass.

'Cheers, Stella. Wow – this one has got quite a kick to it!'

'I figured you needed it, after all the drama I caused at Foxton. I'm so sorry I made yet another gaffe.'

'Look, it appears you've learned your lesson,' Alex generously replies. 'Let's just forget it and move on.' He takes another large swig of his Pimms and lapses back into silence as the boat continues its gentle course along the secluded stretch of canal. On one side, cows gaze impassively at us as they cool their legs in the shallow water near the bank, clearly more appreciative of its refreshing qualities than the spectators at Foxton were earlier. On the other side, the fields are mostly given over to crops, apart from a paddock inhabited by a small group of horses. Wearily and uselessly the poor animals try to keep the flies away with repeated head tossing and tail swishing. Clearly this is an exercise in futility, I reflect, but what is the alternative? You can't just let the flies win, now can you?

Out of the blue, Alex decides to strike up a conversation.

'Actually, it was quite funny,' he laughs. 'Those chavs weren't expecting that, on their day out! It was quite a soaking you gave them. I expect they'll stick to the soft play centre next time they fancy a family trip.'

'I'm glad I kept you amused back there,' I reply, wondering when my husband got to be such a snob and bending down to retie my shoelaces, which have somehow worked their way loose.

'While you're down there!' Alex quips, giggling like a naughty schoolboy.

I ignore him and do a double bow in each of my shoelaces. I've always been good at tying knots; they taught me well in the Girl Guides. I'm not so good at untying them, but that doesn't matter, right now. As Alex manoeuvres to avoid a boat heading in the opposite direction, I quickly tie a clove hitch in the mooring rope, which is draped over the tiller pin, slip the loops over his dangling left foot, then stand upright.

'Another time, stud. More Pimms?'

'Yeah!' cries Alex enthusiastically. 'Bring it on!'

Back in the galley, I resume my grim conversation as I prepare more Pimms and grind more pills. 'This second dose,' I explain to the imaginary Alex, 'is for obeying your girlfriend's orders about where to take me on holiday. No romantic destinations – how could you be so weak? You're going to regret being so submissive, I predict. Also, my darling, it's for remembering my dream holiday destination in The Maldives – then promising to take your girlfriend there, once you have left me. That was a particularly nice touch.'

I tip the second pile of powder into Alex's glass of Pimms, add another slug of gin, stir the opaque liquid and top both glasses with the usual fruit and veg. Then I open the galley window, reach down and drop the pestle and mortar into the canal, where they immediately sink below the surface of the murky water. I put my pills back by the bedside, grab both glasses and return to join my husband.

'Whaz that noise? I heard a kind of plop,' Alex asks, sniggering childishly as he says the last word.

'Nothing – I was just feeding the ducks,' I reassure him.

'You got a good heart.'

'I did have, once,' I murmur.

'Wha?' Alex eagerly gulps his Pimms. 'Christ, this drink's bloody good.'

'It's nothing – doesn't matter. Look, Alex, I'm feeling a bit weary. It has been a trying day, so far. I'm going to nip downstairs for a power nap, so I'll be nice and refreshed by the time we moor up for dinner.'

'S'not a problem – laters.'

'Oh – and Alex?'

'Wah?'

'I've got something to tell you.' Gently I take hold of my husband's shoulders, whisper a few words in his ear, then step back to gauge his reaction. I'm gratified at the devastation on his face as he processes what I have told him. Then I have another idea. This wasn't in the original plan, but I decide to go for it anyway. What the hell.

'In the spirit of full disclosure, Alex, there's something else I should tell you.' Again, I whisper in his ear, stand back and feel a pang of remorse as my husband's face creases up and tears course down his cheeks. The feeling only lasts a moment, though; I recover quickly, and make my final choice.

'See you later, darling.' Gently I kiss Alex on the cheek, nudging the mooring rope into the canal with my foot as I do so. Then I immediately turn my back and retreat to the bedroom, where my pills and a large glass of neat gin are waiting for me. I swallow enough pills to guarantee swift oblivion and wash them down with the gin. Then I lie back on the bed and say a silent 'thank you' to Chris for the heads up.

I barely hear the sound of the prop straining furiously as it fights to free itself from its bonds and obstructions. The noise of the boat hitting the metal piling at the side of the canal is quite faint and seems to come from a long way away, perhaps from the far end of a long tunnel. The muted clash of metal on metal is the last thing I hear before the darkness takes over.

NANCY

8 GOODBYE TO ALL THAT

Right. Let's get one thing straight before we start. I'm going to tell this story my way. I know there's others in this book who like to use big words, like they've swallowed a bloody dictionary or something, but that's not my style. OK granted, I do kind of mess around with words for a living, or at least I used to, but that's when I'm writing my songs, which is totally different. No offence, but books just aren't my thing.

When I said I would do this they offered me a ghost-writer, but I said no. A ghost-writer would either make me sound all posh, like others I could mention, or else like a bleeding Pearly Queen. Truth is I'm neither. You can tell I'm not exactly royalty from reading this, but I'm no Cockney Sparrow neither. I was born within the sound of Bow Bells, true enough, but that was pure chance. We didn't stay in one place for very long, our family. I travelled all over England as a kid, and all over the world later on. I might have a few rough edges, but I tell you what; I could buy and sell everyone else in this book. Not that money means shit, at the end of the day.

That reminds me. They promised to correct my spelling and I promised to tone down my language. I can see I have already let a few curses slip through, but it could be worse. No f-bombs or c-words – at least not yet. That's a relief. Tell you what – I'll just carry on and try to keep my potty mouth in check, alright? Now, where was I? Right, the story. Come on, Nancy, start the sodding story before they all turn up their toes and die of boredom. Sorry.

OK here we go. It all begins on an important day for me. And like I usually do when something important is happening, I balls it up before I even start, by waking up with a monster hangover. When I open my eyes, it feels like the cast of Stomp is having a rehearsal in my head and my stomach is like a washing machine on a spin cycle. I look over at Johnno, but his side of the bed is empty. Guess he didn't even make it home and crashed out somewhere. Christ, what a mess.

I drag myself out of bed, crawl into the bathroom and just manage to make it to the toilet before I chuck up. Afterwards I feel a bit better, but I still need help to get me through the morning. No – not that kind of help. You really don't think much of musicians, do you? Not chemical help. I've never been a drugs girl, me. Booze and weed, that's all, no matter what anyone else is taking. Oh, and fags, of course. What I meant was help from my altar – where my heroines live. Heroine, right? With an 'e'. Just so we're clear.

I stagger downstairs to the kitchen, make myself a black coffee and take it into the music room. What I call my altar is a big sort of collage that covers the whole of one wall above my pink grand piano. It's got photos, tickets, drawings and song lyrics on it, that sort of thing. There are loads of handwritten notes up there from people who even you will have heard of. Those pretentious twats at my record company would probably call it a 'mood board' or something like that, but to me it's my altar. And you know what? All the people on my altar are women – the sisters who changed the face of music. Still don't get what they deserve compared to men, of course. Anyway, without them I would never have ended up being a musician. Mind you, my family's got something to do with that as well. Specially my Dad.

I look up at them all – from Maddy Prior and Aretha Franklin to Poly Styrene and Joan Jett. Dusty Springfield. Patti Smith. Tina Weymouth, the pocket rocket with a brilliant touch on bass. And then I pray. 'Ladies, I am not worthy. But some of you have been here, right? Help me, please. Just help me get through this morning's meeting with my bastard record company. Make them love my new songs, agree the concept for my new album and give me a half decent budget. That's all I ask.'

Chrissie Hynde stares at me from under her long fringe. The same one she's had for the last forty years. She don't look too hopeful.

An hour later and I'm not looking half bad, even if I say so myself. The smoky eye, as the make-up artists call it, is always my friend when I feel like crap. As for my clothes, I've gone for some old friends which have seen me through a lot of gigs over the years. One of my leather waistcoats – always a good call. They say only Kate Moss can wear a waistcoat with nothing underneath, but I beg to differ. I can rock it. Kate would agree, I'm sure. It helps that I'm a bit skinny like her. I always have been. Food has never bothered me much. A burger here and there, that'll do me. Sorry – back to the clothes. Straight leg jeans, cowboy boots, about a million bangles, hair all down and sort of messy. Not that I have much choice there. Sorted. I might feel dog rough, but I look rock rough - and that'll have to do.

By the time the car comes to pick me up I've got my shit together and

I'm ready. Now I should say I'm not one of those musicians who gets a bloody car everywhere. When I'm off duty, I can go all over the place without being recognised. It's easy. Hair up, wig or hat on, shades, different clothes, then just walk around like a normal person. Get the tube or the bus. Madonna does it. Prince William does it, for God's sake. So do I, although I don't have security guys with me all the time like they do. That would do my head in. Of course, it helps that I live in north London, where luvvies and celebrities are two a penny.

Anyway, the car pulls up outside my house, which is in Richmond Crescent, Islington. Posh enough for you? Thought so. I walk down the steps and see a curtain twitch at a window across the road. The people in that flat only moved in recently and haven't got used to having me as a neighbour yet. Most of the other neighbours don't give a damn. We mainly keep ourselves to ourselves.

As we sit in a traffic jam on Rosebery Avenue, on our way to the West End, I put my headphones on and listen back to my songs for the new album. I still love them all – that's a relief. Sometimes, you know, I write some stuff on one day, record it and think it's great, then listen to it again the next day and know it's shit. Press the delete button. But not these songs – they're different. They have all stuck. I really think this album is going to be my best yet.

I feel pretty good by the time I walk into reception. Suzi, who has been the receptionist at the record company for about a million years, stands up and gives a low bow, when I come in. Just for a joke, like. I'm not that bloody important. God knows she sees plenty of people who are way more famous than me.

'Baroness. Long time, no see.'

'Well, this album has taken a lot of writing, Suze.'

'Yeah, Nancy, I'm sure you've been cloistered away like a nun, writing from morning till night. No partying, no drinking – nothing like that.'

'Yep. All work and no play – that's me.'

We smile at each other as she hands me my pass. She's nice, Suzi, she really is. Not like most of the others in that place.

'He's waiting for you in his office. Go on up – and good luck.'

I press the button for the lift. Suzi has never wished me good luck before. It doesn't feel like a good sign.

The Gatekeeper, as I like to call him, is leaning back in his chair with his feet on his desk. Trying to look all casual, but I know he's not. The guy's never relaxed, especially when it comes to money, which is all he cares about at the end of the day.

'Nan. Lovely to see you. Take a seat. Coffee? Black, as usual?'

See how he calls me Nan, as though we are friends? Don't be fooled. You may as well try and make friends with a bleeding Komodo Dragon.

The coffee is good, though, I have to say. It comes from a poncy machine in the corner of his office which probably cost five grand.

'Right – let's get straight to it. The songs. I like them; the lyrics are strong, as I have come to expect from you over the years, although I didn't understand one of the song titles. On the Cut – what does that mean?'

'The cut is what people used to call the canals, back in the day. Some people still do.'

'Nan. Your fans are not going to know that.'

'Don't be too sure. Also, since when did people need to understand every word of the sodding lyrics?'

'Well they won't understand the album title, I can tell you that. Chi Shugra - what's that all about?'

'It's a Romany term, meaning…'

'Look, I don't care what it means. Your supposedly gypsy heritage is old news. Change it. Anyway, back to the songs. Some of the melodies really resonated with me. Cornucopia, in particular. And the chorus on Take Me Back – it gave me an earworm which lasted all day. It could be the first single, I think.'

He carries on like that for a while. Talking about my songs and how good they are. If you were in the room, I bet you would think he really liked them. I know better, though. I have known this guy for a lot of years, and I can tell when he is building up to something.

'So, in summary,' he says finally, with his fingers pressed together in a sort of steeple to make him seem all thoughtful and intelligent 'it's a solid body of work which will appeal to your current fan base.'

'Sounds like you think it's bloody boring.'

'Boring, no. Your work is never boring, Nan. But you need to understand that people just aren't listening to albums any more. They haven't been – not for a long time. That long spiel you emailed me about the different options for the running order. Complete waste of time. No one gives a shit. Running orders no longer matter. The punters just download or stream individual tracks. They don't care whether Cornucopia comes before or after Eight Miles Down. The idea of an album as a holistic concept just isn't valid, these days. Sorry to break it to you.'

'So, what are you trying to say? Are you saying you're not going to make it?'

'Of course, I'm not saying that. As ever, you have the company's full support, Nan. What I'm trying to get across is that this new album won't win you any new fans. From the company's perspective, it just isn't very commercial, which has to be reflected in the budget we allocate to its production and promotion.'

Here we go.

'So how much are we talking?'

He names a figure and I nearly fall off my bloody chair. And not in a good way. The number is a small fraction of the budgets for my previous albums. This is the bit where I need to watch my potty mouth, for the book. Just add the 'f' and 'c' words yourself. Use your imagination.

'You've got to be joking. I can't work to a poxy budget like that. Don't try and tell me that's all you've got to give me.'

'Nancy, we do *not* have a bottomless pit of money – and we have to prioritise the more commercial artists. I'm sorry, but that's how it is. We're not a charity.'

'No shit. Tell me – what "more commercial artists" are we talking about?'

'Well, there's The Enbys, for a start.'

Of course. The Enbys. They all identify as non-binary, which is where their name comes from, so you can't exactly call them a boy band, but that's what they are, really. You're expecting me to diss them, but I won't. True, their songs are probably written for them by a bloody computer program, but they are commercial, no doubt about that. They all look great and their voices can easily be autotuned in the studio, so they sound OK. Add some really talented backup singers and they could even perform live. But they probably won't be around in two years' time and The Gatekeeper knows that. He knows he's got to throw money at them now, so he can make a killing before their so-called fans move on to the next big thing. Meanwhile, I've been in the business for nearly thirty years, but that means nothing to him.

'This is constructive dismissal,' I reply, leaning forward and trying to sound all controlled and business-like. What I really want to do is yell my head off, or knock his block off, but I know neither would help.

'Don't throw contractual stuff at me, Nan. Christ. We have a 360-degree contract with you, but you simply refuse to play ball. You haven't toured for years and you will only play the festivals you want to play. As for merchandising – don't even get me started. Worst of all, you refuse to maintain any sort of social media presence.'

'I've been creating a bloody album, for God's sake!'

'That's not enough any more, Nan. I'm sorry.'

'Also, I don't want my life to be put out there on social media for every bugger to see.'

'Next you're going to tell me you want your music to speak for itself.'

'I want my music to speak for itself.'

'Nancy, wake up. It's time to enter the twenty-first century. We're nearly a quarter of the way through it already, and it's time you joined in – or else you're finished.'

When I hear that word – finished - something inside me snaps and I just go ballistic.

'You're right – I am finished! Finished with you. Finished with your record company. Finished with this industry. You can take your bloody 360-degree contract and stick it!'

'You can't do that, Nan. Your contract isn't up for renegotiation until next year.'

'What did you say earlier – "don't throw contractual stuff at me" – right? Well I won't, but my lawyer will. And as you well know, I've got a shit-hot lawyer.'

I raise my middle finger in the air, feeling powerful. 'Swivel 360 degrees on that, my friend.'

All this time, The Gatekeeper has not moved. His feet are still on the desk and he's still leaning back in his chair.

'I'm sorry you feel that way, Nan.'

From his face I can tell he's not sorry at all. I had been feeling good about telling him where to stick his contract, but when I take a closer look at his face, I don't feel half so good no more. You know why not? Because his face tells me he is relieved. It tells me this meeting went exactly the way he wanted it to. All I can do is try and have the last word.

'Don't call me Nan, you snake. It's The Baroness, to you.'

As he yells back something about having the copyright on my name, for Christ's sake, I storm out of the room. I've got no other option. In any case, I'm sick to my stomach with the whole thing. I preferred the hangover I had earlier, to be honest with you. In reception I say goodbye to Suzi. Of course, she's not surprised to see me go. She knows everything that goes on here.

'They're a bunch of shits,' she whispers into my ear as we hug each other. 'I'd tell them where to stick it as well, but I've got a big mortgage to pay – plus three kids and a waster of a husband to support.'

That gets me thinking.

Thankfully the company's driver didn't get the memo about how the meeting went, so he's waiting for me as I leave. On the way back in the car I have a bit of a cry, I'm not ashamed to say. The driver takes no notice. He's seen it all before. Then I dry my eyes and think how lucky I am not to have Suzi's life. A whole bunch of people depending on me. As the car heads east towards Islington I hatch my escape plan. All things considered, I don't think it will be difficult to get away from everything. Good bloody riddance to it all.

As I walk into the house, I smell bacon frying in the kitchen upstairs. Looks like Johnno is back. Trying to nix his hangover with a full English. Good luck with that, mate. As I climb the stairs, I feel sad. This isn't going to be an easy conversation. It has got to be done, though.

I stand in the kitchen doorway for about half a minute before the guy even notices me. When he does, he jumps in the air and nearly drops his pan of egg and bacon on the floor.

'Christ, Nan – you nearly gave me a heart attack! How long have you been standing there?'

'Long enough.'

'D'you want some eggs and bacon? I've made loads.'

'God no. I think I'd puke.'

'So, you're hungover too, then. I just thought I'd eat my way through it.'

'Whatever works for you. What happened to you last night?'

'I finished up crashing on the sofa at Mike and Ali's. Can't remember how I got there, to be honest. Did you get home OK?'

'Must have done.'

'Have you been out?'

My soon-to-be ex-boyfriend is no Columbo, as you can tell.

'Yes, I have.' I point to my waistcoat and jeans. 'Different clothes from yesterday – see? That has got to be a giveaway.'

'Got me there. Where have you been?'

'Remember I said I had an important meeting with The Gatekeeper at his office, to discuss the budget for my new album? Cast your mind back to last night. When we left the house, I said I was only going to have a couple of drinks at Nigel's party, so I'd be fit to take on The Gatekeeper in the morning?'

'So that plan worked well, then. How did the meeting go?'

'Probably as well as it could have done. Basically, the budget he suggested was an insult, so I told him where to shove his contract. I'm done with him – and his bloody record company.'

'You're not serious.'

'I am. Deadly.'

'Nan – that sounds like career suicide to me.'

'Not to me it doesn't. Call it a tactical withdrawal from the music industry. And from everything else.'

I should mention that all the time we have been talking, Johnno has been shovelling eggs, bacon and toast into his face. He eats like a pig but hasn't got an ounce of fat on him. Mind you, he is young. Very young. Call me a cradle snatcher if you like – I don't care. Also, he's a drummer, so he burns up a lot of calories at band practice. And his band practises a lot. They're trying desperately to land the kind of deal I have just walked out on. I can't expect him to understand what I have done.

The words 'everything else' have actually made Johnno stop eating for a minute. He has twigged there's more going on here than just the budget for my album. He thinks it might affect him. He's right, of course.

'What do you mean – everything else?'

'Johnno – I'm saying goodbye to the industry and I'm going away from here.'

'How long for?'

'Indefinitely. I'm going to rent the house out for the moment, but I'll probably sell it in the end. I'm going off grid. Back on the canals. Back where I came from.'

'Nan, this is a big step and it's the wrong move, believe me. I think you should take some time and reconsider. Don't do anything hasty. Wait until you have calmed down, then call The Gatekeeper and tell him you're sorry. Get your lawyer to sort something out. It's not too late to turn this around, I'm sure.'

I just look at him and shake my head.

'Johnno – it has been fun, right? But you and the band are going places. You're building a loyal fan base. It's only a matter of time before you get the break you deserve. Just focus on that. You've made a few good contacts through me and we've had a great time. But now we both need to move on.'

Johnno looks really hurt and I guess I could have been more tactful. I have never been any good at this sort of thing.

'You make it sound like I was just using you to get on in the industry. I resent that, Nancy.'

'I didn't mean it like that. I'm sorry. I really am. I know you're not that sort of person. You're a top bloke and I've enjoyed being with you.'

'Yeah, me too. You're a class act, Baroness – better than you know. You just need to like yourself more. Sorry for the amateur psychologist BS, but I still think you're making a mistake. You have been done over by The Gatekeeper and he has hurt you, so you're responding by running off, going back to your roots or whatever, but it won't work. It never does. You can't go back. You have to keep on moving forward, whether you want to or not.'

'Thanks for the pep talk, Johnno, but I'm not changing my mind.'

'Fair enough. I'm not going to beg. I'll go and stay with Gaz – I'm sure he'll let me crash there until I can afford a place of my own. You know how to find me if you want to get in touch. I hear the phone signal is pretty bad on the canals, though. I won't hold my breath.'

We hug each other briefly, then off he goes to pack his stuff. I stay in the kitchen, crack open a bottle of JD and wait it out.

A couple of hours later Johnno is gone. In the meantime, I've taken it easy with the JD. Watch out, Nancy, your halo's going to strangle you if you're not careful. I've had a bit of a cry – another one – plus I've made lots of phone calls. Basically, I've dismantled my life. I've briefed my lawyer, put the house up for rent and told all my closest friends what I'm doing.

It wasn't too bad, actually. Most of my friends thought I was mad, but a couple were quite positive, which surprised me. My old pal Stevie, who's always been away with the fairies, said he thought my decision was 'in tune with the zeitgeist', whatever the chuffing hell that means. Another good mate called Justin is the complete opposite of Stevie. A businessman through and through. Brain full of bloody spreadsheets. He said the music business was fast becoming a 'disintermediated industry' and my decision was 'commercially and artistically sound'. Nope, don't understand that either. It wasn't all doom and gloom though. That's my point.

My lawyer, Valerie, was OK about it, I think. She loves a good scrap, that girl, so I reckon she's looking forward to taking on The Gatekeeper and his merry band of record company snakes. And as for the estate agent, he practically bit my hand off. Houses like mine don't come up for rent very often and he's got a bunch of ex-pat clients who'll be fighting over it, or so he says.

My most difficult call was to Dave, my drummer. Dave and I have worked together for decades – almost from the beginning. He's an incredible drummer I have to say. He collaborates with me on the odd song but really, drumming is his thing, rather than writing. Talking of things, the two of us did have a bit of a scene for a while, but for one reason and another we decided in the end not to mix business with pleasure. Amazingly, our music partnership survived the break-up. I get on well with his current wife, Janice, who has been really good for him. He had a problem with drugs and booze, but she helped him clean up. Anyway, to cut a long story short, we've stuck by each other through everything, so we're pretty close, as you can imagine.

Dave's take on it is that he understands why I walked out on The Gatekeeper and the industry, but he doesn't believe it'll be forever. He says he knows the row has been brewing for years but thinks I'll definitely be back. He makes me promise to stay in touch. He says he has other potential projects in the pipeline, but I'll always be his first priority. He reminds me of everything we've been through and reassures me the two of us will be back working together again before I know it. I don't try to put him right. I just hope those other projects work out for him. We both have a bit of a cry but hang up as friends. It's a tough one, though.

My conversation with Marcus, my bass player, was much easier. Marcus has been with me for the last three years since my previous bass player, Nicole, left to join another band. I don't think most people realise how often musicians switch bands but honestly, it's just like bloody musical chairs sometimes. Marcus is a case in point. He's a lot younger than me but has played in more bands than I've had hot dinners. He has also played bass for a load of West End musicals. You've probably been to at least one of them. He's very good, I admit, so he's rarely out of work, but even then, he's got that covered. When things go quiet on the music front, he has a handy little side hustle in IT. The guy's a dab hand at web design, apparently.

Predictably, Marcus is unfazed by my decision. He wishes me all the best and says he hopes we can collaborate again in the future. Before I even put the phone down, I sense he has moved on. Good luck to him.

It's the same with the other musicians I work with. I should explain that me, Dave and Marcus basically form The Baroness – the core band, in other words. You don't need a cast of thousands in my opinion. Look at The Police for a start. Incredible sound from just those three dudes. Having said that, from time to time we do pull in session musicians and backup singers to help create the sound we want. I call all our regular people and those I manage to reach react just like Marcus did. They cut their losses and focus on where their next pay cheque is coming from. They're just guns for hire, in the end.

After that I go back to more mundane stuff. My next call is to my cleaning company, to give the house a good once over. In other words, to de-Johnno it, basically. I'm a lot tidier than you probably imagine, but Johnno was a bit feral, I have to say. The place needs cleaning up, so we don't frighten off those ex-pat punters.

After my conversation with Johnno and all that phoning, I'm done talking. I open up my laptop and Google 'narrowboats for sale in London'.

9 WATER GYPSIES

Right. At this point I need to fill you in a bit. It feels like the right time, now there's just the two of us. Grab a drink and settle down. 'Are you sitting comfortably? Then I'll begin', as some woman on the radio used to say.

Good. So, I basically grew up on a narrowboat. We're not talking one of those flash pleasure boats you see on the canals these days. Ours was a proper commercial boat, used for moving cargo around the country. Me, my brother and my mum and dad were all squashed into a little cabin at the back. Probably sounds horrible to you but I didn't know any different. To be honest, I loved it. We'd fight like cat and dog sometimes, what with being so cooped up, but we always made up pretty quickly.

So, we were among the last of what some people call 'the water gypsies'. We travelled all round England, dropping a load off here and picking one up there. My Dad used to claim we were actually real gypsies. According to him we had some Romany blood, some Irish ancestors or whatever. His stories tended to vary depending on how much he'd had to drink on that particular day. Who knows which parts were true? Maybe the whole lot was made up. He was full of shit, my Dad. Or Irish blarney, if you want to be kind. But he was a loving Dad. He was full of energy and fun. I loved him to bits.

My Mum was the sensible one. When the canal work dried up, as it did from time to time, she'd find jobs for them somewhere else. Sometimes they'd pick fruit on farms in the countryside. At other times my Dad would do some casual labouring and she'd work shifts in a factory. That's why we were here in London when I was born. It's just as well, or she would likely have given birth to me on the bloody towpath. A boating job had fallen through, so my Dad got some temporary work in the East End to keep the wolf from the door. That was how it was back then. We mostly lived hand to mouth when I was growing up, but that was my normal.

Needless to say, my education was a bit hit and miss. My Mum wangled permission for us to be home schooled and she taught us to read and write. We did quite a bit of maths too. Mum was pretty good with figures. She needed to be, or we would never have had a penny to our names. Cash tended to slip through my Dad's fingers, especially when he was in the bar. But beyond the basic three R's, we mainly just learned practical stuff. I'm pretty well clued up on the workings of the diesel engine and can single crew any narrowboat you like, no problem. Another thing I learned about from an early age was music.

My Dad loved his music. He played quite a few different instruments – mainly the guitar, ukulele and harmonica, although he could bash out a decent tune on a piano if he came across one in a pub. Surprisingly, he actually knew how to read music. I never found out how he learned this. He liked to keep a lot of his past a secret, my Dad. I think he fancied himself as a man of mystery. Anyway, he taught me and my brother to play guitar pretty much as soon as we were able to pick one up. I loved it and could play a few basic chords by the time I was four. He got me this little guitar from somewhere and I wouldn't put it down. Mum used to have to tear it from my hands at bedtime, but my brother was the total opposite. Guitar playing wasn't his thing. That's a story for a whole other time, though. If you don't mind, I'll leave my brother out of the picture for now.

Mum didn't play any instruments, but she did have a lovely singing voice. She taught how me to sing and that was it – I was hooked. She also passed on to me her love for all the old female singers from way back when, by constantly singing their songs as she stood at the tiller or at the tiny sink in our boat's cabin. She had great range and could have a pretty good crack at a wide variety of songs by everyone from Sarah Vaughan to Ella Fitzgerald and Doris Day. She loved jazz and swing, in particular, but was also quite keen on folk and country. When she was having a go at a song by Dolly Parton or Tammy Wynette, she would try out a dodgy American accent which didn't really work, but she would nail the tune every single time. She didn't like to perform in public, though. If she saw a boat coming towards us when she was singing away at the tiller, she would shut up pretty pronto. It's a shame really. I think she'd have been brilliant.

Without meaning to, Dad and Mum set me on course for my future career, between the two of them. Playing guitar, singing and writing songs – that's what I did, every spare minute I had. In other words, when I wasn't working the locks, steering the boat, peeling spuds or doing a million and one other chores. Once I got a bit older, I would sing and play alongside my Dad outside various pubs along the cut, whenever the weather was fine. I would lay down my little hat and people would drop in their coins. Dad made a lot more money with me around, so that was all good. He was happy.

Gradually I started to make a bit of a name for myself within the boating community. It's a close-knit group and they were quite proud of me. I was a bit of a bloody child prodigy, on the quiet. People would occasionally give me sheet music, and one or two even let me have their guitars. Then, as I got older, I started to get requests to perform in my own right. Not just in pubs, but with the little theatre companies that tour the canals, and at various waterways festivals and boat shows. Without ever meaning to, I had built myself quite a following by the time I was in my teens.

As time went on, I began to get a bit more conscious of the image I wanted to portray. You know what teenagers are like. I wasn't too worried about the way I looked – unusual, I know - but I was obsessed by what to call myself. I thought my real name didn't have any star quality to it. I figured 'Nancy Parkinson' was never going to set the world on fire although, thinking about it, having a dull name never did Brad Pitt any harm. Whatever. I wasn't happy with my real name, so I set about choosing myself a stage name.

When I wasn't actually playing music, I always had my transistor radio on while I was doing my chores. My brain absorbed tunes and lyrics like a sponge. It still does. I would probably be like bloody Einstein if you cleared all that stuff out of my head, but I wouldn't be without it. Anyway, one of my favourite songs, back in the day, was that golden oldie Killer Queen. I pictured the woman in the song, and I wanted to be like her. She sounded so stylish and sorted. Like me, she never kept the same address, although I doubt this was because she lived on a narrowboat. Unlike me, she spoke just like a baroness, which I found fascinating. What did a baroness speak like, anyway? Who knows, but it didn't matter. I had my stage name. I became The Baroness.

The summer I turned eighteen, my dad and mum had various jobs lined up, both on and off the canals. All these jobs were near the Birmingham Canal Network – the web of waterways which criss-crosses the city. Birmingham has more miles of canals than Venice, did you know that? Good luck with finding a gondola, though, although you should be able to bag yourself a Cornetto. Anyway, I digress. The fact that we were going to be in Birmingham for the whole summer meant I could get some regular gigs at a number of different pubs in the city centre. Girl and guitar stuff. Playing covers of well-known songs, plus a few of my own I sneaked in. To bring in the tourists and keep them there. Putting loads of cash behind the bar. And that's where it happened. An A&R guy from a big record company, the same one I just ditched, came into one of these pubs, on his way to a gig at a larger venue nearby. He listened to me for a bit and liked what he heard. Then later, when his proper gig turned out to be rubbish, he came back to the pub where I was playing. I was just finishing my set when he arrived. He wandered up and introduced himself, gave me his card and it all went from there.

Over the next year, the record company built a little band around me, and the cycle began. Album, tour, album, tour. Rinse and repeat. Somehow, I managed to avoid being eaten alive by it all. My dad and mum had taught me to stand up for myself and fight my corner, which helped. Also, the record company liked my name – The Baroness – plus my songs and my looks, so they didn't try to reinvent me too much. My grungy, girl and guitar style worked back then. I was in the right place at the right time, with the right look and the right sound.

It's a different story now, as my meeting with The Gatekeeper showed. Many years, many albums and a few wrinkles later, it seems as though I have reached my commercial sell-by date. So, I'm going to rewind the tape and go back to my old life on the canals. Would you listen to me? Rewind the tape. What's that all about? Maybe The Gatekeeper's right – I haven't caught up with the twenty-first century yet. And you know what? Right now, I don't care. It doesn't matter a damn what century you're in when you're on a narrowboat.

Thank you for listening.

10 SHINY AND NEW

Right. Back to the story. You know how when something bad has happened and you wake up with an 'oh shit, what have I done' feeling, but you can't remember why? Then it all comes rushing back a few minutes later? Well that's how I feel when I wake up the next morning. I don't panic though – I just hold my nerve and lie there until I feel calmer. I know I made the right decision. The worst part is Johnno, and that's definitely the right way round. He's a decent guy, but I'm well shot of my record company.

It's amazing, isn't it, how a hot shower makes you feel better, even when things are a bit crap? Half an hour later I'm all cleaned up, the coffee is on and I'm feeling like things are looking up. I make a mental note to self – Nancy, make sure there is a shower on your new boat. Needless to say, that's a luxury we never had on our commercial boat, back in the day. Thinking about it, I'm sure none of us smelt lemon fresh most of the time, to be honest. That's one aspect of boating I don't feel the need to revisit. My music might be a bit grungy, but I do keep myself fairly clean nowadays, you'll be relieved to hear.

While I'm drinking my coffee, I put in a call to my accountant and sort out the money side of things. Where to invest the rental income from my house, for a start. How to arrange the money transfer for the boat. Day to day living expenses, that kind of thing. You probably imagine a lot of artists aren't clued up about money and you're right. Many aren't, but I am. Like I said earlier, my Mum taught me to be good with figures. Also, when you've been poor, like I was growing up, you don't take a penny of it for granted when you do make some cash. At the same time, you know you could manage without it, if push came to shove. Anyway, whatever. My accountant Rob and I talk a lot. I'm a pretty hands-on client. I invest my money wisely and donate a lot to charity. And I don't buy stupid shit, neither. I get most of my clothes from Camden Market. I love fossicking away down there. My only luxuries are my guitars – you really don't want to know how many of those I have got – plus the pink grand piano I told you about. I spray painted it myself. And my huge bed – I did shell out a fair bit for that. Otherwise, all my furniture comes from the same websites everyone uses. Even you. Got a Billy bookcase? Thought so. I've got several.

Anyway, I've just put the phone down when the doorbell rings. I'm not expecting anyone to call round, so I keep the chain on when I open the door and peer through the gap, then remove the chain and fling open the door when I see Val, my lawyer, on the doorstep.

Now as I said before, Val is a shit-hot brief who loves a scrap, but you wouldn't know it to look at her. True, she does wear expensive clothes. Tailored, masculine trouser suits, that's her style. The thing is, she always looks as though she has slept in them, you know what I mean? She couldn't look groomed to save her life. Not that she gives a damn. She has always, and I mean always, got a fag on, so her skin is a bit yellow, and her roots always seem to be growing out, and not in a trendy, dip-dyed kind of way. 'I've got grey roots; so sue me,' she would say. Also, that girl loves her chocolate. How anyone can eat a Star Bar or a Creme Egg and smoke a fag at the same time is beyond me, but our Val manages it, no problem. Like me, she drinks black coffee during the day, but then she switches to single malt of an evening. She's always sharp as a tack the next day, though. This morning is no different.

We head upstairs to the kitchen, where I pour her a coffee and stick a large ashtray between us on the kitchen table. Val puts out one cigarette, immediately lights another and hands me the pack.

'I just thought I'd drop round and check you weren't killing yourself, Nan.'

'No, I'm fine,' I reply. 'I had a bit of an "oh shit" moment when I woke up, but I'm over it now.'

'Look, Nan – are you sure about this? You know I can screw a better deal for your new album out of those bastards. Yesterday was just The Gatekeeper's opening salvo. I know how he operates, and I can come right back at him today. I worked up a response overnight. You've got a lot of leverage contractually. I can take you through the details if you like.'

I don't normally smoke in the mornings, but I take one of Val's cigarettes and light up. The nicotine goes straight to my head, like I'm a novice smoker or something. I suddenly realise I can't remember the last time I ate anything. That might have something to do with it.

'No Val, you're alright. Thanks for putting in the work, but I've thought it through, and I really do want out. Just negotiate my exit and we'll take it from there.'

Val looks at me shrewdly. She has known me a long time, so not much gets past her.

'You're really serious about this, aren't you?'

'Yes I am. There are a few nice boats for sale in a marina out east. I've already made an appointment and I'm going to head over there this afternoon. If I like the look of one, I'm going to buy it, then that's it. I'm off. Don't you dare go anywhere though, Val. Whatever happens from now on, I'm going to need my bloody lawyer, you can be sure of that.'

'I'll always be your lawyer, Nan. I owe you, after all. As you know, I made partner off the back of the work I did for you, and the fees I earned from you.'

Val stubs out her fag and winks at me. Then she fishes around in her giant work bag and pulls out a Twirl.

'Yeah right. That's all I mean to you. I'm just the client who got your name on the letterhead. Not.'

'You're right of course, you old cow. You know you're much more than a client to me. I'll never stop being your lawyer. Not after everything we have been through together over the years. I'm sure the adventure isn't over yet, either. Make sure you stay in touch – and I'll be sure to visit you on that boat of yours.'

Val polishes off her Twirl and chases it with a handful of Minstrels. She finishes her coffee, shoehorns in another fag and then heads off to her office. I have no doubt she'll visit me. She always keeps her promises, does our Val.

After Val leaves, I sit in my music room and practise. I practise right up until it's time to go and look at the boats. I play guitar and pick out a few tunes on my piano. It doesn't matter to me that I'm leaving the industry behind. Playing music is still what I do, every spare moment. And that's not going to change, whatever happens. I'm going to miss my piano when I'm on the boat, but I'm going to cram as many guitars as I can in there. I'm looking forward to playing guitar by myself in the evenings. Weather permitting, I'll be out on the towpath. Hopefully in the middle of nowhere. That sounds pretty bloody perfect right now.

In the meantime, I have to schlep across north London to bag myself a boat. So, I pop on my favourite auburn wig and some of my clothes which are designed to make me invisible; a hoodie, some skinny jeans and a pair of trainers. Then I shove a few bits and pieces in a rucksack and head off to Angel tube.

On the way I make a pit stop at my local greasy spoon for a burger. It wouldn't do to pass out on the tube, after all. I have been existing on alcohol calories for the last few days and even I know that's not good. I'm starting to feel a bit rubbish. Time for some protein.

Nico, the café owner, has got to know me very well over the years. I'm not much of a cook, so I show up there on a regular basis.

'Nancy! Good afternoon! Nice wig. I prefer the blue one though. Blue is my favourite colour. Your usual?'

'Yes please, Nico. Oh, and chuck in a milkshake, while you're at it. I could use the calcium. Strawberry one.'

'Ooh – on a new regime, then? Healthy living?'

'Yeah, right. You know me better than that, Nico.'

As I suck my milkshake through a straw like a kid, I think about telling Nico I'm going away, but decide against it. I've had enough goodbyes over the past couple of days. Instead I quickly eat my cheeseburger with extra pickles and read a dog-eared copy of the Metro that a previous customer has left on my table. It is full of what Val would call 'absolute drivel'. There's a piece in there on the Enbys, which talks all about their clothes and their style. It barely mentions their music. That's probably just as well.

Afterwards I hop on the tube at Angel and change at King's Cross. After that I've got quite a few stops to travel on the same line, so I stick my headphones on and zone out. Like I said before, no one bothers me because no one recognises me. People see what they expect to see. Black hair and leather waistcoat – The Baroness. Red hair and hoodie – Nancy Nobody. Easy.

I have to say I regret my choice of outfit when I arrive at the boat sales office next to the marina. From the moment I walk in, it's obvious the two blokes behind the counter don't think I can afford a boat or am serious about buying one, even though I made an appointment. I clock the look they give each other. The look which clearly says 'let's not waste time on this chick'. I'm tempted to walk out, but I'd only be shooting myself in the foot. My quick Internet search showed that they have the best selection of narrowboats in London. So, I swallow my pride. I tell myself it's just one transaction. I don't have to marry the old geezers.

'Now, Mrs. Parkinson. Can you give us an idea of what you are looking for?'

'Miss. Not really. It's been a long time since I've been on a narrowboat. I'm sure they've changed quite a bit. Just show me a few and I'll decide what I want.'

Cue a big sigh from Geezer One.

'We have a lot of boats here, *Miss* Parkinson. Could you at least give us an idea of your budget?'

Ha.

'How much is your most expensive one?' I enquire sweetly.

'Our most expensive boat, Miss Parkinson, is on sale for £167,950.'

'OK. Then let's start with that one and work downwards.'

Well, that's got their attention. I'm sure they now think I'm a money launderer or something, but the prospect of selling an expensive boat makes them scurry around, grabbing various sets of keys from the cabinet at the back of the office. They stop short of tugging their forelocks, but only just.

As we walk over towards the boats in the marina, I forget to be annoyed. I can feel a sense of excitement building. Even though these are pleasure boats, the sort my family and I used to look down on when I was a kid, it doesn't matter. There is a smell about them which takes me back to my childhood. It makes me feel safe, somehow. As I climb aboard the first narrowboat and clock the slight sway as it rocks on the murky canal water, it feels like I am coming home. Then I take a look around me and realise this boat could not be more different from the cramped cabin where I used to live, squashed up against the rest of my family. Obviously, things have moved on a bit, to put it mildly. If I didn't know better, I'd think I was in a bloody apartment in Canary Wharf. One of those pads where merchant bankers live during the week, before they hop in their helicopters and fly off to The Cotswolds, or Monaco or wherever, for the weekend. It doesn't feel like a narrowboat, that's for sure.

The two old dudes talk me through the equipment on board this thing and I get more and more gobsmacked as I go on. In the galley, for a start, there's a washer/dryer hidden away tastefully in a kitchen cabinet. I'm about to be a bit sniffy about it, then I think about the indefinite boat trip I plan to make. This would mean no visits to the launderette. No trying to find a launderette, in fact. There aren't many left, that's for sure. No washing your knickers in the sink at 3am. Time for an attitude adjustment. A washer/dryer on a boat is officially a 'good thing'. That's my view and I'm sticking to it.

We then move on to the saloon, which is lit up like Blackpool Illuminations, with fancy lights everywhere you look. I'm told they are all complete with dimmer switches, should you want to create a more relaxed or romantic vibe. As if. The audio-visual equipment includes, and I kid you not, a flatscreen TV and DVD player, plus a music centre, complete with surround sound speakers. In the corner is a wireless router which apparently provides high speed Internet access on even the most remote parts of the canal network. So much for going off grid.

As I check out the bathroom, I remember a basic shower was the most I had hoped for. This bathroom goes so far beyond that - it's unreal. With its flash shower cubicle and free-standing washbasin, it would not be out of place in sodding Claridges. The rest of the boat is suitably flash, and I can see the two geezers smiling at each other. Like they know the little lady is impressed by the fixtures and fittings. Fancies a nice washing machine and a convenient place to plug in her hair dryer. Time to surprise them a bit, so I start firing questions at them about the engine. After all, the thing's no good if it can't go anywhere. To be honest, I just want to have a bit of fun with them. Maybe change their view of women a bit. I'm sure the engine works just fine.

A few questions in, I can tell they have a bit more respect for me now. After they've got over their shock that a woman could know so much about diesel engines, they take me to the engine room at the back of the boat and let me look under the bonnet, so to speak. All good there, as I expected. Then it's their turn to surprise me by showing me the controls. It's all touch screen, for shit's sake. The engine starts at the touch of a button. There are digital gauges which display the levels of fuel and water in the tanks. Now where's the fun in that? It takes the guess work out of knowing when you're about to run out. Removes the thrill of running on vapour, hoping you'll make it to the next source of fuel before you conk out completely. Or being unable to brush your teeth because you couldn't be bothered to fill up at the last water point. I'm just kidding, obviously. The technology is bloody brilliant.

I'm such a pushover, aren't I? Happily waving goodbye to my traditional boater's principles as soon as I'm shown some shiny new gadgets. The old boys haven't finished yet, though. Like good salesmen, they have saved the best until last. The thing only has remote control! Using an app on my phone, I can turn on the boat's central heating and lights from any location you like. I could be in a hotel room in Tokyo, but if I feel the urge to light up, or heat up, my narrowboat, I can make it happen by simply pawing away at my smartphone screen. I picture myself in a pub somewhere on the cut, blowing the froth off my first pint and thinking my boat might be a bit chilly when I finally get back. That it might be easier to find in the dark if I were to switch the lights on. No problem, Nancy! Just a quick tap on your phone and it's all sorted.

I think my Dad would be turning in his grave if he could see this boat. Actually, he'd be spinning like a chuffing top. My Mum would lap it up though, I reckon. She had to do most of the work, so I'm pretty sure she would appreciate all the practical labour-saving devices. The poor cow would have killed for a washing machine, back in the day.

There's just one thing which does make me have second thoughts. The boat has a bow thruster. Dodgy old name, I know. What it does, in case you don't know, is shove the bow of the boat across when you're in a tight corner, to make it easier to manoeuvre the thing. Traditional boaters tend to diss them. They say they're for people who can't steer properly. They also complain they're too noisy and disturb the peace of the canals. I'm not sure I want a boat with a bow thruster, but once again I stop and give it some thought. I know I can steer, for a start. I don't need to prove anything to anyone. What's more, if you're trying to turn your boat in windy weather, it can be tricky, however good a boater you are. The thing can easily morph into a sixty-foot-long metal sail, meaning it's a sod to handle. I won't have anyone to help me when that happens, so a bow thruster could come in useful. I tell myself it's the equivalent of having a crew, but without the headache of having to put up with another person on board. That's how I persuade myself to have one. I say a silent 'sorry' to Dad's memory for having sold out. Then I trot off after the two guys to check out the other top of the range narrowboats.

In the end I narrow (sorry) my choice down to three boats. Each one has all the luxury and technical wizardry of the first boat. The boys take me on a short test run in each one and they all handle perfectly. All three would fit the bill a hundred times over. I decide that, despite all my questions about engines, wiring and those sort of things, it's going to come down to a very girly decision based on colour, style and name. Well, I've got to decide somehow, haven't I?

So, there's Anuket, first of all. The name means 'Goddess of the Nile', or so the geezers tell me. I imagine having to spell it for the lock-keepers at every staircase I go through, but that's not really an issue. I could cope with that. The boat is painted in lovely shades of blue and green. Very tasteful. Then there's Rosie. Not the most original name in the world, but it suits her. Even though she is as hi-tech as the others, she is fitted out in red and green to look really traditional - Rosie and Jim style. Of the three boats, she's the one which looks most like the boat I grew up on. Lastly there's the first boat I looked at. All done out in gunmetal grey and black, with big old pretend rivets on the side, like it's an industrial craft or something. Load of old crap really. It's no more industrial than the other two. It looks really fierce, though, and it has got a name to match. Warrior.

There's no contest really, is there?

So off I go, back to the office with my two old mates. We're quite friendly now and I'm about to go up even further in their estimation. I tell them Warrior is the one for me. I negotiate a modest discount, just for form's sake. Then I take my phone out of my rucksack, call my accountant and arrange for him to transfer the money over to them. That's a nice moment, I have to say. I practically have to pick those two up off the floor. I'm sure they thought I would either 'get back to them' or produce a carrier bag full of fifty-pound notes. Anyway, they rush around making me coffee as I fill in all the paperwork. They help me sort out my boat licence and my insurance. They offer me a mooring at their marina and are disappointed when I refuse. I explain I'm planning to be a continuous cruiser. Sounds a bit suspect, but that's what it's known as. Always on the move. That's going to be my new life.

I arrange to pick up the boat in two days' time. Afterwards I head back home to pack up all my personal belongings and deposit them in a secure storage facility, so I can leave my house nice and empty. A plain page for the new tenants to write on. It won't take long, I don't think. As I mentioned before, I don't think I'll have a heap of stuff to put in storage. A whole load of guitars – the ones I can't fit on the boat. A bunch of clothes, make-up and shit like that. A few pictures I don't want the tenants touching. And my pink piano – they're not getting their hands on that. Plus, my files with all my sheet music in them. Oh, and my altar, of course. I'll have to dismantle it. No way are they getting their hands on my altar.

11 SHE'S LEAVING HOME

I can hear you laughing from here. Two days to clear my house and put my belongings in storage. 'What is she thinking?' you say. You're right, of course. Turns out I have ten times more stuff than I thought and the storage isn't as easy to arrange as I expected. In the end it takes me four days instead of two, but you know what? I'm going to skip past the whole tedious business of moving out. I think we've already established I'm no domestic goddess. I'm cool with that. I don't want to write about a load of house move crap and you don't want to read about it. Or if you do, go get one of those books with a shoe on the front cover. Where the flawed but charming heroine always bags her handsome prince in the end. In the meantime I'll carry on with my story.

So, after four days, off I go to pick up Warrior. My two mates at the marina take forever to show me the controls in mind numbing detail but eventually I'm allowed to leave. I feel a bit nervous, I don't mind admitting, as I carefully steer my way out of the marina, trying not to crash into anything. OK I had a test run before, but I'm still pretty rusty and I don't want to give those guys the last laugh by ballsing things up before I've even started. That would really kill my vibe.

Once I'm out on the canal, which thankfully is nice and quiet, I relax a bit and stop trying so hard. I have checked the waterways guide and there are no locks for the next few miles, so I make the most of it and put Warrior through his paces. Compared with my family's old commercial boat, steering this miracle of modern bloody technology feels like driving a Ferrari as opposed to an old banger. Obviously you can't really compare a narrowboat, which only travels at four miles per hour, with a shit off a shovel Ferrari, but you know what I mean. Everything is as smooth as silk. Everything works. The thing doesn't even make much noise. There's no thick black smoke, no smells, no banging and crashing. No people yelling at each other. It's all so quiet and civilised. Not at all like the boating I'm used to. And yet, the canal feels familiar. It feels right. It feels like coming home. I had the sense to stock the cool-box and move it to the back of the boat before I set off, so I grab a cheeky beer, spark up a fag and chill out. For the first time since my meeting with The Gatekeeper, the world seems an OK place.

It doesn't last, of course. My mood changes pretty soon. After a while I recognise Victoria Park on my right and realise I'm in Hackney. To my left, not far away, is Mile End and beyond that is Bow, where I was born. Wherever I have travelled in the world, London has always been home, so I feel the city tugging at my heartstrings as I prepare to leave it. Then I look ahead, spot my first lock and immediately forget all that sentimental crap. I bloody well hope I can remember how to do this.

If you have ever been boating, I'm willing to bet you were with at least one other person. If you were lucky, you had kids or friends on hand to help you with the locks, although I guess that could be a mixed blessing. Anyway, what I'm saying is, even if you had to work the locks on your own, someone else was probably steering the boat while you did it. Am I right? Well let me tell you – solo boating is a whole other ball game. If I'm wrong and you have boated on your own, I salute you and will buy you a cold one if I ever meet you. Also, you can probably skip the next paragraph where I describe how to work a lock by yourself. On the other hand, you might want to check and see if I'm doing it right. You gnarly old solo boaters can be picky bastards, in my experience.

So here's what I do when Warrior and I arrive at my first lock. First I pull up at the lock moorings and secure the boat to one of the bollards using the middle rope. Then I run down the towpath to check the status of the lock. It's empty and I'm travelling uphill so the lock is – in my favour. Even if you're not a boater, I know you had this concept explained to you before, so keep up. Anyway, it's a big double lock and I can go in on one gate because I'm a good steerer who has only had one beer. So I open the gate. Then I run back, untie Warrior and steer him into the lock. Next, holding on to the middle rope, I climb up the ladder which is built into the wall of the lock. As you can imagine, the rungs are all slimy with water weed. Nice. Once I reach the towpath, I run back and close the gate, then dash to the front end of the lock and carefully open the paddles. I try my best to hold the boat steady, using the rope, as the lock fills. I don't want to destroy Warrior's perfect paintwork before I have even started, by crashing him against the sides of the lock. Once the lock is full, I open one of the front gates and close the paddles. Then I jump back on board, still holding the rope. I steer through the open gate and tie up at the lock moorings on the far side. Then I run back and close the gate. Finally I return to my boat, untie it, get back on and away I go. Not forgetting to stow the middle rope carefully on the roof, of course. You don't want that thing falling in the water and getting tangled around the prop.

Does that sound like hard work? It bloody well is, I can tell you. So you'll understand why I'm not going to be doing any thirty lock days like some of you holiday have a go heroes. I'm going to be a five-hours a day girl, taking my time and asking for help wherever I can get it. On the way, I'm not going to talk much about locks. I'm sure you'll be relieved to hear that. I'll also skip the bits where nothing much happens and the boat just sort of drifts along in the middle of nowhere. If you like that sort of thing, and granted it is relaxing, they've got videos of it on You Tube which you can watch. Right, I'll press on.

When I reach the top lock at the far end of Victoria Park, I see two skinny young dudes standing there. Jeans hanging off their arses, hoods pulled up, earphones in. They take no notice of me or my boat as I steer into the lock, but they do look vaguely amused as I climb up the ladder and scramble clumsily onto the towpath. They shoot each other a look which clearly says, 'look what that crazy old bat's doing'. I suppose I do look old, to them. Anyway, I quickly wipe the smile off their faces by handing them the middle rope and asking them to hold Warrior steady while I close the gate and fill the lock. I don't think anyone has ever given these two any responsibility in their lives and they both cling to the rope, watching Warrior like a hawk and looking deadly serious, until the lock is full and I have closed the paddles and opened the front gate. I thank them, ask them to close the gate behind me, then hop back on board and chuck them a couple of cold cans of beer for their trouble. They scurry towards the gate, clutching their cans to their chests as though they can't believe their luck. When I look back a couple of minutes later, I see they've popped them open and are drinking away, standing in exactly the same place as before. Their encounter with me is probably going to be the highlight of their day. Poor sods. Being a teenager can be dead boring.

Shortly afterwards I turn right onto Regent's Canal, work the next lock on my own, then continue heading west. To my left is Haggerston, followed soon after by the famous hipster hangouts of Hoxton and Shoreditch. I remember when those areas were dog rough and best avoided, even by people like me, who reckon they know how to handle themselves. Now the houses there cost top dollar and you have to take out a mortgage on your dinner. How things change.

All the time I'm thinking this stuff, I'm trying to push away the thought that soon the canal will be going through Islington. The homesick feelings are starting to bubble up and I know they're only going to get worse. Islington has been my home for the last fifteen years and I still love it. I'm not leaving on this boat because of Islington. And if I don't keep a lid on this homesickness, I won't be leaving at all.

I manage to hold it together as the boat emerges from under New North Road Bridge. It helps that I have to change course pretty smartish to avoid a group of schoolkids in canoes, who are traumatising a mother duck and her chicks. No, sorry, I got that wrong. It's not a duck. It's one of those birds whose faces look like the mask from that film called Scream. A white face on a black background. A coot. That's it, the bugger. The one with the yellow legs and the big grey feet. As you can see, David Attenborough's got nothing to worry about, with me.

Anyway, the canoeists and their instructor gaily follow me into the next lock, which is a bit worrying. I don't want to capsize some schoolkid's canoe. That would really ruin my day and I guess the instructor wouldn't be too impressed neither. Luckily there's a lock-keeper on duty and between us we work the lock without killing any of the kids. Or the teacher.

Once I'm back on board and have no further distractions, the homesickness really starts to hit home, if you see what I mean. We're now in Islington proper and on a sunny afternoon like this, there's no better place to be, in my opinion. On the towpath, groups of runners charge past, logging PBs and holding business meetings at the same time. Normally I'd think they were tossers but now, as I'm about to leave, I find myself admiring them. Especially as I can barely run from one end of a lock to the other. I really must quit with the ciggies at some stage. Once I've got my head together.

As Warrior cuts his way through the bright green duckweed floating on the surface of the canal, I watch a group of childminders pushing Silver Cross buggies along the towpath and take in the trendy apartments in the converted warehouses around Wenlock Basin. That's where the parents of the Silver Cross babies probably live, pulling sixty-plus hours a week in some office just to afford the mortgage and the childcare. Not to mention the pram. Next comes the great expanse of City Road Basin, away to my left, with the new skyscrapers behind it which seem oddly out of place. They look like they belong in Shanghai or Dubai, not on City Road. That's not my Islington. Here on the right is the Islington I love, where some well-meaning bunch of community workers have planted a herb garden on the towpath. I can smell the basil from here. Anyone can come down and snip of a bit of rosemary, or sage or whatever, to put into their pot with their dinner. That's my Islington – a square-knitting, blankets for Syria kind of place, with some fine old pubs and a few wine bars, paninis and posh coffees thrown in for good measure.

Talking of which, the café just below Danbury Road Bridge is doing a belting lunchtime trade. It's full of office workers making the most of the nice weather. Some of them are trying to work, squinting at their sunlit laptop screens and struggling to make out what that supposedly vital email is actually saying. Most have given up, though, and are just soaking up a few rays. The girls have kicked off their sandals and turned their sun-glassed faces to the sky. A little dog is lapping water from a bowl which the café owner has thoughtfully put out for him. Bright droplets of water splash everywhere as he enjoys a messy drink. Suddenly all I want to do is moor up and join those people and that dog. Call my estate agents and tell them to cancel the rental agreement. Drink a posh coffee and then walk home. It would only take about fifteen minutes, unless I stopped for a nice refreshing pint in the Island Queen on the way. Get back the rest of my guitars and my pink piano. Forget this whole stupid idea.

I literally count to ten to force myself to keep going. I look ahead and see the mouth of Islington tunnel approaching fast. Waiting to swallow me and Warrior up. The tunnel passes practically underneath Angel tube station and comes out near the bottom of Pentonville Road, just above King's Cross. Once I emerge at the other end, I'll have passed my house and Islington will be behind me. After that, I tell myself firmly, there will be no going back. No more homesickness or soppy nostalgia. Onwards and upwards – or westwards and then northwards, to be more accurate. I grit my teeth and force myself to carry on into the tunnel. Once I'm in there, under cover of darkness, I have another cry, I'm ashamed to say. I'm turning into a right wimp, aren't I? I've cried more in the last week or so than I have in the last five years.

Of course, it's not over yet, is it? I'm not out of the woods. As the canal wends its way round the back of King's Cross Station, I try to distract myself by people watching. Some self-consciously cool dudes, probably from the You Tube office just up the road, are sunning themselves on the steps at Granary Wharf. Nearby, there's a photo shoot going on, with a bunch of heavily fake-tanned models dressed totally inappropriately for summer, in long fake fur coats and masses of bling. Sweating away to get the right shots for the winter edition of some magazine. The inside of those coats will look like an explosion in a marmalade factory by the end of the shoot. The poor cows look as though they're about to pass out with the heat and I can't help but feel sorry for them. I always hated photo shoots – for album covers, magazine features and the like. I don't feel at all nostalgic for that part of my career. The Enbys are welcome to it.

Further on, the gasworks at St. Pancras has been converted into fancy apartments and the side ponds of the nearby lock have been planted up with loads of colourful water lilies. It's a far cry from the scene I remember as a child; the grim, filthy gasworks and the oily, reeking canal water. The place is practically a nature reserve now, but as I head west, the upmarket, des-res vibe starts to dwindle and the amount of graffiti on the walls and bridges gradually builds up. I spot a small group of grubby tents pitched on the towpath to my right. Shopping trolleys are parked outside, containing all the worldly goods of the tent dwellers. A cyclist with some very impressive dreads rides by and I catch the familiar, sweet smell of weed. Truly Dorothy, you are not in Kansas any more. Around here, offices turn their backs to the canal, rather than their faces. It's more like it used to be when I was a kid and the canal was a dirty embarrassment. Not something which you'd happily pay an extra hundred grand for, so you could see it from your kitchen window every day of the year. It's grimy here and a bit edgy. You would definitely think twice about walking along here at night. I love it, though. Almost as much as I love Islington. It's Camden, of course. My old stamping ground.

At Camden Lock I get lots of help from a lock-keeper and a group of eager tourists, so I have plenty of time to gaze longingly over towards Camden Market and The Stables, my favourite places for shopping, browsing and just generally hanging out. A wave of nostalgia hits me again. There will be nowhere remotely like this out in the Shires, that's for sure. I look at all the boats moored along the towpath and admire my fellow boaters with their many piercings and tattoos, their faded denim and distressed leather. I realise sadly that soon I'll see no more of their kind. Where I'm going it'll be all fleeces and Breton tops, paired with trousers with elasticated waistbands. What am I doing? I feel a surge of panic, and things don't get any better when I reach Dingwalls Wharf, home to the iconic club of the same name. I have played there plenty of times over the years, particularly in the early part of my career. Always with Dave behind me on drums, solid and reliable. Everything was such fun back then – so new and exciting. I'm still not sure exactly when things changed. I hear the haunting, folksy sound of a girl's voice coming over the speakers, entertaining the throng of tourists. She sounds a bit like Dido. Maybe she is Dido. Immediately I want to be up there myself, singing and playing guitar. More than that, I want to identify myself as one of these people around here. They're my own kind. I suddenly feel the urge to carry something of Camden with me on my journey. That's when I finally crack. I moor Warrior just west of the wharf and make my way back through the crowds to Chalk Farm Road.

Now I haven't got much ink, I have to tell you. More than the Queen though, I imagine. Unless Her Maj hides it well under all those pastel coat dresses. Definitely less than Amy, the ultimate Camden girl. She's on my altar, of course. Sorry, I'm going off topic again. The point I'm trying to make is, I've got enough ink to have a favourite tattoo parlour where they know me. I duck and dive through the mass of bodies which always crowds Chalk Farm Road and get there as quickly as I can. Luckily Kevin, my most trusted tattoo artist, is working today. He blows me a kiss as I take a seat and wait for him to come free.

I know exactly which tattoo I want. I'd like a little flock of birds, symbolising freedom. I want an image that signifies my escape from everything that has been bringing me down over the last few years. I want four birds in my flock. One for each member of my family. Me, Mum and Dad plus my brother, who I haven't really told you about yet. Kevin tattoos the birds so they fly across my left collarbone. Before he starts, he checks to make sure that's where I want them. He points out that it's very bony there, so it's going to hurt. Good, I think. Bring it on. It'll distract me from all the other pain I've been feeling today. A distraction is just what I need.

A couple of hours later and I'm good to go. Armed with a box of dressings and a big tube of nappy rash cream to help the tattoo heal, I return to the boat. My collarbone hurts like hell but overall, I feel much better. I untie and head off immediately down the long, lock-free stretch of canal that borders Primrose Hill and London Zoo. It's so weird, I always think, chugging past those aviaries full of exotic birds. I feel glad I'm freer than they are, as symbolised by my new tattoo. I'm also happy to be putting north London behind me. I push on through Maida Vale tunnel and past Little Venice, without stopping to take in one of the most famous spots on the canal network. Likewise, I'm not tempted to divert down towards Paddington Basin, another place that has been gentrified beyond belief. It's all very nice around here, don't get me wrong, but it's west London and I have no connections to this place. Other than the fact that The Gatekeeper and lots of his cronies live around here, which is a very good reason for me to move swiftly on. I continue heading west until I reach the Grand Union Canal, the industrial backbone of the canal network. It feels good to be back, but it has been a long day and I've had enough. I moor up in the first suitable spot after the junction and prepare myself for my first night on board my boat.

As I open a can of beer and start rolling a spliff, I can't get rid of the thought that tomorrow I'll be heading out into the suburbs. Acton, Perivale, Alperton, Northolt. Apologies if you live in any of those places, but even the names make me depressed. I either like to be right in the centre of a city or out in the countryside. Even if I'm living in a squat, or a caravan, and believe me I've done both. Anything in between just makes me want to escape as fast as possible. I'm sure suburbia works for loads of people, as so many of you live there, but it's not for me. So, if you don't mind, I'm going to smoke a nice relaxing joint and drink a couple of beers, then get an early night. I want to crack on first thing tomorrow and put the London suburbs far behind me.

12 GIRLS ON TOP

The best thing I can say about the next day's boating is there are no locks. It's a 'get your head down and get on with it' kind of day. I use the guidebook to check on progress and go as fast as I can. Which is not very fast, obviously. Especially as I'm always careful not to bother anyone else. I kill my speed when I meet a boat going the other way, or see someone fishing, and I always pass moored boats on tickover. Whatever you think of me by now, in this respect at least I'm not a complete tosser, I promise. I remember what it was like on our working boat, when mugs and plates would crash onto the floor because some selfish git couldn't be bothered to slow down. I wouldn't inflict that on someone else.

As Warrior chugs his way along the canal, I check out the various tourist attractions along the route. First up, on my right, is the beautiful Kensal Green Cemetery. Not. To my left is a huge expanse of very scenic railway sidings and beyond that is Wormwood Scrubs. I know a few people from way back when who have done a stint in there. Most of them were friends with my dad. A bit further on I reach Park Royal, which used to be home to the Guinness factory until they demolished it. Now Guinness isn't my kind of beer, but the building was worth saving. Art Deco it was, just like the Tate Modern. Whoever decided to knock it down made a naff call, in my view.

There's more industry further on, plus a few green spaces, but they're all depressingly man-made and manicured. Golf courses and the like. I can't wait to be out in the countryside. Give me the wilderness any day. There's something about the control-freakery of a perfectly striped green lawn. It makes my flesh crawl.

By mid-afternoon I've had enough. There's a stonking great business park on my right; a bunch of faceless corporate monoliths with their plate glass and gleaming metal. To my left is the appropriately named Grave Wharf. It's not the most attractive place to moor, but I'm in a rubbish mood and almost want to tie up somewhere crap so my surroundings match how I feel inside. I'm also knackered, so I find the first suitable place and then do what I always do to make myself feel better. I play guitar, for hours on end. At times like this it never fails to help. I'm sure you have your own remedy that you turn to when you feel shite. Maybe it's baking or writing computer programs. Algorithms or whatever. Writing books, even – although for the life of me I can't see why. Too much like hard work, in my opinion. Maybe you like playing with your kids. Or going down the pub and getting lashed. Swinging, if that floats your boat. Playing guitar is what works for me, every time.

The next morning, I feel slightly better. I make another early start and soon pass the turning for the Slough Arm of the canal. You remember how I wasn't tempted to make a detour down to Paddington Basin the other day? Well I'm even less inclined to re-route to Slough. I'm sorry, Slough dwellers. I'm sure there's lovely stuff to be found in your town, but I'm going to give you a miss.

So on we go, me and Warrior. I'm getting quite fond of him already, I have to say. The fact he doesn't break down is a big part of it. Our old boat was forever conking out and I don't miss having to tinker with the engine every five minutes. By the way, I guess the purists among you are wondering why I refer to Warrior as 'him' rather than 'her'. You wouldn't wonder if you saw him, believe me. Not with his grey industrial paintwork and all his rivets. The stark lettering on his side. The complete absence of roses and castles and anything which could be classed as pretty. Warrior is definitely a bloke. He's a mean old punk too. You couldn't put pots of flowers on his roof or anything like that. His engine probably would cut out in protest if you did.

Today I've got the odd lock to keep me busy, but they're spaced quite wide apart so I still make good progress. By early evening I find myself alongside some pleasant enough lakes, so I decide to moor up. I see from the guide that there is a shop nearby so I walk down and stock up on baked beans, sliced bread, sausages and beer. Back on the boat, I have my first go at using the cooker and make myself beans on toast. I don't even burn the toast, which is pretty good going for me. Afterwards, I make myself a nice big JD and coke for pudding, pick up my guitar and decide today has not been that bad. Things are looking up a bit.

The next day starts off much the same but after a couple of hours, things get tougher. There are more locks and there never seem to be any boats wanting to go through them at the same time as me, so I have to do most of the work myself. As I'm sure you have realised by now, I'm not exactly a paragon of health and fitness so I get tired quite quickly, but I press on and do you know what? All that physical work actually helps with my head. Over the course of the day my hard labour on the locks stops me from thinking about anything else. Gradually I put some mental distance between me and my showdown with The Gatekeeper, along with some physical miles. By the time I moor up for the night near Kings Langley, I'm all in of course, but I feel more content than I have in ages. I make use of my fancy onboard shower then play guitar all evening until my hair is dry. I sleep better than I have in ages.

The next morning is similar to the previous one, although there are more people around as I work the locks through Hemel Hempstead. This means I get some help for a change, which is nice. The flip side is, I meet a few people who think they recognise me. It's no big deal, really. I can handle it. They say things like 'I'm sure I know you from somewhere, but I can't think where' and I reply that lots of people make the same remark and I just seem to have that kind of face. One which people think they know. Then I pull my baseball cap down a bit further and they generally let it go. As I've said before, people see what they expect to see. And no one expects to encounter someone like me on the canals. You know, far bigger stars than me have happily chugged along on a narrowboat for weeks, without any hassle at all. Harrison Ford, for instance. I kid you not. He and Calista Flockhart did the entire Llangollen Canal one year, for their summer holidays. It's one of the most popular canals, but no one bothered him, and you know why not? Because the last thing you expect to see on the Pontcysyllte Aqueduct is bleeding Han Solo. You literally don't believe your eyes.

Having said that, I'm just coming out of Hemel when I spot a lovely looking pub on my left and decide I deserve a couple of pints of real ale as a reward for all my hard work. I do one more lock for good luck and find a good place to tie up for the night. Then I wander back, buy myself a beer and take a seat outside by the canal, to watch some other people boating for a change. After a few minutes, I clock the guys at the next table looking in my direction, whispering to each other and giggling. Not cool, boys. Then I hear one of them daring his mate to come over and speak to me. Eventually this bloke sidles over and says:

'I'm sorry to bother you, but are you that singer? The one who used to be called The Baroness?'

'I get asked this a lot, but no. I just happen to look like her. I was even approached in the street one day by a guy from an agency who wanted me to be a Baroness lookalike, but I said no. Not my thing.'

'You should have said yes!' goes the bloke. 'Those lookalikes earn a good wedge, or so I hear. Oh well – I'll leave you in peace. Enjoy your beer.'

He returns to his mates and they all have a little conflab.

'Oh well, never mind,' says the one who dared his friend to approach me. 'Her music's crap, anyway.'

'No, it's not,' argues one of the others, 'it's better than that Gangsta rap you listen to. Makes my ears bleed, that does.'

'Hip hop,' says the first guy through a mouthful of crisps, spraying crumbs everywhere. 'Not Gangsta.'

'Well, I like her too,' says the one who spoke to me. 'I've got a couple of her CDs at home. Melanie left them behind when she moved out.'

'Well good for you,' says hip hop guy. 'Anyway, it's not her, so whatever.'

They move on to another topic. I finish my beer and leave. Like I say, this stuff is easy to deal with, but I make a mental note to dig out one of my wigs plus a change of clothing next time I visit a pub. It just makes things simpler.

By the next evening I have worked my way through Berkhamstead and am heading up towards Tring. Berkhamstead was nice but the towpath was fairly quiet, so help was in short supply. The exception was a couple of runners, who stopped to help me open and close a pair of lock gates. They had obviously been caning it on their run as they were both hot and sweaty, so I was impressed they were kind enough to help and told them so. I was even more impressed by the girl's hair, which was dark like mine, but amazingly curly and springy, even after all that sweating. That girl could spend hours in the mosh pit and when she came out, her hair would still be shower fresh. I can't say the same for mine. As they ran off, she smiled at her companion, who was a nice-looking guy. You could see that, even through all the sweat. A real love smile, it was. Made me think of Johnno and all my other failed relationships. I'm rubbish at love. Really, I am.

I plan on finding a quiet mooring place and having yet another night in with my guitar, but then I spot another canal-side pub and decide to tie up nearby and check it out. To be honest, I'm not so different from you boozy holiday boaters who just spend the whole time cruising from one pub to another. Nothing wrong with that, you pissheads. I salute you. I have already passed up quite a few decent alehouses in Berkhamstead today and have done a shedload more locks so I reckon I deserve at least a couple of pints. This time, though, I'm going to take more care not to be recognised. I don't need the grief. So, I rummage round in my cupboards and pop on a blonde wig, a pair of pedal pushers and an orange cold shoulder top which The Baroness would not be seen dead in. When I'm done, I look in the mirror and a sort of skinny, flat chested Dolly Parton stares back at me. If you can imagine such a thing. It's a bit of a weird outfit, but at least I'll be anonymous.

Half an hour later I'm sitting in the corner of the pub, minding my own business. It's busier than I expected, and I soon find out why, when the barman picks up a microphone and asks the punters to get into their teams and take their seats for tonight's pub quiz. Just my luck. Time for a sharp exit, as they say. I'm swigging away at my pint – I'm not one to waste perfectly good beer – when this woman walks over to me.

'Excuse me – I'm sorry to bother you…'

Uh-oh, here we go. Note to self, Nancy. The blonde wig is not as effective as you think.

'…but we're one short on our quiz team. I wonder if I could persuade you to join us? All the other teams have got six people but one of our team couldn't make it. It would be great if you could take her place for tonight.'

The woman points to a table on the other side of the bar where her four team members sit with their glasses of Prosecco, looking hopefully in my direction. Normally I'd just say 'no' and head off, but something stops me. Maybe it's the relief of not being recognised. Maybe I'm a bit lonely, if I'm being honest. Anyway, instead of brushing her off, I smile at her and say,

'You're going to regret this. I won't be any good, but I'll have a go.'

'Brilliant! Thank you so much. I'm Susan, by the way.' She grabs my hand and shakes it vigorously, beaming at me. Then she turns and gives a thumbs up to the rest of the quiz team, who look ridiculously excited to have recruited me. That feeling's not going to last, I can tell you now. The poor cows could do so much better.

And so it turns out. After the first couple of rounds the Girl-Rillas – that's their team name – are definitely regretting their decision. I haven't answered a single question on current affairs or TV soaps, which is hardly surprising as I know zip-all about either subject. I nip to the bar before the next round begins and buy a bottle of Prosecco for them and a pint for me. It's the least I can do, given my dismal performance. Then things start looking up, because the next round is on music. The barman plays a whole bunch of intros and we have to identify the artist and track. The Girl-Rillas answer a few correctly, but I answer all the ones they don't know and correct them a couple of times when they get it wrong. At the end of the round I am certain we have got every one right and I feel quite proud of myself. Tragic, I know.

The next round is on history and I answer a couple of those questions too. I'm not a total ignoramus. After that comes sport and once again, I'm crap, but a couple of the women are big sports fans, so we seem to do OK. Then it's all over. Time to swap score sheets and tot up the numbers. I find myself feeling quite keyed up about the result and realise I've had a right laugh with the Girl-Rillas. I'll be drinking bleeding Prosecco next. No, scrub that. I'll never swap beer for Prosecco. It's not going to happen.

Anyway, it turns out the result is a draw between the Girl-Rillas and a team called The Commuters. Susan explains how our opponents all travel to London each day from Tring station and got to know each other on the train. Poor sad bastards. The barman announces that there can only be one winner, so the two teams will be given a tie-break question and the team which answers correctly will claim victory. As we wait for the question to be read out, I actually feel nervous. What a stupid cow I am.

'So the tie break question is…' the barman announces slowly, obviously trying to ratchet up the tension, 'what is the capital of the American state of Louisiana?'

Immediately I'm transported back in time. Me, Dave and the rest of the band are messing about in one of the hotel rooms after our concert. It was a great gig and we are all happy, in that spent way you feel when you have just played and sung your heart out to a fantastic audience. It's a hot, humid night. All the windows are open. We are getting stuck into a few bottles of Bourbon and just jamming, like we always do. We agree that in this town, there is one song we just have to try. I give it my very best Janis Joplin as I launch into the first few bars of 'Me and Bobby McGee'…

'New Orleans,' Susan whispers urgently and I snap back into the present. 'I've been there. I'm sure it's the state capital of Louisiana.'

The others nod in agreement, but I shake my head.

'It's not,' I say. 'The capital of Louisiana is Baton Rouge.'

The other Girl-Rillas look at me sceptically, then at Susan. I don't blame them. I'd go with my team captain's answer any day rather than trust some stranger with a dodgy blonde barnet.

'How sure are you?' Susan asks.

'I'm certain,' I reply and she nods.

'OK. Let's go with your answer.'

The Girl-Rillas look at me like they will be mightily pissed off when I'm proved wrong, but they clearly don't dare to disagree with their captain.

'Right, let's have your answers,' chivvies the barman. 'I'm going to go gents first for a change. Commuters?'

'New Orleans!' calls out the captain of The Commuters, sounding pretty damn confident. The Girl-Rillas frown at Susan, then at me, like they knew Susan was wrong to trust me.

'Girl-Rillas – what's your answer?'

'Baton Rouge,' replies Susan, sounding far less confident than her opposite number.

'OK – thank you to both teams. And the correct answer is…'

The barman draws out the tension for a long moment. I think he reckons he's on bloody Strictly or something.

'…the correct answer is – Baton Rouge!'

Well the place goes mental and I go from zero to hero in an instant. Those Girl-Rillas are hugging me and each other, screaming and jumping up and down. Susan yells in my ear that they've been doing the quiz every week for the last couple of years and this is the first time they've won.

'How did you know the answer?' she asks.

'I guess you don't remember the Janis Joplin song,' I reply. 'Written by Kris Kristofferson, but Janis nailed the cover version.' Then I do something a bit stupid. Something I would never have done if I hadn't been high on the moment, with a few pints under my belt. I let her have the first line – the one which mentions Baton Rouge. I really give it some welly too, in true Janis Joplin style, which has an instant effect. The whole place falls silent and everyone turns to look at me.

Then the barman leans over the bar and calls, 'Come back on Tuesday at seven, love – for open mic night. With a voice like that, you'll be a shoe-in.'

There are murmurs of agreement from around the bar, then the celebrations start right back up again, but Susan is not minded to let it go. She makes the point, quite rightly, that it still doesn't explain how I knew Baton Rouge was the capital rather than New Orleans, but I just ignore her and order another pint, this time with a JD chaser. The prize for the winning team is of course a bottle of Prosecco. It lasts about two minutes and the Girl-Rillas follow it up with a couple more. I stick around and drink lots more beer and JD. Eventually I wobble back down the towpath well after closing time, unable to remember when I had last had so much fun. Unable to remember very much at all, to be honest.

13 CLOSE ENCOUNTERS

The next morning, I wake up with a cracking hangover, of course, but I make myself get up and push on. I'm impatient to be out in the proper countryside now. I want to get past Leighton Buzzard and in particular Milton Keynes, which I'm expecting to be a low point on my journey. I played the National Bowl a couple of times. Nothing wrong with it as a venue but the town did my head in, with that bloody grid system they have there. I want to crack on and put MK in the rear-view mirror, even if I do feel like crap.

Today the first few miles are lock-free, which gives me some time to sit quietly beside the tiller and let the painkillers kick in. As I chug along, I glance at the guidebook and notice I'm on the summit of this particular stretch, so I'll be travelling downhill through the next bunch of locks. For obvious reasons I'm all about reducing effort today, so I prepare to perform a little trick called thumblining, which can only be done going downhill.

Right I know I promised I wouldn't go on about locks, but indulge me for a moment, while I explain how I blitz through Marsworth Locks so quickly. First I attach some shorter ropes to the cleats on either side of the boat, making sure they are not long enough to get snagged on the prop. As I've said before, a rope tangled around the prop is a Very Bad Thing. Believe me. Then, when I get into the lock, I tie the ropes around the two front gates using a special knot whose name I have forgotten, if I ever knew it in the first place. I can remember how to do it, that's the main thing. It's also a minor miracle given the shite state I'm in. Next, I shut the back gates behind Warrior, open the paddles and hop back on the boat. Now here's the clever bit. As the lock empties and the boat descends, the ropes tighten up and I keep the pressure on by using the gears. Then, as soon as the water levels equalise, the tension on the ropes pulls the gates open so I can drive straight out. As Warrior passes through the gates, the ropes detach themselves thanks to that mystery knot.

Thumblining is a handy little trick but it's not without its problems. Often the ropes drop into the water when they detach so you have to drag them out, which is why it's important they're not long enough to drift back towards the prop. Also, you still have to close the paddles and the gates if there's no one around to help, meaning you have to tie up, get off and run back. Luckily Marsworth is a popular spot. There's a café and a couple of pubs plus a reservoir on the left, so the place is full of day-trippers, birdwatchers and other narrowboats and I get a lot of help. Maybe people are impressed by my solo boating and thumblining. More likely they just feel sorry for me as I must look dead rough. I'm wearing sunglasses the size of dinner plates and no one recognises me, which is hardly surprising. Hungover me is a far cry from what I look like when I've been retouched for a magazine or an album cover.

That night I make like a nun. Well, a nun who just smokes a few fags of an evening, has herself one small beer then goes straight to bed. No weed, even. It's the same the next day. I go through Leighton Buzzard like a dose of salts, moor up in the middle of nowhere, play guitar and sleep. Rinse and repeat. That's why, by the time I get through Fenny Stratford and segue straight into Milton Keynes, I'm ready to re-tox. I'll get MK out of the way first, though. As I explained, it's not my kind of town.

Or so I thought. As it turns out, I misjudged Milton Keynes a bit. Or the parts which border the canal, at least. The town planners have designed the place with about a million canal-side parks, lakes and the like. Wall to wall green space; not a concrete cow in sight. It's all a bit contrived for my taste, but it's a lot better than I expected. There is one surreal moment, though, when I figure those town planners have gone completely barmy. At one point the canal actually forms a bridge that goes over a dual carriageway. So, there we are, Warrior and me, chugging along up in the air, while all this rush hour traffic is driving past underneath. It's just mental.

I don't stop in MK. I consult my trusty guidebook and decide to tie up for the night in a village called Cosgrove, which sounds more like my kind of place. There is a weird old pedestrian tunnel underneath the canal, connecting the towpath on the right with what sounds like a decent pub on the other side. That could work. So, I pass through Wolverton, just to the north of MK. It's all gritty and industrial, with a cool canal-side mural. From there it's just a short hop across an interesting old aqueduct and I arrive at my destination, as the satnav says when you're nowhere near where you're supposed to be.

The pedestrian tunnel is tiny, with a low roof, so I have to duck my head as I scurry through on my way to the pub. After a few days on my own since the crazy quiz night, I feel the need for some company. I do like plenty of time to myself, just me and my guitar, but there are limits.

I've chosen my auburn wig tonight. I'm done with my blonde trailer trash look for the moment. I'm dressed in an old T-shirt, plus my trusty Craghoppers and my leather hiking boots, which are all beaten up but dead comfortable. I reckon I'll blend in well with the boaters and other punters in the pub. Also, my tattoo has healed nicely, so it's on show for the first time. I really like it. In fact, I've never regretted any of the tattoos I've had done. No lasering for me. Mind you, I've never had a guy's name tattooed on my arse or anything daft like that. I always make sure I'm stone cold sober whenever I walk into the tattoo parlour.

It's the first thing the barman remarks on when I walk into the bar. Nice tattoo. Then we're off; comparing ink as far as we can without removing any items of clothing. It's quiet in the pub so he doesn't have anything much to do but talk to me. When he does have to serve someone, he comes back to me straight afterwards. He's cute, so it's no hardship, although chatting to a good-looking dude does make me think of Johnno. He hasn't been in touch since he left my house and I don't blame him.

The barman has an accent, which is always a good talking point. I ask which part of Germany he's from and discover he grew up in Hamburg. His name is Andreas, although the pub customers mostly call him Andy. He moved to the UK to be with his English girlfriend, so he says. They got married but divorced after five years of marriage. She met someone else and that was that. Andreas tells me he was heartbroken - and strapped for cash. He didn't do too well out of the divorce settlement and couldn't afford a house or flat, but he didn't want to go back to Germany. So, he moved onto a decrepit old boat he bought from a friend of a friend. Now he works in the pub at night and restores the boat during the day. He smiles at me as he says he's doing OK, but his eyes tell me the pain is still there.

There are a lot of men like Andreas on the canals, in my experience. Divorced and flat broke. I listen to his story, drink beer and supply a few sketchy details about Nancy, the continuous cruiser. In truth I don't need to fabricate a whole lot. He wants to talk, and I let him. It's not all about his life story; we discuss our views on heavy metal, for a start. Like so many German guys, he's really into it. We also chat about Hamburg. I've played there a few times, so I know the city centre quite well. I explain to Andreas how I used to travel there regularly for conferences and exhibitions in my former life, when I was a brand manager for a food manufacturing company. I can make up these stories at the drop of a hat. I've had loads of practice, after all.

It's getting late and nearly all the customers have left. Andreas is loading glasses into the dishwasher at the other end of the bar. I think about what to do when he asks me to join him on his boat for a nightcap and decide I'll accept. I reckon I can read people and I'm pretty sure Andreas is one of the good guys. I feel even more certain when we try to snog each other as we walk back through the pedestrian tunnel. The kiss is really awkward as the roof of the tunnel is so low and our heads are bent. It's hard to be passionate when you're hunched over like Quasimodo and we just end up laughing. I feel comfortable with him. It's going to be OK.

As I do the towpath walk of shame the next morning, I decide I was right. Andreas is one of the good guys. A bit too well behaved for my taste, in fact. Don't get me wrong; he was lovely, and we had a great time, but he's not really a one-night stand kind of person. Whereas I'm not averse to it when I'm single. I don't have a problem walking away the next day. Andreas is clearly the relationship type, though. I could tell from the way he kept hinting I should stick around for a while and the look of regret he gave me after he hugged me for the last time. I hope he gets over his ex soon and finds someone new. In the meantime, I'm not sure whether I made things better or worse for him. Better, I hope, but who knows?

At first, I feel a bit subdued as Warrior and I continue heading north, but I've finally got the open countryside I was after. There's plenty of time to look at it too, as there are no locks for miles. Initially, I don't appreciate the views, but soon enough I start to feel better. I don't waste much time brooding over relationship stuff and I hope you don't either. At lunchtime I work my way through my first flight of locks without incident until I reach the famous canal-side village of Stoke Bruerne. If you haven't been, I suggest you check it out. I haven't stopped there since I was a kid, so I tie up near one of the two lovely pubs and have a pint and a massive cheese and pickle sandwich. Afterwards I feel a bit nostalgic for my childhood on the canals, so I have a quick dash round the waterways museum. I look at the old pictures of working boats just like the one I grew up on, which gets me thinking about my mum and dad. They're both long gone, but you never stop missing them, do you? Then my thoughts turn to my brother and I decide it's time to get back on the canal. There's a different kind of darkness awaiting me up ahead and I'd rather face it without his memory as a travel companion.

The darkness I'm referring to is the three kilometres of pitch black that is Blisworth Tunnel, one of the longest on the canal network. It seems to go on forever and you get ambushed all the time by fat drops of cold water falling from the tunnel roof onto your head. It's surprisingly quiet, though. I only meet one boat coming the other way and the rest of the time I amuse myself by singing. I enjoy the sound of my own voice echoing back at me. It reminds me I can at least do one thing well, even if I constantly screw up in all other areas of my life. Two things I suppose. Singing and playing guitar. That's about it.

As I emerge from the tunnel at the other end, the sun is piercing through the canopy of leaves overhead, sprinkling the water with all these little droplets of light. For the first time on this trip I really feel connected with nature. I know the village of Blisworth is nearby, but I don't notice it.

All I can see around me is water and trees. There will be no more suburbs for me and no more towns for ages. Not until I reach Leicester, in fact. Just villages, and most of these aren't even visible from the canal. This bit's going to be great. I'll enjoy lots of open space and really make some progress. I'm still not sure where I'm progressing to, but at the moment that doesn't matter to me.

That night I moor up just north of the Northampton Arm. Val rings up to give me a progress report on her negotiations with the record company and we talk for half an hour. There have been a few stumbling blocks, but I know she will strike a good deal for me in the end. She talks me though the main points and I can hear her puffing away on a fag at the same time. She sounds as though she is loving every minute of the legal bunfight and she's welcome to it. As always, I feel grateful to have her on my side but I'm glad I can leave her to it and escape. We make tentative plans to meet in Leicester once I get there. She says she needs me to sign a few documents, but I know what she really wants is to check up on me and make sure I'm OK. As well as my lawyer, she's a loyal friend. Like I say, I'm lucky.

The next morning, I get up really early. It isn't sunny like yesterday, but I'm not bothered. I boat like a crazy woman, ignoring the temptation to stop at the pretty villages which lie close to the canal. There aren't any locks on this stretch, and I make good time. I imagine Warrior as a little black dot racing across the pages of the guidebook. Today it feels as though he has wings on his prop.

When I reach the next set of locks I really luck out. Just as I'm approaching the bottom lock, a boat pulls out of the large marina on the left-hand side of the canal. The man at the tiller waves at me to indicate he would like to partner up with Warrior and me and I give him the thumbs up. Good timing, mate. Then it just gets better and better. A woman and a young girl, both holding windlasses, appear on the towpath and wave at him. His wife and daughter, I guess. They must have walked round from the marina. Anyway, they trot over to the lock gates and open them so we can steer the boats straight in. As I pull alongside him in the lock, I offer my apologies.

'Sorry I can't supply any crew. I'm boating solo I'm afraid.'

'No worries, love. My two enjoy working the locks. All you need to do is steer…'

He falls silent as he stares at me and I realise what I have done. Or not done, rather. I haven't seen a soul all day, so I haven't bothered to disguise my appearance. Not so much as a baseball cap or a pair of sunglasses. I should have got myself sorted before I reached the locks, but I was so focused on making progress that I forgot, and now it's too late. I can tell he recognises me, but I can't do anything about it. Shit. There are seven locks in this flight so I'm going to be with him for a long time. I wonder how I'm going to get out of this one.

'I'm sorry for staring,' my companion says. 'It's just you look exactly like that singer – you know, The Baroness? My son is such a big fan of yours. Hey Carol, Angela! Doesn't our friend here look like The Baroness? I'm Frank, by the way. Nice to meet you.'

Now that's a relief. They just assume I'm not her. That often happens, to be honest. I'm pleased I'm not going to have to spend the next seven locks making up cover stories.

The older of the two women smiles down at me. 'She certainly does, Frankie. I'm sorry love, you must get this all the time. Our son, Martin, is a huge fan of The Baroness. That's why we couldn't help but notice the resemblance.'

Frank bends down and shouts through the engine room door into his boat. 'Martin! Come up here and tell me who this lady looks like!'

Oh, bloody hell. I thought they were just going to let it go, but it seems I was wrong. A few seconds later a boy's face peers around the door from the engine room. A little boy with Down Syndrome. When he sees me, he breaks into a huge beaming smile. I guess Martin is aged about ten. He's wearing a Superdry hoody and has brown hair cut in a floppy fringe.

'Martin,' his father asks. 'Who does this lady remind you of?'

Abruptly Martin's face disappears.

'I'm sorry.' Frank sounds puzzled. 'I don't know why he ran off like that. He's not usually shy around strangers.'

'I'm sorry for frightening him off,' I reply, feeling a bit bad for deceiving this nice family who are helping me through the locks.

Suddenly Martin reappears. It seems I haven't frightened him off after all. He's still beaming as he holds up three of my CDs, one after the other, pointing at my face on each of the covers. Frank looks proudly at his son and ruffles his hair as we steer out of the first lock and head towards the second, which is not far ahead, just the other side of a canal bridge. Frank graciously waves me ahead, letting me go under the bridge first. By the time I reach lock number two, Carol and Angela have opened the gates and I can steer straight in. As their boat approaches, I hear Martin singing one of my early hits. He gets most of the lyrics right and he's in tune. He waves at me as the boat enters the lock and I make a snap decision. Once our two narrowboats are wedged alongside each other in the lock, I say I'm just going down to the galley for a moment. I guess they think I'm going to pop the kettle on or maybe grab a bottle of beer.

When I return with two guitars Frank looks confused. 'Do you do karaoke …or something?' he begins. Then the penny drops.

'This has got to be our secret, OK? No pictures or anything.'

'I wouldn't dream of it,' he says earnestly, and I believe him. Like Andreas, he's definitely one of the good guys.

As I start playing the song which Martin has just been singing, the look of delight on his face makes me stop caring whether they take pictures or not. However, I do notice Frank shakes his head sternly at Angela when she takes her phone out of her jeans pocket. At the end of the first song I hold out my hand to Martin and he eagerly jumps across onto Warrior's back counter. I lift him onto the roof of the boat, where he remains for the next five locks. Once we are secure in each lock, I play him another song or two as it fills. Sometimes he sings along with me and sometimes he just listens. After every song I get a round of applause and another big smile. He really is the perfect audience.

As we steer into lock number six, Frank calls out to me.

'You might want to stop after this lock. The top lock is right outside a pub, so you'd probably be recognised by someone if you carried on. Obviously, Martin would love you to carry on singing all day – in fact we all would – but we understand you don't want a load of hassle.'

'Thanks Frank. You're a gent. Can you pass me Martin's CDs, please?'

I run down to the saloon for a pen, bundle my hair into a baseball cap and put on my huge shades. Then I return to the back counter, write personal messages to Martin on the front covers of the three CDs and hand them back to Frank. Finally, I hold my arms out to Martin for a hug. He wraps his arms round my waist and squeezes tightly. When I eventually hand him back to his Dad it's a good job I'm wearing shades as my eye make-up has definitely run. I don't need a mirror to tell me that underneath my sunglasses I look like Alice Cooper. On a very bad day.

'We'll never forget your kindness to our little boy,' Frank says as we enter the last lock. That doesn't make the Alice Cooper situation any better. Nor do the hugs which Angela and Carol give me when the lock is full, and I'm on the same level as them.

As our two boats leave the lock side by side, I glance at the pub on my left. The customers at the picnic tables outside are enjoying their cool evening drinks. At last, the sun has broken through the clouds and they're taking the opportunity to catch a few rays. I think I'll join them. I could use a drink or two. I reluctantly wave goodbye to Martin and his family. It's the end of another canal brief encounter. Spend enough time boating solo on the canals and you'll have lots of them.

I manage to tie up just a few yards beyond the pub and down my first pint quickly, then linger over my second, watching the boats going through the top lock. Sometimes I get up and open or close a gate if I spot a boater who's short of help. After all, people sometimes do the same for me and I'm in a generous mood. My impromptu concert for Martin has left me feeling better about myself than my night with Andreas. Don't worry, though. I'm not going to go all moral on you. That'll never happen.

14 BAD DARTS

While I drink my beer, I do a spot of people watching. At the next table a couple with two kids are eating dinner. The sprogs are demolishing industrial quantities of chips and staring blankly at their iPads while their parents indulge in some light bickering. Meanwhile another couple come out of the pub and walk towards me. The woman is tall and very striking, with short funky blonde hair. She's way too stylish for this place, that's for sure. In one hand she holds an Aperol Spritz while the other clutches an enormous, neon pink handbag. Her companion follows in her wake with his beer and they take their seats at an empty table close by. Once they're settled, the woman rootles around in her bag and extracts a guidebook. I listen with amusement as she regales her other half with descriptions of nearby stately homes and craft centres which she would like them to visit on their trip. The man listens patiently then gently explains, in a warm American accent – midwest, I think – that he would rather come back to the pub tomorrow and enjoy a couple more beers in the sunshine while she does the cultural stuff. I'm with you, mate. They have a bit of a discussion about this but eventually agree to pursue their separate interests. I get the feeling they've had similar conversations many times before and I admire their ability to compromise. I've always struggled to adapt to anyone else, personally. I guess that's how I ended up here on my own.

I finish my drink and walk back to the boat, then carry on a bit further, turning right just after the pub, onto the Leicester Arm of the Grand Union. My family often used this stretch of canal when I was a kid, so it feels familiar right from the start. I tie up for the night alongside some crusty old boats which look as though they haven't moved since I was last here with Mum and Dad. Then I sit on Warrior's roof and have a smoke while I watch the sun go down. I'm planning a quiet night in as I want to make a very early start tomorrow. I've got a staircase to do first thing. It's called Watford Locks and is a pretty spot, as I recall, despite being right under the M1. You need to hit it early though, especially in summer, or you can get stuck there for half a day.

In the morning I'm on the move early, as planned, so I get a place near the head of the queue before the locks have even opened. Staircases worry some novice boaters, but are good news for me, as they are always manned by volunteer lock-keepers. When I book Warrior in, I chat the guy up a bit, telling him I'm a solo boater, and he promises that he and his colleagues will give me plenty of help. Result. I have to wait my turn, though, so I cook the last of the sausages and sit on Warrior's roof to eat breakfast. The sun is burning off the morning mist as I eat. Looks like it's going to be lovely weather, which is helpful. Today is going to be a long one.

By mid-morning I get through Watford Locks and continue heading north. The guidebook reminds me I have over twenty miles of lock-free cruising ahead of me. Happy days. I settle in for some laid-back boating, past a load of old haunts which bring back childhood memories. Not all of them good ones, I have to say. Soon afterwards Crick Tunnel provides me with another chance to exercise my vocal chords. It gives me a right soaking too, like Blisworth Tunnel did, but afterwards I soon dry off in the hot sun. As I pass the wharf at Crick I'm tempted to stop and grab an ice-cream, or maybe even check out one of the village pubs for a lunchtime pint, but I stay strong and press on. I've got a destination in mind for tonight, but I need to motor if I'm going to make it. Also, those Crick pubs bring back too many memories. Mostly of Mum having to drag Dad out of there after he'd had one too many and started upsetting the locals. He was a great guy, my dad, but he was a Jekyll and Hyde when he was on the sauce. For the same reason I give Yelvertoft, the next village, a swerve. Once Dad came back from the pub there with a bloody great goose he had bought for the price of a pint. He expected Mum to pluck and dress the thing in our cabin, which was chock full at the best of times, then roast it in our tiny oven. Mum was not impressed. Another time he returned with a black eye, which didn't faze any of us. Situation normal, as far as we were concerned.

After Yelvertoft it's just open countryside for the rest of the day. I chug a couple of beers, enjoy a cheeky spliff and commune with nature. At one point I disturb a heron standing like a sentry on the towpath. As Warrior approaches, it flaps away lazily and takes up a new position just yards further down. Then, as the boat rocks up again, it just moves on and repeats the process. This continues for some time and I start to wonder just how far I'm going to herd this bird. Eventually, though, the heron twigs what's going on and glides away across the fields. Majestic, that one, but not too bright.

As the day wears on, the heat builds. Cows stare wearily at me from their shady canal-side retreats under the trees. Tossing their heads and flapping away with their tails at the clouds of flies swarming around them.

They're wasting their time, poor sods. Those flies aren't going anywhere.

As I get closer to the Welford Arm of the canal, I start wondering whether to make the slight detour I have been planning. Down to a pub at the end of the arm, where there is usually some fun to be had, if I remember correctly. I think about changing my plans and pressing on towards Foxton, as I've sort of got the boating bit between my teeth, but then something stops me. Just short of the junction, I catch a flash of electric blue to my right and turn my head just in time to see a kingfisher whizz past. It feels like a reminder to stop and smell the roses. To enjoy the beauty all around me. It's going to be a lovely evening and I should take a break. So I swing Warrior's tiller to the left and he obediently arcs right, down the Welford Arm. It's my first detour on this trip and I figure it's about time.

It's not much of a diversion, in fact. The Welford Arm is less than two miles long, so it doesn't take me far out of my way. It's a popular place, though, so I'm not surprised to find myself following another boat down the canal. But I am amazed to see that the guy at the tiller can't be more than twelve or thirteen. I'm not joking, honest. A cool little dude with bright blonde hair. There's a small lock halfway down and he solos it, no problem. I do the same and catch up with him at the end of the arm as he's nipping skilfully into a tight mooring space. He's got pole position right next to the pub, the crafty little sod. Are boaters getting younger, I ask myself, or am I just getting old? I realise I'm going to have to retrace my steps and grab a mooring further back up the canal, then walk to the pub. I'm not too chuffed by this. As I'm sure you've gathered by now, I'm not exactly a fan of physical exercise. I think about calling off my visit, but then I hear music and laughter drifting across from the beer garden. I look over and see a whole bunch of people partying in the sunshine. Someone is playing a squeezebox and they're all singing away. Sounds like they've had a few, even though it's only early evening. This is just what I've been looking for. I think I'll go and join them.

After I've moored up, I put on an old cotton peasant dress and my blue wig. It's mental, this wig, but I reckon no one will look at it twice around here. It's that kind of place. Then I grab one of my guitars, put my sunglasses on and wander off down the towpath in search of some fun.

So, the reason why I've come down here is, this is one of the pubs where me and Dad used to sit outside, sing and play guitar together when I was little. Either we'd play by ourselves or jam with anyone else who happened to be around. Most times there would be a few crusty old boaters with musical instruments trying out some tunes. A little canal-based theatre group used to tie up there too, from time to time. I don't know if it's still going. I hope so. Anyway, I grab a pint and follow the noise out to the beer garden. A homemade sign tied to a tree tells me one of this rabble has their

70th birthday. I look around for the birthday boy or girl and don't have much trouble spotting him. There he is, the fella. Singing away in a Grade-A black country accent. He reminds me of my dad's friend Billy from Wolverhampton. He's wearing a wide-brimmed boater's hat. So far, so normal, but on top of this hat is what looks like a food cover. You know, one of those things you use to keep the flies off when you have baked a cake. Totally random. Attached to this cover is a badge proclaiming he is seventy today, but he looks nowhere near that age to me. I really must be getting old.

Anyway, they're a friendly bunch, this lot. As soon as they spot my guitar, they call me over to join them. I'm introduced to the squeezebox player; we agree on a few songs and it goes from there. The drink flows freely and the weather cools as the sun dips below the trees. Someone lends me a jacket and we carry on playing and singing. Birthday boy's wife, as generous as she is friendly, orders up trays of fish and chips for the party guests and all the hangers-on like me. Once it gets dark, she lights some lanterns and produces a huge birthday cake, complete with sparklers. Squeezebox and I strike up 'Happy Birthday to You' accompanied by much drunken roaring. The pub has a late licence and it's well after midnight when we all totter off to our respective boats. It has been a really nice night. Good uncomplicated fun. It's what you need, sometimes.

Another day, another hangover. As I leave the Welford Arm the next morning I'm paying for that night of fun, big time. I turn north towards Foxton and decide what I need right now is a quiet few days. I'm going to take things easy and look after myself for a change. So, I drink a flask of tea during the morning to perk myself up, then stop for a lunch break, which is very rare for me. I even eat. I heat up a can of tomato soup. Real comfort food. I don't have a beer to go with it. I don't even smoke anything. Not so much as a single fag. What this means is, by mid-afternoon, my body is feeling relatively temple-like. Which is just as well, considering what's waiting for me around the next corner.

I mean that literally. I'm just chilling out and digesting my soup when Warrior rounds a bend and there it is. A boat, slewed sideways across the canal right in front of me, blocking my way. Untied and floating free, with no one in sight. Its mooring rope descends, taut and vertical, from the rear of the boat, while the other end snakes towards me through the murky canal water. It looks as though part of the rope is tangled round the prop. Bad darts.

I slam Warrior into reverse gear to take the speed off and avoid crashing into this other boat. Then I pull over to the side and tie him up. On Warrior's roof I have a long pole with a hook at the end. It's part of a set of what is quaintly named 'deck furniture'. By standing on the canal-facing side of my boat, I discover I can just about reach the other boat's middle rope with my hook. It's a good job the canal is not very wide here, so the rogue boat is quite close. I drag the middle rope off its roof and pull it towards me through the water, until it is close enough for me to reach down into the murk and grab it. Then I tow the boat clear of Warrior by pulling on the middle rope. I use a couple of my spare mooring pins to tie it to the piling just in front of my own boat.

This whole process takes a while and is a right faff, but it's not as strenuous as you might think. Not even for someone like me, who is unfit and has not quite recovered from her hangover. Granted, the boat probably weighs between fifteen and twenty tonnes, but obviously it is floating, so the water takes most of the strain. Even so, I need a little breather once I'm done. Apart from anything else, I could use a few moments to decide what to do next.

Usually, when a boat is drifting in the canal like this, it means one of two things. Either the mooring ropes have worked themselves loose, or the boat has been untied deliberately by a bunch of pissheads or naughty schoolkids. However, this tends to happen in towns and cities, not in isolated rural locations like this. So, the first option is the most likely in theory, but it's rare and I don't think it has happened here. How do I know? It's quite simple really. When boats come untied, it's usually when there is no one on board. The owners are generally away, and the boat is all locked up, but unfortunately that's not the case here. The door which leads into the engine room from its back counter is wide open. It has been hooked securely to the side of the boat. I can see that from here. There's nothing for it, is there? I'm going to have to step aboard and find out more. I'm not looking forward to this, I'll tell you now. I'm no have-a-go hero.

I climb quietly onto the back counter of the boat, then sit down on the steps in the engine room and listen. Nothing. Not a sound. After a couple of minutes, I stand up carefully, then walk slowly down the steps towards the door leading into the boat's cabin. As I pull open the door, inch by inch, the first thing I see is the corner of a flower-patterned duvet. Gathering all my courage, I peer cautiously around the door into the bedroom. What I see makes me slam the door shut again and lean breathlessly against the outside, shaking and sweating. It takes a few moments before I can summon the strength to open the door and take a proper look at the body lying on the bed.

It's a woman. She's probably a few years older than me, but no more than that. When I first saw her, I thought she was dead, but as I look closer, I realise she isn't. Panic over. She's just crashed out, big time. I've seen hundreds of people in her state, over the years, so I know what I'm looking at. It's odd, really. She looks a bit like me. Or rather, what I might have looked like in a different life. She's dressed in a striped T-shirt and denim shorts. Probably from Boden or Joules. Somewhere like that. Her hair is dark, like mine, but highlighted tastefully with coppery red and twisted up in a scrunchie. I figure she's a bit heavier than me, although that's not difficult. She has got a good figure, actually. A real hourglass job.

I take Mrs Hourglass by the shoulders. She's definitely a Mrs, by the way. There's a stonking great diamond solitaire on her finger plus a thick platinum wedding band studded with more diamonds. I give her a little shake and say something stupid I don't doubt. Something like, 'Are you OK?' Anyway, whatever I say, it works. Mrs Hourglass opens her eyes and looks at my face like she can't work out what the hell is going on. Hardly surprising, really. We stare at each other for a moment, then she smiles.

'Hello, Baroness,' she says.

15 THELMA AND LOUISE. NOT.

Mrs Hourglass tries to fall asleep again. Her eyelids flutter briefly, then close, and her head flops forward. She looks like a worn soft toy that has lost the stuffing in its neck. I have to shake her quite roughly to keep her awake. 'Look, I need to find out what happened to you and your boat. So I can help you.'

The woman smiles a lazy, dopey smile. 'Well, in that case, just ask my husband. He's the one with all the answers. You'll find him at the back of the boat.'

'No, I won't. There's no one aboard except you and me. I found your boat drifting sideways across the canal, with no one at the tiller.'

Well that wakes her up. It saves me the bother of having to slap her. Or throw a glass of water in her face.

'But – I don't understand. Alex was driving the boat when I came down here for a nap. He can't have just vanished. He must be here…'

Suddenly she's up and off. Running through the saloon and galley in a right panic. Calling his name over and over, her voice getting louder and shriller by the second. I don't know where she thinks he's hiding. He's not about to emerge from a bleeding cupboard. There's nowhere to hide on a narrowboat. As if she has just twigged this, she turns around and charges past me in the other direction, to check the engine room and the back counter. As though I might somehow have failed to notice her husband on the way in. When she comes back, it seems like it's starting to sink in. The fact that he's gone. Her eyes have opened very wide and are staring right past me at something only she can see. Looks like it's scary, whatever it is.

'Let me get you a glass of water. I'm sure we can work this out.' I'm not sure at all, to be honest, but I need something to do. As I fill the glass, I wonder why I'm getting involved. I really don't need the hassle, but on the other hand, I can't just abandon her here. I can hear her sobbing in the bedroom, and I leave her to it for a moment, before I go back in there. I'm

113

no good at comforting damsels in distress, so I decide to opt for the practical approach instead.

'Here you go.' I hand her the glass. 'Try not to upset yourself. Look, I'll take a walk along the towpath in both directions to see if I can spot – Alex, was it? Then I'll come back, and we can decide what to do next, if I don't find him. Is that OK?'

Mrs Hourglass nods and I make a quick exit, relieved to escape into the open air. First, I walk back in the direction I've just come from. I check carefully all along the towpath and in the hedgerows. I even scramble through every gap into the fields on the other side, to make sure the guy hasn't wound up there somehow. I find nothing, though. Just cows and sheep. A couple of boats go past in quick succession and in opposite directions. I call out to them, but neither crew has seen anyone on the towpath for miles, so I turn round and go the other way. As I walk back past Warrior, I resist the urge to fire up the engine and flee. Instead I carry on against my better judgement, listening carefully as I pass the rogue boat, but all's quiet. It's then I notice the boat's name for the first time – Two's Company. Not the most appropriate name right now, if you get my drift.

I continue northwards, up the towpath in the direction of Foxton, and I haven't gone far when I spot it. A large, reddish brown stain, right there in the dirt, where the grass has been worn away by the walkers and cyclists. It looks quite fresh to me. Of course, there could be a simple explanation. A fox or a dog could have enjoyed a tasty rabbit meal earlier on. There's bound to be lots of rabbits around here. And foxes too, no doubt, plus dogs of course. If I'm being honest, though, the stain looks too big for that. There's no bones or fur scattered about, neither.

I check the area thoroughly but there's no sign of anyone around, so I walk back to confront Mrs Hourglass. I don't know what, if anything, I'm going to say to her about the bloodstain on the towpath, but when I return to her boat, I find she has pulled herself together amazingly well during my half hour absence. In the end, she makes it easy for me. I don't need to mention the stain at all.

'Thanks for coming back,' she says when she sees me. 'If I were in your position, I think I'd have been tempted to leave me to it.'

'I can't deny it. I did feel like running off at one point, but my conscience got the better of me in the end.'

'Well, I'm grateful it did – and I'm sorry for being so pathetic earlier. While you were away, I did some thinking, and I concluded I have to face the possibility that Alex might have had some sort of – accident – while I was asleep. So, I suggest I ring round all the local hospitals and find out if he has been admitted. Now I know you've checked the area and haven't found him.'

'Good idea. Your mooring rope is wrapped around the prop, for a start, so something must have gone wrong for that to have happened. Why don't you make the calls while I untangle the rope, then we'll take it from there?'

I think we're both relieved to have something to do. She immediately starts pawing away at her phone. Googling the hospitals, I guess, to get their numbers. I leave her to it, go and get my lovely new toolbox from Warrior and set about removing the mooring rope from the prop. As I mentioned before, this is a right bugger of a job, so it takes me a while, even with my shiny new tools. Gradually I cut away and remove bits of rope, but it's a real struggle. The rope has the prop in a deadly embrace, the bastard. My arms quickly get soaked with filthy canal water.

Mrs Hourglass has come out onto the towpath to get a decent phone signal, so while I work, I get to listen in to her conversations with the various A&E departments at the hospitals. I quickly gather she's drawing a blank every time. As I work, I think about what to do next if she doesn't find her husband, which is what seems most likely to happen. Eventually she falls silent and I remove the last shred of rope. Then I walk over for an update. As I approach her, she shakes her head.

'I've called every hospital within a hundred miles of here. Leicester, Peterborough, Nottingham, Derby – the lot. None of them has admitted anyone with my husband's name.'

I'm glad I've thought this through. 'Right,' I begin, trying to sound decisive. 'I suggest you try the hospitals again in the morning. Meanwhile, I reckon you should head back to base, so you can pick up your car as soon as possible and get where you need to be – more quickly than you can on a narrowboat. Where did you start your trip?'

'Allenby Marina, this side of Leicester.'

'Got a guidebook on you?'

She trots off obediently, returning a minute later with the guidebook. She locates the marina easily and I marvel at how calm and focused she seems, after her initial outburst.

'OK. Allenby Marina is about a day and a half away, if you push it. What you need to do is get back to Foxton before dark tonight, then head through the locks first thing tomorrow and push on northwards from there. I'm going north myself, so we can partner up. That way you won't have to solo the locks north of Foxton which would be hard work, if you're not used to boating alone.'

Whoops. Whatever I said, it has stopped her being all calm, like she was a minute ago. She looks bloody terrified now and clutches my arm in a panic. Her voice comes out as a sort of strangled squeak.

'No – you don't understand! I can't – drive a narrowboat. My husband does all that. I just work the locks, and I can't even do that very well. I make tons of mistakes. This is my first time on a narrowboat, you see. I'm a complete beginner.'

Oh, Christ. What have I got myself into? I can't leave this novice boater here. On her own, stranded and shit scared in the middle of nowhere. I take a deep breath. I know I'm going to regret this, but I don't have much choice. The woman is staring at me in desperation, her big eyes brimming with tears.

'OK, I see. Don't look so worried. I'll grab a few things, lock up my boat and take you back to Allenby in your boat. Then you can give me a lift back here in your car. Can't say fairer than that.'

'Oh, thank you so much!' Mrs Hourglass grabs hold of me and gives me a big hug. 'You are very kind. I'm so lucky it was you who rescued me.' Then she stands back and holds out her hand. 'I'm Stella, by the way.'

'Nancy.'

'Oh yes. I vaguely remember Hugo telling me your real name was Nancy.'

'Look – I'll just go and get my stuff. I'll be back in a minute.'

Shit. In all the confusion, I forgot Stella called me Baroness when she first woke up. And now I've gone and given her my real name. Oh well – it can't be helped. I guess being recognised is the least of my worries at the moment.

Back onboard Warrior, I shove a few bits and bobs in a bag. A change of clothes, a bottle of JD, a couple of packets of fags and my stash. The clothes are the least important items, to be honest. I think everything else will be bloody essential. I also take Warrior's spare rope, to replace the mangled one on Two's Company. Then I lock up my nice new boat and set the burglar alarm. Sorry - I forgot to mention that before, when I was describing all the technical gizmos on board Warrior. It even has a burglar alarm which talks directly to your phone. I didn't realise I was going to need it quite so soon, but there you go.

As I walk away from Warrior I feel gutted. We haven't had much time together and I didn't count on us being separated so early in our voyage. Still, it should only take a couple of days at most to deliver Stella to Allenby Marina and get back here. I try and cheer myself up by telling myself it's only a blip in my journey and hopefully I will earn some karma for helping out a sister. Who knows? Maybe it will balance out some of the crappy things I've done to people over the years. In the cosmic scheme of things.

Back on Two's Company, Stella has gone into full 'hostess with the mostest' mode.

'Hi Nancy – welcome back!' she trills. 'Now the dining suite converts into a double bed, so you will be quite comfortable tonight. Thankfully there's plenty of food in the fridge, so we can have dinner when we moor up later.'

'OK. Thanks. Let's head off. We need to get in the queue for Foxton Locks.'

the boat like that, without even tying it up? It's bloody dangerous, for a start. Also, have you checked whether anything is missing from the boat? Surely, he would have to take a few essentials with him, if he was going to do a runner?'

'I believe Alex wanted to make it look like an accident – to throw me off the scent. That's why he didn't tie the boat up. And as for his stuff – I have checked and it's all on board.' Stella waves her arm in the rough direction of the boat. 'Wallet, car keys, laptop, clothes – the whole lot. All except for his phone. He always keeps his phone in his back pocket, like a teenager. Doesn't want me looking at it, for obvious reasons. Of course, he can do anything with his phone. As long as he's got it with him, he can just walk away.'

'I'm sure he wouldn't do that to you, Stella.'

'Are you? You don't know Alex. Or what he's capable of.'

Now I really don't know what to think. I could ask more questions, but I remember my promise to myself not to get involved, and this latest conversation has already got me far more embroiled in the domestics of Alex and Stella than I'd like to be. I look over at Stella, who is slumped in her folding chair, asleep. No problems with insomnia tonight. Hardly surprising, after today's diet of wine, sleeping pills, whisky and weed. Not to mention Prosecco, I'm willing to bet, and maybe Pimms as well. She'll need a trip to bloody Champneys, or wherever people like her go, after all this. We musicians get a bad press when it comes to mind altering substances but really, some of these middle-class housewives put us to shame.

Having said that, I do skin up a solitary spliff to smoke before bedtime. Just to give me a few minutes to myself. Then I wake Stella up and herd her back onto the boat. As I make up my bed in the saloon, I hear her stumbling around between the bedroom and bathroom, giggling and knocking things over. I really shouldn't have let her smoke that ganja. Now and then she calls out to me. Like we are two friends having a sleepover or something.

'You know that song, Nancy, about there being fifty ways to leave your lover?'

'Yes,' I sigh.

'There's someone in it called Sam, who makes a plan…'

'Stan.'

'What?'

'The guy's called *Stan*, Stella.'

'Whatever. Anyway, I think they should add a line in there that goes – "jump off a boat"…'

I've heard enough. 'Stella?'

'Yeah?'

'Go to sleep.'

'Oh, OK – goodnight.'

Stella's not feeling quite so chirpy the next morning, but I show no mercy. I always say the only way out is through, and I want to get through this ordeal as quickly as possible. That's why, as soon as the lock-keepers come on duty, I'm there to book Two's Company in. When I get back to the boat, Stella has the coffee all ready. She looks a bit rough, but she's functioning. Thankfully she doesn't raise the subject of breakfast.

As we head towards Foxton Top Lock, Stella confesses to me she opened the paddles in the wrong order on the way up and flooded one of the side ponds. She's worried the lock-keepers will remember her and give her a hard time, but I put her mind at rest. I tell her they see hundreds of boats every week and didn't react to the boat name when I booked in. They deal with plenty of incidents like that, I say, so they're unlikely to remember her. It's not like they blacklist people or anything. And even if they do recall what happened, it's likely they'll give her more help, rather than less, as they'll be worried she might screw up again. In all likelihood, it'll be a different crew on duty from the day before. To be honest, I can't believe she's worrying about such trivial stuff when her husband is missing, but there you are. Relationships are complex things. Way too complex for me.

In the end, Stella needn't have worried. We get through Foxton Locks without any unfortunate incidents. The lock-keepers give us plenty of help and Stella concentrates like crazy on opening the red paddles before the white ones. Red before white and she's alright. You can see it in her face, how determined she is not to make a mistake. I do believe her precious Alex could turn up right now and she wouldn't even notice he was here.

By mid-morning we have left Foxton behind, but we still have a long way to go before we reach Allenby. Not to mention the twelve locks which lie ahead. I consult the guidebook and see there are no locks for a bit, so I suggest to Stella that she might want to call the hospitals again.

'Good idea,' she replies. 'I'll just make us some more coffee first, if that's OK with you, Nancy?'

'Coffee would be good.' Why is she treating me like I'm her boss or something? I'm not complaining, though. I need all the caffeine I can get, today.

A few minutes later, Stella reappears with two steaming mugs of coffee and a plate of chocolate mini-rolls. 'I didn't think you would want a full English, but I imagine a mini-roll might hit the spot?'

I smile at her. She's getting the measure of me, no question. 'Several mini-rolls might.' As we snaffle the whole plate between us and sip our coffee, I find myself telling her about my lawyer Val and her love of cigs and chocolate. Often at the same time. Then I suddenly twig I'm revealing more about my life than I normally would to a near-stranger. She has got that sort of face, does our Stella. A face you open up to. I need to be careful, so I cut the chit-chat short by reminding her to hit the phone, and she does as I say. We sit either side of the tiller as the boat chugs along and Stella struggles to get a signal and then reach the right person in each hospital.

An hour later and we are no further forward. I mean, Two's Company has made some progress up the canal, but Alex hasn't shown up at any of the hospitals. I'm starting to fear the worst and I reckon that Stella is too, from the grim look on her face. To give her something to take her mind off the fact that her husband is missing, or maybe even dead, I suggest she call the office at Allenby Marina, to warn them we're coming and make sure they have a berth ready for us. I don't think we'll arrive until long after the office has shut. Marinas aren't generally known for their flexible working hours.

Stella obediently calls up the marina and speaks to a person called Ron. I know this because she uses his name about a million times during the conversation. I marvel at how composed and frightfully polite she sounds, for somebody whose husband has probably either jumped ship or drowned. I guess these social skills are just second nature to her, after a lifetime of conditioning. She tells Ron she is awfully sorry to bother him, but her husband has gone missing. She sounds as though she is apologising for breaking a glass on the boat and is offering to pay for a replacement. She gives Ron her name and checks he remembers her, and Alex. Clearly, he does. She listens for a while, then thanks him. Over and over again. She can't believe how helpful he is being. She is so grateful and so sorry to put him to all that trouble. She will see him later, and so on. Eventually she hangs up.

'Ron is going to get a berth ready for us at the marina. He lives there, on his boat, so he has promised to look out for us and help us tie up, when we arrive.'

'Great.' All I can think about is whether we'll get there early enough for Stella to drive me back to my boat tonight. I know, I'm a selfish cow. Anyway, I'm not holding my breath. Asking Stella to drive an unfamiliar route, in the dark, when she's going through something like this, wouldn't be the kindest thing. Also, I'd like to get there in one piece.

We sit in silence for a while, then out of the blue Stella remarks,

'I was thinking earlier that it's a very smart move on your part. I mean, dispensing with the services of your record company and taking full responsibility for your own career.'

'What do you mean?' Where the sodding hell did that come from?

'You mentioned your ex-record company last night, so I assumed you had decided to go it alone, like lots of other artists. After all, music is fast becoming a disintermediated industry, so you might as well take advantage, especially when you have such a well-established brand.'

'That's funny. One of my friends said almost exactly the same thing.'

'There you are then. So, what's your plan?'

'I haven't really got a plan.' In spite of myself, I tell Stella the bare bones of the story about my row with The Gatekeeper. As I said, she has got that sort of face. When I mention I wouldn't play ball by going on social media, she is very sympathetic.

'I can understand why not, when your record company is pulling the strings. But now you're free of them, you can use social media to your advantage. Portray your chosen version of your authentic self, the one you want your fans to see. Sure, you'll attract some trolls – that's unavoidable, for someone with a profile like yours. But at the end of the day, it's about who you want to communicate with your fans. Yourself, or a record company? Or a bunch of random individuals who set up fake accounts in your name?'

When I remain silent, Stella challenges me. The submissive, polite person who brought me a plate of mini-rolls, and apologised to Ron for inconveniencing him, has taken leave of absence. Or so it seems.

'So, you didn't make a strategic decision to take control of your own career. You just ran away.'

'Something like that.' I've had enough of discussing my music career with Mrs I've Just Swallowed a Business Self-Help Book. She doesn't notice, though. It's almost as if she's talking to herself.

'No matter. Whatever the reason, it could be a good decision, even if it wasn't exactly planned in advance. There's no harm in taking a career break, at the end of the day. Leave the fans wanting more, then come back and re-engage them with your very own, digitally-driven enterprise.'

She's on a roll now, warming to her theme. As we approach the first of our twelve locks, she starts describing in more detail how she thinks I can revive my career by rebranding myself as an independent recording artist. She trots off to work the lock, which she does perfectly, without any slip-ups. Then she comes back and carries on talking. I don't have to say a thing. Clearly my career fiasco provides her with a perfect distraction from her own problems. Shortly after lock three she disappears into the cabin, returning a minute later with a notebook. Then she starts doodling. She draws some sort of rough diagram and adds words all around it. Christ alone knows what she's up to.

'I thought you said it should be a digital business?' I can't resist teasing her.

'Touché, but I still find it easier to get my initial ideas down on paper. Also, I couldn't use my laptop in this sunlight. I wouldn't be able to see the screen. Anyway, I'm just drafting a mind map for you, to capture all the points we have been discussing.'

That you've been discussing, you mean. 'Stella. How do you know all this stuff?'

'I used to be an IT consultant before I had the kids – and afterwards, for a bit. Since then, I have tried to keep up to date with all things digital. Technology and maths have always been my thing. Also, I have a business plan for my own digital advisory service. On a very small scale. To give me a new challenge, now the children are nearly off my hands. I haven't launched it yet, though. I've never quite found the confidence to go for it. My daughter, Imogen, is constantly nagging me to get started. So, where were we? Ah yes, your USP...'

I don't need to say anything much during the afternoon. I just steer the boat in and out of the locks and pootle on down the canal. The odd 'that sounds interesting' or 'that's a fair point' is all she wants from me. Between working the locks, scribbling in her notebook, Googling stuff on her phone and wittering on about my bright future, Stella is gainfully employed, and so avoids having to confront the problem of her missing husband. Just like I'm saved from having to make polite conversation. It's what she would call a win-win situation. I half listen to what she's saying and have to admit some of it sounds quite sensible. Creative, even. Clearly, she doesn't know anything about the life of a musician, even though she claims to have dated some record company dude for a while, but her ignorance of the business is quite helpful. It gives her a fresh take on things. I'm forced to admit there's a decent brain lurking inside that well-coiffed head of hers. Especially when she's not out of her tree on pills, booze and weed.

With just two locks to go, I notice the little notebook is nearly full. Stella goes back down into the boat once again, and when she reappears, she is obviously hiding something behind her back. She is smiling proudly like a child who is about to show his mother a painting he did at school.

'Ta-da!' With a flourish, she produces a bottle of champagne and two glasses. 'I thought some proper bubbly was in order, to celebrate the creation of your new business plan.' Expertly she pops the champagne cork, without spilling a single drop. Evidently, she has done this many times before. She fills both glasses, hands one to me, then clinks hers against mine and takes a big gulp. There goes my chance of a lift back to my boat tonight. Oh, well.

'Cheers, Nancy. Here's to the next phase of your brilliant career. I'm glad I had the opportunity to provide you with some professional advice. It's the best way I could thank you – for everything you have done for me. I promise you, this book will be much better, and more useful to you, than my cooking!'

Stella makes a big show of handing the notebook over to me and I realise I'm supposed to look at it, so I put my glass down. 'Hold the tiller for a second, Stella.'

Gingerly she takes hold of the tiller and I have a flick through. I see page after page of detailed notes, diagrams and graphs. Key points are underlined or circled. There are web addresses and recommendations for further reading. Videos to watch. Ted talks to listen to – whatever they are. On the last page, there's a step by step action plan advising me what to do next. It's divided into short, medium and long-term activities. I'm getting quite absorbed in the book when suddenly Stella squeaks with alarm. The boat is heading straight for the bank. I grab the tiller from her, set Two's Company back on course and smile at her.

'Looks like you're better at business than boating. Actually that's not fair. You're fine at working the locks – you just need to learn how to steer. Anyway, cheers for this.' I wave the notebook at her. 'For the business plan – and the champagne. I promise I'll read the plan properly, when I get the chance.'

As we approach the second last lock, Stella jumps off at the lock moorings and I drain my glass of champagne. It's not bad, I have to admit. Not my drink of choice, but better than Prosecco.

The last part of the journey to Allenby is spent in a pleasant champagne brain fog. It never lasts, though, does it? Wears off dead quickly. Just leaves you feeling a bit headachy and wondering what that was all about. By the time we go under the footbridge that forms the entrance to Allenby Marina, the champagne bottle is empty, and Stella appears a bit subdued. I guess she is not looking forward to seeing this Ron person and telling him what has happened. She has managed to avoid the Alex problem for most of the day, but now there's no place to hide. Especially as Ron has clearly been looking out for us. As soon as we enter the marina, I see a man leave a boat and run along the perimeter path, shouting and pointing at an empty slot between a couple of other hire boats. I glance over at Stella. 'Ron, I presume?'

'Yes' Stella replies. 'He's very – keen.'

He certainly is. The guy bustles and fusses around, helping us tie up and clumsily trying to say how sorry he is about what happened. Stella is gracious and polite, as ever. She introduces me, explains how I helped her, and I can see Ron looks relieved. It could have been much worse, from his point of view. The boat could easily have ended up in a bad state if I hadn't intervened. He obviously realises he got off lightly, with only one mooring rope to replace. When I explain how the rope was wrapped around the prop and I had to cut it free, Stella tells him to deduct the cost from her deposit, but he's having none of it. She's got enough to deal with, he points out. He's a decent sort of bloke, our Ron. Even though he's a bit of an old woman.

Talking of which, as we stand on the path beside the boat, discussing the rope issue, a little old lady with a powder puff of grey hair walks towards us. She's carrying something in her hands. Very carefully, like's she has just discovered a bleeding Ming vase floating in the canal and has brought it to show us.

'Hello, Stella me duck. I'm so sorry to hear – about your troubles. I'm sure you and your friend haven't had time to cook today, so I've made you a casserole. I hope you enjoy it. Come on now, Ron.' She takes Ron's arm firmly and leads him away. 'Leave these ladies to settle in. They need to relax and get some rest.'

Stella and I look at each other, then at the casserole.

'Let me guess. Not your thing?' She smiles at me and I admire her for trying to be cheerful, despite everything.

'Dead right,' says a man's voice behind me. 'Our Nancy has never been a casserole kind of girl.'

I recognise the gentle Irish accent immediately and turn around to greet its owner. 'Dan!' I cry, holding my arms out for a hug.

'Nancy. Good to see you. And who might you be?' he asks Stella over my shoulder.

'I'm Stella.'

Dan releases me and Stella shakes his hand.

'I had a – spot of bother – on the canal, and Nancy was kind enough to leave her boat behind and accompany me back to the marina.'

'So you've chucked it all in as well, have you, Nancy?' Dan asks me.

I notice how Stella looks relieved when Dan shows no interest in her problems.

'Sort of. It's a long story.'

'Well, if you have, you're in good company. You can't move on the waterways for musicians, these days. There's another in this marina, in fact.'

Dan names a guy I know slightly, who wrote an iconic 90's pop song and played saxophone in a couple of successful bands. Decent bloke, as I recall. Apparently his royalty payments are enough to finance a pleasant existence in Allenby Marina, where he and Dan regularly jam together and play in the house band, along with a bunch of eager amateurs.

'So how come you wound up here, Dan?'

Sorry, I should explain. Dan is a talented session musician. He plays a mean rhythm guitar and has a good voice. He accompanied my band on a couple of tours and was popular with all of us. A good guy – and a safe pair of hands. One of the roadies falls sick, Dan will happily offer to lug some kit. That kind of bloke.

'Like you said, it's a long story, and you two have got a casserole to eat. Why don't you both come over to my boat afterwards? I've got lots of beer on board and it would be good to catch up.'

'I don't mean to be rude, but I don't feel much like socialising, tonight,' says Stella. 'I'm going to leave you to it. Like you say, you'll both have lots to catch up on.'

'Alright, I'll come over for a beer later,' I reply. 'I can't stay long, though. I've got an early start in the morning. What's your boat called? So I can find you.'

'That's the one.' Dan points at a grey and black boat moored nearby. It looks a bit like Warrior, funnily enough, although it's older and a bit shabby compared with my shiny new toy.

'Well, that figures,' I laugh. The name of his boat is Slowing Downe. That's Dan's last name. Downe. Daniel Fergus Downe is his full name. I remember it from the tour paperwork.

Back on board Two's Company, Stella and I eat about two mouthfuls of casserole each. Then she helps me set up my bed.

'I hope you didn't refuse Dan's invitation because you thought you'd be in the way,' I remark as she tosses me a pillow. I know what she could be thinking. Like we're in a bloody high school romance or something. 'There's nothing between us. No history or anything. He's just someone I worked with, that's all.'

'No – it's not that. I just need some time alone. To process everything that has happened.'

'Process'. How these people talk.

'OK. Well, look. I'll just be an hour or so. Call me if you need anything.'

'I'm unlikely to get a signal, but thanks anyway. Oh – and Nancy?'

'What?'

'That man definitely fancies you.'

Now I promised right at the start I wouldn't curse, so I won't tell you what I call Stella as I throw the pillow right back at her head.

Dan and I spend a fun couple of hours together, talking and laughing about old times. We drink a few beers and make a modest dent in my stash. We even have a mini jam session. He wants me to stick around for a few days, to meet the marina house band, but I say no. I want to get back and reclaim Warrior as soon as possible. To his credit, Dan doesn't push it. In fact, he offers to give me a lift back to my boat the next morning, so I can put all this behind me, and Stella can get on with finding out what has happened to Alex. It's a kind offer that's typical of Dan, and I can't accept quickly enough. I'll have to fit in with him, though, as he's got the electrician coming over to fix a wiring problem on his boat. Apparently the guy has a packed diary, like most good tradespeople on the canals, so Dan can't predict exactly when he'll show up. That's fine by me. I'm happy to be flexible in return for not having to rely on Stella for a lift. The woman's got enough to deal with.

By the time I return to Two's Company, Stella is in bed and all is quiet. I suspect a wine and sleeping pills combo. It's not very late, after all. Like I promised her, I didn't spend too long on the boat with Dan. And in case you're wondering, there wasn't any funny business neither. For a start, the Andreas episode is still fresh in my mind and besides, the last thing I need right now is more complications. So, I just curl up in bed and try to read Stella's notebook, but after a few minutes my eyes start to close. Not that her notes are boring; I'm just knackered. It has been a long couple of days.

16 ARRESTED DEVELOPMENT

The next morning, I literally wake up and smell the coffee. Stella, clearly back in hostess mode, is shuffling around the galley in her slippers.

'Morning!' she says brightly. 'Would you like some coffee? Now I don't want to alarm you, but I'm about to make some bacon sandwiches. You know, like real food? Could you manage one, before I give you a lift back to your boat? I know I shouldn't fuss, but you really don't eat properly. I'd like to send you off with some decent food in your stomach.'

Weirdly, I am hungry, which I almost never am. Not first thing, anyway. Also, even I know that the four mini-rolls I ate yesterday, washed down with champagne and beer, don't exactly equal a balanced diet. 'Bacon sandwich would be great,' I reply. 'But you'll be pleased to know you don't have to give me a lift. Dan's going to drive me. He offered, and I thought it would save time for you. So you can concentrate on finding out what has happened to Alex.'

Now I know I'm leaving soon and can't be delayed further, I feel ready to ask Stella that awkward question about the police. I quickly get dressed and finish my coffee. Then, as she's pouring me a refill, I raise the subject.

'Stella. I've been giving all this some thought overnight. You and Alex, I mean. And I've got to admit I think it's time you got the police involved. I'm not a big fan, as you can imagine, but they'll investigate this whole thing properly. Find out what really happened.' As I talk, I'm mentally crossing my fingers behind my back, thinking about all the unsolved cases out there. The rozzers don't exactly have a one hundred percent track record. But then, who does?

'Oh, I don't think they'd be any help.' Stella waves her hand dismissively. 'It would just be a domestic issue, to them, so I doubt they'd be interested. After all, we know Alex hasn't been taken to hospital, so it's pretty clear he has left me. OK, he picked a funny way to do it, but that's Alex for you. He doesn't behave like everyone else. He prefers to stand out.'

I can tell she's putting on a brave face, so I try and be gentle. Without meaning to, I've got to like her, sort of, and I don't want to upset her. Then again, I don't want to let her off the hook neither.

'Look, Stella, I don't mean to sound morbid, but there could be another explanation for all this. Even though it's unlikely, you've got to face the fact that Alex could have drowned. I know the canal's only three feet deep, like I said before, but it has been known. Or maybe he was abducted.'

'But who would want to do that?'

'Who knows? Maybe he made some enemies. Through his work, or something. People you don't know. Anyway, what I'm saying is – the police can dredge the canal. Send their divers in. At the very least they could rule out the drowning scenario. I can't force you to contact them, but I think the time has come to get them involved.'

Stella says nothing. She just stares into space, mechanically flipping the bacon rashers in the pan. Eventually, she looks at me and nods.

'You're right. Looking back, I should have called them as soon as you found me, but I wasn't thinking clearly. Then, afterwards, I just hoped I would find the answer myself – one way or the other. Also, I thought maybe Alex would call. So I would know for certain he had gone. I assumed he would at least care enough to put my mind at rest. Calling the police would have made it all seem so – official, somehow. To be honest, I admit I've been procrastinating. What worries me about contacting the police now is they might ask why I didn't call them in the first place.'

'They probably will ask you that. But they also know people don't behave logically in times of crisis. They've seen it all, believe me. They'll understand how you weren't your normal self.'

'OK. I'll call them after breakfast. I'll phone the children, too. It's time I faced up to all this properly. Ketchup or brown sauce?'

Stella assembles two massive bacon doorsteps and we sit down together on the unmade bed to eat. It's bloody delicious, I have to say. As I shove huge chunks of bread and bacon into my mouth, Stella grabs the notebook she used to draft my supposed business plan and scribbles something on the inside front cover. I notice she has been crumbling the bread from her bacon sandwich into bits, without eating a thing.

'My contact details,' she says. 'If you have any questions about the business plan, or if you would like some more advice, just get in touch. Anytime, no charge of course.' She puts her hand on my arm and adds, 'I'll never forget how you helped me, when I was in such a mess. In all the world, I could not have chosen anyone better. You have been absolutely amazing.'

Now I've never been comfortable with personal compliments, unless they're about my music. So I just mumble something at her through the last of my sandwich, then start clearing up ready to leave. First, I make up the bed and convert it back into a dinette. Then I pack my few things into my bag. I leave Stella the rest of the JD. I guess she might need it. Weirdly, I feel a bit sad to be leaving her. I'm sure the feelings will disappear as soon as I get into Dan's car and we drive away.

Stella washes the dinner and breakfast dishes and I dry. The woman's in danger of domesticating me, but I'm sure it will all go to pot once I'm back onboard Warrior. We're standing side by side in the galley, beavering away, when there's a knock on the side hatch.

'That'll be Dan. He probably wants to arrange a time to give me a lift.'

I'm wrong, though. When Stella opens the side hatch, I see a middle-aged man with a thatch of grey hair and a ruddy face with a map of thread veins across his cheeks. A drinker's face, just like my Dad's.

'Good morning, ladies. Could you both to come up to the marina office as soon as possible? There are some forms we need you to sign.'

'We?' Stella replies. 'Where's Ron? He's the person I've been dealing with – him and Joyce.'

'It's their day off today. I'm Eddie – Ron's business partner.'

'OK, Eddie. We'll come up to the office in just a moment. I'll bring Joyce's casserole dish with me, when I come. I just have to dry it up.'

Eddie gives Stella a puzzled look, then turns and walks away from the boat.

I can't imagine what forms Eddie wants me to sign, but I pull on my boots and follow Stella out of the boat a few minutes later.

'Might as well get all the paperwork out of the way,' she reasons as we walk up the path towards the office. 'Then I can just tidy the boat up and leave. Once I've spoken to the police, obviously. I figure it's too early to call Hugo, what with him being five hours behind, now he's in the US, so I'll ring him later. Also, I've decided I'll delay speaking to Imogen until I get home. I'd rather tell her face to face, I think.'

Dan is standing on the back counter of his boat with a cheery-looking dude in a boiler-suit, sporting some creative facial hair. The electrician, I hope. When he spots me, he waves and walks along the jetty towards us.

'Good morning. Aubrey has just arrived. He says he'll be about an hour, then we can head off to your boat. I'm looking forward to a guided tour, when we get there. You can show me all those fancy gadgets you were telling me about last night.'

'What is with you blokes? There's nothing you like more than a shiny new bit of kit. Guitars, motorbikes, boats, whatever. Fitness trackers, even. New gear. It always gets you boys going.'

Dan laughs and gives me a cheeky wink. 'Says the woman who has just bought a brand-new boat bristling with tech.'

'Whatever. Look, some guy called Eddie wants to see Stella and me in the office. Something about paperwork. We'd better head on up there. I'm ready to go after that. I'll come and find you in about an hour.'

'OK, Nan. See you later.'

As soon as we're out of earshot, Stella nudges me and whispers: 'I still think he fancies you.'

'For Christ's sake, Stella. What are we - fifteen years old?'

We're still smiling as we open the door and step into the marina office.

As soon as I walk through the door, I know something is up. Eddie is talking quietly to a couple standing at the counter with their backs to us, but he looks up when Stella and I come in and the couple immediately turn around to face us. The man is tall and barrel-chested, with dark hair shaved close to his head. There's a bit of a gut on him, but you wouldn't want to mess, trust me. The woman is small, wiry and hard-faced, with blonde hair pulled back tightly in a Croydon Facelift. Both of them are wearing North Face hiking jackets, jeans and trainers. Honestly. When will the undercover rozzers learn how conspicuous they look in those outfits? To some of us, anyway. Stella is oblivious, bless her. She just carries on smiling until Croydon Facelift approaches her, flips open her wallet and holds her badge in front of her face.

'Stella Marie Pitulska?'

'Er – yes?'

Croydon turns and looks at her colleague, who smiles knowingly.

'Funny. We thought you might say that.'

'What do you mean…' Stella begins, but Croydon raises her hand and cuts her off.

'Can you listen carefully to what I have to say. You are under arrest on suspicion of stalking, contrary to the Protection of Freedoms Act 2012. You do not have to say anything, but it may harm your defence if you do not mention, when questioned, something which you later rely on in court. Anything you do say may be given in evidence.'

'Stalking?' Stella looks round at me, frantic. Like she has just landed in a world where all the rules are different. Which she has, of course. 'But I don't understand…'

'I suggest you leave the "there must be some mistake" speech for when you have a lawyer present,' the man says. Then he turns to me. 'You were with this woman, or so I hear?'

'That's correct, Sir.' I'm all business now. That's the way to handle the cops, I find.

'In that case, we are going to require you to give a statement. I need to ask you not to leave the area until you have provided it. May I have your mobile number, please? We'll be in touch to make the arrangements.'

So that's it. My dream of escaping on my narrowboat goes up in smoke, for the second time in days. Tears of frustration spike my eyes as I obediently share contact details with the male cop. Then I stand alongside Eddie, outside the marina office, as they put Stella in the unmarked car. Barrel Chest places his hand on her head with its dark, shiny bob. He pushes down firmly as she gets into the back seat, to make sure she doesn't hit her head if she starts struggling. Which she doesn't, of course. As the rozzer slams her door, she looks so submissive. So small and frightened. Then, as the car drives away, she stares at me through the window, tears streaming down her face. 'Help me,' she mouths.

I have no idea what's going on, or what Stella has done. I don't want to get involved; never have done, as you know. But it's way too late for that now. As I turn and walk away from Eddie, towards Dan's boat, I dial a number I know by heart and press the phone to my ear.

DAWN

17 CONFLICT OF INTEREST

I'm halfway through the late shift when the call comes in from the Control Room. The operator tells me a man was admitted to the Infirmary at around 5pm in circumstances the doctors regard as suspicious. Apparently, he won't be fit for interview until tomorrow morning at the earliest, but the surgeon who performed the emergency operation knew to call it in as soon as possible. I recognise the doctor's name. It's not the first time he has contacted us about a patient in his care, so he understands the procedure.

Of course, I could just write up the crime report and leave it for the day shift to handle in the morning, but as I listen to Maddy from the control room describe the nature of the man's injuries, and the location in which he was found, I feel myself getting drawn in, despite the extra workload it will mean for me. I should say at this point that there is no shortage of crimes to investigate here in Leicestershire - or anywhere else in the country, for that matter - but most of them are routine violations which experienced detectives like me have resolved countless times before. It's rare for me to be presented with a scenario which is truly intriguing and could really test my skills. I'm sorry if that sounds arrogant; it's not meant to be. Most of my colleagues feel the same way. Stay in this game long enough and you develop a sixth sense for the few incidents which are different, and I have a feeling this could be one of them, so I decide I don't want to leave it for someone else.

When I finish my conversation with the control room, I pick up my coffee mug and go into the kitchen for a strong black coffee to keep me alert through the rest of my shift. It appears someone has microwaved a fish dinner in here recently, and the place smells putrid. If I were in charge of such things, I would ban certain types of food from all the communal kitchens here at police headquarters. Haddock would be right at the top of my list. I escape as soon as I have poured my coffee, return to my desk and put in a call to my DI.

'Andrew? It's Dawn.'

'DS Burrows, as I live and breathe. What can I do for you?'

'I'd like your permission to change my hours so I can work the day shift for the next few days. A call has just come in from the control room and I want to follow it up myself.'

As I explain the details to my immediate superior, DI Andrew Gillespie, I hear the rustling of sweet wrappers, followed by some rhythmic chomping noises on the other end of the phone. Andrew still struggles with the smoking ban in the office, even though it has been in place for goodness knows how many years. In all this time, he has never got used to it, and has acquired a serious wine gum habit to keep him going between cigarette breaks. I estimate he eats at least three in the time it takes me to brief him.

'OK. I can see why you want to lead this one. As usual, you're as keen as mustard. Look, I don't have a problem with you changing your hours, but you'll still need to cover your evening shift as well. I can't get anyone to replace you. Not at such short notice.'

I was expecting this. 'That's OK. I can handle the extra hours.'

'I know you can, Dawn. But I do feel obliged to mention a concept called work-life balance.'

'Ah come on, Andy. You don't care about work-life balance. You just want to have the best people working on every case.'

'And you just want a DI's post, when one becomes available. It'll happen, Dawn, believe me. You passed your Inspectors' exams with flying colours and you've impressed the decision makers. You've done all the right things. You don't need to kill yourself trying to get promoted. A suitable opportunity will come along sooner or later. You just need to have a little patience.'

'Understood, Boss, but while I'm waiting, I might as well work the interesting cases.'

'Sure, but you also need to take some time off here and there. Hang out with that boy of yours.'

'That boy, as you call him, doesn't even notice I'm there, half the time.'

'Of course, he does. Dawn - take this on, by all means; but don't let the job consume you. Any more than it already has. That's what I'm saying. Believe me, it will only get worse, once you're a DI.'

'OK, Boss. Point taken.'

'Also, Dave Langley is on days tomorrow. Assign him to the case and get him to do most of the legwork. In every one of your performance reviews you have been told delegation isn't your strong point. It's time to change that, if you want to make a success of your promotion, when it comes.'

'Will do. I'll link him to the crime report and brief him first thing tomorrow.'

I hang up the call and start to enter the information from the control room into the case management system. It takes a while, as the system is on a go slow. It's running like a dog – a big, fat, plodding dog. You don't get this on any of the TV police dramas, do you? IT malfunctions don't usually figure much in the plots of those shows, but they should do, for the sake of realism. After all, detective work is not all car chases, breathless pursuits through gritty urban landscapes and rapid-fire conversations shouted across crowded offices. In fact, it's not often about any of those things. Most of the time, it's an officer sitting quietly at her desk, tapping away at her keyboard, like any other wage slave. There will be probably be a pot plant next to her computer, plus a couple of family photographs, and a collection of chocolate bars in her desk drawer. Also, while we're on the subject, crime detection is very rarely about sudden flashes of inspiration which miraculously happen to provide the key to solving the case. In fact, when it comes down to it, the job is mainly about procedure, attention to detail and lots of hard work, with a generous side order of admin thrown in for good measure.

Towards the end of my shift the phone rings again. It's an old friend of mine, PC Aditi Chauhan. We did our training together when we first joined the police, but Adi opted to remain in uniform and become a traffic cop. It's not my idea of fun, but she loves her job and is absolutely brilliant at it. We still meet for a drink sometimes, along with other members of our training cohort, if they can make it. We also have a sort of informal 'Come Dine with Me' arrangement, where we occasionally cook a posh dinner for each other, when the planets are aligned, and our shifts allow. This time, though, it's definitely not a social call; I can tell immediately from her tone of voice.

Adi tells me she and her partner just pulled over a car, as one of its brake-lights wasn't working. They breathalysed the young driver, who was well under the limit, so they just told him to get the brake-light fixed and would have left it at that, except Adi happened to notice a smell of cannabis in the vehicle. As I said, she's a very talented officer, and never misses a trick. Anyway, she and her partner searched the driver and his two passengers, but found no drugs on any of them, so they ran a swab test on the driver, which again came back negative. The three explained they had merely been in a room at a party where cannabis was being smoked, and the passengers did not appear stoned, so Adi sent them all on their way with a few well-chosen words on the dangers of drugs. All of which would be fine, except one of the passengers was Craig, my son. He and Adi met briefly a couple of times when she came to my house, and she recognised him. Sounding concerned, she says that she thought I ought to know and hopes she has done the right thing. I thank her and reassure her I would much rather know what my son was up to.

Later, on my way home to confront Craig, I tell myself to keep things in proportion. My son was at a party where drugs were present, and could have partaken himself, but that isn't the end of the world. He is, after all, a seventeen-year-old boy, so I need to be realistic and accept he's probably going to experiment at some stage. As usual when there is a problem with Craig, I feel guilty and blame myself. I worry my split from his dad could have affected him more than he let on at the time. Craig was only thirteen when Fraser and I broke up, but he acted as though he wasn't that bothered, and his schoolwork didn't suffer. It remained as distinctly average as before. Overall, he just carried on as normal, but I worry he is now starting to pay the price for putting on a brave face. I also rebuke myself for not giving him enough attention and for not forcing Fraser to spend more time with him.

My ex-husband is in the job as well but is a long-serving constable with no intention of ever going for promotion. He rarely puts in extra hours; unlike me, as you saw earlier. In fact, my career ambitions were what caused the rift between us, and ultimately destroyed our marriage. That's what Fraser would say, anyway. He resented the extra time I spent at work and used it as an excuse to justify his affair with one of my colleagues. When I eventually found out, I tried hard to forgive him, and we went for counselling. We both promised to change, but the damage was done, and we soon went back to our old ways. I was reluctant to scale back my work commitments, and Fraser responded by leaving me for a younger, more compliant woman, who thankfully is not in the job. Wendy is a full-time mum to their twin baby girls, and my ex is devoted to all three of them. I know he loves Craig as well, but he has not spent enough time with him lately. Maybe this incident will serve as a wake-up call for both me and Fraser; a reminder that our boy needs our love and support. He might be taller and stronger than both of us, with designer stubble and an impressive collection of band T-shirts, but I suspect there's a little child somewhere under that cool exterior, crying out for attention.

By the time I reach home I'm ready to have a civilised conversation with my son about what happened earlier this evening, but of course, it doesn't work out like that. In my experience, when it comes to teenagers, things rarely go according to plan. I find Craig in the kitchen, demolishing a huge jam sandwich, and try to initiate a mature, constructive discussion, which actually goes something like this,

'Hi, sweetheart. How was your evening?'

'OK, I s'pose.'

'Anything interesting happen?'

'No – why should it?'

'So there's nothing you want to tell me.'

'What are you on about, Mum?'

'I'm *on about* the fact that Cory's car was stopped by a traffic patrol on the bypass this evening and you were a passenger…'

'Hang on - how did you know…'

'You didn't recognise my friend Aditi, did you? PC Chauhan. But she remembered you, and she thought I ought to know she detected a smell of cannabis…'

'She had no right…'

'She had every right! And she obviously made the right call when she dropped you in it, seeing as you clearly had no intention of telling me about the incident…'

'Listen to yourself, Mum! There was no *"incident"*, as you call it. A broken tail-light. A smell of dope from a spliff smoked by someone we don't even know. I don't see what's the big deal…'

'The *"big deal"*, Craig, is you were planning to hide from your mother the fact that you had been stopped by the police!'

'I wasn't hiding anything. I just didn't think it was worth mentioning…'

'Of course, it was worth mentioning! Particularly given the job I happen to be in…'

'Oh, I get it! You and your bloody job. You don't care what I was doing – you're just worried it will make you look bad at work!'

We carry on like this for quite some time. Craig accuses me of only caring about my job, and I try unsuccessfully to convince him otherwise. My words sound pretty hollow, I have to say, given the decision I made at work earlier. Craig yells at me, accusing me of not trusting him and interfering in his life, and I yell right back. I know they say never to sleep on a quarrel, but Craig and I are both too stubborn to back down, and we eventually retreat to our respective bedrooms, angry and tired. The last sound I hear before I fall asleep is the relentless thud of Craig's beloved indie rock being played at an ear-bleeding volume through his headphones, so it is audible even through the bedroom wall that separates us.

I wake at half five, feeling disappointed by the way I handled things. I'm the adult here; I shouldn't have allowed our discussion to descend into a shouting match. So I do what I normally do when I need to sort my head out - I pull on my trainers and go for a run. A few laps around Abbey Park are just what I need. As I jog slowly up the road to warm up, my brain fog gradually begins to clear, and I decide to talk things over with Fraser and ask him to spend more time with Craig. I also make a mental note to ask Dad to come around a bit more often during what remains of the school holidays. My son gets on well with his grandad, who lives a bus ride away on the other side of town. The two of them like to share a pizza and play a few card games. It would be good for Dad, too. Like his grandson, my father is an expert at pretending he's OK, when, really, he's not. Since my mum died last year, he has insisted he's doing fine, and he has plenty of friends to keep him company, but of course he's not fine. He's lost without her. Some time with Craig won't fix the situation – nothing will – but it will help.

As I begin my first circuit of the park I think about Mum, and how I have taken to running without headphones since she died. My mum loved all kinds of music, and in the weeks following the funeral every song on my running playlists seemed to remind me of her and bring on a fresh flood of tears. So, I decided it was safer to listen to the background mix of traffic noise and birdsong for the time being, until the pain of losing her eases off, which it shows no sign of doing. I would give anything to get rid of the hurt and keep the memories, but the opposite seems to be happening. Mum's face is imprinted less distinctly in my mind's eye every day, while I feel the loss of her more keenly as time passes. It's as though the truth of it is only just starting to sink in, even though she died nearly a year ago. Weirdly, the thing I remember most clearly is the feel of her springy, wind-resistant hairstyle, when I would pat her playfully on the head after one of her frequent visits to the hairdresser. Her crash helmet, we used to call it. A mass of rigid, lacquered curls, teased and fused into a glistening brown dome that sat on her head like the shell of a tortoise.

I'm sorry – I've gone right off the point. I'm supposed to be telling you about the interesting case I'm working on, and instead I've ended up waffling on about my dysfunctional, grief-stricken family. I'm now running through the section of Abbey Park that borders the canal, which reminds me it's time to get back to work and stop using you as an unpaid counsellor by boring you with my domestic trivia. Just bear with me while I get Craig sorted out, then I'll get back to the story, I promise.

Eventually I run home, have a quick shower and put on a plain navy trouser suit and a white shirt. Professional but anonymous; just right for today's interview with the patient. I haven't worn a police uniform for over ten years, and that suits me just fine.

When I walk into the kitchen to make a coffee, I'm astonished to see Craig sitting at the kitchen table, slurping a bowl of Crunchy Nut cornflakes. He's not usually up for at least another couple of hours in the holidays. When he sees me, he waves his spoon at a large mug of coffee and a plate of peanut butter toast on the worktop. His cheeks bulge with cornflakes and a dribble of milk descends slowly from lip to chin.

'Are these for me?'

My son nods.

'Thanks, sweetheart. A perfect post-run snack.'

I decide not to say any more. I know a peace offering when I see one, and I don't want to spoil it by saying the wrong thing and reigniting last night's argument. Instead I eat my toast, drink my coffee and pull my hair back into a scrunchie, ready for the day ahead, then I'm ready to go. I don't wear make-up to work, as a rule; I reserve it for special occasions and particular people. Before I leave, I exchange texts with Fraser and arrange to meet him in the staff canteen at HQ when I arrive. Now that's one person for whom I always stay barefaced, these days. I wouldn't even waste my cheapest lip balm on that man, but I need to talk to him about Craig, so needs must.

Talking of which; when my son realises I'm about to leave for work without giving him a hard time, he visibly relaxes. Thinking he's off the hook, he decides to have a go at teasing me.

'Mum,' he quips, 'you should try a high ponytail. You know, like Beyoncé and J-Lo - and loads of the girls at school. It would really suit you, even though you're a bit older, obviously.'

'Thanks for the advice but, first of all, I am much younger than J-Lo and second of all, you've just convinced me to have my hair cut in a nice, flattering, layered bob.'

'Chicken.' Craig flaps his elbows, makes a clucking sound and gives me a cheeky grin.

'Have a good day – and no more drama, right?'

'Chill, Mum. I've got band practice this afternoon, then I'm staying in tonight. Just me and the Xbox. That's it.'

'Sounds perfect. I'll stay in touch. Call or message me if you need anything.'

'OK, Mum. Don't fuss.'

Right, let's get to work.

18 CURIOUSER AND CURIOUSER

Half an hour later I walk into the staff canteen at HQ and see the former love of my life, the man I thought I'd be with forever, sitting at a table by the window, chowing down on a full English. Obviously, Fraser's appetite has not been adversely affected by any concern for his son. My ex hasn't noticed me yet; his head is down as he troughs away, so I buy myself a black coffee and a protein bar for later, in case I don't get time for lunch, then go over to join him.

'Good morning, Fraser.'

'Dawnie. Nice to see you. Sit yourself down.'

I can't believe he still calls me Dawnie after everything that happened between us, but there you are. He's contented now, so he has given the past a nice coat of rose-coloured paint and filed it away. I wish I could do the same.

'I can't stay long. I'm starting a new investigation this morning...'

'Of course, you are.'

I decide to let that remark go. I haven't got the time, or the energy, for another argument.

'Fraser, I'll cut to the chase. I need you to spend more time with Craig. I know you're busy with the twins, I get that; but please make time to come over and see him more often than you have been doing of late.'

I explain about last night as Fraser finishes the last of his eggs and bacon. Putting down his knife and fork, he finally gives me his full attention.

'I don't think you should make too much out of this, Dawnie. It could be nothing. Craig might never have even touched drugs. We need to show we trust him, rather than getting on his case all the time...'

'I'm not on his case, I'm just concerned...'

'I know you are. So am I. But I don't think it will help if I start showing up at your house and giving him the third degree...'

'But you've got to do something! Make more of an effort…'

'And I will. But in a less obvious way. He and his band have got a gig in the community centre on Saturday night, haven't they? I saved the date on my phone. I'll pop along there once the twins are in bed and go backstage afterwards with a few cans for the band…'

'He's seventeen, Fraser.'

'Get real. The boy and his mates like a beer. Also, Tigers are at home to Harlequins in the first game of the season. I'll buy tickets, so Craig has something to look forward to. You know how miserable he gets when school starts.'

'That's not for a while, though.'

'I know, but in the meantime, I'll take him out for a burger or a Nando's. Regularly, like I used to, before the twins came along. You're right, Dawn. I have let things slip in that department.'

'You certainly have.'

'What I won't do, though, is lecture our son, or spy on him. It's bad enough for him, having two police officers as parents, without us treating him like one of our clients.'

Fraser makes quotation marks with his fingers as he says the final word, and I gulp the last of my coffee.

'OK, I understand. The main thing is to spend more time with him. Thanks for agreeing to do that.'

'You're welcome, Dawnie.'

I know I shouldn't be thanking my ex, just for doing right by his own son, but I'm stunned by the fact that he has admitted being in the wrong, so I'm inclined to be generous. In all the years I have known him, Fraser has hardly ever apologised or accepted the blame for anything. Maybe he is mellowing, or maybe it's just guilt, but I don't care either way, as long as Craig gets the benefit.

'I've got to go but, for the record, I like your music, rugby and fast food strategy. It could work, I think. Just share the dates with me, won't you? So I know when Craig's going to be out.'

'Ever the control freak,' my ex replies, but he's smiling as he says it. 'Will do. Now off you go and start that investigation. Good luck with it.'

As I turn my back on him and walk away I find I'm smiling, too, so while I'm in a good mood and before I immerse myself in work, I put in a call to my dad, who happily agrees to check in with his grandson. I don't bother to tell him the reason why I'm asking; I decide he doesn't need to know.

I'm just logging on to my computer – a long and tortuous process – when I spot DC Dave Langley walking towards me. If the Leicester Tigers front row are ever short of a forward, they could do worse than Dave. He's what you might call a big unit, with a massive chest and huge guns. He could easily do the Incredible Hulk thing and rip his cheap work shirt apart, just by flexing his muscles. He's a bit chubby around the middle, due to the typical detective's diet of doughnuts, burgers, sandwiches and crisps, but the overall impression is still one of power and strength, reinforced by his severe crew cut and mean resting face. However, like so many supposedly tough guys, Dave is a real softie underneath. He dotes on his children and his little dog, and he's devoted to his wife; they met in school and have been together ever since. There are no divorces or affairs in Dave's past, which is quite unusual, in our line of work. Most importantly for me, he's a hard-working detective with a keen eye for detail. I'm lucky to have him working with me on this, and I'm grateful to DI Gillespie for recommending him.

'Morning, Sarge. I just checked my workflow queue and see you've assigned me to your new case. Sounds like it could be interesting. I brought you a coffee. Got time to brief me now, or should I come back later?'

'Now's fine. Pull up a chair.'

I take a look at the coffee, which is black, of course. That's the sort of attention to detail I was talking about. I haven't worked with Dave for at least a year, and he still remembers how I take my coffee. I can't give him any more information than is already on the system, but I run through it anyway, and Dave takes a few notes.

'So, the patient is male, probably in his forties. He was found on the canal towpath by a cyclist, a few miles south of Foxton. Apparently, he was barely conscious and had already lost a lot of his blood due to his injuries, which are pretty horrific, as you will have read. Anyway, the cyclist called an ambulance and he was rushed into A&E at the infirmary, then straight in for emergency surgery, which lasted several hours. As of last night, the doctors hadn't even discovered the man's name, as they had to keep him very heavily sedated following the operation. The consultant heading up the medical team is Mr. Dixit...'

'Isn't that the surgeon who operated on that little girl, last year? The one who was mauled by a dog? Dreadful business.'

'Yes, that's him. He was an expert witness as well, during the trial. He has been involved with a few other cases too, over the years, so he knows when to contact us, if something doesn't seem right when a patient is brought in. He said our man might be available for an initial interview this morning, but he'll be groggy and might not make much sense.'

'So how do you want to play it, Sarge?'

'I want us to show up while he's groggy and not making much sense, so we can catch him while his guard is down and see what he says. It might just have been an accident that caused his injuries, but then again it might not. Also, I need you to track down the ambulance crew and the cyclist and arrange for us to interview them.'

'Do we have a name for the cyclist? Any contact details?'

'Nothing, Dave. The ambulance crew were fighting for this man's life, so exchanging numbers with the cyclist wasn't exactly a priority. You'll have to get creative with that one, I'm afraid, but it should be relatively easy to identify the crew members.'

'Sure. I'm ready to head off to the infirmary whenever you are. I'll make a start with my enquiries on the way.'

Leicester Royal Infirmary is near the city centre, and the rush hour traffic at this time in the morning is horrendous. We're in an unmarked car, and this isn't an emergency situation, meaning I can't switch on the blues and push past the commuters, so I have to curse and fidget my way through the traffic jams, like everyone else. Dave makes good use of the time, quickly finding out the names and numbers of the ambulance crew who brought our man in. Unfortunately, they are on a rest day today, but he makes arrangements for us to interview them tomorrow. As things stand, there's no justification for interrupting their rest day, but that might change once we have interviewed the patient.

Eventually we arrive at the infirmary and track down Mr. Dixit, who explains that the patient is still extremely drowsy. He doesn't think we'll get much out of him, but we can see him for a maximum of ten minutes and come back later in the day, if we like. In the meantime, he will stay close by and let us know when our time is up.

The lights of the intensive care unit are kept deliberately low and, as usual, I'm struck by how quiet the place is, compared with the other wards. The happy clamour of the maternity wing and the hubbub of the surgical wards are absent here. The struggle between life and death is conducted at a muted volume, and the ongoing soundtrack provided by the beeping, whirring hospital equipment becomes hypnotic after a while. If you listen to it long enough, you will start hearing the tune of some long-forgotten pop song, and the resulting earworm will stay with you all day.

Our man is in a bed at the far end of the unit, screened off from the other patients by the usual plain blue curtains. A nurse pulls one aside, motions for us to enter, then leaves us to it, and we take a seat on either side of the bed.

He is lying motionless, with his eyes closed, and the first thing I notice about him is he's very good-looking. It's hard to look attractive when you're pumped full of sedatives and lying in a hospital bed, but he manages to pull it off. I'm sure, in his normal life, he's a real head turner, even if he's clearly well into his forties. He will probably be regarded as hot for many years to come, and be lusted after by women far younger than himself, whilst female beauties of the same age resort to Botox, fillers and dermabrasion, in a vain attempt to hold onto their looks, and end up looking like puffy, expressionless clones. For an instant I feel grateful I'm not pretty or rich enough to engage with that kind of nonsense.

You might think me unprofessional, remarking upon the patient's looks before anything else, but believe me when I say looks are often a factor when it comes to solving crimes. They motivate people to behave in a whole variety of ways.

Suddenly there is a slight movement in my peripheral vision.

'Someone's awake,' says Dave quietly.

I turn to face the patient. 'Good morning, Sir. I'm Detective Sergeant Burrows and this is Detective Constable Langley. We'd like to ask you a few questions about how you have come to be in hospital. We know you have undergone a serious operation and need to rest, so we won't keep you long. Is that OK?'

The man nods, and Dave flips open his notebook.

'First of all, can you tell us your name?'

For a moment our man is silent, then he opens his mouth to speak. His voice, when I hear it for the first time, is a faint croak, and Dave and I automatically lean in to catch what he is saying.

'Alex.'

'Thank you. Can you give us your surname?'

There is a long pause while Alex frowns, clearly concentrating hard. Then he looks at me, with tears in his eyes.

'I - don't know. Can't remember.'

'That's OK. Do you recall anything at all about what happened to you? Before you were found on the canal towpath?'

Another long pause.

'I was - on a boat.'

'A narrowboat?'

Alex nods.

'Was anyone with you?'

'No – all alone.'

'Can you tell us the name of the boat?'

Alex thinks for a moment, then shakes his head.

'Do you have any idea about how you came to be lying on the towpath?'

'There was an accident. I - fell off the boat. That's all - I don't remember…'

'That's OK. Don't worry. Just take your time. Is there anyone you'd like us to contact? To let them know you're here?'

'Yes.' To my astonishment, Alex reels off a mobile phone number. 'My partner,' he says.

I look over at Dave, who is scribbling furiously. He nods to confirm he has written down the telephone number. At that moment Mr. Dixit returns.

'I think we should leave it at that, for the moment. My patient needs to get some rest.'

'That's fine,' I reply. 'Alex, thank you for your time. We'll get in touch with your partner and tell – her?'

Alex nods.

'…tell her you're here.'

'Thank you.'

Then, as Dave and I stand up to leave, Alex suddenly looks alarmed. He reaches out his hand and tries to grab my arm, so I sit back down.

'Is something the matter?'

'There's a woman – my ex. She won't leave me alone – stalks me. Says she's my wife. Don't let her find me. I don't want her to know where I am!' Alex thrashes around frantically as Mr. Dixit calls for the nurse and asks her to bring something; more sedatives, I guess.

I look Alex in the eye. 'I won't let her find you.'

'Thank you.' Instantly he calms down and closes his eyes.

I look over at Dave, jerk my head at the gap in the blue curtains, and we both go and wait outside. When Mr. Dixit emerges, having administered the sedative, I intercept him.

'So, as you heard, the patient's name is Alex. Apparently, he can't recall his own surname, but he recited his partner's phone number from memory, at the drop of a hat. How is that possible?'

Mr. Dixit takes off his glasses and wipes them. 'After a patient has been through severe trauma, and has been anaesthetised and heavily sedated, their memory is often adversely affected in ways which can be unpredictable. Fragments of memory come back to them gradually, often in a seemingly random way, and not in the order you might expect. For instance, we had a young girl in here a few months ago with severe head injuries, following a riding accident. For days, she couldn't tell us the name of her school, but she kept repeating the mathematical formula for the solution of quadratic equations, which is quite complex. She always got it right, too, even though maths was her worst subject. What I'm saying is, we still have a long way to go in understanding how the brain works, Sergeant Burrows. It can appear to operate in ways which are – illogical.'

'Thank you, Mr. Dixit. We'll contact his partner and ask her to meet us here. Can we come back and see Alex again this afternoon?'

'You can, but only for a short while. I'm sure you understand I can't allow your investigation to jeopardise my patient's recovery.'

'Absolutely. We'll see you this afternoon.'

As Dave and I retrace our steps through the labyrinth of hospital corridors, I ask him what he thinks.

'To be honest, Sarge, I was ready to dismiss it as an accident, until he mentioned the stalker. Now I don't know what to think. In my view we should keep an open mind until we have found out more.'

'Indeed. I'll call the partner and arrange for us to meet her in the hospital reception. I want to make sure we talk to her before she sees Alex.'

Once we're back in the unmarked car, I call the number Alex has given me and tell the woman on the other end of the phone the news about Alex. I use some well-worn phrases, telling her his injuries are serious, but not life-threatening. I refuse to be drawn on specifics; I'll let Mr. Dixit fill her in on the details. As you would expect, she is distraught, and it takes her a couple of minutes to recover her composure. I get a sense of her strength as she battles to regain control and work out what she needs to do. She explains it will take her about three hours to get to the hospital. I arrange to meet her in reception, give her my mobile number and a brief description so she can spot me, then make a mental note to return in two and a half hours, just in case she is early. It's essential I don't miss her.

On the way back to HQ, Dave and I discuss next steps. We agree he will post an appeal on the force's Facebook page and Twitter feed, asking for the cyclist who found Alex to come forward. The local media should pick up the posts, and maybe we'll get lucky. I also ask him to update the case management system with the extra information we have gathered this morning and to upgrade the initial crime report to a full-blown case. I feel tempted to make the changes myself, as I know admin is not Dave's strong point, but I resist, mindful of my promise to Andrew that I will learn to delegate better. I'll check all his updates later on, of course. Ever the control freak, as Fraser said.

For now, my priority is to deploy a team to search the section of canal south of Foxton. If Alex is telling the truth, there should be a narrowboat around there somewhere, unoccupied and floating free. If the team can find it within the next few hours, before I meet up with Alex's partner, then we might be getting somewhere.

19 BAD COMPANY

As soon as we arrive at HQ, I commandeer a meeting room so I can make a private call; I don't want anyone to listen in on this conversation. The person on the other end of the phone is a superintendent called Alan Hamilton. We have managed to keep our relationship secret for the few months we have been together, and neither of us is ready to go public just yet. There is nothing to hide, really; we both divorced years before we got together, but as he is quite senior and I am going for promotion, we have agreed to be discreet. The last thing I want is to be accused of nepotism, and in my experience, people are still quick to make that allegation when a woman is successful in her career.

Alan and I had arranged that I would stop by his house tonight, after my late shift. As I'm sure you can imagine, we are forced by our jobs to keep some strange hours, or we would never get to see each other, but this time I need to cancel. I explain about Craig, the new investigation, and the extra hours I have volunteered to work, and say that, for the next few days, I need to spend my limited spare time with my son. Al is sympathetic, like he always is, and I know he understands; after all, he has a huge workload and two teenage children, who have not always been angels. Everything seems fine, and I am about to hang up, when he tells me to wait a moment, as he has something to say. His tone of voice is suddenly grave, and my stomach lurches.

'Dawn – once this investigation is over, you and I need to sit down and have a proper talk.'

'What about?'

'Let's leave it for now. You've got enough on your plate. Just call me when you have time to speak face to face. Somewhere off site.'

I agree, but a feeling of dread washes over me as I hang up. I really like Alan; we have a rare combination of great chemistry and mutual respect, plus we make each other laugh, which in my experience is essential. I have been happy with him these last few months, and I thought he felt the same, but it seems as though I might have been wrong. Since my marriage ended, this has happened to me every single time; as soon as I start to trust someone, and allow myself to get close to them, they back off, dump me or cheat on me. I admit I have sometimes been a bit of a commitment-phobe since my divorce, so perhaps they relish the chase, but then quickly tire of the everyday reality of a relationship.

I sit at the meeting room table, stare blankly at my phone and feel my emotional defence mechanism clicking into place, piece by piece, until my emotions are enclosed in a virtual suit of armour. It just happens automatically now, with no effort on my part; after all, I have had plenty of practice. Iron Man couldn't be better protected, but I don't feel like a super-hero. I just feel numb and sad, but it's better than the pain of rejection, and I can distract myself with work, which is what I usually do in these situations. So, I return to my desk and attack my email inbox until it's time to return to the hospital. On the way, Dave and I prepare the questions we plan to ask Alex's partner and by the time we arrive, I have pushed Alan right to the back of my mind. We also check in with Gillian Lonsdale, the DC in charge of the towpath search, to see if they have located the unoccupied boat, but sadly they have found nothing so far.

We arrive in reception well before she could possibly get here, given the distance she has to travel. Plastic cups of scalding hot coffee burn our fingertips as we scan the patients and families who are constantly disgorged through the revolving doors. Almost exactly three hours after we first spoke, the woman appears, and we spot her immediately. It is not difficult; for a start, she is dressed better than anyone else around her, in pristine navy tapered trousers, a striped Oxford shirt and loafers. With her slim figure and long red hair, she looks like a poster girl for Gant or Crew Clothing. She radiates confidence, which is impressive, given what I told her earlier on the phone. It only takes her a few seconds to spot us, and when she does, she strides across reception, her right hand outstretched.

'Good afternoon, Sergeant Burrows. I'm Jennifer Knight.'

'Good afternoon, Jennifer. May I introduce DC Langley?'

Jennifer shakes hands with Dave but does not take her eyes off me.

'I hope you don't think me rude, Sergeant Burrows, but I'm desperate to see Alex and talk to his doctor, as I'm sure you understand. Will this take long?'

'Not at all. In fact, we'll take you up to the ICU now. We can talk on the way.'

'Thank you, Sergeant. I'll try to help wherever I can.'

As we navigate the maze of hospital corridors, I warn Jennifer that Alex has little memory of what happened on the canal yesterday and might still be groggy from his meds. Then I raise the subject of his ex.

'Perhaps you can help us with this. Before we left Alex this morning, he mentioned a woman with whom he once had a relationship and who he claims has been stalking him. He seemed terrified she might track him down and made us promise not to tell her where he is, should we encounter her. Does this ring any bells with you at all? Has Alex mentioned to you any problems he has been having with an ex-girlfriend?'

Jennifer stopped dead and turned to face us.

'Yes, of course. Every day I see the effect of it on him. Sorry - let me give you some background. You see, Alex left her for me. I'm not proud of it, but these things happen, and Alex tried to manage it as sensitively as he could, but she won't let it go. I've told Alex several times that he should go to the police, but he always said he could handle it...'

Jennifer suddenly falls silent and stares into the middle distance. I see Dave is about to speak and discreetly raise my hand, warning him to keep quiet. I find you must resist the temptation to fill the vacuum, if you want to uncover what is really going on.

'Oh my God. Do you think she might have had something to do with Alex's accident?'

'We can't rule anything out at present, and we are pursuing every possible line of enquiry.'

'Well in that case, let me help you by telling you everything I know about her, and exactly what she has done to Alex.'

She starts walking briskly down the corridor as we tag along, pointing her in the right direction at each junction. Dave scribbles in his notebook as she describes a sustained campaign of stalking against Alex, which aligns perfectly with the definition of stalking we use. Fixated, obsessive, unwanted and repetitive behaviour; it's a textbook case. She shows me some examples on her phone; texts and emails which Alex has forwarded to her. She also volunteers a comprehensive description of the stalker, whom she has apparently seen in numerous photos. Dave and I barely need to ask any questions; it's rare we encounter such a willing and eloquent interviewee. She does not stop talking until we enter the hushed environment of the ICU, where suddenly her confidence seems to desert her. She looks very young and frightened as she surveys the rows of curtained cubicles. Clearly Dave and I provided a welcome distraction from the grave reality of her partner's injury, but now she is about to confront what lies behind one of those curtains and it scares her.

At that moment Mr. Dixit walks into the ICU and I make the introductions, then he leads us over to the cubicle by the window and ushers Jennifer inside.

Dave and I wait on the other side of the curtain and listen as the couple are reunited and as the consultant explains the full extent of Alex's injuries. I guess you would probably withdraw discreetly at this intimate moment, unless you are also in the job, in which case you would do like us and make sure you catch every word that is said. We don't hear anything untoward, though; Alex says nothing, but there are lots of tears from Jennifer, as you would expect from someone who has just realised that her life has been shattered.

Eventually Mr. Dixit emerges from the cubicle and motions for us to join him on the other side of the ward.

'The patient is still in a lot of pain, I'm afraid. Overall, I'm sorry to say he's not doing as well as we would have liked at this stage. We have recently had to administer some more pain relief, so he's still not making much sense. I'm hoping his condition will improve, now his partner is here. That often happens, in my experience.'

'Can we go in and see him?'

'Only for a few minutes. Like yesterday, I'll tell you when your time is up.'

Alex looks pale, but Jennifer looks worse. Her confidence and poise have evaporated, and her eyes are red rimmed from crying. I sit down opposite her and remember I have agreed to delegate, so I lean back in my chair and observe them both, while Dave asks the questions. He enquires whether Alex can describe his ex in more detail than he was able to yesterday, and the patient croaks a brief response, with every word seeming to require a huge effort of will. Although his description is more sketchy than that given by Jennifer earlier, it is consistent with that of his partner, albeit somewhat kinder. For instance, the figure which Alex haltingly describes as curvy was dismissed by his partner as dumpy. However bad the stalking might have been, it appears to me it has not entirely extinguished the affection felt by Alex for his ex-girlfriend, and I wonder if Jennifer has noticed the same thing.

Apparently, Alex still cannot recall his surname, but the ever-helpful Jennifer is happy to oblige, while warning us that his ex, should we track her down, might claim to be married to Alex and share the same surname. The woman has done this before, according to Jennifer, who obviously finds some comfort in imparting information to us. She starts to explain how the names we hear will be slightly different, as Polish surnames end in an 'i' for a man and an 'a' for a woman, when Alex waves his arm to silence her. He looks animated, as though something important has suddenly occurred to him, and we lean in eagerly to listen. It takes some effort, but finally he speaks.

'Alan B.'

'Who do you mean, darling? We don't know anyone called Alan...' Jennifer seems as puzzled as we are.

'Not – a person. Place.'

Dave and I look at each other, bemused. Then Dave has a light bulb moment.

'Do you mean Allenby, as in Allenby St. Giles? A little village just to the south of Leicester? Couple of nice real ale pubs?'

Alex shakes his head.

'Near – Allenby. The boat place…'

Dave starts pawing away at his smartphone screen. After a few seconds he raises his head, a look of satisfaction on his face.

'Allenby Marina. Just outside Allenby St. Giles. Home to a couple of hundred privately owned narrowboats, a service wharf – and a boat hire business.'

'Was this where you hired your narrowboat, Alex?' I ask.

Alex nods, looking exhausted, but visibly relieved to have conveyed the information. Grabbing Jen's hand, he attempts a smile that looks all dopey; I guess it's down to the drugs.

'Two's company,' he murmurs.

'That's nice,' Jennifer replies, although she looks a little puzzled at his turn of phrase; I imagine she blames it on the drugs, too.

Alex looks frustrated. 'No – name. Two's Company.'

'Was that the name of your boat, Alex?'

Alex nods in response, just as Mr. Dixit pops his head around the curtains.

'Time's up, I'm afraid.'

I open my mouth to protest but he shakes his head vehemently, so Dave and I thank Alex and Jennifer for their time and obediently follow the consultant out onto the ward.

'I am very concerned about my patient right now, Sergeant Burrows. I know you will want to return and see him again, but I must ask you to delay until at least tomorrow afternoon. He needs some time to work on his recovery and to be with his partner. I'm hoping that will help.'

I agree to give Alex some more time, trying not to let my frustration show. Then Dave and I return to HQ to regroup and work out what to do next.

The first thing I do is check in with DC Lonsdale for an update on the towpath search. Like my friend Aditi, Gill is incredibly thorough, so I'm confident she will find the boat, if it's there.

'Hi Gill – any joy in the search for our narrowboat?'

'Still nothing I'm afraid, Sarge.'

'Well, don't despair, as I now have a name for our missing boat. It's called Two's Company.'

'Bit of a daft name, Sarge, but not the worst I have come across today, by any means. I haven't seen it, though.'

'How do you know?'

'Because we have logged the name of every boat we have seen on this stretch of canal, both those which are moored up and those that have driven past us – in both directions. I'll email you the list of names – I'm looking at it now. Two's Company isn't on it.'

I told you she was thorough.

'Good job, Gill. I suggest you extend the search area two miles further south, in case the boat has drifted more than we thought, then call it a day. Let me know if you find anything, otherwise just write it up.'

As I put the phone down, I look at my watch and see that the day shift is about to conclude. Dave walks over to tell me he has checked our social media posts about the cyclist and, although our tweet has been retweeted and our Facebook post shared numerous times, both by the local media and by the general public, no useful information has yet come to light. We decide to give it some more time, and I tell Dave I will focus on planning tomorrow's interviews with the ambulance crew and the staff at Allenby Marina.

'Would you like me to call and make an appointment at the marina, Sarge? Before I book off?'

'No. Let's just turn up. I don't want to give them any opportunity to concoct a story.'

'Why do you think they would want to do that?'

'I don't know, but it's always a possibility. You can't be too careful. What time does the marina open for business?'

'Nine o'clock.'

'OK. Let's meet here first thing. Early, before it gets light. I'll confirm the exact time later on.'

Once Dave has booked off, I quickly nail my interview preparation, then brace myself for tackling the mountain of admin that awaits me. I'm just on my way to the kitchen for some coffee, to give me the boost to get started, when I have an idea. Luckily it's the summer time, otherwise it would be a non-starter. I rush back to my desk and check out Google Earth to find out if it could work. I don't know what we police officers ever did, before Google Earth came along. Anyway, the results look promising, so I grab my car keys and tell my colleagues I'm going out for a while.

The rush hour is pretty much over, so the traffic isn't as bad as it was this morning, and soon I'm working my way through the suburbs, leaving the city behind. Now I told you earlier that hunches are rare in policing, which they are, and this is no hunch. I prefer to call it a legitimate line of enquiry, based on information received from a less than reliable source. I hope it proves worthwhile, as my admin backlog is not getting any smaller; I can almost feel the number of emails building up in my inbox as I drive through the peaceful Leicestershire countryside. I park the unmarked car down a quiet country lane in a lay-by I spotted on Google Earth, close to a rustic brick bridge that spans the canal.

It's a beautiful evening; the air is still and the humidity of the summer day is slowly receding, as the harsh glare of the sunlight gradually fades into the gentle radiance which makes photographers call this time of the evening the 'golden hour'. Anyone would feel inspired to take a few pictures on their phone, I think as I stand on the canal bridge and take in the view. I hold up my mobile and click a couple of times, just in case anyone is watching. Then I walk down the path to the side of the bridge, onto the towpath.

I wander along the towpath for about five minutes and take a few decent shots. First, I snap a passing narrowboat, whose crew give me a friendly wave, and I wave back, wondering why perfect strangers always wave at each other, just because some of them happen to be afloat. I have no idea, but we all do it, don't we? It's as though boating encourages us to revert to an earlier, kinder era, when people raised their hats to one another in a polite greeting, everyone knew their neighbours, and there wasn't such an urgent need for people like me. Next I take a close-up of a gorgeous profusion of wildflowers at the canal's edge, followed by a shot of two curious cows at a watering hole on the opposite bank, their front hooves planted firmly in the mud as they stare at me with their bottomless brown eyes. Then I walk round a bend in the canal and am treated to the picturesque sight of Allenby Marina, with its boats of many colours, on the other side.

The boats are moored in orderly rows, alongside jetties covered with chicken wire. Picnic tables are dotted here and there, each occupied by a small group of boaters with wine or beer glasses clutched in their hands. Others stand at a communal barbecue, fussing and prodding with their forks, whilst a few stride purposefully from boat to table, carrying piles of plates or bowls of salad. The smell of grilled meat fills my nostrils and my stomach growls its response. I make a mental note to pick up a late-night snack for me and Craig as I take a few shots of the moorers and their boats.

'Lovely evening!' remarks a dog walker as he passes. 'You'll get some good photos, that's for sure!'

Let's hope so, I think to myself. At first my task appears impossible, but then I notice that the hire boats, easily distinguishable by their striking blue and green livery, are moored in a designated area at the far end of the marina. There are big gaps between the boats; the majority are obviously out on hire to people seeking a peaceful summer staycation. I lift my phone, zoom in and work my way through those that remain, reading the names painted on their sterns which, luckily for me, are facing the canal. Eightsome Reel, Four Square and then, there it is - Two's Company. Instantly I feel the warm glow of satisfaction that comes from getting it right. For a moment I allow myself to feel smug, as I run off a few shots of the boat. Then it gets even better, as a dark-haired woman climbs out of a hatch in the side of Two's Company and walks down the jetty with her back to me. I snap a couple of photos of her before it occurs to me that this woman could not remotely be described as dumpy, or curvy, even, like Alex said. Her skinny jeans hang loosely on her narrow hips and her shoulder blades make sharp angles under her T-shirt. I'm confused; clearly this is the marina, and the boat, that Alex took such pains to tell me about, but this woman doesn't look like the person he and Jennifer described to me.

I'm losing the light, and with it my reason for being on the towpath, so I turn around and walk back the way I came, taking a few random shots on the way, to keep up appearances. Once I am back in the car, I call Dave and tell him I have found the boat.

'But how did it get there, Dawn? Allenby Marina is well north of Foxton, and the accident happened several miles to the south, so you have got all those locks in between, plus a really long stretch of canal.'

'I don't know. Maybe it had something to do with the woman I saw getting off the boat.'

'Our stalker!'

'Not so fast, Dave. I got a good look at this woman and she does not fit the description given by Jennifer and Alex.'

Dave is silent as I describe the woman I saw. In the background, I hear the clatter of dishes and the sound of children laughing. It sounds as though the Langley children have been allowed to stay up for a late supper, as it is the school holidays.

'Do you want me to come over, Sarge?'

'No need. It's getting dark, so the boat isn't going anywhere tonight. Let's stick to our original plan; I just wanted to keep you up to date.'

'OK – thanks. Good job, Sarge, by the way. I can see why you're tipped for greater things…' there is a smile in Dave's voice as he teases me, and I smile back.

'Just bugger off and have your tea, Dave. Give my love to Sophie and the kids. See you tomorrow.'

Back at the office, I blitz a surprising amount of paperwork during what remains of my shift. I even find time to call Craig, who I expect to be doing a late turn on his X-box, as he promised earlier. I'm wrong, though; apparently my Dad has shown up to keep him company and is planning to stay the night. I'm delighted to hear this, and my son is equally happy when I ask him to order pizzas and ice cream as a late-night feast for the three of us. On the drive home, I reflect that, despite my fears for my relationship with Alan and my frustrations over this odd new investigation, it hasn't been a bad day.

I arrive home to find Craig and Dad sitting side by side on the sofa, with a big bowl of tortilla chips on the coffee table in front of them. My dad is holding a can of John Smith's, while my son is swigging from a can of

Coke. They are both engrossed in the darts, and Craig barely looks up when I come in, but my dad stands up and gives me a hug.

'The pizzas have just arrived, love. I put them in the oven to keep warm, and I left the ice cream out on the worktop, to soften up a bit.'

As we eat our pizzas and I stare, unseeing, at the darts, I imagine an alternative family evening. One where I get home at a decent hour, then prepare a nutritious, home-cooked meal, which we eat at the dining table, whilst having an actual conversation. Maybe Dad would tell me how he is getting on at bereavement club or regale me with tales of his pub quiz team's latest victory. Maybe Craig would manage to string two syllables together. Maybe Mum's death would not be the elephant in the room. Then I tell myself to stop this pointless daydreaming, appreciate the two flawed people I love so much, and enjoy what I have.

Craig has left a half-eaten slice of pizza on the arm of the sofa, but for once I don't get on his case. Instead, I finish my slice of pepperoni, go into the kitchen and fill three cereal bowls to the brim with salted caramel ice cream and chocolate sauce.

20 LEGAL AID

It's still dark when I get up for work the next morning. I have only managed to snatch a few hours' sleep but, even so, I feel alert and alive; I'm fizzing with energy, thanks to the tail end of last night's ice cream sugar rush, plus a hefty adrenaline buzz. I dress in the type of clothes I usually wear when I don't want to be recognised as a police officer – jeans, a T-shirt and trainers, with a lightweight hiking jacket to combat the early morning chill. Then I creep quietly down the stairs, out of habit rather than necessity; it takes a lot more than a creaking floorboard to rouse my son or my father when it's this early. Once in the kitchen, I make a flask of strong black coffee, scribble a quick note, with lots of kisses scrawled at the bottom, then slip silently out through the back door, locking it behind me.

On the way to HQ I call Dave and arrange to pick him up in the car park. I don't want to run the risk of being waylaid by a colleague, which could easily happen if I actually enter the building. To reach HQ, I only have to make a short detour off the route from my house to Allenby Marina, and we're way ahead of the rush hour, so we'll reach our destination hours before the marina office opens, but I'm not taking any chances. I want to make sure Two's Company does not leave the marina before we get a chance to interview its occupant. I'm certain the woman did not notice me last night, and I can't imagine why she would decide to abscond in a hire boat at first light, but I don't want to risk losing her.

As I drive into the car park, I immediately spot Dave, a daypack on his back and a bag of takeaway food in his hand. He's not an easy man to miss, even though the car park is dimly lit, and he's wearing an anonymous outfit which bears a distinct resemblance to mine. Once we are underway, he gets stuck into his all-day breakfast roll and places a couple of my favourite protein bars on the console between us. Like I said before, he's the thoughtful type. As I drive out of the city into the countryside, I run through the game plan I devised last night, answer his questions and make a few adjustments, until we are both absolutely clear on what we are about to do and our respective roles.

The sun is just sketching a line of luminous pink above the black horizon as we drive into Allenby St. Giles. As I noticed last night, the place is conveniently situated on a modest hill overlooking the canal, which meanders its silvery way through the valley below. Thus, the southernmost edge of the village provides a useful vantage point from which to observe the marina from a distance and spot any boats which enter or leave from either end.

After driving around for a few minutes, we find a quiet country lane on the outskirts of the village, with a good view of the marina, then park up on the grass verge and get out our binoculars. We climb up onto the roof of the car and each fix our sights on one of the two marina entrances, which are gradually becoming visible in the early morning light. Should anyone happen to drive past, we will appear to be nothing more than a pair of keen birdwatchers, who have got up first thing to watch the birds taking flight into the rose glow of the sunrise.

I always find surveillance makes me hungry. It's not the most exciting task for someone as impatient as me, and the boredom inevitably drives me to eat lots. One Christmas I ploughed my way through an entire selection box while waiting for a suspected drug dealer to emerge from his flat. As I stare through my binoculars at the marina entrance, I make short work of my two protein bars and have to ask Dave to dip into his stash of chocolate. We share a couple of Snickers and a Dime Bar, along with my flask of coffee, but see little sign of life in the valley below. A solitary boat passes by, heading south on the canal, a few dog walkers make their way along the towpath and a pair of moorers emerge from a boat called Jezebel, to clear up the detritus from last night's barbecue, but that's about it. No narrowboats leave the marina and, when I zoom in on Two's Company, I can discern no signs of life.

Eventually, after what feels like about two days, it's time to head down to the marina and surprise the office staff. On the way, my adrenaline starts spiking and my stomach ties itself in nervous knots. I start to regret the chocolate binge, but otherwise I feel great. This is the part of the job I love best; the part that makes all the administration, waiting games and frustration worthwhile. The bit where we make things happen and, if things go to plan, maybe even solve a crime.

A few minutes later we walk into the marina office, show our warrant cards and introduce ourselves to the grey-haired man behind the desk, whose name badge identifies him as Eddie. He has the ruddy complexion of a heavy drinker, and certainly looks as though he had a rough night last night, but the appearance of two undercover police officers instantly perks him up. Clearly, it's the most exciting thing that has happened to him in ages and he's immediately all ears, eager to help.

Dave explains we would like to speak to the person on board the hire boat called Two's Company, without giving advance warning of our presence either to her, or to the other occupants of the marina. Even though we're in plain clothes, similar to those worn by many of the boaters I saw last night, I'm conscious we are strangers in what is probably a close-knit community. We're bound to be conspicuous if we go walking around the marina, whereas I want to keep a low profile. Fortunately, Eddie has a solution.

'I could nip down to the boat and ask them to come up here to the office. I could say there are some forms I need them to sign.'

'Good idea,' Dave replies. 'By the way, if you fancy a change of career, we're recruiting,' he quips, but I silence him with one of my looks, then turn to Eddie.

'You said "them", just now. Are you telling me there's more than one person on that boat?'

'That's what I was told.' Eddie nods vigorously. 'When my partner Ron handed over to me last night – it's his day off today, you see – he informed me there had been some sort of accident, that the lady's husband had disappeared, and she and her friend were looking for him, like. He said to help if they asked for it, but to leave them be, otherwise.'

Dave and I look at each other and he wordlessly defers to me.

'Eddie, please go down to the boat, like you suggested. Ask the two of them to come up here as soon as possible, but don't make it seem too urgent. Just act nice and normal and relaxed. Do you think you can do that?'

'No problem. Leave it to me.' Eddie is obviously fired up by his new task and is eager to be part of what he sees as an exciting and dramatic situation, but he remembers to curb his enthusiasm and act naturally as he ambles down the path towards the hire boats. Meanwhile, Dave does not need telling what to do next.

'I'll get the bins.'

A few seconds later he returns from the car with a set of binoculars, which he trains on Two's Company and the surrounding area.

'There's no way anyone can escape along the towpath, Sarge. The path is on the other side of the canal and the bridge is too far away. There's no choice but to come up the path in this direction or cut across the grass. Either way, we'll be able to intercept if necessary.'

'Let's hope it doesn't come to that.' I'm quite a fast runner, and always ace my bleep test during our regular fitness assessments, but I don't want to have to give chase today. To me, that would mean we had failed.

Dave responds by starting up a running commentary on the scene as it unfolds.

'Right – our man Eddie is just approaching the boat. He's walking down the jetty – now he's knocking at a hatch door located approximately halfway down the length of the boat. Hang on – yes, someone has just opened the hatch, but I can't get a look at them. They must be standing well back inside the boat.'

He adjusts his position, trying to get a better view.

'Still can't see anyone – and now it's too late. Eddie is walking away, and the hatch has closed.'

'Right. Keep your bins trained on the boat and let me know as soon as anyone emerges.'

A few minutes later Eddie opens the door and walks back into the office.

'How did it go?'

'Alright, I think. The wife was a bit surprised to see me, as she has only dealt with Ron and his wife Joyce up until now, so we haven't met before. Also, the other woman questioned why she needed to sign any forms but, overall, they were OK. They'll be on their way in a few minutes, as soon as they have finished washing up their breakfast.'

Dave grins as he continues to stare through his binoculars, knowing I'll be frustrated at having my investigation held up by boaters' domestic chores. Meanwhile Eddie offers to make coffee, then potters off to put the kettle on. I'm relieved to have a couple of minutes' respite as I suspect our Eddie might be the inquisitive type, and I'm not in the mood to face a barrage of questions. It turns out I'm right; as soon as he returns with the three mugs of coffee, he starts trying to find out more. I sip my coffee and fend off his relentless enquiries until Dave calls out, 'OK – they're on their way. Two of them. Heading up the path in our direction.'

'Let me take a look.'

I grab the bins from Dave and train them on the two women approaching the office. One is the skinny, dark-haired woman I saw last night. The other woman also has dark hair, but she's not skinny. Neither is she dumpy; Jennifer's description was uncharitable and inaccurate. When Alex described her as curvy, he got it about right. For some reason I can't fathom, she is carrying what appears to be a casserole dish.

'That's her,' I tell Dave. 'The one on the right, holding the dish.'

As we hear their footsteps crunch on the gravel path, we turn our backs to the door and address ourselves to Eddie, who now looks anxious.

'Just keep talking to us and act natural,' I say to him in my most reassuring voice. 'Pretend we've come to hire a narrowboat or something.'

As the women approach, I hear them chatting away, then one of them bursts out laughing. They are still talking when they open the door. Dave and I wait for them to walk in and listen for the sound of the door closing behind them, then we both turn around at the same time.

The skinny one realises immediately that we are police officers; I can see it in her face. Her smile disappears in an instant and she fixes us with a dark, wary look. Then she glances at her companion, who is still smiling. Either she doesn't have a clue what's going on, or she's doing an excellent job of pretending to be oblivious.

I hold my warrant card up to her face and the smile disappears. She gasps in shock and drops the casserole dish, which crashes onto the wooden floor, but remains intact. Good old Pyrex.

'Stella Pitulska?' I remember that thing Jennifer said, when she was trying so hard to be helpful. Polish surnames end with 'a' for a woman and 'i' for a man.

'Er – yes?'

I glance over at Dave, who smiles thinly. 'Funny – we thought you might say that.'

'What do you mean?' the woman begins, but I have heard enough.

'Can you listen carefully to what I have to say. You are under arrest on suspicion of stalking, contrary to the Protection of Freedoms Act 2012. You do not have to say anything, but it may harm your defence if you do not mention, when questioned, something which you later rely on in court. Anything you do say may be given in evidence.'

'Stalking?' the woman does a pretty good job of appearing not to know what I am talking about, but Dave is not convinced.

'I suggest you leave the "there must be some mistake" speech for when you have a lawyer present,' he says. Then he turns to the other woman, exchanges contact details and instructs her not to leave the area until we have interviewed her and taken a statement. She's obviously not impressed, but she remains composed and compliant. I get the impression this isn't the first time she has dealt with the police; she knows how to handle us.

Her friend, on the other hand, is anything but composed. Sobbing and shaking, she puts up no resistance as we usher her into the back of the unmarked car. As I drive away, I look in my rear-view mirror and see Eddie's face, its ruddy tones temporarily bleached by shock. Standing next to him, the skinny woman watches us for a moment, then turns away without a word and puts her mobile phone to her ear.

In the back seat, our charge is still sobbing loudly. Dave tries to get her to calm down, but she is oblivious to his efforts, so eventually he shrugs, gives up and turns back to me.

'Dawn – did that other woman remind you of anyone?'

'Funny you should say that. She kind of looked like a singer my mother used to be keen on. Mum had loads of her CDs. I can't remember her name...'

'The Baroness?'

'Yeah – that's it. Nice voice. My mum used to try and sing along, but she was completely tone deaf and she made a right old racket. I always used to tell her to shut up. I'd give a lot to hear that racket again...'

'I'm sorry, Dawn.'

'No – I'm sorry for going off the point,' I answer briskly. Sympathy always makes me uncomfortable and I'm embarrassed to have let my guard down momentarily in front of a colleague. 'Anyway, I don't suppose for a minute it's her. The singer, I mean. What name did she give?'

'Nancy Parkinson. I guess she's not exactly going to call herself The Baroness, in real life. Definitely a stage name, that one.'

'Exactly. Anyway, what would someone like that be doing on a canal in Leicestershire?'

'True enough. Stranger things have happened, but I admit it's unlikely. Hang on a minute – my phone's vibrating.'

Dave pulls his phone out of his pocket and is mostly silent as he listens to the person on the other end. When he eventually hangs up, he looks at me in amazement.

'Well, what do you know?'

'Who was that?'

Dave names one of the leading, and most expensive, law firms in the country.

'The caller's name was Valerie Lewis. She was phoning on behalf of her client, one Nancy Parkinson, who has instructed her to arrange legal representation for our friend in the back of the car here. Ms Lewis explained how she doesn't intend to handle the case personally, as she specialises in – get this – entertainment law, but to expect a call from one of her colleagues in the firm's criminal practice within the next hour. That person will travel up from London today and will, of course, want to be present when we conduct our interviews.'

'Entertainment law, you say?'

'I do.'

'Extraordinary.'

Dave calls over to the woman in the back seat, who is still in tears.

'Looks like you made a good friend, out there on the narrowboat. Apparently, your mate is hiring a lawyer from one of the top firms in the country to represent you – and she's picking up the tab. You obviously made quite an impression.'

The sobbing stops for a moment, then continues, all the way to the custody suite, where we book her in and explain to the custody sergeant that we'll be back to interview her later, once her brief has shown up. By which time, with any luck, she will have stopped crying and calmed down. The custody sergeant takes one look at her, realises she is unlikely to cause any trouble, and tries to soothe her as he leads her away. As I watch her retreating figure with its slumped, shuddering shoulders, I almost feel sorry for her, until I remind myself how deceptive appearances can be. It's easy to seem devastated when you have been caught out and, if the accusations against her are proven true, she has, at the very least, made two peoples' lives a misery for a long time.

Now our suspect is safely in custody, we haven't got any time to waste, as Dave reminds me by tapping his watch.

'Time to go, Sarge. We need to leave for the hospital now if we're going to be on time for our interview with the ambulance crew.'

'OK, let's go. On the way, give Mr Dixit a call and arrange for us to talk to him, and the other doctors who helped perform the operation. I just want to confirm a couple of points with them, once we have spoken to the paramedics.'

Half an hour later, the two of us are drinking machine coffee in a windowless room just down the corridor from the main A&E reception, with the crew of two who brought Alex in. Rory Gardiner and Helen Simpson are almost a carbon copy of me and Dave; he is large and burly, whilst she is small, wiry and probably stronger than she looks. Both their expressions are grave as they describe the state Alex was in when they arrived on the scene.

'He had obviously lost a lot of blood...' Helen begins, before Rory interrupts her.

'...but the thing is, there wasn't that much of it on the towpath. I think he must have struggled for quite a while to drag himself out of the canal, and been bleeding into the water all that time, if you see what I mean...'

'Yes, I do. Thank you.' I find amateur detectives like him irritating, although they can be useful sometimes. I turn to Helen, feeling annoyed on her behalf for the interruption, but she doesn't seem bothered; she's probably used to it.'

'You were saying...'

'Oh, it's nothing, really. He was drifting in and out of consciousness, so he didn't say anything we could make out, apart from to ask how he fell.'

'That's right.' Rory nods his head emphatically. 'That's all he said, several times over. "How did I fall?" or "How could I fall?" That sort of thing. Other than that, he made no sense, which is what you would expect, given the extent of his injuries. I'm surprised he managed to say that much, to be honest.'

'Thank you; that's very helpful. Now can I ask you both about the possible cause of his injury? In your professional opinion, is there any way it could have been inflicted deliberately, with a weapon?'

'You mean an axe, or a machete, that sort of thing?' Rory is matter of fact in the manner of someone who has seen it all before - or wants to you to think he has.

'Something like that, yes.'

The two paramedics shake their heads in unison.

'No,' Helen states flatly. 'A blow administered deliberately would have inflicted a relatively clean cut, whereas this was the opposite. The edges of the wound were all ragged and torn. I've never seen anything like it.' She winces at the memory, evidently not as keen as her colleague to seem impervious to the trauma she has witnessed.

'I have,' says Rory, proud to be able to upstage Helen. 'I used to work in Australia as a paramedic, up in tropical North Queensland. We once rescued a guy from the ocean who had been bitten by a shark. A big one, maybe even a Great White, we reckoned. Anyways, this man's wound looked very similar – all ragged and torn, as Helen says. Not a clean cut at all.'

'OK. So, given that there aren't, to my knowledge, any Great White Sharks in the Grand Union Canal, I figure there has got to be another explanation, in this case.' Out of the corner of my eye, I see Dave is trying not to smile.

'Yes, of course.' Rory is quick to venture a theory. 'My guess would be machinery of some kind. I would have said farm machinery, if the accident hadn't happened in the water, which it clearly did. I mean, the guy was wet through, when we found him. It definitely wasn't an axe, though, or anything like that.'

Mr. Dixit and his team of surgeons are in total agreement with the paramedics.

'The edges of the wound were completely shredded,' the consultant confirms. 'If there was ever an opposite to a clean cut, this was it. That's one of the reasons why we had to take the approach we did - and perform a massive blood transfusion, despite the possibility of complications. It's also why the patient's recovery will be less than straightforward, with a high risk of infection. You're the detective, Sergeant Burrows, but as a medical professional, it's my opinion that this kind of trauma is highly unlikely to have been inflicted deliberately, with a weapon.'

'Thank you, doctors. You have been extremely helpful. Mr Dixit, could we possibly have a quick word with Alex, while we are here? We don't want to conduct another interview; we would just like to bring him up to date with progress on the investigation.'

'You can see him for a couple of minutes but try not to make him anxious. His partner is with him, which has helped a lot, and he's making some progress, but I'm still not satisfied with the pace of his recovery. You'll find him a little vague, as before, due to the medication.'

The consultant is not wrong; Alex barely acknowledges us when we enter the cubicle. He opens his eyes for just a few seconds, then promptly shuts them again, so I address myself to Jennifer, who is as pleasant as ever.

'Good afternoon. I won't keep you long. I just wanted you to know that, this morning, DC Langley and I took into custody a woman calling herself Stella Pitulska and claiming to be Alex's wife. We have good reason to believe she's the woman who you say is responsible for stalking Alex.'

Jennifer nods with quiet satisfaction. She puts her hand on Alex's arm and says quietly, 'Did you hear that, Alex? They've arrested her. She can't come after you any more.'

Alex nods, reaches over and squeezes Jennifer's hand, then lets his own hand drop back onto the bedsheet, as though this is all too much effort. Jennifer glances up at us, then nods at the gap in the curtains, and the three of us step outside.

'I'm sorry,' she says as soon as we are out of earshot. 'I know you probably expect me to look happier and more excited to hear this woman has been taken into custody. Don't get me wrong; I appreciate all your efforts, I really do, and I'm relieved she can't do Alex any more damage. Right now, though, my main concern is his recovery – or lack of it. Mr. Dixit is worried about his condition. Did he tell you that?'

'He did,' Dave replies. 'And we understand completely why you're not exactly going to be celebrating right now, however much progress we have made. We'll leave you to it. We just wanted to keep you up to date.'

'Thank you.'

The near silence of the ICU suddenly feels oppressive, and I can't wait to leave it behind. As I shut the door behind me, I look back through the glass panel and see Jennifer is still outside Alex's cubicle in the main ward, watching us depart.

The convoluted route along the hospital corridors is quite familiar to us now; we barely need to consult the colour coded signs, so we focus instead on our phones as we weave in and out of the flow of patients, visitors and staff, who all seem to be walking in the opposite direction. As usual, it appears, we're swimming against the tide.

'Any word from the London brief?' I ask Dave.

'Yes. He just this minute texted me. It's not good news, I'm afraid. It seems there has been a fatality on the East Midlands line, somewhere near Kettering, and all the trains are delayed, so he won't be here for at least a couple of hours. Just our luck. What do you want to do next, Sarge?'

'I suggest a quick trip to your fast food vendor of choice. Preferably one which does good coffee. Then, after that, I feel a celebrity interview coming on.'

'Can't wait. Eat your heart out, Hello magazine!' Dave has a spring in his step as the revolving doors of the hospital rotate at speed and eject us into the balmy warmth of the summer afternoon.

21 MELTDOWN

When we get back to the marina, we check in briefly with Eddie, who is clearly still in shock from what he witnessed earlier. He tries his best to waylay us with rapid fire questions and offers of tea, but we swiftly make our excuses and head down the sloping path towards Two's Company, where Nancy Parkinson has promised to meet us. When Dave called her from the car, he put her on speaker so I could listen in. She sounded composed, but not exactly forthcoming. As we approach the boat, I tell myself it will take all our combined interviewing skills to avoid coming away with the bare minimum of information. I suspect Nancy is very smart, and I'm sure that's all she plans to give us.

As soon as we knock on the window of Two's Company, Nancy opens the front door to allow us in. Judging from her expression, the word 'invite' is not appropriate here. When I step into the cabin, to my surprise I see a man sitting at the dining table. He is dressed in a battered Radiohead T-shirt, which showcases his muscular pecs and an impressive set of guns. His hair is that Celtic shade of brown which always looks as though it has been tinted with henna, but definitely hasn't, in his case. This is not a man who would colour his hair. He stares at me and Dave, his expression grim and his jaw, predictably adorned with reddish stubble, set firm. When he speaks, it's with a lilting Irish accent. My mum, God rest her soul, would have been putty in his hands at this point. She would probably have used some ridiculous, archaic term like 'dishy' to describe him. I keep my mouth shut and sternly remind myself to focus.

'Do you want me to stay, Nancy?' the man asks.

'No, you're alright, Dan. I'll come and find you when I'm done.'

Reluctantly Dan takes his leave, bending low to fit his tall frame through the front door. Nancy watches him as he departs, then indicates the bench seat he just vacated.

'Take a seat.'

Dave and I obediently sit alongside each other, while Nancy positions herself opposite us, like a panel interviewee. She stares suspiciously at Dave's laptop as he fires up the voice recording software and recites the standard form of words we use to open an interview. Then she wastes no time.

'Right. What do you want to know?'

It's a brusque opening salvo from a witness who wants to get on the front foot, control the interview and dispense with it as quickly as possible. Dave and I glance briefly at each other; this is what we were both expecting. We agreed in the car that I would take the lead, initially at least, and that open questions were the way to go.

'Please start by describing to us the circumstances under which you first met the woman who calls herself Stella Pitulska.'

Nancy obliges, and promptly surprises both of us. Despite her aggressive demeanour, she is actually very forthcoming about how she found Two's Company floating sideways across the canal as she travelled northwards in her own boat. She describes how she woke Stella up, then searched for her husband in both directions, up and down the towpath. How she offered to return to Allenby Marina with her in convoy, but met with a horrified response from Stella, who claimed to be a novice boater. How she reluctantly packed a few essentials, locked up Warrior, her own boat, and agreed to steer Two's Company back to base, on the understanding that her new friend would give her a lift back as soon as they arrived.

'And look how that turned out,' she finishes wryly. 'So much for my good deed.'

'We'll get you on your way as soon as possible,' I say in my most reassuring voice. 'You're being very co-operative, so we'll try and help you in return.'

'Well, doesn't that sound cosy.' Nancy raises an eyebrow and gives me a sardonic look; a clear warning not to get too comfortable.

Discreetly I kick Dave's leg under the table. Time for him to have a go.

'That was all very interesting, thank you,' he begins, 'but what I don't understand is – how did Stella manage to sleep through it all? Whatever happened to her husband, it ended with the boat floating about all over the canal, and probably ricocheting against the metal piling on both banks, which must have made a fair amount of noise. I don't get how she failed to wake up.'

'Booze and pills,' Nancy stated flatly. 'Stella told me how she and Alex had both drunk a right skinful at lunchtime. She said they went to the pub while they were stuck waiting at the locks, so you can always investigate whether anyone saw them at Foxton, if you want to make sure my story checks out. There are only two canal-side pubs there, so it won't be too much of a stretch for an experienced detective like yourself.'

Dave is about as keen as I am on witnesses being sarcastic and telling him how to run the investigation.

'What about the pills?' he growls.

'Stella told me she took some sleeping pills as well. Her GP prescribed them, plus a load of anti-depressants and painkillers. Your standard medical kit for a middle-class woman, approaching the menopause, who doesn't want to feel too much.'

That's my cue to jump in. 'And what was she trying not to feel, on this particular afternoon?'

'She just said she wanted to make sure she got some sleep. She hadn't had a decent night's sleep for months, she told me. She blamed it on her time of life.'

Dave leans forward. I can see he senses we haven't heard the full story. Not yet.

'What else, Nancy? What else did she want to block out?'

Nancy is silent for a moment. She bends her head and picks absently at a frayed rip in her jeans, through which a bony kneecap protrudes, bisected by a faded scar. Then she looks up.

'Stella said she had found out her husband was having an affair. She claimed to have heard him talking to this other woman on the phone. She didn't think Alex had twigged that she knew for certain, although she said he did realise she suspected him of cheating. Obviously, I don't know how true any of this is, but that's what Stella told me.'

'And you believed her when she told you she was married to Alex?'

'Yes, I did. I had no reason not to. Still don't. And for the record, I think your charge of stalking is way off. God knows where you dreamed that one up.'

Again, Dave is unimpressed. 'Let's just say we are privy to some information which you don't have, Ms Parkinson.'

'Well, good for you.' Nancy fold her arms defiantly and I start to worry we're getting nowhere. I administer another swift kick and try a different tack.

'Please can you tell us, Nancy, what led you to hire a very expensive lawyer to represent Stella?'

'In my opinion, Stella is – an innocent – and I'm choosing my words carefully here. I'm not saying she *is* innocent – I'll let you rozzers work that one out for yourselves. What I mean is – she has led a very sheltered life, until now. A privileged, affluent, middle class existence. I bet she has never come across a police officer before in her life, let alone a custody suite or a courtroom. She needs help, in my view. Someone to fight her corner. When you arrested her and took her away in your unmarked car, you saw the state she was in. I made a decision right there and then, as you drove away. I figured I was in a position to help, as I knew a good brief and could afford to pay the legal fees. So I did. Help, I mean.'

'Do you like her, Nancy?'

Nancy smiles. 'Yeah, actually I do. I wasn't expecting to and, believe me, I tried not to like her, but I do.' Then the smile abruptly vanishes. 'But I don't like her enough to lie for her, if that's what you're driving at.'

'No one's suggesting you're lying,' I reply hastily. 'We just want to get to the bottom of things, that's all. Just going back a bit, can you tell us how Stella behaved, after you failed to locate her husband?'

'Well, first of all, she was quite practical in how she tackled things. She called round all the hospitals to see if Alex had been admitted. I got the impression, though, that she didn't expect to track him down. She seemed convinced he had done a runner and tried to make it look like an accident. She was even sort of relieved, if you get my drift, when the hospital option was ruled out. Then, after that, she got very – domesticated.'

'How do you mean?' Dave looks puzzled.

'She was constantly fussing around me. Making my bed up, cooking food that neither of us could eat. That kind of thing. Anything to distract her from what was actually going on. The fact that her husband had probably binned her. I'm just guessing here, obviously, but she seemed like she was in denial the whole time. Or trying to be. I think that was the reason she liked having me around. Apart from the fact that I could steer her boat. I saved her from having to face up to her own problems.'

'How so?' I ask. Finally, we seem to be getting somewhere.

Nancy regards us suspiciously.

'You guys know I'm a musician, right?'

'Yes, we worked it out. We're both fans, as it happens, but we didn't want to embarrass you by asking for selfies, autographs, that kind of thing. Maybe later.'

Nancy glares at me like she can't work out whether I'm being sarcastic or not.

'Well, anyway. Whatever. My lawyer tells me that this has made the press now, so it's not exactly a state secret and you might as well know. I ditched my record company recently. I told Stella all about it as we were travelling along on the boat. You get lots of time to talk, out there on the canals. So she gets really enthusiastic, saying it's a great opportunity for me to take ownership – that's how she talks – of my career and produce and distribute all my own material using digital channels, social media, that kind of thing. Then, before I know it, she gets this notebook and starts preparing a business plan…'

Dave and I stare at each other in disbelief.

'I know,' Nancy says, 'it sounds mental, given the circumstances, but it turns out Stella was a consultant of some sort, back in the day, like her husband. She gave it up when the kids came along, but it sounded to me like she always missed it. Anyway, she kept her hand in. Stayed up to date with what she called emerging technology, as well as business theory, that kind of thing. Whatever floats your boat, I guess. As we travelled along, she scribbled away in her notebook and came up with this very detailed business plan for me. A lot of it was spot on, which is quite an achievement for someone who knows almost nothing about the music business. I'd probably use some of it, if I wasn't done with that scene forever. Sorry, I've gone right off the point. What I meant to say is, the plan kept her occupied for a while and distracted her from the problems in her own life. That's what she was trying to do, in my opinion. Pretend none of this actually happened.'

'You mentioned kids?' Clearly Dave has heard enough about business plans.

'Yeah – two.'

'Can you tell us any more about them?'

'Just a little. We didn't talk about them much. The older one's a boy, I think. He's in the US, working at one of those summer camps they have out there. The girl's staying with a friend. That's all I know.'

'Names?'

'Oh, Christ. Now you're asking. Standard issue posh names. Take your pick. The boy was – Giles? Something like that? Daisy for the girl? I really can't remember.'

'And did she make any attempt to contact them, while you were together?'

'Not that I know of. I think it would've made it all too real, you know? Telling them what happened. She was trying to put it off as long as possible, I reckon. Like I said, she was in denial. Sorry – I don't know anything else about her children.'

'Don't worry. You've been very helpful. Really.' I decide to risk a smile. 'We won't take up much more of your time, I promise. Just one more thing. Do you have any idea why Stella didn't report her husband's disappearance to us?'

'It's like I said earlier,' Nancy replied. 'She has led a sheltered life. The police are just not on her radar. It's hard for people like us to get our heads around, but I don't think it ever occurred to her to get in touch with you. For the record, I did recommend she contact you, but then you showed up anyway.' Another wry smile.

'OK, fair enough.' Dave glances at me; it looks as though he thinks the interview is coming to a natural end, and I'm inclined to agree. However, I'm encouraged by Nancy's implicit inclusion of Dave, when she used the phrase 'people like us', and I get the feeling there's something she isn't telling us. Perhaps not even intentionally. So I have one last go.

'Before we leave, Nancy – is there anything else that struck you as a little strange, or out of the ordinary, during your time with Stella? Anything spring to mind?' Presence of the abnormal; absence of the normal. That's what we always look for.

I half expect Nancy to dismiss this question with a curt 'no' - but she doesn't. She appears to give it some real thought, for a moment or so, then she replies.

'Yes, there is, now you ask. Sorry, I forgot to mention it. Cast your mind back to the beginning of the interview, when I described how I found the boat floating in the canal. When I approached it, I noticed the rear mooring rope was wrapped tightly around the propeller, which meant the boat wasn't going anywhere. Now experienced boaters know that removing a rope, or anything else, from around the prop is a total pain in the arse and can take hours, so they're careful to avoid it happening.'

'What causes a rope to get tangled around the propeller?'

'Negligence and ignorance, basically. For example, the crew might have left the rope in a place where it can slip off the side of the boat, or be knocked off, say by someone's foot as they walk past. Looping the rope around the tiller pin is a possible cause of the problem. People think it looks cool, but it's not a smart move. To be fair, though, it's quite rare for a rope to start off wound around the tiller pin and end up tangled around the prop. Most of the time it's fine.'

'So, do you think Alex was just careless?' Dave asks.

'Well, that's the thing. From what Stella told me about Alex, it sounds like the guy is the opposite of careless. A nerd, even. Fussy about details and obsessed with doing things properly. I think it's unlikely he would have let his rope get tangled around the prop, unless he wanted it to happen. For instance, if he wanted to disable the boat and make it look as though there had been some sort of accident.'

This time it's my turn to get a kick from Dave. Clearly, he wants to carry on with more questions. 'I see. Very interesting. Let me ask you something. Do you think it's possible Stella could have tangled that rope around the prop, instead of Alex?'

Nancy laughs. 'Not in a million years. The woman doesn't know one end of the boat from another. It wouldn't ever occur to her.'

Dave looks sceptical. 'Are you sure? Are you certain Stella is the novice boater she claims to be?'

'One hundred percent,' replies Nancy emphatically. 'Sure, she has learned how to work the locks, but she's not very confident and she still makes mistakes. As for steering, forget it. I asked her to man the tiller once or twice, just for a couple of minutes, while I went to the toilet and looked at that business plan I mentioned, but she was really reluctant and, each time, the boat ended up tacking all over the place. One time we nearly collided with a boat coming the other way. The crew were not impressed, let me tell you. Also, Stella was useless at helping me moor up and she had no idea how to fill the water tank. I had to do everything myself. No, I'm certain it would never occur to her to wrap a mooring rope around a prop deliberately.'

I expect Dave to leave it there, but he doesn't. Really, I have no idea where he's going with this line of questioning, but I decide to let him carry on.

'OK, Nancy, last question. Let's say, for the sake of argument, that a careless or inexperienced boater lets her – or his – mooring rope fall over the side. In your opinion, is there any chance this same negligent person could get tangled up in the rope and end up falling, or getting dragged, overboard?'

Nancy reflects for a moment on Dave's question. 'You know, I've been boating for a long time; since I was a kid. I grew up on a boat, so I know what I'm talking about. I've heard of this happening, but it's extremely rare, and it's not something I think Alex would've allowed to happen, for all the reasons I already mentioned. In theory it's possible, but I reckon it's highly unlikely.'

'OK. Thanks for clearing that up.' Dave looks over at me and it's obvious he's done, so I stand up to leave.

'Thank you for your time, Nancy. You've been very helpful.'

'Yeah, well. I don't like doing this kind of thing, as I'm sure you realise, but I want to help Stella, so I've given you as much information as I can.'

'You're going to like this even less, Nancy, but it would be very helpful to us if you could remain in the marina for the time being, just in case we need to talk to you again tomorrow. Now I can't force you to do this, and we could always telephone you, but we know how bad the signal can be on the canal network and we don't want to risk being unable to contact you. It goes without saying that we'll let you to go on your way as soon as possible.'

'You know,' sighs Nancy 'I could've just left her there and carried on down the canal, couldn't I? Saved myself all this hassle. I kind of wish I had, now.'

'I'm sure you do,' says Dave. 'But you're not that sort of person, are you?'

'No. And now I've gone and got myself involved, I might as well finish what I started. Help her where I can. So, I'll stay put.'

'Thank you.' Dave looks as relieved as I feel. This has gone much better than either of us expected. He terminates the interview with the standard form of words and flips his laptop shut.

'Just off the record – I'd take another look at that business plan if I were you, Nancy.' Dave shoves his laptop into his backpack and hoists it onto his shoulder. 'Keep on making music. I'm sure you've got lots of fans out there who are eager to listen – myself included.'

I've heard enough; we haven't got time to waste on this. I give Dave one of my looks and he immediately falls silent.

'Thanks for the career advice.' Nancy replies, smiling thinly as we take our leave. 'I'll wait to hear from you.'

On our way back to the car we call in briefly at the marina office to let Eddie know we're leaving. Again, he tries to delay us with questions, to no avail. He's clearly desperate to know what has just been said aboard Two's Company, but he's destined to be disappointed, I'm sure. We tell him nothing and I'm sure Nancy will do the same.

Dave takes over the driving and, predictably, makes a pit stop at the village shop in Allenby St. Giles to stock up on chocolate. Then, on the way back to HQ, we do a quick debrief.

'Well, she was a lot more co-operative than I expected,' Dave begins. 'I never thought she'd agree to stick around for another day. I mean, I imagine she's pretty clued up on her rights as a witness. She knows we can't force her.'

'True enough, but then again she might have another incentive to stay put,' I reply, handing Dave a Double Decker, which I've just unwrapped for him.

'How d'you mean?'

'Come on, Detective. The man? Ripped physique? Irish accent?'

'Oh yeah. Sorry. I can see why you might have looked twice there, Sarge,' replies my colleague with a cheeky grin.

'That's not the point.' I try to sound stern, but I can tell Dave is not convinced. 'Right, let's summarise what we found out. First of all, Stella claims to have two children, a son and a daughter. One working in the US, the other staying with friends. Let's explore that when we interview her, then we can do the research afterwards to see if her claims check out. Hopefully by the time we get back into town her brief will have shown up and we can crack on with the interview. OK, Dave – what else?'

'Apparently, she self-medicates with alcohol and abuses prescription drugs, which could explain why she was out of it when Nancy found her on Alex's boat, after he disappeared. Also, Nancy clearly believes Stella's claim that she is Alex's wife.'

'More than that – Alex's wronged wife…'

'With good reason to take revenge…'

'Hang on, Dave. Let's not get ahead of ourselves …' I protest, but Dave is warming to his theme and I decide to let him carry on for a moment.

'Dawn, I think the key thing we have got to establish is - who exactly is the person in our custody suite? Is she a stalker who has made life a misery for her ex and his new partner, and could possibly pose a threat to them?

Or is she a troubled wife with possible addiction issues, whose husband had an unfortunate accident while she was under the influence?'

'In which case,' I interrupt through a mouthful of Snickers, 'why didn't Alex give us her number when we first encountered him in hospital?'

'Good point. Or, is she a jilted wife whose husband devised a creative, but rather strange method of staging a boat accident to provide cover for his desertion?'

'An accident that went wrong, if so,' I add. 'I mean, no one would willingly choose to do that to himself.'

'Exactly. It's bizarre, I have to say.'

'Quite a range of options.'

'Hang on, Dawn, I haven't finished. I think there's another option; one where the woman in the custody suite is neither an innocent victim, nor a predatory stalker. Where she turns out to be something much worse.'

'Go on. I'm intrigued.'

'You know all those questions I was asking? About the rope getting wrapped round the propeller?'

'I admit, I did wonder where you were going with that line of questioning...'

'Yeah, well. Thanks for letting me run with it. Here's the other option. Let's assume for the moment our Stella is actually Alex's wife, who has found out he is playing away and decides to take revenge. Here's what she does...'

As Dave continues talking, I start to regret having eaten that Snickers. Don't get me wrong; I have attended a lot of nasty crime scenes and been first to arrive at a couple of fatalities. I have a strong stomach, but nevertheless I feel slightly queasy as I imagine the scenario described in gruesome detail by my colleague.

'OK. It's a theory – and it's consistent with the nature of Alex's injuries.'

'Exactly, Sarge. And if I'm right, we're no longer looking at a stalking charge. We're talking attempted murder.'

'...which would be incredibly difficult to prove, without a confession.'

'I know, Dawn. I suspect I'm wrong. I really hope I'm wrong, to be honest. I wouldn't wish that on anyone. But I just wanted to tell you what was on my mind.'

'Sure. I appreciate you raising it, but let's keep it between ourselves for the moment. After all, we have no evidence to support it, and theories without evidence are just hunches. And you know what we think about those...'

Just then my phone rings. It's the custody sergeant, and the news is not good. Apparently, after we left her earlier, Stella became increasingly agitated, culminating in a major meltdown which left the Sergeant with no choice but to call in the medics. The doctor promptly put her under sedation and left instructions that she would not be fit to be interviewed for the next couple of hours. With impeccable timing, her lawyer then showed up, straight from the train station, only to be told he couldn't see his client. Obviously, he wasn't exactly delighted by the news, but apparently checked himself into a hotel and agreed to return later, when instructed. I feel some sympathy for him; he has been beset by the sort of multiple delays which so often hold up our investigations. One thing's for sure, though. He will have ample time to prepare for the forthcoming interview with his client – and with us.

22 RECOVERY

As I hang up my phone, Dave's immediately rings. He listens in silence, then confirms that we are on our way back to HQ and will go straight to reception when we get there, to check the number of the interview room.

'What was that all about?' I ask him.

'It seems our social media campaign has finally delivered a result. Our cyclist, the one who found Alex on the towpath, has just turned up in HQ Reception – with her mum. They are taking them to an interview room, but we need to talk to them soonest. The girl's very upset, by all accounts.'

'How old is this girl?'

'Fifteen.'

'Ah. Helpful of her to bring an appropriate adult with her.'

'Exactly. Saves us having to find one.'

'I was hoping to run those background checks on Stella and her supposed children, but I guess that will have to wait.'

'I could always run the checks, Sarge, while you conduct the interview?'

'Thanks for the offer but, given the age and possible vulnerability of the witness, I think we should both be there, to provide support to the girl and her mum. We can run the checks afterwards, before we go back to the custody suite to interview Stella.'

As always happens when I have to interview a juvie – sorry, a juvenile – I can't help putting myself in the parent's position and wondering how I would react if Craig had witnessed something similar. I ask myself how well I would cope and how good I would be at supporting my son, and I don't much like the answers I get back. Despite all the training I've had – I was a family liaison officer, earlier on in my career – I suspect Craig's grandfather would be more helpful to him than me, these days.

As Dave and I open the door to the interview room, the young cyclist and her mum spring nervously to their feet. I hold out my hand to the mother and then to her daughter, giving them what I hope is a warm and reassuring smile. The girl's handshake is limp, and her hand is clammy with sweat.

'Good afternoon. I'm Detective Sergeant Dawn Burrows and this is Detective Constable David Langley. Thank you very much for coming in to see us.'

'That's alright,' the mother says. 'I'm sorry it has taken us a while to get in touch, but Chloe here didn't tell me anything about what she saw. I thought she was acting funny, these last couple of days, but she kept telling me she was fine and to get off her case. You know what teenagers are like. Anyway, this morning, we were both in the kitchen when it came on the local radio, how they were appealing for witnesses to come forward and all that, and Chloe just bursts out crying and says she's the person you're looking for. Kept it from me, she did.'

The woman casts a worried glance in her daughter's direction and Chloe glares back at her, clearly uncomfortable at being talked about, then puts her head down and stares fixedly at the floor.

'That's quite understandable.' I smile in Chloe's direction, hoping she will look at me. 'I've got a son not much older than you are. I'm sure he'd have done exactly the same thing, in your position. It's not easy to talk about this kind of thing, is it? Even to your mum.'

I look over at Chloe to see if my words have made her feel more comfortable, but it's hard to tell, as she continues staring at the floor and scuffing the toes of her trainers against the well-worn carpet. I notice Dave has set up the laptop ready for the interview, so I give him the nod to indicate it's time to begin.

'OK, let's make a start. Can please you confirm your names for us?'

'Sorry, I should have said earlier. I'm Susan Thursfield and this is my daughter, Chloe Grayson. Her dad's name. We split up six years ago and I got married again last year.'

'Thank you, Susan. Now, if it's OK with you, Chloe, we're just going to ask you to describe, in your own words, what happened two days ago on the canal towpath, and what you saw. Just take your time, and if you need to stop and take a break, just let us know.'

The interview with Chloe is a long, drawn out process, punctuated by lots of tears and frequent requests for a break. Gradually we establish that Chloe was cycling home from her friend Lauren's house when she came across Alex lying on the towpath, barely conscious. Chloe immediately called 999 and used the what3words app on her phone to pinpoint her exact location. I'm impressed by this and tell her so.

'I wish more people were as clued up as you, Chloe. You could well have saved that man's life by using that app. Given the relatively isolated location, it could have taken the ambulance crew ages to find you, if you had just tried to describe where you were. You should be very proud of your daughter,' I add, turning towards Susan.

'I am proud of her. You did really well, love. I just wish you had told me sooner.'

'Don't worry about that,' I reply. 'You had the courage to come forward and you're here now. That's what matters. Chloe, can you recall whether you saw any other people on the towpath while you were waiting for the ambulance to arrive, or whether any boats passed by?'

In the end, Dave and I don't get much from the interview in return for our time. Chloe did not see any other people or boats while she was waiting with Alex on the towpath. She mostly talked about Alex's injuries, which was understandable, but gave us nothing new. The only really useful thing to come out of the interview was that Chloe confirmed, unprompted, what the ambulance crew had reported Alex as saying. Like Rory Gardiner and Helen Simpson, Chloe recalled Alex asking repeatedly, in his barely conscious state, 'How did I fall?'

After what feels like hours, Dave and I bid farewell to Chloe and Susan and leave the interview room. We're just on the way back to our office to do the background checks when we run into my DI, Andrew Gillespie, in the corridor. As you might have gathered, given I haven't mentioned him since the start of this investigation, Andrew is a hands-off kind off boss; with me, at least. Since I passed my Inspector's exams, he has treated me almost like a peer and usually lets me get on with it but, now he has seen us both, he decides he wants a quick update and diverts us to the canteen for a coffee.

Over coffee I explain to Andrew how we have placed Stella under arrest on suspicion of stalking and taken her into custody but have not yet been able to interview her due to her meltdown. I summarise our interviews with Alex, Jennifer, Nancy, Mr Dixit and his colleagues plus the ambulance crew and, lastly, Chloe and Susan. Andrew listens carefully, without interrupting, as he sips his mug of black coffee and chews his way thoughtfully through a few of his customary wine gums. When I eventually stop talking, he remains silent for a minute, then gives me a hard look.

'From what you've just told me, Dawn, I'd say this was an accident, pure and simple. This whole stalking business is a bit suspect, in my opinion, and I doubt you'll be able to make the charge stick, particularly once this fancy, top dollar brief gets stuck in. My advice would be to get it wrapped up as soon as possible. You're working all hours on something that is not going to pay back.'

'You could well be right,' I reply. 'We should know a lot more once we have interviewed Stella. I'm expecting a call any time now from the custody sergeant, giving us the word to go. I promise you, Andrew, I'll call it as soon as I feel confident enough to do so. In the meantime, Dave has formulated a theory I think you should hear about. It might be nothing, we both agree on that, but we also think it means the case could be worth a little more of our time.'

Dave stares at me in astonishment. After I urged him earlier to keep his theory between the two of us, the last thing he expected was for me to invite him to reveal it to Andrew. However, there is an element of self-preservation here; I don't want my DI to think I am wasting time on a case that is probably just a simple, but tragic accident. I need him to realise there could be a lot more at stake.

Andrew listens closely while Dave explains his theory. While Dave is talking, he does not reach for a single wine gum.

'I see. So if your theory is correct, Dave, we're looking at attempted murder.'

'Yes, sir. That's what we concluded. Of course, we're probably way off track, but just say, for the sake of argument, that we're not, then…'

'Sorry to interrupt, Dave, but I've just seen a missed call come up on my phone from the custody sergeant. Andrew, I'm guessing the interview with Stella is on, so we need to go. I don't want her lawyer to get to her before we do.'

'Of course not, Dawn. Give me an update tomorrow and go home straight after the interview. You look exhausted, and if this case does turn out to be attempted murder, you'll need to conserve your energy. You know how these things go; it'll be a marathon, not a sprint.'

'I'll run those background checks after the interview,' Dave offers. 'It's time I pulled a late night for a change, rather than you.'

'Thanks. I probably should go home and check in with Craig.'

As Dave heads out of the canteen, Andrew collars me for one of his quick pep talks. 'Work life balance, Dawn – and delegation. Am I wasting my breath, here? I suspect you and Dave have been doubling up for most of this investigation. Do less and get him to do more. Call me tomorrow and let me know what's happening - or drop by my office. I'm being serious. You're an exceptional officer and I don't want to see you burn out.'

Andrew leaves and I call the custody sergeant back as I hurry after Dave. Happily, Stella is now fit for interview. I instruct the sergeant to delay informing her lawyer for at least fifteen minutes, to give us time to reach the custody suite first. I want to make sure Dave and I are present when Stella's lawyer encounters her for the first time.

Half an hour later, Dave and I are sitting side by side in the custody suite reception when her lawyer walks in. Even before he opens his mouth, I know it's him. For a start, he is wearing an impeccably tailored suit, a rare sight around here. On his left wrist is an understated, and therefore probably hugely expensive, IWC watch. In his right hand he holds one of those high-spec leather laptop bags, in marked contrast to the battered rucksacks Dave and I carry. His dark hair is slicked straight back from his face and his brogues are highly polished. He's young but is trying hard to look older and give an impression of gravitas. He doesn't quite pull it off.

Dave and I walk over to introduce ourselves. Conscious of my jeans and North Face jacket, both slightly grubby after a day in the field, I flip open my warrant card to confirm my status and shake the lawyer's hand firmly. 'Detective Sergeant Burrows.'

'Alastair Young,' he replies curtly. 'I'd like to see my client.'

'Of course. She has been brought up to an interview room. We'll take you there now.'

On the way to the interview room, I try to make conversation. 'I understand you've had a trying day, Alastair, what with the train problems and the doctors' verdict on your client's fitness for interview. We'll do our best to ensure there are no further delays.'

Alastair does not reply. Clearly, he's not one for small talk. I'm sure all he wants is some time alone with Stella, but I'm not going to give him that option.

As soon as we step into the interview room it's obvious Stella has had a very bad day. I'm not surprised the doctors prevented us from interviewing her earlier; in fact, I'm amazed she has been judged fit for interview now. Her eyes are red raw from crying, her face is puffy and mottled, and her arms are wrapped tightly around her body. Although the interview room is warm and stuffy and her T-shirt clings damply to her back, she is shivering. She doesn't stand up when we come in, nor does she acknowledge us in any way; she just looks up at the three of us, her expression a mixture of fear and resignation, as though she is wondering which person will land the first blow.

Alastair sits down opposite his client and holds out his hand, which Stella ignores. This lack of response does not seem to bother him. Briskly he introduces himself, names his firm and confirms to Stella he has been hired by Nancy to represent her. There is no warmth in his voice, no empathy in the way he addresses his client, and I suspect each case merely represents for him an intellectual challenge; an intriguing puzzle to unpick and solve. Not a people person, then. When I observe how Stella instinctively recoils from Alastair, I sense an opportunity for me to find out more than I might have done, had she immediately placed her trust in him.

'Can I get you any tea or coffee?' I ask gently. 'I see you already have some water.'

Stella shakes her head in response.

'OK. Just let me know if you change your mind. Now, as you can see, my colleague DC Langley has set up his laptop. It has voice recording software, to enable him to record our conversation. What I'd like you to do, in your own time, is to describe to us the events leading up to this morning, when we arrived at Allenby Marina. Go as far back as you think will be useful, to help us understand what happened. Just take it at your own pace and, if you need to take a break at any point, just tell us and we'll be happy to stop for a few minutes.'

Stella regards me suspiciously. I suspect she has watched too many police dramas and was expecting an aggressive interrogation with quick fire questions, lots of shouting and accusatory fingers pointing right in her face. She never imagined she would be invited just to talk. Alastair does not intervene, and Stella does not look at him for confirmation that it is OK to proceed. She just sits silently for a moment, looking marginally more composed than when we first entered the room. Eventually she begins to speak. Alastair records her monologue on his phone and busily takes notes. I just listen.

Once she gets going, Stella talks for a long time, at a low volume and in a flat monotone. The voice recording software will pick up her every word, though - I'm confident of that. First, we hear how she never wanted a narrowboat holiday, but was forced into it by her husband. She then goes on to describe her various mishaps on the canal and I resist the temptation to ask her to move the narrative along a bit. I can't risk her falling silent, now she has begun talking. Things get more interesting when she describes how she had suspected her husband of infidelity for some time, citing a range of supposed clues including suspicious phone calls, purportedly from clients, plus his reluctance to let her use his phone when her own was on charge. She mentions one particular incident at Foxton, when she observed him on the phone while she was working the locks and apparently saw the guilt 'written all over his face'. I'm not convinced, but she maintains her suspicions were later confirmed when she reportedly overheard a phone conversation between her husband and his lover. As she recounts what her husband allegedly said, she starts to lose what little composure she has, so I pass her a box of tissues and suggest we take a breather. While she's getting it together, I lean back in my seat and sneak a quick look at Dave, who discreetly raises an eyebrow and assumes a puzzled expression. I imagine he's thinking the same as me; that unexpectedly, Stella's story so far is wholly consistent with the account given by Nancy in her interview.

When Stella is ready to talk again she apologises, rewinds her narrative and describes how she and Alex had been drinking quite heavily that lunchtime in one of the canal-side pubs below Foxton Locks, then continued after the locks when, devastated by the conversation she had so recently overheard, she mixed both of them some strong cocktails. She breaks into sobs as she describes how she suddenly felt unable to cope and decided to take refuge in sleep, with the help of a hefty dose of sleeping pills which she had on prescription from her doctor. After that, she apparently passed out on the bed from the combination of pills and alcohol and remembers nothing more until she was woken by Nancy.

The rest of Stella's account is also almost identical to Nancy's. Her voice shakes as she describes how she phoned round all the hospitals then, when she discovered no record of her husband being admitted to any of them, concluded he had abandoned her. She refers to Nancy's company as being both a comfort and a distraction at this difficult time and mentions in passing the business plan drafted in her notebook as the boat headed north, back to Allenby Marina. When she admits she could not bring herself to tell her children what had happened, I decide to apply a little subtle pressure.

'Would you like to speak to your children now, Stella?'

'No – not yet. I'm still not ready. To tell them would make it all too real. I know you think I'm in denial – and you're right, I guess. I'm finding it hard to accept what has happened.' Then, unexpectedly, she becomes belligerent. 'Although the two of you don't think any of what I have just told you is true, do you? For some reason, you think I'm a stalker.' For the first time, Stella turns to face her lawyer. 'Have you any idea where they got that notion from?'

I decide to jump in quickly. Here goes. 'Stella, what if I told you the man you claim is your husband is currently in the intensive care unit in Leicester Royal Infirmary, where he is in a stable condition, but recovering from serious injuries? His partner is at his bedside. In separate, consistent accounts, both of them have described a sustained campaign of stalking waged against them by a person we believe to be you. The ex who could not accept your relationship was over, and Alex had moved on.'

'My client does not wish to respond…' Alex protests, but Stella holds up her hand to silence him.

'Yes, I do wish to respond.' Her voice is shaky, but defiant. 'I wish to respond by describing his supposed partner to you. If I'm correct, she has long red hair, a slim figure and a slight Mancunian accent. Answers to the name of Jennifer.'

'So, you've met her?' I ask in my most neutral tone. Out of the corner of my eye, I see Alastair's furious expression as he glares at Stella, the client who is ignoring his advice and possibly implicating herself in the process.

'Yes, I have. Just once. She introduced herself to me at a corporate event hosted by my husband, where I had been presenting the prizes. An event attended by hundreds of people, most of whom saw me up there on stage, if you want to check I'm telling the truth. I had no contact with her before the event, nor have I communicated with her since then. Hardly the actions of a stalker, wouldn't you agree? In fact, it seems to me I was right all along. My husband has left me for someone else and, if that wasn't bad enough, they both appear to be colluding to implicate me in a crime I didn't commit.'

'Why do you think they would do that, Stella? What possible motive could they have?'

'DS Burrows, do not ask my client to indulge in speculation.'

Again, Stella holds up her hand to silence her lawyer. 'It's alright, Mr. Young. I'm not going to speculate, because I have absolutely no idea.'

'Then I suggest we terminate the interview. Thank you for your time, Stella.' I glance over at Dave, who is already closing the interview, speaking quietly into the microphone on his laptop.

'May I now have some time alone with my client?' Alastair says curtly. He appears irritated at having been ignored and overruled by Stella. I'd be interested to know what he is going to say to her.

'Of course.' I head for the door. Dave flips his laptop shut and follows me outside.

'So, what do you think?' I ask him as we walk back towards reception.

'Her story is completely consistent with what Nancy told us,' he begins, and I nod in agreement. 'However, they did have plenty of time to work on it, while they were on the boat.'

'When they weren't busy writing business plans.'

'Quite. It could all be true, though. I actually reckon she really is his wife and, frankly, I don't think for a moment the stalking charge is going to stick. I don't think she has been stalking Alex and Jennifer, but neither do I think she is an innocent victim in all this.'

'Why do you say that?'

'Because she didn't ask about his injuries. When you told her Alex was in the ICU and was serious, but stable. I would expect a wife, even if she hated her husband for cheating and walking out on her, to ask for more details about how badly he was hurt. Unless, of course, that wife didn't want to know the full extent of his injuries, for some reason…'

Dave abruptly falls silent as Alastair walks into reception and heads straight for us. 'That was quick,' he mutters under his breath.

'DS Burrows, DC Langley, I don't believe you have sufficient evidence to detain my client and I will be petitioning to have her released from custody. Goodnight to you both.' He stalks out of the building through the automatic doors, which swish shut behind him.

Dave watches him disappear down the street, then turns to me. 'Dawn, you look exhausted. Andrew was right. Why don't you go home and see Craig, and I'll head back to HQ and run those background checks? I'll call you as soon as I have the results.'

'OK, if you're sure. Let's meet first thing tomorrow and work out where we go from here. I'll drive you back to HQ then I'll call it a day.'

When I arrive home, I find the house empty and in darkness. Craig is out and his mobile goes straight to voicemail. I resist the temptation to leave a message; I know anything I said would undoubtedly come out all wrong and be likely to put him off coming home, if anything. I'm about to text instead, when I look up and spot a photo of my mum nestling among the takeaway menus and other detritus pinned to our kitchen notice board. It feels like a sign, somehow.

'What would you do, Mum, if you were me?' I ask. I remember how good she was at keeping the lines of communication open, all through my rebellious teenage years, mainly by following a 'light touch' approach and by trusting me. Her answer comes back loud and clear. I put down my phone, grab a glass from the kitchen cabinet and retrieve a bottle of wine from the fridge.

'Good call, Mum. Cheers.' I raise my glass to her, then walk through to the living room and flop, exhausted, onto the sofa.

I must have fallen asleep soon afterwards, because the next thing I see is Craig standing over me, with my phone in his hand.

'Your phone was ringing when I came in. Probably work, as usual. I'm off to bed.'

My son spots his opportunity and disappears upstairs before I have a chance to wake up properly and ask him why he is out this late. I decide to let it go and respond to the three missed calls from Dave.

'Hi – I'm sorry for not picking up. I crashed out on the sofa with a glass of Pinot and left my phone in the kitchen.'

'Quite right too. Glad to hear it. Anyway, I've run all the background checks on Stella and they're consistent with what she said at interview. She is Alex's wife and they do have two kids. Hugo and Imogen.'

'Posh middle-class names, just like Nancy said. Christ. Pity we didn't get the chance to run the checks earlier. Never mind – we are where we are. I'll call Alastair Young now and tell him we're releasing Stella from custody. If you could speak to the custody sergeant and do the admin, that would be great. Let's meet first thing tomorrow and work out what to do next. Top of my list is another visit to Alex.'

'I agree. And Dawn – just because she is his wife, and we've had to release her from custody, doesn't make her innocent.'

'No, but it doesn't mean she is guilty, either. Let's sleep on it and start afresh tomorrow.'

23 DECISION TIME

The next morning, Dave and I meet in the HQ canteen at a relatively civilised hour. Over breakfast, we plan how to handle our forthcoming interview with Alex. We take our time; both of us agree we want to ensure Jennifer is present at interview, so there's no point us showing up at the hospital before visiting hours have begun. Afterwards, we return to our desks and the prospect of some fascinating case administration and email wrangling.

While my computer is booting up, I have plenty of time to send Craig a text message, asking if he will be around for dinner. I try my best to sound casual, to avoid the usual accusation of getting on his case. I justify my enquiry by saying I plan to drop in at the supermarket on the way home and need to know how much food to buy. A minute later I receive a brief response. My son will be out and won't need any dinner. He signs off with a kiss, though, which is something, I guess. I fire back the 'thumbs up' emoji plus a kiss of my own and resist the temptation to ask what time he will be home.

Eventually it's time to depart for the hospital. I head over to Dave's desk, where my colleague is staring fixedly at his screen. In his hand is a garish coffee mug with 'World's Best Dad' emblazoned on the side. How nice it must be to have young kids who are still uncritical enough to give you presents like that.

'Shall we go?'

'Yes – this stuff can wait. Just give me a minute to log off.'

Dave and I drive to the hospital in almost total silence. We have planned the interview as far as we can and we both know it would be pointless to go over it all again. We can't predict how it's going to pan out and there is nothing more we can do to influence the outcome, so there's nothing left to say.

As intended, we arrive at the ICU soon after visiting hours have begun.

The nurse on reception is on the phone and clearly under pressure. She recognises us from previous visits and waves us straight through. On the ward itself, there is no sign of Mr Dixit or any of his colleagues. So far, so good. I offer up a small prayer as I pull aside the curtain and, for once, the planets are aligned. Alex is sitting up in bed and Jennifer is seated in the chair next to him.

'Good morning Alex. Jennifer. May we have a word with you both?' I try to keep my tone light and conversational; I don't want to give the slightest hint of what I'm about to spring on them.

'Of course, Sergeant Burrows. Constable Langley. Would you like me to find you a couple of chairs?' Jennifer is as charming and gracious as ever.

'No, thank you. We're fine.' I'd rather remain standing over them, although I'm sure they are both well practised in body language and probably see straight through my rather obvious tactic. Dave and I have agreed he should go first, so I just keep silent and wait.

'Alex, the reason we're here is to inform you that, late last night, we released Stella Pitulska from custody. Her lawyer arranged for overnight accommodation for her in the city centre and she is free to return to Allenby Marina, or indeed to the marital home, should she choose to do so.'

'The – what? I don't understand...'

Jennifer looks over at me for clarification, but I ignore her and address myself to Alex.

'As DC Langley said, we released Stella from custody. We did this as soon as we established that she is, in fact, your wife – just as she claimed to be.'

Jennifer jumps to her feet, clutching her bag in front of her as though it could somehow defend her from what she has just heard. 'Alex. Tell them they're wrong – that they made a mistake. Tell them!'

Her last words are shouted at top volume and I worry we might have attracted the attention of a nurse, but no one appears.

Alex shakes his head and stares fixedly at his bedclothes. 'They're not wrong, Jen. I'm sorry. I should have told you.'

Jennifer looks over at Dave and me, her eyes full of tears. She opens her mouth to speak, then her self-preservation instinct appears to kick in as she apparently makes a conscious decision to maintain her dignity. Without another word, she pushes aside the curtain and leaves the cubicle. I listen to the sound of her heels clicking loudly on the hard floor as she walks rapidly towards the door. She doesn't stumble once.

Dave pulls the curtains back together. As I sit down in the warm chair Jennifer has just vacated, my colleague catches my eye and winks. Luckily Alex is still staring down at his bedclothes and doesn't notice.

'Right, Alex,' I begin. 'Now it's just the three of us, why don't you tell us why you claimed that Stella, who we have now established is your wife, was stalking you?'

Alex is silent for a few moments. Slowly and deliberately, he pours himself a glass of water from the plastic jug at his bedside. Dave and I wait patiently, happy to give him all the time he needs to recover from Jennifer's abrupt departure and formulate the latest twist in his story.

'It's complicated,' he finally says.

'Go on.'

'Well – there was a woman who stalked me persistently – back in Leeds. I met her in a bar. We had a brief affair, then I called it off and she took it really badly. She started harassing me and continued for a long time – well after I started seeing Jen. Anyway, I did tell Jen about Stella when we first got together although, as you just saw, she didn't know we were married and I told her we had split up, which wasn't strictly true. I should say that, by mutual agreement, Jen and I were both very discreet about our relationship and our colleagues had no idea we were together, so no one had any reason to tell Jen the truth, even if they knew it, which they probably didn't. I never discuss my personal life at work.'

Alex pauses for a drink of water and Dave and I glance briefly at each other. My colleague looks vaguely amused as I pass the baton to him.

'So, what happened next?' he prompts.

'When I received the abusive calls and texts and Jen was around, I would tell her they were from Stella. I changed the contact details on my phone so it would look as though they came from her, if Jen happened to see my screen.'

'And why did you do that?'

'I know it might sound odd, but I figured Jen would be OK with one recent ex, but two – well, it wouldn't look good. Obviously, it has all backfired now, to say the least, but basically I was just your classic arrogant idiot. I was very successful at work and I made the mistake of believing my own publicity. I thought I could have it all – the loyal wife, great family, beautiful girlfriend and amazing career. I convinced myself I was clever enough to make sure my girlfriend never found out about my wife – or vice versa.'

'And that your girlfriend didn't find out about your ex-girlfriend,' Dave can't resist adding.

'That's right. When you put it like that, it sounds pretty shabby, I admit.'

'Look, Alex. We're police officers, not vicars,' I remark. 'We're in no position to make moral judgements and it's not our job to do so. Frankly, if marital infidelity were a crime, half the police force would be behind bars. We're just trying to determine whether or not a crime has been committed.'

'Can you tell me, Alex,' Dave continues, 'why you gave us Jennifer's mobile number when we first interviewed you, rather than Stella's?'

'It's quite simple,' Alex replies quickly, a look of relief on his face. 'You must remember how out of it I was, from all the painkillers. For some reason, it was Jen's number that came to me through my brain fog, rather than Stella's. I'm amazed I was able to remember anyone's telephone number, but her number just sort of popped into my head. I guess it's because I call her so often.' He smiles sweetly at me and I can see why his charm might still work on some women, but I don't smile back. It's time to turn up the heat a little.

'As I recall, you said at the time that you were alone on the boat when your – accident – happened, although at the same time you also expressed concern about your stalker. It sounds to me that, even whilst under the influence of painkilling drugs, you were still able to focus on keeping your story straight with Jennifer, to ensure she didn't find out about Stella.'

'That's just not true!' protests Alex, suddenly animated for the first time during our conversation. 'I'm sure Mr Dixit will confirm how heavily sedated I was at the time. I just told you exactly what I remembered. If I was confused back then, it's because of the meds. I'm still taking them now, of course, although the doses have been reduced.'

'I still find it surprising,' says Dave, 'that it was Jennifer's number you remembered, rather than Stella's.' I'm not sure why my colleague is going back over the same ground. It wasn't in the interview plan, but I let him run with it for the moment.

'As I said before, I call her a lot. More than I call my wife, that's for sure. Jen and I are very close, or rather we were. I suspect the first part of this interview has changed all that.'

'If you were as close as you say, don't you think it's likely that your wife would have found out? She appears to be an intelligent woman. I suspect it's entirely possible she knew about you and Jennifer.'

'No. I don't believe she did.' Alex looks complacently at Dave. 'It's fairly easy to hide these things, in my profession. Especially when one is working away from home during the week.'

'I appreciate that, but what about when you and your wife were together constantly, as was the case during your recent narrowboat holiday? Until the accident, of course.'

'That changed nothing,' Alex insisted. 'I was always very careful. There's no way my wife could have found out.'

'Did Jennifer call you while you were on holiday?'

'Yes – not very often, though.'

'And did you answer those calls?'

'Yes – but only when Stella wasn't around.'

'Do you think there is any chance Stella could have overheard you talking to Jennifer on the phone, and drawn her own conclusions?'

'Absolutely not!' Alex shouted. 'I never talked to her when there was the remotest possibility that Stella could have been within earshot!'

'So, there's no chance your wife found out and tried to take revenge? To settle the score by harming you?' Dave stands squarely in front of Alex and folds his arms.

Alex struggles upright in bed, a look of astonishment on his face. 'Am I to understand this is what you're driving at? You think my injury wasn't caused by accident. The two of you imagine Stella might in some way have engineered it?'

'Exactly.'

'No – that's not possible. Not in a million years. Stella is incapable of doing something like that. She loves me – or at least she did. I guess she feels differently now. Anyway – she's the kindest, most caring person in the world. Very family orientated. She would never do anything to hurt me or upset our children. No – it was definitely an accident. I shouldn't have had so much to drink. It was my fault.'

'So, you never for a moment suspected Stella might be responsible?'

'Not for an instant. How could she be? She wasn't even there when it happened! She was in the cabin, fast asleep.'

I can sense Dave's frustration as he steps closer to Alex's bed and looks down at the patient. He glances over at me and I shake my head, almost imperceptibly. There is no point in him sharing his theory. It would get us nowhere. I decide to try another tack.

'Alex. Answer me this. Did you fabricate a false accusation of stalking to punish your wife for harming you?'

'No, I did not! How can you even think that? How do you people come up with these ridiculous ideas?'

'Years of experience, Alex. I'm no longer surprised by what people are capable of doing to each other – and to themselves.'

'Furthermore,' I continue, 'did you invite your girlfriend to collude with you in creating this fabrication, in order to bolster the credibility of your story, with the ultimate aim of getting your wife arrested and remanded in custody?'

'Of course not! How could I have done that, when I was in a hospital bed, pumped full of drugs, and Jennifer did not even know Stella was my wife, as you discovered earlier? Look, this whole business on the boat was a total accident, I swear, and thanks to your investigation, my private life has been shattered. My marriage is undoubtedly over, as is my – relationship. And that's before we even get to my injury. I have physical and emotional scars from which I will never heal. I think I have suffered enough, don't you?'

'I would be tempted to agree, Alex, if it weren't for the fact that your story has got more holes in it than a string vest.'

Another faint smile from Dave.

'I'm not even going to waste my time picking it apart. Instead I'd like you to cast your mind back to an event you hosted, not long ago in Leeds. An event where your wife presented the prizes and your girlfriend was in attendance, along with hundreds of potential witnesses. Apparently, Jennifer even introduced herself to your wife after the awards ceremony, although I'm told you were elsewhere in the room at the time, so you might not have witnessed the encounter. Do you see where I'm going with this?'

Alex is silent.

'Alex, I'm sure I don't need to tell you that, if you are convicted for wasting police time with a false accusation of stalking, you could face a fine, or even a custodial sentence.'

'Look – Sergeant Burrows. Constable Langley. I can see my account doesn't quite stack up, but I assure you I didn't mean to waste your time or make any false accusations. I have been very confused, due to the trauma of my accident and the drugs I need to combat my excruciating pain. I'm sure Mr Dixit and his team will confirm that. Also, I was desperately trying to limit the damage to my personal life; without success, as you will have noticed. I just didn't want either Jennifer or Stella to get hurt. Neither of them deserves it. As for me – I admit I'm a cheat who has lied to the people he loves, but I'm not a criminal, I swear. In fact, I…'

At that moment the curtain is pushed aside, and we are interrupted by a young man dressed in a navy polo shirt and black trousers. He walks round to the side of the bed with the light and bouncy gait of a person for whom fitness is a way of life. I bet he doesn't have a secret stash of chocolate in his desk drawer.

'Hi Alex – it's time for your session!' he announces brightly. 'I'm Fraser Coutts, Alex's physiotherapist,' he explains, turning to me and Dave. 'I'm working with him on his rehabilitation.' He smiles openly at us, clearly unaware we are police officers. He is also oblivious to the tense atmosphere in the cubicle. 'You're welcome to wait here,' he offers, 'until we come back.'

'No that's fine – we're all done,' I reply, ignoring the look of incredulity on Dave's face. 'We'll leave you in peace. See you again soon, Alex.'

I walk away across the ward, with Dave trailing reluctantly in my wake. As I turn to step through the door I look back and catch sight of Alex, just visible through the gap in the curtains. He sits patiently on the side of his bed. His right foot is clad in a white surgical compression sock and he swings it idly back and forth like a child. Then the physiotherapist brings his zimmer frame and supports him as he stands upright. As he takes his first tentative step forward with his right leg, his weight resting heavily on the frame, the left leg of his pyjama bottoms flutters and flaps alongside, empty and useless.

Back in the car, I remain silent as Dave navigates his way through the busy lunchtime traffic, back towards HQ. My colleague makes no attempt at conversation; I'm sure that, like me, he needs time to reflect on what he has just heard and seen. Only when he pulls into a parking space which has conveniently just been vacated near the front door of the building does he finally ask the question.

'So, what now, Sarge?'

'I'm going to recommend we NFA it.'

'Are you serious? No further action on a possible attempted murder and a possible attempt by the victim to fit up the perpetrator?'

'You just said it, Dave – possible, in both cases. And how would we prove either of them? Let's start with the attempted murder. The supposed victim swears it was an accident. The supposed perpetrator wasn't even present when the incident took place. There were no other witnesses and there's no forensic evidence. And as for the fit-up, as you call it – there's ample evidence of the huge quantity of mind-altering drugs that have been administered to Alex over the last few days. OK, so his story is wildly inconsistent, but there is always going to be one plausible explanation. The meds. No jury would convict him, beyond reasonable doubt, of wasting police time, particularly given the horrific nature of his injuries. All we would be doing is wasting even more police time – and money. I know our instincts tell us otherwise, but I'm calling it. Come on – let's go and find DI Gillespie. I bet he agrees with me.'

Andrew Gillespie is obviously not happy with whatever is on his screen. As we approach his desk, he chomps savagely on a ballpoint pen and jabs his forefinger in the direction of the monitor.

'All out of wine gums, Andrew?' I enquire, nodding towards the mangled pen.

'Trying to quit the sodding things,' he growls. 'I've put on half a stone. Would you look at this, Dawn? I'm sending the person who wrote this statement straight back to school. It's about the cannabis factory we discovered recently, up on that industrial estate. Talk about hiding in plain sight. Anyway, notice how our esteemed author here spells the word "illicit". E-L-I-C-I-T. Even worse, he seems unable to distinguish "you're" from "your". I give up.'

'Tell him – or her – that's it's the difference between knowing your shit and knowing you're shit,' I quip. 'In the meantime, can we distract you for a minute?' I point towards the glass walls of the meeting room in the corner which, miraculously, appears to be vacant.

'I would like nothing better.' Andrew gets up from his desk and ambles towards the meeting room. Dave and I follow.

As soon as we are settled, I bring Andrew up to date with progress on the case, tell him about the interview with Alex and give him my recommendation of no further action. Then I hand over to Dave, to allow him the opportunity to share his reservations. Andrew listens patiently to both of us, without interrupting, then is silent for a moment or two, before giving us his verdict.

'Dave, I understand why you have a problem with Dawn's decision. You have a great policing instinct and you hate to see bad guys – or girls – get away with anything. But Dawn's right, in this case. NFA is the correct decision. We could never secure a conviction. We would just be wasting police time and money. You know what, though? From what you've told me about these people, they'll punish themselves perfectly well, without our help. Don't quote me on this, but I do believe in such a thing as karma.'

As Dave and I stand up to leave, Andrew calls me back. 'DS Burrows – a word, please.'

Dave shoots me a quizzical look as he leaves the room and I shrug my shoulders briefly in response.

'I just wanted to say, Dawn, that your confident NFA on that odd little case was the decision of an outstanding DI. Well done. What's more, a DI who should be setting her sights on promotion to DCI at the earliest opportunity, just like me.' Andrew smiles and lobs his broken ballpoint pen into the rubbish bin in the corner of the room. 'You know your shit, Dawn. Without the apostrophe. Now get out of here – and remember to book off on time, for a change. Have yourself an evening.'

When I return to my desk, Dave bustles over. 'Everything OK with DI Gillespie?'

'Fine. He's impressed with how we both handled the case, so well done. Now let's just write it up, agree the outstanding actions, then draw a line under it.'

'Sure. For the record, I do understand your decision to NFA, even though it hurts. I hope we get to work together again soon, Sarge. Even though things turned out the way they did, it has been a pleasure.'

'I hope so too, Dave, and who knows? We might even get a result next time.'

I'm just about to begin my final updates on the case when I reflect on my DI's advice and decide to do something else first. It takes me a minute or two to pluck up the courage, but eventually I convince myself I'm better off knowing than not knowing. I walk down the corridor to one of the small meeting rooms and pick up the desk phone in there. I'm worried that if I use my mobile, Alan might screen out my call if he sees it's me and doesn't want to talk. I'm sorry if I sound paranoid but, as I said before, I have a bad feeling about this.

When he answers the phone, Alan is as professional as ever. 'Superintendent Hamilton,' he says briskly.

'Alan. It's Dawn.'

'Have you finished with that case?'

'Just about to sign off on it. Andrew Gillespie agreed with my decision to NFA it. Do you still want to have that talk you mentioned?'

'Of course. Are you free tonight?'

'Yes, I am, as a matter of fact.'

'Excellent. Have you been to that new French restaurant which has just opened up in town? Le Perdrix, I think it's called.'

'No, but DS Gamage took his wife there the other week for her birthday dinner. Serious wallet ache, apparently. He moaned about it for most of the following day, although he did admit the food was superb.'

'I'm not worried about the price. I'll book us a table. We should be able to get one, seeing as it's mid-week. I'm going into a meeting now, so I'll text you the details. See you later.'

'OK. See you later, Alan.' As I put down the phone, I decide it surely can't be bad news, if he has suggested a fancy French restaurant as the venue. I'm annoyed with myself at how relieved I feel, and how much I care. So much for trying to keep a lid on my emotions.

To distract myself from these inconvenient thoughts, I return to my desk, log on to my PC and get stuck into the final case notes. As I type, I wonder to myself whether I will ever be tempted to go on a narrowboat holiday. It could be relaxing, I guess - in circumstances other than those I have just encountered.

I am just about to hit OK for the last time, and consign the case to the archives, when my mobile pings with an incoming SMS. I expect it's from Alan, like he promised. His text messages to me are always scrupulously professional, as befits a superintendent communicating with a more junior officer. There is never the slightest hint of our relationship. In fact, were you to read the messages he has sent to me so far, you might well think he doesn't even like me.

I pick up my mobile, click on the messages icon and stare at the screen in surprise. I can't believe what is written there:

'Le Perdrix is booked for 8. I'll pick you up from your house at 7.30. Can't wait to see you.'

The message concludes with two kisses.

TWO YEARS LATER

24 MUMMY DEAREST

A few of us were asked to give you an update – you know, on how we are all doing, two years later. They thought you might like to know how we have coped, since Daddy's accident. Not everyone took them up on their offer, and to be honest, I wasn't exactly keen to go over it all again. It was my counsellor, Rachel, who persuaded me in the end. She thinks writing it all down like this will help me finally 'achieve closure and move on'. Her words, not mine. Don't get me wrong; Rachel is lovely. I couldn't have managed without her, especially in the early days. I just can't bear all that psychobabble. It does my head in.

Anyway, eventually I gave in and said yes, so here I am – a different person from the girl I was two years ago. You might not realise it at first, if you saw me, as I look more or less the same, although I have a few more tattoos now. My favourite is on the inside of my left wrist. It's nothing fancy – just a simple, interlocking symbol which means 'survivor'. I look at it every time I feel I can't cope, and it reminds me I can. Somehow, I survived what happened, and so did everyone else. We're all still here, although some people are doing better than others.

I admit I did really struggle for a while, just after it happened, which is why Rachel was brought in to help me. With her counselling, and a lot of support from my best mate, Sam, and her family, I started to turn things around. Eventually I began studying again, and even did OK in my A levels. Not brilliantly, but well enough to get a place on a fantastic textile design course at Manchester School of Art, where I'm now one of the top students in my year. I don't mean to sound boastful, but I'm proud of what I have achieved at college.

Sam is at Uni in Sheffield and we see each other lots at the weekends. We're always hopping on the train from one city to another; lucky they are so close. We go clubbing and shopping, as you would expect, but sometimes we get off the train right in the middle of the line and go rock climbing in the Peak District. At night we stay over in a bunkhouse and drink beer with the other climbers. It freaks Daddy out a bit, to be honest. He's dead scared I'll fall and hurt myself when I'm climbing, which is understandable, I guess, given what happened to him. Mostly, though, he keeps his fears to himself and lets me live my life. He's cool – or at least he tries to be. I've even trained him to stop calling me Minnie. I'm not Minnie any more. I don't even like being called Immo. I've ditched all those tragic pet names; these days I just use Imogen. My real name. The one Mummy and Daddy chose for me.

I think that's quite enough about me. I guess you want to know how Mummy is doing. After all, she was the one who was hurt the most by all of this. It was bad enough for her that Daddy had that awful accident on the narrowboat. I still think she blames herself a bit, even though she was in bed asleep when it happened. Then, if that wasn't enough for her to cope with, Daddy said afterwards he couldn't come home, and he wanted a divorce. That was harsh. I always thought my parents were happy together, but I guess an accident like that changes a person and anyway, you never know what is going on in someone else's ship. Sorry, relationship. I'm trying to keep teen slang out of this, as Rachel said you probably wouldn't understand it and anyway, I'm getting too old for it now.

The whole thing was made even worse for Mummy, as Daddy 'moved on', as Rachel would say, quite quickly afterwards. He hooked up with his new partner, Jen, just a few months after his accident. I honestly expected Mummy to fall apart completely, as she had never seemed a particularly strong person to me. When I was growing up, she always allowed Daddy to dominate her and make all the decisions, plus she would get lashed on wine whenever she had a bad day. But I have to say, she really surprised me. She turned out to be so much stronger than I thought she was. All through the divorce proceedings and the sale of the house, she stayed on top of things, then she downsized to a little cottage not far from where we used to live. She even started her own business, which she had been talking about for years, but had never actually done anything about it, even though I was always nagging her to get back out there. She's really very intelligent and she was kicking her heels at home, especially as we got older.

Mummy's new business is a digital advisory service. She helps people, mostly older people, I have to say, who are scared of technology, to become tech savvy and engage with the digital world. There is no shortage of customers – I mean, Surrey is full of people who grew up using quill pens, or whatever. It's never going to make her a fortune, but it gives her something to do and I think she enjoys it. Some of her clients have gone on to be quite active on social media, and a few have set up their own websites and even self-published books, created blogs and podcasts, that kind of thing. It's lit, sorry cool, what they have done, and I'm proud of Mummy for helping them.

I think there might even be a man in her life. She has mentioned a guy she sees now and then, but I don't know if it's going anywhere. I believe he's called Chris. The funny thing is, she told me he has a narrowboat. You would think she would want to keep well away from those things, given everything that happened. I don't know whether she has been on it, but even so. It's different with Daddy and Jen; they are not really into staycations. They prefer exotic beach holidays in places like Tahiti and The Maldives.

That's nearly all I've got to say about Mummy. On the surface, she seems OK, but I sometimes catch her looking really sad. She doesn't think I notice, but I do. Also, I check the recycling bin when I visit, and there are always lots of empty wine bottles in there. It does worry me, as most of the time I'm not around to check up on her, what with being away at college and everything.

It was different when I was growing up. Mummy and I lived in each other's pockets. A lot of my friends didn't get on with their mothers, but mine was more like an older sister than a mother. She gave me lots of advice, then picked up the pieces when I didn't take it. I'll always remember her holding back my hair as I puked up in the loo after drinking too much on a night out. Sure, we had lots of rows, but I always knew she had my back, and she never told Daddy what I had been up to. Back then, Daddy still thought I was his perfect little girl and it was Mummy who really knew me. She loved me in spite of all my flaws and mistakes, and I loved her back – so much.

We went through a really rocky patch when I found out she had told my biggest ever secret. The one only she knew about and had promised she would never reveal to anyone. At first, I thought I would never be able to feel the same way about her or trust her again; not after what she told him. But Rachel did a lot of work with us both, until gradually we put the whole painful incident behind us. It wasn't easy, though. I guess we've all been through a lot of pain, since that narrowboat holiday.

Which brings me on to Daddy. As I think you know, I didn't find out about his accident until a few days after it happened. Mummy and Daddy both said they couldn't face telling me and Hugo at first, and we both understood that. I felt bad, though, as I had told Sam how nice it was that they hadn't called for a while. How I was enjoying a break from them. Anyway, when they did tell me, and I first visited Daddy in hospital, after he had been moved out of intensive care into a private room, he cried a lot. So did I, obviously. At first, I thought his tears were all down to the accident, but eventually, after a few visits, he said something else was upsetting him as well. That was when he told me he knew about my abortion. I figured he could only have found out about it one way, but I needed to know for sure. So, I asked him if Mummy had told him, and he said she did.

After that, we had a few difficult conversations, it has to be said. There was lots of shouting and tears from both of us. Good job he had a private room. Daddy was deeply hurt that I didn't confide in him when I got pregnant, but he was even more angry with Mummy for keeping it from him. I guess it was one of the reasons for his decision to ask for a divorce, but I'm sure there was a lot more to it than that. I have just accepted the fact that I will never know the whole truth about why they split. Whatever; the surprising and really positive outcome from all of this was that Daddy and I got to know each other a whole lot better and became really close. I would never have built such a strong relationship with him if he had continued to imagine I was his perfect little girl. He had to see me as a flawed person, who has problems and makes mistakes, in order to get to know me properly. The same was true for me, as well. I had to discover my real Daddy, and I'm glad I did.

So now the two of us talk about everything – his life with Jen, my counselling sessions with Rachel and his rehabilitation. Of course, we also discuss less heavy stuff, like my studies, my friends, films and music. He has seen all my tattoos and, while he doesn't exactly love them, he accepts it's my body and my decision.

We also talk about Hugo, my brother who, by the way, was one of the people who turned down the offer to write about his experience. I had suspected for years he was gay, and he says he tried to confide in me a few times, but always changed his mind at the last minute, as he thought I was too young to understand. How lame is that? Eventually, as you know, he came out to Mummy during the narrowboat holiday and asked her to tell Daddy, which she did. Like me, my brother wasn't that close to Daddy back then, so he thought it would be best coming from her.

Of course, Hugo's news was a bit of a shock to Daddy, but he's totally cool with it. Like me, Hugo now gets on better with Daddy, because he doesn't have to tell lies any more, or hide who he really is. It helps that Daddy and Jen really like Rob, his boyfriend. He and Hugo are both in their final year at Uni, up in Scotland, and have been together since around the time of the accident. Rob is American and he's lush, I have to say. Hugo has done well for himself. Also, Rob's parents run a boutique hotel in upstate New York, and we have all been to stay there at least once. That's what I call a result.

Coming back to Daddy, I think the accident has actually been good for him in a way, however mad that may sound. For a start, he resigned from that firm, which basically owned his life. He is freelance now and, with his track record, he can pick and choose his contracts. He still earns shedloads of money, but he gets to decide when and where he works – and with whom. He and Jen don't work together any more. She left the firm at around the same time as he did and landed herself a great job in Manchester. So, Daddy makes sure he works mostly in the North West, so he can get home most nights. He doesn't want to be away too much, especially not with the baby on the way. Their house in Wilmslow is lovely, with plenty of space for me to stay over, whenever I want to escape from the city, and for Hugo and Rob, too, when they're down from Scotland.

Daddy also does more exercise, since his accident. From the start, he was determined his disability was not going to hold him back. He has always been a gym bunny, but now he's a runner as well. He has done loads of 10Ks and quite a few half marathons and has raised lots of money for charity. Like me, he enjoys being in the mountains, these days, so we are doing the Three Peaks Challenge together this year. I'm so proud of him.

So I'm just about done. In many ways, life is good; maybe even better than before, weirdly. That's not to say I don't have good days and bad days. There are still days when I can't get out of bed, wash, eat, study, or take care of myself in any way, but these are isolated days now, rather than whole weeks. I still pre-load with vodka before going clubbing but give me a break. I am a student, after all. The one thing I'm not interested in right now is a relationship, but who knows? Maybe I'll change my mind about that as well, one day. There's always hope. As Rachel says, 'once you choose hope, anything is possible'.

Talking of Rachel, she was right, annoyingly. It has been really helpful to write all this down. I must remember to thank her.

25 BACK IN THE LOW LIFE

Hello again. As you might have gathered, they talked me into giving you a heads up. I said you could find most of it out by Googling me, but they were having none of it. Also, Stella didn't want to play ball. She wants to put the whole thing behind her, poor cow. Not surprising, really, but I feel I owe it to her, to make sure her story gets told properly. It's the least I can do, after everything she has done for me.

Before I fast forward to the present, like they want me to, I'm going to take you back to the day after those two rozzers took Stella into custody. One of the cops who arrested her, DC Langley – although I call him Dave, now – showed up at the marina that afternoon and tracked me down on Dan's boat, where the two of us were having a cheeky beer and a jam session.

Rozzer Dave explained that the stalking charge had been dropped and Stella had been released from custody. Honestly, he could have given me the news over the phone, instead of coming all the way out to Allenby, and I told him so. He made some lame excuse about witness support, but I wasn't fooled and anyway, I already knew what was going on. Stella had come by a few hours earlier, to pick up her car and say goodbye, thanks for hiring the lawyer for me, that kind of thing. I tried to stop her from driving home, as I didn't think she was in any fit state. She was really tearful and shaky, but she insisted she was OK, and off she went. She wanted out of Allenby Marina as quickly as possible.

Rozzer Dave, on the other hand, was quite happy to hang about, and I signed a couple of CDs he had brought with him. For his wife and kids, he said. I reckon was what he came for, really. He asked me to let him know if I was doing any local gigs, but I told him not to hold his breath, as I was done performing. I was wrong about that, though, as it turned out.

Two years on, whenever I announce a forthcoming gig on Twitter, Rozzer Dave is one of the first to retweet. He's always liking and sharing my Instagram and Facebook posts and he's often in the audience at my local gigs, along with his wife. Back in the day, if you have told me I would have a cop as a superfan, I would never have believed you. Funny how things turn out. Now and then he DM's me with random crap he thinks might interest me. For instance, when that other rozzer who arrested Stella, the one I called Croydon Facelift, but whose name is apparently Dawn, got married. Like I care. The only interesting part of his long message was the news that her husband moved to another force so as not to mess up *her* career. Makes a change, I suppose.

As you will have gathered by now, I eventually took Stella's advice and resumed my music career. It took a lot of persuading, I should say - mostly from Dan, but also from other musicians around here. Anyway, I finally gave in and put into practice some of the recommendations from that bloody business plan of hers. I put my own spin on it, of course. If I was going to come back, after everything that happened with The Gatekeeper, it was going to be on my terms. So I bought a beaten up old widebeam – like a narrowboat, but twice the width – and had it converted into a studio, customised to my exact requirements and fitted out with all the latest digital technology. It's moored here at Allenby and it's where I create and distribute music, the way I want to. No record company required.

Dan plays on nearly all the tracks I lay down and has also co-written some of the new songs. My old buddy Dave – Drummer Dave, not to be confused with Rozzer Dave – often comes up from London to join in, and we have teamed up with a whole raft of local musicians, as well. It's amazing the number of talented players and performers there are around here. Some of them are neighbours, moored up near us here in the marina. There's a 90's pop star who's chilling, gigging at local venues and still earning royalties from his old hits. He plays saxophone on some of our tracks. It's like the canals are a magnet for all sorts of artists, even more so than when I was a kid.

I have also finally got to grips with social media. It's fine now I have control over what I put out there. These days I have my own Twitter and Instagram accounts, a Facebook page, the lot. Dan and I have even set up our own You Tube channel. The number of views and followers we have is never going to keep Taylor Swift up at night, but it's respectable and growing steadily, according to Dan, who likes to monitor and analyse these things. He says the people who follow us, download our music and view our videos aren't just from our 'core demographic', as the record company tossers would put it. We're acquiring new fans, all the time. People who never knew we existed before, or never cared, even if they did know. It's brilliant.

It's not all rosy, though, in the crazy world of social media. It definitely has its downside, for me. I constantly get trolled, as you can imagine. You wouldn't believe the abuse I get – or maybe you would. The death threats. The sick people out there who wish me harm and tell me in graphic detail how they would like to inflict it. And that's before you even start on the rumours. Apparently, I've been in rehab several times, nearly died from a drugs overdose on more than one occasion and had every eating disorder and STD known to man, along with a sex change. I just try to ignore it. It helps that I have a thick skin, and the positive vibes I get from people far exceed the amount of crap that comes my way. It seems there's a lot of love out there, for me and my music, so I try to focus on that, and forget the trolls. They're just a sad bunch of muppets with nothing better to do.

But enough about me. It's Stella you really want to know about, isn't it? Well, I'm pleased to report that we're still in touch. Mostly by phone or email, although we do sometimes get together when I go to London. She never comes to see me in Allenby, for obvious reasons. Like me, she has started her own business, which she runs from home. These days she lives in a small cottage, not far from the house she used to share with Alex and the kids.

That was a strange business. Her and Alex. Turns out he had a nasty accident, while Stella was crashed out. Horrific actually. Fell off the back counter of the narrowboat and lost half his leg on the prop – and half his blood. He was hammered, obviously. The emergency services found him long before I showed up, thanks to a young cyclist who knew the right app to use. She probably saved his life. Of course, he was barely conscious and was rushed straight into emergency surgery, which lasted for many hours, which was why the hospital reception had no record of his admittance, when Stella called up. No one even knew his name at that point and there wasn't any time to worry about paperwork; they were all too busy trying to keep him alive.

So, Stella was wrong; Alex hadn't deserted her. But she was right about the other woman, and you know what? The bastard did end up jumping ship, as it were, and he and this woman are still together. And if that wasn't bad enough, he made out to the kids that the two of them only hooked up a couple of months after the accident, so the kids wouldn't know he had been cheating. And Stella went along with it. Why? What age are these kids – five years old? They're students, for Christ's sake. I can understand why Alex didn't want them to know the gory details, but Stella? I have no idea why she would want to protect him, after what he did to her, but she won't explain it to me and I don't think it did her much good, in the end. I get the impression she sees a lot less of her children than she used to, before the accident.

It doesn't help that she's the only one of her family who still lives in Surrey. Her daughter is at art school in Manchester, not far from where her dad lives with his new squeeze, and her son is at university in Scotland. She tells me she has a whole bunch of friends in the area, back from when she and Alex were together, but I get the impression they are mainly dinner party friends, you know what I mean? Shallow. Not the kind of people you can have a real conversation with. Also, get this; some of them have apparently ghosted her, as they don't like to invite a single woman to their poxy parties. Why not? In case she nabs one of their middle-aged, paunchy stud-muffins? It's pathetic. There's one woman – Madeleine, I think her name is – who seems like a genuine friend, but I get the feeling Stella is lonely sometimes. When we talk on the phone, she's often quiet and subdued, although she always seems pleased to hear from me. At the end of the day, though, we're never going to be close friends. We're too different, and we don't have enough in common, but in spite of that, it does feel like we went through something together, so we have a bond, or whatever tragic name you want to give it. I'll always look out for Stella.

And we do have a laugh, now and then, it has to be said. For instance, once my download sales and YouTube views started to ramp up, they inevitably caught The Gatekeeper's attention, and I heard on the grapevine that the CEO of the record company gave him an absolute bollocking, for letting me go. Anyway, to cut a long story short, he found out where I was and came up to Allenby, trying to get me to re-sign. He must have been really keen; it takes a lot to drag his sorry arse outside the M25. As you can imagine, I took great pleasure in telling him where to stick it, and I told the whole story to Stella, the next time we spoke. The only thing is, I used his real name by mistake, when I was talking to her. I won't reveal it here. And it turns out Stella used to go out with the snake, back before she started dating Alex. Small world. Typically for The Gatekeeper, he dumped her the minute a sexy backing singer glanced in his direction. That was back when he had a bit more to offer a girl, looks-wise, than he does now. Not surprisingly, Stella loved the story of how I rejected his – strictly professional – advances. She was pleased to see him get back some of the crap he normally dishes out. She's one of those people who believe in karma, is our Stella. If I'm honest, so am I.

So, to sum it all up, I get the feeling life isn't much fun for Stella, these days, and I hope it gets better. In my opinion, she has been through a lot, and she deserves a break. At the moment, her business is almost all she has, and she needs a bit more play in her life, to balance out the work.

I'm glad to say my life isn't all work. As you know, I ditched my London existence to explore the canals, where I grew up, and I haven't abandoned my plans. OK, so I'm based at Allenby Marina, these days, but Dan and I take a nice long trip on Warrior whenever we can. We did the Leicester Ring this year. No smutty jokes from you. It's got nearly a hundred locks and loads of beautiful countryside, with a few gritty urban vistas thrown in. Most importantly, there are plenty of decent pubs, although some of the ones I remember from my childhood have closed down, which is sad.

When we go off on one of our adventures, we leave Dan's boat behind. It's a bit shabby and the engine is unreliable. Sometimes it lives up to its name – Slowing Downe, remember? – and on other occasions it's more like Breaking Downe. So we take Warrior. Dan doesn't mind; he's the first one to admit he has got used to the creature comforts on board my boat. Even so, we plan to hang on to both boats, as we like our own space. Particularly me. I need time to myself, or I'd go mental, and my music would suffer.

I guess you will have gathered from all of this that Dan and I are more than just fellow musicians and business partners, but don't get too excited. Don't buy a bloody hat. We both like to keep things nice and casual, and I can't see that changing any time soon.

As far as gigs go, we also like to keep things low key. We only play small, intimate venues, even though we could fill much larger places. We just prefer it that way. The same cannot be said for my ex, Johnno. He and his band eventually landed their dream record deal and, as you probably know, they're doing very well for themselves. They triumphed at Glastonbury last year and they have just finished a sell-out European tour. I'm chuffed for them. It's great to see a genuinely talented band break through. I speak to Johnno sometimes; mainly to tease him about his new heartthrob status, which embarrasses him a bit, although he always comes straight back at me, calling me a 'crusty old boater'. Even though I dumped him out of the blue, there are no hard feelings, I'm pleased to say. It helps that he's currently dating a Victoria's Secret model.

In a way, I guess Johnno's right. Despite the fancy shower cubicle on board Warrior, I can't remember when I last washed my hair. As I write this, I'm cosied up to the wood burning stove, wearing one of Dan's moth-eaten jumpers and a pair of jeans which are ripped at the knees. From wear and tear, not as a fashion statement. Perhaps Johnno is right, and I am an old boater at heart, but I've learned over the last two years that I don't have to choose between career and canal. In a way, I've got Stella to thank for giving me a shove in the right direction. I'll remind her of that, next time we speak.

One last thing. I know I said a few times that I'd tell you about my brother, but I forgot. OK, I know I should put this right, but you'll have to give me a break; I'm not up to it at this precise moment. Another time, maybe. For now, I'm done gazing in the rear view mirror. The only way I'm going is forward.

26 ALL'S WELL

Received wisdom apparently dictates that there is always one person in a marriage who loves more, and it was true, in my case. It was definitely me. I knew it and was comfortable with it, and my wife knew too. Needless to say, it suited her just fine.

I remember the night when I first met her, at the firm's welcome party. It was lust at first sight. As Stella shook my hand and introduced herself as my work buddy, I thought how stunning she was, and how unaware of it she seemed. Usually I find that beautiful women, when you first meet them, generally pause for an instant and watch for your reaction, but not Stella. She was straight down to business, telling me all about her early days with the firm, sharing advice and introducing me to our colleagues.

By the end of the evening, I was smitten. No – scrub that. Horrible, soppy, women's magazine word. You'll have to excuse me; I'm not used to writing this sort of thing. Business reports and presentations are what I usually write, and I keep those as concise as possible. I'm out of my comfort zone here and I'm struggling to find the right tone. The word I'm looking for is 'obsessed'. Stella ticked all my boxes. She was highly intelligent – and intellectual, which I definitely wasn't. She had a sparkling sense of humour and was obviously liked and respected by all her colleagues. I can't begin to describe how dazzling I found her. I decided then and there that I had to have her, but clearly it would be bad form to come on to her at the welcome party and anyway, I knew what the response would be. She hadn't flirted with me once; unlike most of her female colleagues, and one or two of the men. I wasn't used to being ignored like that. My looks usually provoked a reaction, and I had worked hard on the charm thing, during my university years, but Stella was immune to both. I believe she thought she was out of my league.

So, in summary, I realised I had a lot of work to do, but I relished it. I have always loved a challenge and I was confident that, in the end, I would get what I wanted. I just needed to be smart and play a relatively long game.

I soon found out the challenge was greater than I had thought. I asked around discreetly and discovered that Stella was taken. No big surprise there, with a girl like that, but the problem was her boyfriend. Apparently, he was a big shot record company guy, who could offer her access to a world which was closed to me. I Googled him and found out he was the real deal, unfortunately. According to his profile on Wikipedia, he had discovered and nurtured a whole raft of fledgling bands and developed them into highly successful international artists. You would definitely have heard of most of them, and probably bought some of their music. Sometimes, when Stella and I met or spoke on a Monday, as part of her work with me as my buddy, she would casually mention a gig she had been to that weekend, or a famous musician she had met. She didn't do it boastfully; just in passing. She had obviously got used to that world, and the people in it, so meeting household names was no big deal to her, which made things even worse for me. My looks and my lines, which usually enabled me to seal the deal with a girl very quickly, were useless in this situation. My rival – I love that word – was not particularly handsome, compared with me, but evidently that didn't matter to Stella. So, I did something I don't normally bother with, and made friends with a girl first. I became Stella's loyal and patient friend.

As Stella was my buddy, I always had a legitimate reason to contact her in those early days, and I made the most of it, frequently asking for advice and meeting her for drinks after work as often as I could, without making her suspicious or looking desperate. My first obstacle appeared at the end of the official three-month buddying period. I had been assigned to a project in Reading, whilst she remained on a client site in London. Without another reason to keep in touch, there was a danger she would have drifted away from me, so I asked her to be my mentor, to keep the connection going. She was flattered, and happy to accept.

After that, I worked hard to find lots of reasons to come into London after I had finished work with my client. Internal projects, helping a colleague with a sales proposal, that kind of thing. When I was in town, I always tried to take Stella out. I started to suggest dinner, rather than drinks, to give me more time with her. Ever the perfect gentleman, I always insisted on picking up the bill. My bank account, which was a sorry thing in those days, as you would expect from a recent graduate, took a big hit, but I didn't care. Gradually, almost without Stella noticing, we were becoming good friends, as well as colleagues, so it was worth it. During dinner, I often made her laugh with tales of my large and colourful Polish family. As the only child of a single mother, she didn't have much of a family life when she was growing up, so she enjoyed experiencing it second hand through mine. To be honest, I haven't been close to my family since I left home. I had outgrown them by then and some of them were just embarrassing, frankly; but I didn't tell Stella that. They came in very useful, back then, helping me to build up trust and present myself as a warm, caring guy.

As we got to know each other better, Stella told me a few things about her boyfriend. Reading between the lines, I got the impression he had been a real player, in the past. It's not surprising, really, given his line of work. There must have been plenty of temptation - and opportunity. I would definitely have taken advantage, had I been in his shoes. However, Stella obviously thought she was the one who was going to change him. Why do women always think that? It just makes me laugh. I knew she was wrong, and I waited patiently for the inevitable to happen. When it did, and the guy ditched her for some backing singer, I was there to pick up the pieces, as befits her faithful and supportive friend. After that, it was only a matter of time.

Even once I finally got what I had worked so hard to achieve, I still made all the running. That was the unspoken agreement between us. The balance of power was definitely tipped in Stella's favour. I had asked, she had graciously accepted, and I should be grateful and keep grafting away to make her happy. I didn't mind, though; she was worth the effort, in every respect, and besides, her feelings for me had grown. I could sense it. She didn't see me as a clean-cut graduate trainee any longer. I had made sure of that; both in the bedroom and out of it.

But I still had to initiate everything. Once we both got promoted – her once and me twice, in quick succession – money became less of a problem. I knew how much she wanted to travel, so I booked a series of holidays for us. I started off with relatively modest mini breaks in Europe, then progressed to long haul, increasingly exotic destinations. California and Tanzania are two that spring to mind. We were beginning to live the dream. Admittedly, the dreamscape was all created by me, but Stella was having a good time. I could tell. Most importantly, so was I.

Anyway, life was good but, even so, the thought that I could lose Stella was always at the back of my mind, pecking away. I had never felt insecure about a woman before, and this new sensation was not something I wanted to live with. I was used to feeling comfortable and complacent when it came to women, and to making a quick exit whenever it suited me, without a backward glance, when a more appealing prospect showed up. The one exception was my schoolboy romance – I hate that word – with a girl called Dosia, who dumped me for some dork. I was pretty cut up about it at the time, but I bounced back soon enough. I was eighteen, for God's sake. The lasting impact of that relationship is that her family introduced me to narrowboats, setting in train an unfortunate series of events.

Sorry, I'm getting ahead of myself. Back to my paranoia about the prospect of losing Stella. As time went on, my fears grew. As a consultant, you meet a lot of new people, and I was tormented by the thought that, one day, she would encounter the person who would take her away from me. If anything, I was more obsessed with her than when we first met, so I made plans to keep her with me forever. I proposed to her on a beach in Mexico, just as the sun was setting, like you are meant to do. I went down on one knee, produced a hugely expensive diamond engagement ring and she said yes, as she had to all my other suggestions.

As soon as we were married, my fears subsided and my confidence grew, which had a very positive impact on my career. I became a lot more forceful, which the partners and client sponsors liked, and I really started to get some results. My latest promotion came with a sales target and I smashed it, every quarter. A couple of the partners quickly noticed, took me aside and told me I should set my sights on joining their ranks. Getting to partner in the firm is a tall order, but they offered to become my mentors and help me succeed. You can have as many mentors as you like, and Stella was still technically one of them, but in reality, she was no longer in a position to provide me with advice. Professionally speaking, I had outgrown her.

As I grew more secure, both professionally and financially, I began to think about the next step, to bind Stella to me even more closely. Even though, as I said earlier, I'm not too bothered about my family, I admit my heritage probably played a part here. For my Polish relatives, marriage inevitably meant children, and I felt the same way. So I told Stella I wanted to start a family.

For the first time in the history of our relationship, I met with some resistance. Stella was reluctant to have children at that point, as she was worried about the impact on her career. Back then, she was gunning for the promotion I had already got, but I reassured her that she could pick up where she left off, when she came back from maternity leave. I reminded her about some of our most senior female colleagues, who successfully balanced children and consultancy, although I neglected to mention their full-time nannies or house husbands. I promised Stella she would have my full support in resuming her career and that it wouldn't be a problem. Eventually, I got my way.

After we had children, everything changed. Or rather, Stella changed. From the start, she focused totally on them. She did return to work for a while, after my son Hugo was born, but her heart wasn't in it, and she never went for that promotion. Then, after my daughter Imogen came along, she jacked it in completely. After that, her life revolved around play dates, after school clubs, that kind of thing. Don't get me wrong; I know that lifestyle works for a lot of women, but I was astonished it was enough for Stella; the dazzling career woman with whom I fell in love. Suddenly, it was like I was married to a different person.

By this time, I was working away from home quite a bit, so I often didn't see much of my family during the week. I missed my children, but I never had any concerns about their welfare, as Stella was such a good mother. Too good, in some ways. She built a strong bond with Hugo, and particularly with Imogen, which would have been fine, except that, in the process, she started to push me out. I'm not sure if she meant to, but she did. When I came home at the weekend, I was not welcomed with any enthusiasm. Gradually, I began to feel like an outsider in my own home.

Don't misunderstand me; we did have lots of fun times together, as a family. We enjoyed some memorable holidays – camping in France when the children were little, then surfing in Cornwall, as they got older. If I scroll back through my photos, I see countless images of happy faces at Christmas times. I see my children posing proudly beside elaborate, themed birthday cakes made by Stella. My iCloud is full of videos of them wobbling precariously on their first bikes and thrashing through the water doing doggy paddle, their orange armbands bouncing up and down on their flailing arms. There is Hugo, playing a sheep in the school nativity play, and there is Imogen, making a din on her violin.

So there were happy times, mainly during the holidays and on special occasions. However, as I grew more successful and spent even more time away, I increasingly felt as though my main role was to finance my family's lifestyle, rather than play an active part in it. Being realistic, I suppose it was inevitable that, with me away so much, Stella would be the centre of my children's world. I just feel she could have done so much more to keep me in their thoughts while I was away, but she didn't. She would always cut my FaceTime sessions short, saying the children were tired, or needed to finish their homework before bed; she always found an excuse to hang up on me. What's more, she never called me unless she had a practical query or needed something. As usual, it was me who had to initiate most of our contact. At the start of our relationship – back when we were just friends, in fact – I used to send her friendly, mildly flirtatious little texts, but by now that habit was long gone. I didn't bother any more; I just stuck to the practical stuff, like she did. Don't take that to mean I had fallen out of love with her, if that's how you want to put it. I still loved my wife, even though I didn't always like her very much. She remained beautiful, if less confident than she used to be, and intellectually she was still in a different league, not that it ever bothered me. I have more relevant skills.

As the years went on, though, I became increasingly resentful of Stella. My children were growing up fast, but I didn't have the kind of bond with them I wanted, and I blamed her for that. It was a different story for her; she and Imogen were more like two sisters than mother and daughter, and she and Hugo had a whole raft of private jokes, from which I was excluded. There were compensations, though. By now I had made partner at the firm, and my reputation in the business community had grown. I frequently accepted invitations to speak at conferences, many of which were overseas. At these events, most of the delegates are unlikely to see each other again, and everyone is in an unfamiliar location, cut loose from their home life, with plenty of alcohol doing the rounds. Inevitably, I was approached by women, and sometimes I took them up on their offers. To be fair, on some occasions, it was me who made the first move. These encounters meant nothing to me. They were merely a quick sugar hit; an ego boost which had zero impact on my marriage. I felt no guilt. Despite my Catholic upbringing, I don't do guilt. As emotions go, it's a waste of time.

When Jen joined my project in Leeds, I realised I wanted more from her than I had from these other women, although ego still came into it. From the start, it was clear she adored me. Far more than I did her, despite her beauty, youth and street-smart intelligence. It was the reverse of my early days with Stella. This time, I was the one with the power, and it felt good. At my instigation, Jen dumped her partner of three years, even though she knew I was married, and I had not promised to leave my wife. In fact, I had no plans to split up with Stella. My extraordinary career success – I was one of the youngest ever partners in the firm – had made me feel like a master of the universe. I thought I deserved it all: a brilliant career, luxurious home, beautiful family and a gorgeous mistress. Curious word, that – mistress. Jen was not my mistress; no one was. Now, I was in control.

Before long, though, there was a subtle power shift. Just a slight one. My feelings for Jen grew stronger, and she picked up on this very quickly. She's an expert in reading people, which is what made her such an excellent comms manager. Anyway, she pushed home her advantage, ramping up her demands. It was only to be expected; a girl like that will never be content with a supporting role. She thinks she deserves to take centre stage. So, to try and contain her, I began to make promises. I said we would get together properly, once Imogen went to university; that we would start a new life. I insisted Stella and I were together in name only and our marriage was effectively over. I told her all the usual things men tell their lovers when they want things to stay the same. We tell them everything is going to change – just not right now. Free beer tomorrow. That's how it works.

And so it went on, for quite some time. Stella didn't suspect a thing, I'm sure of it. I was very careful to ensure she never found out and, to her credit, Jen never tried to force the issue by letting something slip. By then she knew me well enough to realise such a tactic would backfire spectacularly. Despite all my precautions, though, Stella eventually discovered something which made her suspicious; I've no idea what it was. It was just before our narrowboat holiday that she first revealed her suspicions to me, although she stopped short of challenging me outright, so I concluded that she did not have any real evidence, and didn't worry about it any further. I told myself that suspecting is not the same as knowing and reminded myself to be even more careful in future.

To this day, I have no idea how Stella found out about Jen for sure, but I know she did. She must have done, or she would never have done such a cold, callous thing. There's a lot I don't understand about what she did, to be honest. For a start, how did she come up with the idea? She knows nothing about boating; I doubt she even realises a narrowboat has a propeller. Also, I can't figure out how she managed to get me so drunk. Let me tell you; I can take my drink. On occasion I used Polish vodka as a tool to get Stella to do what I wanted, and she always got way drunker than me, much more quickly. How could the situation have been reversed, this time? On wine and Pimms? Bloody Pimms, for Christ's sake? OK, I know she mixed them strong, but normally I can drink that stuff all day long and remain in control. It just doesn't stack up.

I was drunk, though. Absolutely steaming but, even so, Stella obviously did not want to leave anything to chance. Before she went off for her exonerating sleep, she delivered a devastating one-two punch, just to remind me how excluded I was from the lives of my children. Left lead – Hugo is gay. Clearly, she thought I would be heartbroken by this news, but I wasn't. I would just have preferred not to find out in a way that was designed to cause me distress. So that first blow was not enough to finish me, but Stella followed it up with a killer right cross – Imogen's abortion. My darling girl, my Minnie – what she must have been through. The terror, the pain, the agonising decision she had to make. And Stella kept it all from me; she shut me out. I can understand why my daughter was afraid to tell me, but my wife? How could she exclude me from this crisis in my daughter's life, then use Minnie's pain as a weapon against me? As Stella turned her back on me, walked down the steps into the cabin, and vanished from my sight forever through the blur of my tears, I understood for the first time her total contempt for me. I was crying for my children, of course, but for something else too; the absolute death of love. The love which only I had felt and which was passively unrequited, over so many years.

That's the last time I remember being at the tiller. The next thing I recall is hitting the water, seemingly in slow motion, as the blue sky, with its stately clouds, revolved lazily above my head. Then the water in the canal thrashed dirty brown and bright red. It's astounding how fast cold water, searing pain and the fear of imminent death sober you up. In a flash of clarity, I realised what had happened and focused all my energy on saving myself. Later, as I lay on the towpath, I resolved to take revenge, if I survived. An idea came to me, through my haze of anger and pain, and I held onto it, as an angel on a bicycle came to save me. Soon after, the ambulance crew took me away, and then everything went black. It wasn't until much later, after I had come round from the operation and been transferred from the recovery room to the ICU, that I retrieved the idea, and decided to act on it.

My top priority was to make sure I did not further damage my children's lives, especially given what they had already been through, and would have to endure in future. For me, it was essential that they never find out what their mother did, nor how their father responded. Within these constraints, I was determined to make Stella suffer as much as I could and, most importantly, let her know I understood what she had done. If I were successful, I would be able to exert control over her, to an extent that I had never achieved during our marriage. Even if I never saw her again, I would pull the strings from afar, and help her to punish herself.

To make all this happen, I needed an accomplice, as I could obviously do very little in practice, from a hospital bed and through a morphine haze. I hoped Jen would respond as I expected. In a way, I welcomed the opportunity to test her devotion, as I resolved never to let a woman get the better of me again. First, however, I needed to find a way to contact her. Fortunately, fate intervened, just as I was failing to think the problem through and fighting the urge to fall asleep. One of the duty nurses pushed aside the curtain that shielded my bed from the rest of the ICU and handed me my phone. Remarkably, it had remained in my back pocket, where I always keep it. She asked me if I wanted my clothes returned to me, but I declined. I was sure Jen would get me some new ones.

The nurse said the phone was unlikely to work, but she thought I might want it, just in case. She tactfully refrained from saying it probably drowned in the canal, like I so nearly did. She was wrong, though. You should know that I upgrade my phone every time a new model is launched onto the market, as it doesn't do for someone in my position to be seen using out of date technology. Also, I'm sure you have noticed the advertisements boasting that the latest generation of phones can survive immersion in water for up to thirty minutes. I never thought I would have to test this capability but, luckily for me, the claim checked out, and I had enough battery life left to make a discreet call to Jen, in the middle of the night, from the privacy of my curtained booth. After I hung up, I hid my phone beneath the mattress.

It was, and still is, the most difficult call I have ever had to make. I could sense Jen's turmoil as she tried to process what she was hearing, without breaking down. She attempted to respond, to say what she thought was the right thing but, even for someone with her communication skills, there is no right thing to say in a situation like this. So I just told her to listen while I described my idea, and what I wanted her to do. After that, she rallied quickly; as always, she was quick to spot her opportunity and run with it. All I could do, in my condition, was give her the sketchiest outline, but she understood immediately what I was trying to achieve. The shorthand we had developed, from working closely together in a high-pressure environment over a long period, was invaluable that night, and Jen's professional skills were essential in the days to come. She is a brilliant communicator and, most importantly, a very convincing liar.

My main role, over the next few days, was to be an unreliable witness. It cost me a lot of pain and slowed down my recovery, as I 'tongued' most of the painkillers that were administered in tablet form, like I had seen people do in those movies about mental institutions. So I was often more lucid than the doctors thought; enough to check with Jen, during her visits, on the status of our plan, and to give the police the appropriate answers to their questions, when they showed up. I was sure the police would get involved at some point, and I was right.

I didn't think we could deceive the police for long, and I was right about that, too. The officers assigned to the case were quick to react to our stalking story and the detailed, carefully fabricated evidence presented to them by Jen. They promptly arrested Stella and placed her in custody, but they were equally quick to release her, once they had ascertained that her claims checked out.

It was enough, though, as I knew it would be. The arrest and the brief spell in custody were quite sufficient to traumatise a person like Stella, who has led such a sheltered, cosseted life. Also, I knew she would understand only I had the motivation, and the means, to engineer her incarceration. In short, she would realise that I knew what she had done. Mission accomplished.

Jen and I knew we were taking a big risk. My stalking accusation didn't stand up to much scrutiny, of course, although Jen managed to lend it enough credibility to engineer the arrest. However, we were always conscious the police would soon deduce what we were up to and probably accuse us of wasting police time, although I had promised to protect Jen if this happened, by insisting I had deceived her into helping me. To mitigate the risk, I played the role of unreliable, inconsistent witness to the best of my ability. It wasn't too difficult, given the state I was in.

There was also what was a lesser risk, in our opinion; namely that the police would somehow work out what Stella had done and charge her with something really serious, like attempted murder. I didn't want that to happen, because of what it would do to my children, even if Stella did deserve it.

Things got rather tense at one point, when the two police officers made it clear that they both suspected Stella of foul play and me of attempting, however clumsily, to frame her for a crime she didn't commit. Frankly, they saw right through me. I recall the senior officer, a woman, describing my story as having 'more holes than a string vest'. That was a nervous moment.

Thankfully, the woman was pragmatic, as well as sharp. After an anxious few hours following my final interview with them, I received a phone call, from the junior officer, I might add, to inform me they intended to take no further action. He sounded unhappy with the decision; it was clear he didn't agree with his boss on this one, and I don't blame him. If I were the senior officer, I would have gone for it.

I can imagine their decision-making process. Even if they did understand the exact nature of the crime committed by Stella, the fact was that the victim denied it had ever taken place. I was careful to ask both my towpath cyclist and the ambulance crew repeatedly how I came to fall off the boat, to convince them it was a simple accident, so they would corroborate my story. Furthermore, any forensic evidence would have long been washed away in the canal, and there were no witnesses. I'm sure they concluded it was impossible to secure a conviction under such circumstances. With regard to my misdemeanours, they probably reasoned that, given the amount of drugs that Mr Dixit and his team would testify as having prescribed, not to mention the severity of my injuries, a jury would conclude I was incapable of acting rationally and had misled Jen, so we were unlikely to be convicted of wasting police time. I'm sure the decision to take no further action was frustrating for them, although perhaps they concluded we were perfectly capable of punishing each other all by ourselves.

On the subject of punishment, I believe I won, in the end. Stella got the worst of it, in my opinion. She has to live forever with the fallout from the snap decision she made, driven by rage, jealousy and alcohol. I don't imagine it was a cool, calculated move. Even now, I believe her incapable of being that ruthless. I'm convinced it was a 'crime passionnel', as the French call it. Fundamentally, Stella is a decent human being, which means she experiences guilt, and I'll make sure she is never free of it. I, on the other hand, feel exonerated by what she did. In a funny way, when she tied the mooring rope around me, what Stella actually did was free me.

There have, of course, been challenges, since my accident, but I have bounced back from all of them. On a professional level, the incident did cause a few raised eyebrows at senior levels within the firm. Those guys are very sharp, and I'm sure they suspected things didn't quite add up, although outwardly, there was a great show of support and sympathy from my colleagues. Not long after I returned to work, some off the record chats took place and I was informed, with great subtlety, that the senior partner promotion was never going to happen, so I left, and Jen followed soon afterwards. In a way, it was the best move either of us could have made. She landed an excellent job in PR and I have my pick of lucrative freelance contracts, interim roles and non-executive directorships.

My disability doesn't hold me back at all. In a way, it was the easiest problem to handle, as it was tangible. I made rapid progress once the police left me alone and I started taking all my meds. Nowadays, I regularly run 10Ks and half marathons, which I never did before, raising large sums for my favourite charities. Later this year, I plan to tackle the Three Peaks Challenge, with my daughter at my side.

Which brings me on to my children. After some very tough conversations, lots of tears and a great deal of hard work from all three of us, I now have the close relationship with my son and daughter which I always wanted. To them, I'm the good guy. Stella's guilt, combined with the fear that I will tell them what really happened, have handed me all the cards. I can get her to agree to anything. For instance, it was easy for me to force her not to reveal my affair to the children, thus allowing me to present Jen to them, after a decent interval, as my new partner. On the other hand, Imogen knows Stella told me about her abortion. My daughter asked me the question, so I had to give her an honest answer, didn't I? And now she knows, she will never again trust her mother completely. That closeness between them has gone. I'm her confidant, now.

It doesn't work quite the same way with Hugo, for practical reasons. He lives in Scotland during term time and spends most of the holidays in the US with his partner, whilst Imogen is studying close by in Manchester. Nevertheless, Jen and I keep in regular contact with my son and his partner and visit them regularly, while Stella sees them less often. We often fly to the US and meet up with them on the eastern seaboard but, since my accident, Stella won't step on a plane. Maybe she has some sort of PTSD. I don't know, and I don't care.

When it comes to the relationships that Stella and I have with our children, it's a zero-sum game. When I win, she loses out, in equal measure. It used to be the other way around, but those days are gone. From now on, I will always win.

You know, if Stella had not done what she did, I would probably have stayed with her. Jen might have left me in the end but, if so, there would have been other lovers to take her place. Believe me, though, when I say I'm happy how things turned out. Now I have a relationship with someone who adores me and where I am the one in control. I call the shots and that's how it will stay. Especially now the baby is on the way; that will really help me nail things down.

So, over to you. Do you think Stella got what she deserved – or did she have a lucky escape? Or am I the lucky one? You decide.

27 TWO'S COMPANY

Please excuse me if this sounds a little rushed. I'm not writing this down like I normally do; instead, I'm recording it on my phone. By the way, I know I said I wasn't going to give you an update, but I changed my mind. You'll see why; or rather, you'll hear. Right, here we are. The train is approaching its final destination. Time for me to get off, making sure I have all my personal belongings with me when I leave the train.

The station has changed a bit since I was last here. There are lots of shiny new shops and restaurants on the concourse, but the platforms still have a slightly shabby, retro look about them, which brings back lots of memories. I just did a double-take, though, when I heard a station announcement being recited in a broad Lancashire accent. Have I really become such a southerner? I was brought up around here, for goodness' sake. Clearly, I have been closeted away in Surrey for too long. I need to get out more.

Having said that, I'm not sure I should be here, but it's too late to back out now. What was it that Shakespeare wrote? 'Screw your courage to the sticking place' or something like that? Anyway, I'm now leaving the station behind me and walking down the curved slope of the approach road onto Piccadilly. The place is a mixture of alien, modern buildings and comforting, familiar red brick ones, but it doesn't feel like my city any more. I suppose that's because it isn't. It's theirs.

The introduction of trams has been a big improvement, I have to say; especially as I want to reach my destination as quickly as possible. I'm going to get on at Piccadilly Gardens, which is just ahead of me. I did my homework on the train, so I know I have two options…hang on, wait a minute…there it is, over there. The Altrincham service, just about to make its next stop on the purple line. Bear with me while I run for it.

Just made it. Note to self; I really must get back in the gym. Even though I lost those ten pounds at Fat Club, plus a few more afterwards, what with all the stress, I'm still desperately unfit. Let's just say improving my cardiovascular endurance hasn't been a top priority over the last two years. Oh look – here we are already. It was only a short hop to Deansgate-Castlefield. I'd forgotten how compact the city centre is, compared with London. Time to get off the tram and I'm still out of breath.

I'm walking up Castle Street now, wondering why she chose a canal-side bar as the venue for our meeting. Was it done deliberately, to make me feel uncomfortable? Or was it meant as some kind of joke? One thing's for sure; she didn't select the location without thinking it through. That's not her style.

Right, here we are. As I expected, it's a trendy, upmarket converted warehouse. On the wall are blackboards displaying a long list of wines, craft beers and expensive cocktails, plus an array of shots. There are grazing boards to share, along with supposed pub classics and an extensive vegan menu. Outside I can see a large terrace, beyond which the murky waters of the canal just about manage to glisten in the midday sun. That'll do nicely. I'll get myself a table out there, before it gets too crowded. By some minor miracle it's a hot, sunny day and I remember how rare that is here, even in the height of summer. It's almost lunchtime, so I imagine the office workers will be pouring in here soon. I had better buy myself a drink and get settled, before the influx. Now, where's the bar?

'Please may I have a large glass of Sauvignon Blanc? Actually, on second thoughts – do you serve wine by the bottle? Great – thank you. A bottle of Sauvignon Blanc and two glasses, please.'

Right, I'm all set. Time to enjoy a nice chilled glass of white wine in the warm sunshine, not far from the towpath. This would all be lovely, if it weren't for the person who's going to be arriving shortly. My heart's racing and I need to think about something else for a moment. I'll try that 5-4-3-2-1 exercise which is supposed to help you deal with stress. A grounding exercise, it's called, or so I believe. You start by describing five things you can see. The first thing that catches my eye is the lock, just yards away, which brings back unpleasant memories of that fateful holiday. It's not a promising start; my stress levels are ratcheting up, rather than down. Let's try again. What else can I see? Yet another reminder, I'm afraid – it's a traditional red narrowboat rising up inside the lock as the canal water floods in through the open paddles. There's a man at the tiller who radiates calm. He definitely looks as though he's done this thousands of times before. He appears to be boating solo which, as Nancy explained to me, is very tricky indeed. He's stepping off his boat now, middle rope in hand, to open the lock gates, so he can continue his journey along the canal. He doesn't hurry; not like I used to. I would run around like a headless chicken, often to little effect. This man does the opposite, working the lock with quiet efficiency and skill. He looks like the quintessential gentleman – tall, grey-haired and slim. He's what Nancy might call a 'class act'. I wonder what it must be like to have been married to someone like him for fifty years or more. A decent man, who doesn't cheat on you and who treats you with love and respect, every single day. Of course, I could be wrong about this stranger. He could be a serial killer. I realise appearances can be deceptive but, somehow, I instinctively know I'm right about him.

Hang on. Here she is, walking towards me, with her beautiful, long red hair displayed to its best advantage in the sunlight, which brings out the subtle flecks of gold in her natural highlights. Her baby bump is neat, round and high, emphasising her narrow silhouette, which appears unaltered by her pregnancy. Both times, I spent nine months flopping around like an elephant seal, but obviously Jennifer is not going to look like I did. Of course, she isn't. From a distance she appears perfect, but as she draws closer, I see she looks nervous. The skin on her neck and chest is blotchy red and the knuckles of her right hand, which clasps a large Prada handbag, gleam white under her translucent skin.

'Hi, Stella. Welcome to Manchester. I wasn't sure you'd come.'

'Neither was I. Look. I can't pretend this is a social occasion. I should warn you that I'm recording our conversation on my phone.'

'Fair enough. I've nothing to hide from you.'

'Makes a change. Sorry – pointless remark. Have a glass of wine.'

'I shouldn't really…'

'I can tell you from experience – the baby can cope with an occasional glass of wine. Just a small glass. They're tough little things, for the most part.'

'OK then. Just a small one.'

'There you are. Now perhaps you would be kind enough to explain why you asked me to come all this way and meet you.'

'I wanted to ask your advice – and to warn you.'

'I see. Does Alex know you're here?'

'No. Absolutely not – and I won't tell him, I promise.'

'Right. So, first of all, what do you want to warn me about?'

'About your new relationship – with this guy Chris. I'm sorry, but Alex knows. Imogen let it slip when she visited us last week.'

'Is that it? Honestly, I can't say I'm bothered, Jennifer. It's early days with Chris and, anyway, Alex has clearly moved on – with you. In fact, we've all moved on. It's been two years, after all. I don't see why it's an issue.'

'You don't get it, do you, Stella? Alex will never let you "move on", as you put it. Not with Chris; not with anyone. He'll find a way to destroy every relationship you have, and he'll stop you from being successful – in any area of your life.'

'I don't see why he would spend the time, or make the effort, when he has destroyed my life already and built himself a new one. I think he regards it as "job done", as he would say.'

'No, he doesn't. He'll never let up, believe me.'

'How do you know?'

'Because he's working against you already. Has been doing for some time, in fact.'

'What do you mean?'

'Your digital advice service. It would be much more successful than it is now, if Alex wasn't using his old network of contacts in Surrey to undermine your professional reputation and dissuade potential clients from signing up.'

'I can't believe he would do something like that.'

'Wake up, Stella. This is Alex we're talking about. It's amazing you've achieved what you have and that your business has even survived, given how he's been briefing against you. I see so much potential in what you're doing, but Alex will make sure you never fulfil it. He's got you right where he wants you and he plans to keep you there. You're stuck for ever - and so am I. Alex thinks he's won, because now he controls us both, plus he controls the story with your children. They only know what he wants them to know, which allows him to play the part of the perfect father…'

'I'm aware of that and I went along with it, for their sake. I didn't want to cause them any more pain. They've been through enough already.'

'I get that, but are you prepared to lose the amazing relationship you have with Imogen, in particular? Because I'll tell you now – Alex believes he has destroyed the trust between you, so you'll never be close again.'

'He's wrong about that, I can assure you. I admit, we went through a rough patch, but we're fine now. Stronger than before, if anything.'

'Even if that's true, Alex won't rest until he has driven a wedge between the two of you, to punish you for what you did.'

'OK, I get it. Alex has the knives out for me, and I'll have to find a way to deal with it – but how is he controlling you? He loves you. I heard him say so on the phone and I could tell he meant it.'

'He loved you too, though, didn't he? But that didn't stop him from turning the screws, once he'd tied you down – and now he's doing the same to me. My PR career was going so well…'

'Let me guess. He put pressure on you to have a baby.'

'That's right. Don't get me wrong; I love the baby already and I wouldn't change him…'

'Him?'

'That's right. I'm expecting a little boy. I wanted a surprise, but Alex insisted on finding out in advance, so he could "put a plan in place". Anyway, I'd rather have waited a few more years before getting pregnant, but Alex got his way in the end. Now he has a convenient excuse for everything. If he wants to stop me from doing something, he just says it's "for my son's sake". That's how he always puts it, "my", not "our". These days, there are so many things he prevents me from doing, because he disapproves of them as "unsuitable for a woman in your condition".'

'So, the cycle is repeating itself, but much faster this time round. I thought something wasn't quite right when I saw your dress.'

'My dress?'

'Yes; I would've expected you to be wearing something more stylish. I mean, when I met you at the wrap-up party for Leviathan, you looked so chic and polished. I know you're pregnant, but maternity wear doesn't have to be frumpy these days. Sorry - I didn't mean it to come out like that.'

'No, you're right. This dress *is* frumpy. I wanted to buy some more fashionable maternity clothes, but Alex wouldn't hear of it. He criticises everything about me these days; my clothes, my make-up, my friends – and especially my cooking. He always knew I wasn't the domesticated type. I thought it was one of the things he loved about me; the fact that I was so different from you – sorry. But now he goes crazy when I can't cook the sort of food he wants to eat.'

'Well, if we were friends, I'd probably teach you a few recipes, but we aren't – and in any case, it wouldn't help. I'm a great cook and I used to make him all sorts of gourmet meals, but he still found fault with everything I did, just like he does with you.'

'To be honest, I could put up with the constant criticism, but it has gone way beyond anything verbal. That's the other reason why I wanted to meet you face to face. To see if he used to do the same to you.'

'What are you talking about?'

'Let me give you an example. Say we're at a dinner party with friends and I'm telling a funny story. One where I tease Alex, just a little bit. If he doesn't like what I'm saying, he'll grab my hand under the table and crush my fingers, as though he wants to break them, until I stop talking. Or, if he's sitting opposite me, he'll put his foot on top of mine and press down so hard that he bruises me. So, I've learned never to speak out of turn and my friends keep telling me my sparkle has gone. I always excuse myself by saying it's because I'm pregnant, but the truth is, I'm afraid to tell them the real reason, in case he finds out...'

'Oh God, Jen – don't cry. Hang on, I've got a bottle of water in my bag. Here – have a drink.'

'Thanks – sorry about that. Anyway, it's even worse when we're alone at home. When he gets angry, he sometimes throws full mugs and plates of food at the wall, so they smash and fall onto the floor, then he storms out of the room, yelling at me to clear up the mess. Last week, I was standing at the bathroom mirror, putting on my make-up, when he walked in and said he wanted to shave. I asked him to wait a moment while I finished up, so he just grabbed my hair and dragged me out of the way. Also – and this is probably too much information – in the bedroom, his behaviour has changed. He's not as romantic as he used to be. Nowadays he's often more…'

'Insistent? Forceful?'

'That's right. Aggressive even, at times. I mean, he never does anything illegal and he wouldn't risk hurting the baby – and he's still nice to me a lot of the time – sorry. This probably all sounds really trivial to you.'

'Of course, it doesn't. It sounds the opposite of trivial.'

'Was he like this with you, Stella?'

'Not so much. There wasn't any plate throwing as the kids were usually around when he was at home and he wouldn't behave like that in front of them. In fact, there was nothing physical at all, except in the bedroom where, I'm sorry to say, I can relate to what you just told me. Look, I've finished the bottle of wine and I'm going to need a second, to help me carry on this conversation. Will you be alright here for a minute? Can I get you anything – some food, perhaps?'

'No thanks; I'm fine. I'll just finish up my glass of wine.'

As I stand at the bar, I look out onto the terrace where Jennifer sits at our table, hunched over her wine glass. She's a mere shadow of the vibrant woman who greeted me at the Leviathan wrap-up party. I know I should feel a sense of satisfaction, of justice having been done, but I don't. I just feel incredibly sad for both of us. When the barman brings my wine, I ask for a glass of tap water and take a couple of pills. As you know, they shouldn't be taken with alcohol, but don't judge me. I think you'll agree this isn't the easiest of lunchtime drinks and I need a little extra help to get me through it. As I return to our table, Jennifer carries on talking as though I had never left.

'…and that's not the worst thing, though.'

'What could be worse than constant criticism and intimidation, with a side order of physical violence?'

'When we moved in together, Alex promised he would only take on local assignments here in the north west, so he could get home every night for me – and now for the baby as well.'

'So, what's changed?'

'Lately, he's started to sign up for projects which require him to stay away overnight. He has also presented at some overseas conferences and accepted invitations to do several more. I can't help thinking he might be…'

'Ah, I see. Less than scrupulously faithful…'

'I wouldn't blame you if you laughed and said I got what I deserved.'

'Honestly? I'm way beyond all that, although I have to say that by moving in with Alex, you've created a vacancy, as someone once said.'

For recording purposes let me just note that, at this point, Jennifer and I look at each other and have a little laugh. Just a small one. I think we're both desperate for a moment of light relief. Then I pour her a second small glass of wine. She puts up only token resistance.

'Oh God, what a mess. Look, you're right. I should hate you and delight in your misery, especially after you tried to frame me and got me arrested, but…'

'I didn't come up with that idea, Stella, I swear! It was all Alex's doing. I just did what he told me – executed his plan, if you like. I regret it now, if that's any consolation.'

'But didn't you see he was controlling you, even back then?'

'It sounds crazy now, but at the time I didn't really think about it. I was so focused on…'

'Doing what you were told? Trying to impress him and prove yourself? Look, I'm not in a position to judge. I was exactly the same. I didn't realise what was happening until it was too late. I believe it's what's known as "boiling frog syndrome".'

'Precisely. You don't notice the heat gradually increasing until you are well and truly poached…what is it, Stella? Are you OK?'

'I'm fine; just thinking what a piece of work my ex-husband is, to come up with a plan like that, when he was fighting for his life.'

'He was out for revenge, which is a powerful motivator for someone like Alex, who's charming on the surface but cunning and utterly ruthless underneath.'

'The winning combination which makes him a great programme director, who will direct both our lives forever, if we let him. You know your career will be finished once the baby comes, don't you? There's no reason why you shouldn't have both, these days, but Alex will make sure that doesn't happen, like he did with me. Just look at what he's done to you. A few years ago, you were a successful, independent woman, living a rewarding life in the centre of a dynamic city. You had a loving partner – Stefan, I think his name was…'

'How do you know about Stefan?'

'I trawled your social media accounts.'

'That figures. I'd have done the same.'

'Anyway, now you're facing the prospect of life as a suburban housewife with a controlling, violent and possibly unfaithful partner. That sounds pretty familiar to me.'

'Of course, it does, Stella. Oh, Christ. What are we going to do?'

'Well, I already tried to do something, as you know – and look how that turned out.'

'It was a bit random, though, you have to admit, but full marks for originality. I'm impressed you came up with the idea on the spur of the moment. Look. Excuse me a minute. I must go to the loo.'

Off she goes. I have to say, I'm relieved. I don't want any more questions about what I did that day, or how I thought it up. It's my fault, I guess, for raising the subject in the first place. I'm well into my second bottle now and, what with the pills as well, things are getting a little hazy. I'm sober enough to realise I have to stop Alex from wrecking what remains of my life, but right now I can't work out how I'm going to do it. Meanwhile, I still don't know where Jen is going with all of this. Uh-oh, she's coming back. I had better try and focus.

'Stella. I need to ask you something.'

'Go ahead.'

'Do you ever wish – that it had worked?'

'You mean…?'

'What you did that day, on the boat. Do you wish you had, well - finished the job, as it were?'

'I suppose it would've made things simpler, I have to admit. What about you?'

'At the time I would've been devastated, of course.'

'And now?'

'Now, with the benefit of hindsight – I think it might've been for the best.'

'So, if I've understood correctly, you wish I had "finished the job", as you put it?'

'Yes. I do.'

We both stare at my phone, which is still recording away. Mutually assured destruction right there, in that innocuous digital device. I top up my glass and stare across the table at my former nemesis.

'So, here we are. Two intelligent, educated women with lots of skills, including our ability to lie convincingly. Surely we can find a way to get ourselves out of this?'

'Before all this happened Alex used to say you were so innocent. He put it down to your privileged lifestyle. I guess he underestimated you.'

'Of course, he did, but he was right, in a sense. I was a bit naïve, but not any more. Particularly not after that spell in the custody suite.'

'Look, I'm sorry about that – and everything else.'

'Sorry's not going to help us now; nor is dwelling on the past. You're no longer the problem – Alex is. We need to find a way to take him on.'

'I wonder what he would say if he could see us talking like this.'

'It would never occur to him that we might get together. After all, he knows he's won, but that unshakeable confidence of his could be his undoing, if you see what I mean.'

'I do, Stella – but what have you got in mind?'

'Just give me a minute to think. I'll be right back.'

Now I'm standing by the canal, playing for time, holding my phone and my glass, which is almost empty. Another narrowboat has just entered the lock. A woman in denim shorts and a striped T-shirt is struggling, pink-faced, to shift the heavy balance beam on the opposite side. She reminds me of myself, learning the hard way during that holiday I now no longer regret taking. All of a sudden, I remember something I was told, back there on the towpath of the Grand Union Canal, by a feisty old lady with a good imagination. Instantly my wine and pill fog clear, and I turn around to face the terrace. As I move, I see Jennifer raise her head expectantly and I hesitate. After all, I was impulsive before - and look where it got me. I'm still not convinced I can trust her, but I guess I'll find out. I swallow the last of the wine, then take a deep breath and start retracing my steps towards our table. Time to explain what we're going to do next. First, though, I have to switch off this phone.

ABOUT THE AUTHOR

Felicity Radcliffe divides her time between a small rural village, where she lives with her husband and dog, and a narrowboat on England's beautiful canals. Union Clues is her second novel.

LET'S TALK FREE STUFF...

Hello - thank you so much for reading Union Clues. I'd really like to know what you thought of it. As I write, I'm already working on the second book in the Grand Union series, so your feedback would be very helpful.

Please feel free to email me at **felicityradcliffebooks@gmail.com** to start our conversation. Alternatively, you can contact me via my Facebook page, Twitter or Instagram. Writing is a solitary process and it can get quite lonely at times, so it would be great to hear from you.

Once we're in touch, I'll share a whole load of free stuff with you. I regularly send out short stories and poems free of charge, and I'll make sure you get a copy of each one. Some of these will be unrelated to Union Clues, but others will explore the lives of the UC characters, beyond the confines of this book. If there are any characters, particularly the minor ones, you'd like to hear more from, please let me know. I'm also planning to launch a newsletter, which I'll send to you as well.

If you have enjoyed reading this book, please tell your friends and ask them to contact me. It makes my day when someone tells me that a friend recommended they read my books. It's also nice when I get reviews on Amazon, Goodreads and Bookbub, so please do leave me a review for Union Clues. Whatever rating you choose to give, I value your opinion. If you're reading this in paperback, obviously you can't follow the hyperlinks, but you can still leave a review and contact me via one of the methods suggested above.

I'm looking forward to hearing from you. Thanks again for choosing Union Clues.

Felicity Radcliffe
April 2020

Printed in Great Britain
by Amazon

84832338R00135